JESSICA WOULD DO ANYTHING TO SAVE THE SHADOWS. *ANYTHING!*

Jessica dumped another finger of whiskey into her glass. "The mill, did you go out to the mill and line up some construction?"

"Trouble out yonder, too, pickets stoppin' niggers from workin'. Some fella came in with a bunch of company guards, brought 'em in Cadillacs; they had sawed-off shotguns, and maybe a machine gun. This Lassiter fella said—"

Jessica spun on her barstool to face him. "Lassiter—Earl Lassiter?"

Her frown smoothed into a smile. Earl was back. Jessica stared into the bar mirror. She'd have to do something about her hair, take care of her nails, find a good dress.

It was strange that Earl should have risen so high, coming off a hardscrabble farm with only a high school education. But not so strange that their paths would soon cross again.

He had always been handy when she wanted him. . . .

BED
OF
STRANGERS

Lee Raintree and
Anthony Wilson

A DELL BOOK

Published by
Dell Publishing Co., Inc.
1 Dag Hammarskjold Plaza
New York, New York 10017

Dell ® TM 681510, Dell Publishing Co., Inc.

ISBN: 0-440-10892-6

Printed in the United States of America

First printing—December 1978

BOOK I
1951

CHAPTER 1

Sand coughed up from the belly of the treacherous Tchufuncta River was silken, ground almost fine as dust; it had swirled so thickly around the tombstones that even wiry Johnson grass had to struggle for breath. Glittering browngray in summer sun, it made the family cemetery neater than Avery Coffield had ever seen it, but he wished he was knee-deep in weeds.

"Ain't much more to go, Mist' Avery," the black said. "Jes straighten the fence where water bent it some; no weedin' to speak of this year."

"Goddamn *sand*," Avery grunted. "River pukes it up, the goddamn river oughta lick away its own mess; that right, Bodie?"

"Yessuh. I swony, never seen high water three years runnin' afore." Bodie looked up from where he was clipping grass from around a tilted monument. "Jes ain't natural."

Avery wiped at his forehead. "Ain't natural that wet, ain't natural this dry; hell—even a crawdad has to tote his own drinkin' water."

Dutifully, Bodie laughed, and went back to clearing the base of the stone. Avery lifted his straw hat to let in some air, and settled it back on his head. Kicking once at the sand, he moved over into the deepgreen shade of a chinaberry tree. From there, he could catch the scent of the river, or was it Lassiter's ditch?

Hell; forty ditches—a hundred—wouldn't do the cotton any good; not now, and not with all that damned sand overlying the rich black soil. Lassiter's piddling little old truck farm had only been touched by flood deposits, and where sand *had* reached, the boy had been smart to put in melons, which thrived in sandy soil.

The ditch had been Earl Lassiter's idea, too; old Ben was just like any other hardscrabble farmer around here: if it got dry, he prayed for rain and cussed the sun. Irrigation was for big corporate farms in country where it didn't rain enough all summer. Only now it wasn't raining *here*, damnit—only early every spring for three years running, and then like a cow pissing on a flat rock, so the Tchufuncta came roaring out of its banks to shovel sand all over hell and back. And when there was another layer of the cotton-choking stuff, the land dried up.

But Lassiter had water now, enough for the vegetables he hauled into town for shipment on the pulp cars to Mobile or New Orleans. Lassiter kept his two-bit operation going because his boy dug a ditch, while Avery Coffield couldn't even get his spanking-new swimming pool filled in time for the party tonight.

"Maybe even the goddamn Indian spring will dry up," he muttered, and Bodie creaked his graying head around to say, "Suh?"

"Nothin'," Avery answered, and leaned against the chinaberry tree to look across the family graveyard to where his daughter sat atop a tombstone, her heels beating a slow and blasphemous tattoo against cracked marble. Heat waves shimmered around her, making her ethereal.

As always, there was a little catch in his throat when he glanced at her suddenly, seeing how golden and shiny she was. But more often lately, there was also a tightening of his belly. She was doing it again, showing too damned much leg and smarting off; she oughtn't do that, especially around the niggers. Hell, old Mason wasn't more than five, six yards away, being careful to keep his eyes on his own black hands pulling weeds. But any man with juice to him could *feel* those long, slender legs flipping around every whichaway. And anybody with a lick of sense knew that niggers started younger and kept at it longer than white men. Anyhow, Mason was just a few years older than Avery himself.

She was just deviling her daddy, Avery thought; she was only being Jessica, headstrong as any hotblooded and unbroken young filly, and come down to it, he wouldn't have her any other way. Temple County girls in her social class were apt to simper and giggle and act like they never had their period yet and wouldn't admit it if they did. But Jess now—she could ride to hounds good as any man, and was a fair hand with a rifle, and could drop a spinner into a far eddy and snag herself a big old green cutthroat any time she wanted.

Trouble was—Avery squinted at her drumming her heels against the tombstone with her head thrown back and her firm young breasts—trouble was, Jess was just turning ripe, filling all up with sweet red juice like a prime watermelon. Avery pushed away from the tree and shook his head; good thing she was going off to college in the fall, because there wasn't any man in the county good enough for her. Unless—he frowned and shook his head again, and walked out into the sun toward her.

It was going to near about kill him to let her go, but there was no holding her now. So ready, so damned beautiful and fiery, and with a deepdown strength to her that nobody sensed but himself, Jess meant to run her own life. All he could do was try to keep her from screwing it up.

"Go help Bodie with the fence," he said to Mason, and waited until the man had moved off, then said, "Jess, damnit."

Seagreen eyes moved lazily behind half-shuttered lids. "Am I desecrating the holy grave, Daddy?"

"You know goddamn well that ain't it. You been shakin' yourself at old Mason, and I could feel the heat clear over yonder."

Jessica laughed, a melody of muted chimes. "Could you, Daddy?"

"Get down off there and pull that towel around yourself. I swear, sittin' out here in a skimpy bathin' suit—"

"Just eager to swim in the new pool, Daddy. It *is* goin' to be ready tonight? Be a shame if the first pool in Temple County, the *only* pool, wasn't any better than a mudhole in the Tchufuncta." She strode away from him before he could answer, her boyish-girlish hips swaying lithely, honeygold hair swinging pendulum down her straight back, calling more attention to the rhythm of her tightly modeled bottom.

A pace behind, Avery pulled up to avoid bumping into her as she stopped suddenly and propped one neat, sandaled foot upon another stone, a smaller one. She said, "This is my favorite; over a hundred years of Coffield heritage commemorated in marble, but only this little bitty headstone doesn't carry a last name. Let's see now—*Sally, 1845–May 9, 1865.* You never did tell me why a slave wench was buried in our lily-white plot, and so close to one Endicott Coffield, too."

"Come on," Avery said. "I want to see about the pool."

She lowered her foot, but didn't move off. "They died a day apart, with her goin' first. You know, somebody might figure Endicott killed himself."

Avery said, "Whatever that wench meant to your great-great-granddaddy, you can forget that idea. No Coffield ever committed suicide. Coffields hang in there like snappin' turtles, but *they* don't even let go when it thunders."

Those special, smoldering eyes cut around at him. "They pull in their necks sometimes, though; hide in their shells?"

He felt it coiling inside, the shameful tightness, the helpless anger. Goddamnit, she could push too far. He said, "I don't want to hear that out of you, Jessica. Nobody knows how it—especially, I don't want to hear it from *you.*"

She was a little girl again, just tomboy enough, just feminine enough, too, suddenly contrite, tucking her chin into the towel and putting her head to one side. "I—I'm sorry, Daddy. I don't know what gets into me. The heat, this drought—I just don't know."

I know, Avery thought; the juices stirring, the heat inside matching the heat outside; hotter maybe, simmering, bubbling so it was about to break through the rind. He knew a sharp knife edge of jealousy, of resentment toward the man who would know the full flavor of that loosing. Then he tried to grin as he led the way from the cemetery, up the gently angled hill toward the big house. God pity the man who wasn't strong enough to stand up to Jessica; if there was any softness to him, she would burn him out and leave only an empty husk. She'd do him like a dirt-dauber did a fat spider, and if she didn't drain him for herself, she'd paralyze the bastard and tuck him into a nest for her young to feed on. He couldn't look around at her half a step behind him; Avery didn't want to picture her with a swollen belly. Not now; not just yet.

When they reached the jeep, she moved around to the other side and ducked gracefully beneath the canvas top. "I used to be scared of the cemetery, even when Aunt Elvira carried me down there and we put flowers on all the graves. Except Sally's, of course. Later on, it got to be a bore, all that fussin' and cleanin' and paying homage to the dead. And when I asked about Sally, she told me it was old Endicott's hunter, that he thought so much of the horse he wanted to have it right there next to him, always."

Avery started the jeep and backed it around. "Your aunt was a fine woman, a pure-D lady."

"Uh-huh; I guess I can understand now why she looked so put out when I said that great-great-granddaddy must have been really good in the saddle."

Slamming down on the gas, Avery jumped the jeep out, wheels spinning in gravel, his teeth clamped.

From the corner of her eye, Jessica watched her father's craggy, gone-to-jowls profile, knowing she'd gotten to him. He usually turned red in the face when she rattled that family skeleton or when the subject even got close to sex. It was funny how she could like him so much, and yet clash with him on just about everything that mattered, and some that didn't.

He was still a handsome man, graying some in his mid-fifties and turning paunchy despite sometimes working in the fields alongside his hired hands. Jessica thought him attractive, sensuously so, even with that petulance around his mouth. Maybe that was a birthright arrogance that came with three thousand rich bottomland acres and the majestic, colonnaded house; it might have been handed down by all those Coffields before him, throwing their shadows across the land since before the Revolution.

Avery Coffield was the biggest planter in Temple County, and controlled other businesses, those he didn't downright own. Anybody could feel that kind of power, especially a woman who admitted that power itself was sexual.

When the jeep pulled up at a side entrance to The Shadows, she slid out, careless about the beach towel supposed to cover her, and stood watching her father move quickly, efficiently, among buffet tables being set up. Of course, he had to check the smallest details— the angle of paper lanterns, how the bar was stocked, even the cut-flower centerpieces. Down at the fields he was one kind of man, sweaty and hearty and not too proud to dirty his hands; on these carefully trimmed lawns he was another man, visibly proud of the great house and its tended gardens, jovial master—but master nonetheless—to scurrying black servants.

Tonight he would be lord of the manor, the casually lavish host, moving among his guests to touch this group and that like some great bumblebee, adeptly pollinating each cluster before moving on. Jessica smiled as she passed between the tables, thinking that few of those upon whom Avery's golden dust had fallen would even realize they had been impregnated.

He grinned at her and put an arm across her shoulders. "What do you think of it, Jess? Mighty fine layout, I reckon."

"Like Adam and Eve's comin'-out party in the garden, if God had the time."

Avery laughed. "Time, hell; he just didn't have the money. But he had his own water master, and we don't. That damned pool ain't half full yet. Hey there, Clayton—can't you get more flow out of that valve?"

"No sir; guess the water level's too low." Squat and blueblack, Clayton hunkered at poolside, his new white coveralls fingermarked in grease.

"Daddy," Jessica said, "the Lassiters have water."

"So has the damned river, but gettin' it from there to here is—" Avery broke off and his mouth twitched. "Might be an idea at that. Say, Clayton—it wouldn't be hard to run a line from the gin to that ditch, and if a man was to tie that juice in to a good pump and lay some plastic hose—"

"Mist' Avery," Clayton said, "that ditch is a good hundred feet on Lassiter land, and you know how ol' man Lassiter—"

"Hell," Avery said. "Ben ain't that trigger happy; ain't been, since that play-pretty moved in to keep his mind on somethin' better. Tell you what—you fill this pool to the brim by this evenin', and your check'll buy you a slick young pretty like Ben's got, least for a night or two."

Clayton sighed and wiped his hands on his coveralls. "Like you say, Mist' Avery; like you say."

Smiling widely now, Avery tugged Jessica into the house. "It's goin' to be all right, Jess. Won't anything mess up your goin'-away party."

She looked at him. "I didn't think anything would. Do I get a drink to celebrate?"

Avery frowned and glanced at his watch. "If you want, but it's a mite early. You got everything all packed?"

Jessica nodded. "More than I'll ever need."

"Damn," he said. "I know you ought to go look around, find your place and all that, but it's two months until school starts and—oh hell, Jess. I reckon I'm tryin' to say it won't be the same around here without you. Not that I want to stop you from growin' up, understand, and every fledgling has to try his wings."

"Or her wings," Jessica said, moving out from beneath his arm and drawing the beach towel closer.

"Sure, sure. And I know you're goin' to fly like a chicken hawk and look down to spot you somebody don't haul pulpwood or run bustskull whiskey, somebody fancy but not a fancy man. Oh hell; it ain't that early, so let's you and me have us a quick one before we have to get dressed."

"You mean a drink," she said, watching him through lowered lids.

Avery blinked and rubbed a big hand across his chin. "A—a drink, yeah. What the hell do you *think* I meant, Jess?"

"I changed my mind," Jessica said, and swept on through the formal living room to skip derisively up the curving flight of carpeted stairs. It was so easy to throw him off track, she thought, and wondered why she got such a kick out of doing it. Maybe it was because she didn't like being called Jess, and hadn't, since she quit being a tomboy raiding other folks' watermelon patches and goober fields. Maybe it was because she was determined to make him see her as a woman grown, and—Jessica smiled as she turned off the hallway into her own suite of rooms—and just possibly she liked to needle her daddy because he knew damned well she was a woman, but kept trying to avoid the fact.

Heeling the door shut behind her, she tossed the towel on the bed and peeled out of her swimsuit, grinning again as she thought how this would shock him, and her mother, too. Genteel young ladies simply didn't stand around stark-naked, not even in the privacy of their own rooms. But Jessica had a good body, one hell of a good body, and she liked to admire it. She did it now, watching the slow pirouette of sleek bare flesh in a full-length mirror, feeling the washing of warm air over her skin and the tingling of fine golden hairs standing alertly separate.

The whores down at Beevo's must stand around bare-assed all the time, she thought; at least, the time they were on their feet. Jessica shivered deliciously, and the points of her coral nipples tightened. Someday, somebody would get wise and put in a whorehouse for horny women to visit, where they could have naked men paraded before them and take their pick; and if those studs were just as black as Beevo's girls, that would be all right, too.

Touching her breasts lightly, she moved on into the bathroom, highly conscious of how her thighs brushed against each other. Bending to turn on the tub taps, she had the feeling that tonight should be something very special. A home-leaving ought to be more significant than a homecoming, and she'd sure as hell see that it was.

CHAPTER 2

He could hear the offbeat laboring of the tractor across the field, and knew the valve job couldn't be put off much longer. Straddling a feeder line, Earl Lassiter watched its muddy water slow to a trickle and wondered what had jammed the main ditch, a log, soft bank crumbling?

He'd clear it in the morning, because if he said anything about it, the old man would have something new to chew on. His father had never fully accepted the ditch, even now when other home gardens and truck patches were brown and scraggly. Ben Lassiter looked upon irrigation as some kind of Yankeefied nonsense.

But maybe Ben could spare money for a set of grinders; in the long run, it'd be cheaper than having the valves done at Hale's Garage, and Earl wanted to try the job himself, anyway. He never had, but knew he could. There wasn't anything about machinery he couldn't handle—except maybe working out those last few wrinkles on the post peeler he was designing. And he'd get them in time, because even if machinery fought him stubbornly for a while, it always gave in to the knowing touch of his hands. Some folks had that feel for horses and stock, but Earl could keep pickups and tractors running with spit and baling wire.

Grinning, he thought that he'd damned well *had* to, or else have a hoe handle grow to his hands. Stepping away from the narrow ditch, he thought briefly of Alvah and how his brother couldn't cut it here—or wouldn't. If Alvah had stayed, maybe Earl could have managed a few courses in engineering. As it was, there just wasn't time, and there'd never been the money. And with Alvah long gone, somebody had to help the old man with the place.

Walking between rows of cabbage that looked solid and good, he could see the sky blotting up red from a sinking sun. There was just a dab of coolness in the air, and he knew a little lift of excitement because Jessica's party was tonight, and he was going. He'd rather go on the sly, without having to flat out lie to his father, but however it came out, Earl meant to be up at the big house, come dark. The bad blood between Ben Lassiter and Avery Coffield was none of his doing, or Jessica's, either. Things changed; folks came out different than they started, like Alvah for instance, but the daddies and granddaddies didn't see it that way. They wanted it all to stay just like it, was, as if anything or anybody had no right to try a different road.

The tractor was already chugging up to the barn, and Earl paused at the path to the old sawmill. It tugged at him every time he walked by, like it was hollering out to him to get the job done. He often had the feeling it was like Lazarus, but dead a heap longer, and begging to have life breathed into its rusted bones again. Simple machinery in the sway-backed old shed, big old motors that had done a good job away back yonder before all the big trees had been logged off. There'd been belts and good steel saw blades, too—edgers and planers and all it took to turn out lumber. But it had all died when the logging outfits moved on, moldering in its tin tomb long before Earl's mother died, too.

He could barely remember his mama. She was pictures in the album, a plain, smiling woman, and maybe some of her was left in the come-down generations of flowers around the house. But that was all. Sue Anne Lassiter had come and done her job and gone, but there had to be more to life than that. There ought to be more than working from can't-see to can't-see and walking tall just because you didn't owe anything to anybody. There was the land, his father said; *my* land, boy, and your land someday. A man walks his own land, he don't have to bend his neck to nobody.

Slinging his shirt over one bare shoulder, Earl bypassed the mill and headed for the house. It didn't seem to matter that there wasn't cash money for anything—a new truck, boots, and for God's sake, don't even mention going off to college. Just be proud you can walk your own land, boy, and it don't matter a damn that the land's hardscrabble and only forty acres of the two hundred sixty able to grow anything but loblolly pine and water oak and bitterweed. It's land, and a man without land ain't no kind of man a'tall.

"Shit," Earl said aloud, because he'd been all over this a thousand times inside his head, and it always came out the same. He didn't want to stay and he couldn't leave, and that was that.

Stopping outside at the pump, he worked the handle and sloshed reddish water in a bucket, so he could wash most of the day's grime from his upper body before going into the house. After supper he'd shower and shave and get into his town clothes, such as they were. Maybe he could pin a sign on them: "These ain't much, but bigod, I walk my own land." Or my daddy's land, and there's a hell of a difference.

The house smelled good, all warm cornbready and strong black coffee and frying sidemeat. Ellen was a good cook who could make do with what she had, but sometimes Earl couldn't help wondering what oysters and alligator pears and such fancy food would taste like. Might be he'd get the chance to sample some up at The Shadows tonight. But his belly tightened more at the idea of tasting Jessica Coffield.

He'd kissed her twice, back when they were younger and she used to run her horse lickety-split through the country, jumping fences and not giving a damn whose they were. But then she'd been flavored with bubble-gum and would rather kiss her big gelding than any old boy. Now would be something else, because he couldn't look at her without getting a knot in his belly and a rising in his crotch. Somehow, no matter where Jessica was or what she was up to, she had the look about her of a filly in heat, like she was dripping clear, hot fluid and all atremble in the legs, she was so ready to spread them for the mounting.

And didn't every slick town boy, every hardup country boy know it? They could *smell* Jessica, the same as a stud horse caught wind of a mare in season, and they came prancing, rolling their eyes and trying to hide the bulge in their pants. But far as Earl knew, none of the young stallions had got Jessica's neck in their teeth—yet.

He ate slaw and turnip greens and cornbread and tomatoes, but passed the shallots because he didn't want them on his breath. Looking up from his plate, he caught Ellen's black eyes watching him, and looked away from her and her little girl to the head of the bare plank table where his father sat chewing in silence.

"Goin' to town tonight," he said. "I'll check with George Hale on that valve job, too, maybe see can I deal on a set of grinders, if that's all right with you."

Ben Lassiter wrapped a browned hand around his coffee mug. "We can swap George corn for the job; he's still feedin' hogs."

"Be better if we had our own grinders," Earl said.

Ben stirred his coffee and left the spoon in. "Sure you don't need 'em for that invention of yours?"

"All right," Earl said, "forget it."

From the stove, Ellen said quietly, "Rhubarb pie."

"Not for me," Earl said. "I got to get ready."

"I'll iron your white shirt," she said.

"Appreciate it," Earl said, rising from the table. He went out across the yard to his quarters in the mill shed. It had been easier on everybody when he'd moved out there, and he'd rigged up his own shower from an old drum. Besides leaving the house and beds to Ellen and his daddy, Earl could work when the notion took him, like it so often did at night.

It wasn't that he resented Ellen; even if she was black, it had been good to have a woman in the house after those years of eating like hogs and living not much better. Alvah now—Alvah didn't seem to care much for her being there, but Alvah had been older and already kind of set in his ways, and wilder than a pissant, when he was of a mind to be.

Folks talked some about her being there, sure. But there was more than one house back off in the woods with a black housekeeper, and it was a pure-D wonder how many of those places had widowers in them. Besides, Ellen had been hard up for a place to stay, knocked up like she was and run off by her hardshell Baptist daddy.

Taking her in meant raising of her youngun, too, but little Marcie wasn't any trouble; she was already being a help to her mama around the house. Next year, she'd be going off to school. Earl stood under the cold water of his shower and remembered that Jessica was going off to school, too; and not like other folks, not waiting until September, but champing at the bit to be gone in the middle of summer.

Well, he couldn't fault her for wanting to take off from Temple County quick as she could. She'd been to New Orleans and Mobile, but there was a need in her to see more, to go farther and faster than anybody else. Just like she rode her horses hard, taking chances and laughing at them that didn't.

But maybe tonight—Earl shivered and it wasn't from chilly water. She'd especially invited him to her going-off party, a promise sliding around behind those eyes of April green that somehow always held the sultry heat of July. He turned off the water and stepped out onto the towsacks he used for a bathmat, scrubbing at his body with a ragged towel. He was scared, damn it. What if he didn't do it right? If there was anybody in the whole world he couldn't stand laughing at him, it was Jessica Coffield.

The bare bulb dangling over a cracked mirror didn't give much light, but he was used to it, and blamed his nervousness for nicking his chin with the razor. He said *shit!* with feeling, and pinched a dab of toilet paper off the roll to stop the bleeding.

From the shed door, Ben Lassiter said, "Reckon you might's well ask George about them grinders. Do you find time, that is."

"See him first off," Earl said, "before I get to horrawin'."

Ben came two steps into the shed, and rolled himself a smoke from a can of Prince Albert. "Do you good to hooraw some. It ain't natural for a boy to spend all his time messin' with machinery. Woman flesh fits better to the hand."

"I'm doin' all right," Earl said, turning his back to put on his shorts.

"Just wear what you got to," Ben said. "White or black don't make no difference, a man ought to protect himself."

"Yeah," Earl said, embarrassed as he climbed into his pants.

Ben leaned against a timber, his leathery face wreathed in blue cigarette smoke. "I know I ain't talked to you much, about women and such, but I figure boys learn on their own. If they don't, there's somethin' wrong with 'em. Course, it don't hurt none to start 'em off right, like I done with your brother. Your ma didn't say nary a word to me for weeks after I carried Alvah out to Beevo's for his first drunk and his first nigger nooky."

Earl pulled on an undershirt. "I ain't Alvah. If I was—" He stopped and pretended to use the mirror.

"You'da lit a shuck," Ben said. "I know. Just talkin', boy. Seems like it ain't all that easy for you and me to talk. But here—" He held out a rumpled bill. "No, don't shake your head at me like a muley cow; a boy needs somethin' in his pocket, and lord knows you don't get to spend much. Just don't spend it on Beevo's stumpjuice whiskey; I know damned well he puts kerosene in it, to give it a bead. Buy a jar from old McNally; Saturday nights, he'll be sidlin' around behind the bus station."

"I ain't much for drinkin'," Earl said.

"Don't hurt a man, now and then; flushes him out, like. Marryin' up with a bottle is somethin' else."

"Alvah didn't exactly do that," Earl said. "He just had to go his own way, Pa."

"We ain't talkin' about him. Thank the lord you and him wasn't two peas in a pod. You just—well, boy—have you a good time in town." The sweet odor of tobacco lingered after Ben was gone, and Earl thought when he took up smoking, it wouldn't be Prince Albert, even though ready-rolls cost more.

His hair wouldn't lie down just right, so he put on more brilliantine and brushed at it. Looked greasy now, he thought, and wiped the towel over his head. When he turned from the mirror, Ellen was standing there with his good white shirt. She had a coat over her other arm.

"This'll be a mite big for you, but it's hot anyway, and once you're inside, you can carry it over your arm."

"I don't need Pa's coat."

"Beats that old jacket of yours."

"*He* give it to you?"

"Not likely. Put on your shirt; there's plenty of starch in it, and best you wear a tie."

Earl eyed her, this trim, efficient black woman who had become a part of his life. She stood proud and looked you in the eyes, which was more than most blacks did, unless they were drunk and hunting trouble. A handsome woman, Ellen; put together with high, firm breasts and long legs; velvety-looking and moving nice. If Beevo had any crib girls like her—

"How come Pa knows where I'm goin'?" he asked.

"I didn't tell him; word gets around. Try on the coat."

Earl let her put it on him, but neither of his two ties seemed to go with it. "He didn't say I couldn't go to The Shadows."

"Could be he learned somethin' about sayin' no all the time."

"Too late for Alvah, I reckon. Coat's too big; I ain't near as wide as Pa."

"You will be. He's acceptin' that, Earl; a man wants his boys to grow up, but it kind of scares him when they start to."

"Ben Lassiter *scared?*" Earl took off his tie and threw it on the cot.

"They's different kinds of scared," Ellen said softly. "And whatever you think, he's glad to have you home helpin' him on the place. One boy in Korea is enough."

"I wanted to go soon's I was old enough. Alvah's been there a full two years, since it started in 1950," Earl said. "Damn it, Pa knows I wanted to, but they'd have kept me this side of the water account of my back. That piddlin' disc or whatever, it don't even show, and it sure don't keep me from workin' my hind end off. Didn't even know I had it until they examined me. Must have happened when I fell off the tractor that time, before you came here."

Ellen picked up the tie and held it in her hands. "You was way too little to be drivin' a tractor. Take the tie with you, in case."

"Somebody had to," he said. "All right, I'll carry the damned tie."

"Just so you won't be out of place."

Earl laughed without humor. "I won't fit in with that bunch. If I had on a fancy white suit and pulled up in a new Cadillac, I still wouldn't fit in, but I'm goin' anyway."

"You got a good name," Ellen said. "That makes up for no big car and white suit."

"Sure," Earl said, shrugging his shoulders uncomfortably. The coat was too heavy for this time of year. "Oh sure—that good name is on the statue of old Colonel Lassiter in the town square, and on all of Pa's medals, but there ain't no brass plate on *Earl* Lassiter's belly. And if there was, it wouldn't buy me a Mason jar full of popskull whiskey. Good names and wore-out land and old traditions—none of that stuff is any good anymore. Goddamnit, the whole world is changin', and the South has got to change with it, or get sloughed off like a garden snake sheddin' its skin.

"You know what that means, Ellen? It means if the old way don't work, find a new way. We got to quit livin' in the past and see there's more to things than sweat and scratchin' and once in a while Saturday nights."

"And more than Beevo's," Ellen murmured.

If she hadn't been what she was and who she was, Earl might have kissed her cheek, because this woman seemed to understand. "It's why I'm goin' on up to the big house," he said. "Avery Coffield is a smart man, and so are some of the others. Maybe I can make him see what a good thing my post peeler will be. If I had the money, if I could order some factory parts made up—"

"Your Pa'd never let you take Coffield money."

"Money don't come ear-cropped and branded," Earl said. "It belongs to whoever holds it in his hands."

"Ben don't see it that way."

"I know," Earl said, "damn it, I *know*."

Ellen drifted back and put her hand against the same heavy timber Ben Lassiter had leaned against. "Takes a spell to get two mules to work in harness," she said. "One has a mind to go thisaway, and the other one won't pull. Takes patience and time, but like as not, before long they're shoulder to shoulder and gettin' the plowin' done."

"And one good tractor can do the work of a dozen mules," Earl said.

"You make do with mules until you *gets* that tractor," Ellen said. She turned and started for the door, walking gracefully with her back held straight. Pausing then, she said over her shoulder, "Course, that don't mean you can't go around pricin' machinery, long as everybody in town don't hear you're in the market. And Earl—one more thing."

"Yes?"

She stood in shadow now, her face hidden, her body only a darkened blur. "You said there's more to it than Saturday nights and Beevo's. Well, I say all the women who ought to be workin' at Beevo's cribs ain't there; some of 'em are runnin' loose."

"What the hell—" Earl said, but she was gone, and he stood glaring at where she'd been before taking off the jacket and folding it over one arm.

He put the coat on the seat of the battered pickup and gunned the motor viciously before driving off down the dirt road toward the highway.

CHAPTER 3

The jacket fit perfectly, tailored just so, and Elliot Coffield loved it. The tartan tie and matching cummerbund were a bit daring for Temple County, but it was what just everybody was wearing up north and out on the Coast. He admired the combination in the upstairs hall mirror, turning his head slowly from side to side to catch the light.

A few of the older men might be wearing dinner jackets, he thought, but certainly none of the younger ones. They'd be content with linen or seersuckers; the kind that would crease up before the evening even got under way. Still watching the mirror, Elliot drew a cigarette from a burnished gold case and lighted it with a matching, monogrammed lighter.

Turning, he peered over the banister into the living room, where his mother was moving among the tables, where pink-jacketed servants were laying out the Georgian silver. The pink livery had been his idea, since the Harveys and Nelsons had their waiters in the usual white. They were the only other families that counted; others, shamed by the size and opulence of The Shadows and the Harveys' Whiteoaks, the Nelsons' Moss Bend, gave their more or less formal parties in the banquet room of The Templars. So gauche, he thought, and moved down the stairs, enjoying the beauty of the room below, the quiet, refined almost-beauty of his mother.

Lila was so smoothly efficient, he thought; she could direct everything and see that all came off well, and you would never see a beading of moisture upon that well-bred face, never find her coiffure mussed. His mother might very well be one of a kind; he had never seen another woman like her, with such calm and poise and impeccable taste. Yet in all these years, Lila Coffield hadn't been able to smooth the rough edges from her husband. Someday, Elliot thought, he would have to ask his mother just why she had married Avery.

In a way, he supposed, he was glad she had; The Shadows was grander than either Whiteoaks or Moss Bend, and coarse as his father often was, still Avery was better than either Sam Harvey or Martin Nelson. He couldn't imagine calling either of *them* his daddy.

"Elliot," Lila said, glancing up from arranging flowers in a delicate bowl. "You look very nice, dear."

He went over to kiss her cheek and smell the faint, ladylike odor of jasmine he always associated with Lila. "Not too nice, Mother? I mean, if it's a bit much, I could go back up and change to my old midnight-blue jacket."

"It's perfect for you, dear," Lila answered, patting his cheek. "I'm so glad you had it done in New Orleans, where there are still decent tailors."

"The cummerbund and tie," he went on, "not garish?"

"*You* would never be garish, darling. Why do you fret so? Oh, I see the roses coming. Excuse me, dear."

"May I help?"

"Why don't you join your father and Jessica in the library?"

Elliot was dismissed and knew it. He hesitated a moment, then realized he was about to drop ash on the rug and cupped a hand beneath the cigarette until he could deposit it in an ashtray.

From the library, he heard the familiar, discordant crashing of the cocktail shaker and their easy laughter, a background for that traditional evening sound. He was a year older than his sister, and heir apparent; why then did the pair of them make him feel so uncomfortable? Why did the evening drink ritual close him off and make him the interloper?

Pausing at another mirror, the one with the lovely old curlicued frame, Elliot lifted his hand and rumpled his hair just a little, pulled his tie slightly askew. Grinding out his cigarette, he forced himself to slouch as he strolled into the library. He had never liked this room, especially the glassy-eyed deer head above the mantelpiece, nor the threatening rows of guns behind glass, nor the cloying scent of old leather and cigar smoke that seemed to permeate the very walls. Years ago, there had been shelf after shelf of books, but most were gone now, the shelves altered to display Jessica's horse-show trophies.

Avery was making a choppy, muscular production of·using the cocktail shaker and chanting, ". . . five . . . six . . . seven . . ."

Jessica drummed her forefingers upon the bartop. ". . . to make a sidecar next to heaven, it's never eight but always seven . . ."

So damned childish, Elliot thought; as if anybody could tell the difference, or cared. They laughed together as if it was the first time they'd used the prattle, instead of the millionth. As he poured, Avery looked up and saw him. Nodding, Elliot walked over to them. His father didn't pour a drink for him, just shoved the shaker his way. Elliot didn't reach for it.

Cocking his head at Jessica, Avery said, "He didn't want the niggers wearin' white coats, but look at him. What you think, Jess—this new jacket too pinched in, or maybe not enough? I mean, that's goddamned important, you know."

Elliot said stiffly, "I can change it, if you want me to."

Avery drank and said, "What does your mama want?"

"She—she said I looked nice."

"Yeah," Avery said, "you look real nice. Ain't you goin' to be late pickin' up Mary Alice?"

Staring at coldly beaded sweat forming on the silver shaker, Elliot said, "I—she said it would be easier if her folks brought her, and I wouldn't have to make the trip."

"I'll be damned," Avery said, snorting. "You're engaged to a girl, a mighty fine-lookin' girl, and you let her folks carry her home in *their* car?"

"I can take her home if you want," Elliot said. He started to unbutton his jacket, but let his hand fall.

"Hellfire," Avery said, "if *I* wanted to take that cute little gal home, the Harveys would be lucky to see her come daylight, and then she'd sure as hell be some mussed. But you—oh goddamn; go on out yonder and help your mama with the flowers or something."

As Elliot stalked from the library, he heard his father mumble, "I want, *I* want; always, it's what I want. Just what in the jumped-up and ass-kickin' hell does *he* want?"

Jessica said, "He does look nice, you know. You might have said so."

Avery refilled their glasses, emptying the shaker.

"He looks *pretty,* and damned if I'll tell him that. Scared of horses when he was a youngun; never even splashed in the mud because he didn't want to get dirty; and to this day, Elliot couldn't hit a bull in the ass with a bass fiddle, much less pick a bobwhite outa the air like you can."

"He has other talents," Jessica said. "Look how he and Mama are making over the old wing. That takes a lot of knowhow, to find exactly the right pieces of furniture for the period. One of those Royal Street antique dealers could sell me half the trash in New Orleans, and I wouldn't know the difference."

"You wouldn't give a damn," Avery said. "You could keep the place runnin', if somethin' happened to me, and keep the niggers on their toes, and you wouldn't let old Sam Harvey skin you at the bank, and if you wanted somethin' done to the house—why hell, you'd hire an interior decorator to do it for you, and turn around and have his hide if he didn't do it right."

Jessica got up from the bar and walked across the library to peer out the window. At times like this, she could talk at her father, but never *to* him. Even if she stood up on a table and screamed it at Avery Coffield, he wouldn't realize that his son was his son, and his daughter his daughter, and he couldn't change one for the other. He'd come pretty close to it with Elliot, she admitted, but he'd never see that for his own fault, either. To be honest, Jessica told herself, Mama had a hand in it, and maybe she did, too. But by the time she got old enough to know it, Elliot was out of reach. If only he wasn't so submissive to Avery, and so—so goddamned bitchy to everyone else.

Across the lawn where oriental lanterns swayed in a welcome breeze, cars were beginning to arrive, purring into the long, curved driveway. Nobody different would get out of any of them, just bodies carrying the same old-old faces, the same old-young faces; there'd be boys she'd known from first grade, and paunchy, raunchy men who'd keep saying they knew her when she was kneehigh to a boll weevil. The women would be worse, primped and powdered wives who'd be all sugary when they said how beautiful she'd grown up, and hating her flat belly and trim behind because their own were sweating in girdles. The girls would pretend not to notice her new green party dress, nor see how lowcut it was, and somebody would be bound to whisper that Jessica was wearing falsies. They'd pretend the dress didn't cost more money than most of them saw in a month of Sundays, that it wasn't the perfect, special shade of April green to set off her coloring.

"Jess?" her father said from the bar. "Want me to shake up another batch?"

Without turning, she said, "No; sidecars won't go well with champagne until after I've eaten." The Caddys kept coming, and that freshly polished Continental of Martin Nelson; there were a few Buicks and Olds, and one dusty Chevy station wagon. That was the Carters, who pretended it didn't matter because he was the high school principal and she taught seventh grade, which gave them some kind of status. After she went off to college, she'd have Daddy buy her one of those sporty MGs, something dashing and very fast. It would be the only one in Temple County when she came home on vacation. Still at the window, she heard Avery leave the room, and the boom of his voice as he began to welcome guests. It was getting dark, but Jessica thought she saw a pickup slow down, then speed up again, as if the driver had changed his mind. Tak-

ing a fistful of curtain, she squeezed it hard. If Earl
Lassiter lost his nerve at the last minute, she would
never forgive him.

Outside, Earl drove by the entranceway again; he
didn't want to park the old truck in with all those new
cars, but he didn't want to call attention to himself by
walking all the way up the drive, either. Pulling into
the drive, he angled the pickup for the turnoff road
that led out back to the toolshed, parked it there, and
cut the lights. He sat awhile, craned around to watch
skylarking boys and giggling girls pile out of cars.
Some of the boys wore open shirts, but all of them had
jackets on. Earl left the tie but put on his coat and
climbed down. For some of the guys, this would be
their last good fling; draft notices came quickly after
graduation.

He thought of Alvah over there, the short notes that
came from time to time, addressed to him and never
Ben. For a couple of years, there'd been only a rare
postcard from far places like Chicago or El Paso or
San Francisco while his brother was bumming around.
Alvah'd never said if the draft caught him or if he
signed up himself, but now he was a Marine in Korea.
Ben Lassiter listened close to the war news on the radio every night, but never said anything about it. Earl
sighed, tried to make the jacket fit better, and crossed
the lawn to where colored lanterns bobbed over well-
stocked tables.

Inside the house, Jessica sulked. She moved from
one chattering group to another, finding nothing new
in any, saying the same old things and hearing the
stock comments. She drank two glasses of champagne
and nibbled at the barbecue; she danced once with

Jerry Brand and twice with Kent Neil, then begged off
and slipped into the library to hide from other silly,
clumsy boys.

"Well," she said, finding Elliot behind the bar,
"isn't the bubbly enough, or are you practicing on sidecars?"

"That," Elliot said with a curl of his mouth, "I
leave to you and dear old Dad."

Climbing onto a stool, Jessica crossed her legs and
asked, "Where is Daddy, anyhow?"

Elliot poured a glass of something brown and icy.
"With that Jew from Boston."

"A Jew—here?"

Elliot tasted his drink and nodded. "I shook this
eight times, and it's better. You mean you didn't know
about our Semite visitor? You mean there's something
Avery didn't tell you? My, my; you haven't even left
home yet, and there seems to be a little crack develop-
ing in that sacred, loving bond between you two.
Imagine how much you won't know in a year or two."

Jessica glared at her brother. "I'll bet he's out by the
pool."

Elliot shrugged. "Look for yourself."

"You really are a bitch," Jessica said. "While I find
Daddy and this Israelite, why don't you do your duty
to Mary Alice? I mean, you could sneak her away from
her folks and drive her home the long way. You can
take out the back seat and have her lie down on it . . .
pull up her dress and snatch down her panties . . .
can't you just see Mary Alice with those plump white
thighs wigglin' and her belly pumpin' . . ."

Elliot's slim hand clenched around his glass. "You
really are disgusting."

"Ain't I?" she laughed, and skipped out of the library.

A black was netting moths and night beetles from the light-dappled surface of the pool. Two girls were wading in the shallow end, their skirts pulled up; a young man sat uncertainly on the tiled edging, his trunks new and dry.

Ira Lowenstein's suit was new, too, smelling of the same store racks where Temple County men bought their own linen suits. Avery Coffield lolled back on a lounge and eyed the man, thinking that was smart of him, trying to blend in with the bunch. But Lowenstein would always stand out, even if he'd been born here; there was an intensity to him, a calculating something that peeped through the eyes. A hurry-up feeling that sat wrong in the jovial camaraderie of the night.

Over his glass, Avery said, "It takes understandin', our Temple County. It's a good place to live, and our people relate in a simple, special way. That's important to us, Mr. Lowenstein."

Lowenstein held his own wine glass lightly in long fingers. "Please—it's Ira."

Avery said, "I call it harmony, Mr. Lowenstein; the harmony and balance of a society that don't muddy up its own drinkin' water. Now maybe you folks up north think different, and you got a right to—up there. Down here, there's a time and a place for everything, and everybody knows where they fit in. Harmony, Mr. Lowenstein."

Lowenstein said, "Just call me Ira; I'm only a businessman like you."

"Like me?" Avery shook his head. "Plantin' comes first with me; business is next. But look here; I'm monopolizin' all your time, and I'm sure some of the other boys got some questions for you." He looked past Lowenstein then, blinking rapidly. "Jess, damnit! That ain't a proper bathin' suit, and you know it."

"The newest thing, Daddy." Pirouetting slowly, she showed him more of its skimpiness. "I reckon your visitor from up north can tell you everybody's wearin' them there."

"Here ain't there," Avery grunted. "Mr. Lowenstein, my daughter Jessica, but I'm not sure I want to claim her right now."

Coming quickly to his feet, Lowenstein held out his hand. "Miss Coffield, any man on any beach in this country would lay claim to you, if he could."

Smiling, her eyes lidded, Jessica murmured, "My; such courtliness from a Yankee."

Avery glanced at the outside bar, the men gathered there drinking heavily and getting louder. He said, "If you put on a robe, maybe you can show our guest around. Carry him down to the spring, maybe. I got to talk to the boys, kind of lay the groundwork for Mr. Lowenstein here."

"Be proud to, Daddy," Jessica said. Hips swaying, she walked past them to the pool house and reached inside, feeling Lowenstein's eyes on her as she slipped into a terrycloth robe and sandals. Turned back to them, the robe hanging open, she said, "But surely he isn't interested in our old legends."

"I'd like to know as much about the country—and its people—as I can learn," Ira said.

Sliding her arm through his, she guided him through the swirling crowd. He was different, a stranger from a far land, and that made him interesting. The man was dark, his hair fitted closely to his head in ringlets; his lips were full, and there was the look of a hawk about him. Jessica brushed her thigh against his as they strolled across the lawns and down the graveled walkway toward the old Indian spring. Daddy had simply used her as an excuse to get the man out of the way for a while, she knew, but it might lead to more than that. After all, it was *her* party, but Daddy was using it as he always did, to talk business and get things done his way.

"Kind of dark here," she said. "Hang on to my hand."

"Gladly," he said, his fingers softwarm but strong around her own. It was a hand that had never known calluses, she thought.

"There's a light at the spring," she said. "See it through the trees? You might not understand about the spring, Mr. Lowenstein."

"Ira," he said. "Why do I get the impression that I'm in a game and don't know the rules?"

"A game?" As they came into the circle of yellow light, Jessica pulled her hand from his. "What kind of game, Mr. Lowenstein?"

"That one," he said. "Always *mister*, a way to set me apart and keep me there."

"Well, you *are* a stranger, but when I know you better, when I know what you're doin' down here—"

"I could be one of the Magi, come bearing the gifts of now, so Temple County can climb out of yesterday."

"Maybe we like it there, in yesterday."

Ira touched her hand again. "Is that why you bought that swimsuit? It's *now*, Jessica, and tomorrow's design will be just as interesting, and probably freer."

She moved away from him, belting the robe about her narrow waist. "Here's the spring, and I know it doesn't look like much, but there's a wonderful story comes with it, a magic story. Reckon that's where the word magic came from, the Magi?"

"Probably."

"But one of the three wise men was black, wasn't he?"

Ira frowned at her. "I think so."

"Well, now," Jessica said, "he might have been an Indian, I suppose. Like the Creeks who were here a long time ago. Our own Magi was a chief named Sow-Hita, and the first settlers got along with him real good."

"Harmony and balance," Ira murmured.

As if she hadn't heard him, Jessica went on, "Until a white girl disappeared and they blamed Sow-Hita for it. One summer night, they lured him here and stabbed him to death, just where we're standin' now. There wasn't a spring here then, but after they buried him so the Creeks would think he just vanished, too, the spring started up. You just hunker down close and watch it, and you'll see somethin'."

Ira kneeled to stare into the water, although he'd much rather look at the girl's slim, tanned legs. But the water stirred itself and bubbled, pulsing like a liquid heart, turning dark, turning the color of blood. He put his hand into it, scooped some to sniff it in his palm, to put his tongue to it.

"Red clay substrata and iron sulfides; some kind of geological fault that allows pressure to build up—"

She took a step back. "That's the way you look at it *now*. I like the legend better, and we'll keep tellin' it that way around here."

Ira stood up and wiped his fingers on a white handkerchief. "And where are the Creek Indians now, the ones whose chief's heart is supposed to be in this spring?"

"Why—they're all gone. I mean, they attacked the whites at Fort Mims and massacred 'em every one. Then Andy Jackson came to clean out the Creeks. There weren't many left, and the survivors were shipped off somewhere."

"Because they resisted change and couldn't adapt," Ira said. "It happens every time a sophisticated culture clashes with a primitive one. Adapt, integrate, or perish."

"Integrate?" Jessica said. "There's another funny word. You sound like a schoolteacher, Mr. Lowenstein. This is my going-away party and I don't want to hear any lectures until I get to college."

"Hey," Ira said. "I didn't mean to upset you. I'm sorry."

"You probably *will* be sorry," Jessica said, and wheeled to stride away up the walk.

CHAPTER 4

He'd been through the house, always on the fringe of some bunch or the other, his eyes daring the town boys to laugh at his jacket. He'd had bubbly wine from a crystal glass and tried some food he couldn't identify, and when he ran into Mrs. Coffield made his howdies to her real polite. Yes'm, he said, they were working hard over to his place, and no ma'am, he hadn't seen Jessica yet.

The swimming pool was something, he admitted. The Tchufuncta River not half a mile away, and the Coffields built them a swimming hole right in their own backyard, where they wouldn't have to worry about stomping on a copperhead or a snapping turtle grabbing on. But he wondered how they'd filled it; only a few days back, one of the Coffield niggers was saying how low the well was.

Uncomfortable, he wandered around the lawns and ate something on a cracker that tasted fishy and looked like blackberry jam. He rinsed out his mouth with more wine and kept looking for Jessica, but ran into Mary Alice Harvey instead.

She was pouty, rared back in a lawn chair with no-body close by. "Didn't expect to see you here," she said.

"Where's Elliot?" he asked. Mary Alice had been a

pudgy, sullen girl all through school. The baby fat was gone now, and she had a pretty good body, but she still kept that lower lip stuck out.

"My fiancé is busy as all getout, helpin' his mama," she said. "Find us some more champagne, Earl. I might's well get good and drunk, for all he cares."

He found a warm bottle on a table and brought it back. Over at the bar, Avery and the banker and Nelson were hollering it up. Pouring wine into Mary Alice's glass, Earl said, "When you two gettin' married?"

The girl gulped at her drink. "Damned if I know. The wedding keeps gettin' put off, and my daddy don't like it any more than I do. *You* wouldn't put off marryin' me, would you, Earl?"

"You and me ain't never been friends, Mary Alice," he answered, his head beginning to feel a little swimmy, "but I sure wouldn't back off from the chance of gettin' into bed with you."

She blinked up at him, her shiny lower lip pouty. "You know how to make a girl feel good, you ol' country boy. I bet you could make her feel lots better, in bed. Tell you what—if my fiancé don't get away from his mama, maybe you and me can sneak over to the river and take us a nice, long swim."

"They got a pool right over yonder," Earl said.

"You got to wear a bathin' suit here," Mary Alice said, and he hid his face behind the wine glass, bubbles tickling his tongue.

"There you are," Jessica Coffield said behind him, and Earl was glad to swing around. "I just *knew* you'd show up, but I guess I kept missing you in all this crowd."

She was beautiful; she wore a swimsuit that clung to her body the way his hands itched to. He could see the push of her nipples against rubbery green material, and down below, the rich mounding, with a hint of a cleft to it.

Mary Alice said, "*I* found him all right."

And Jessica answered, "Keep tryin', dear. Maybe you won't have to ride home with your mama, after all."

Warm and cool at the same time, her hand was on Earl's, and he followed her happily, the whole evening coming alive with her presence. The lanterns were brighter, happier, the music more lively. His throat tightened when he saw they were moving away from the crowd and down toward the Indian spring. The smell of her perfume went all the way down into his groin, and the light, sometimes brush of her thigh against his own made Earl go hard. So many years of tomboying, then of easy flirting, but now—now all the promises made by Jessica's eyes and body were about to come true. To be so near that fulfillment shook Earl, and he tried to keep his hand from trembling.

He thought they'd turn off before they got to the spring, ease into some grassy spot guarded by tall hedges, but she kept walking, right on into the circle of light at the spring itself. Jessica stopped there and turned into him, pressing the soft, supple length of her body right up to him, so he could feel her breasts mashed to his chest, feel the rounded cleft lifting and pushing against his crotch.

Nibbling at his lips, Jessica's mouth was sweet and fiery, making him catch his breath and tighten his arms around the slim, firm body. Her tongue was a quickwet flame, darting between his teeth, seeking his answering tongue, and below, Jessica's hips made little short swings, back and forth, up and down. Earl's hands slid down across them and found the wondrous, surging melons to cup.

When he could breathe, when he could tear away his mouth, he said, "Let's—let's get outa this light."

Her hands were all over him, inside his shirt, down his belly, back out again so that she could roam searching fingers over his upright shaft. "No," Jessica panted. "Let's do it here, right here by the spring."

Earl fought to keep from going off in his pants. "Damn, Jessica, you know we can't. Suppose somebody came down the path and saw us? Your old man, anybody—"

"Are you scared?" She had his fly unzipped now, and her hand seared him. "Are you afraid to take a chance, Earl? I thought you weren't afraid of anything. Come on, Earl; come on and do it to me—right here and right now."

"Jessica—" Pulling at her, legs spread apart and awkward, he tried to draw her off into the shadows. "Oh, damn! I want you so much, need you so much—"

She jerked back, sending him off balance. When he looked up, she had stripped off her bathing suit and was standing, hips outthrust, crossed arms cupping her breasts, taunting him. Lamplight gleamed upon the honeyed curls of her mound, reflected from her tapered thighs. "Then *do* it!" Jessica commanded. "Do it to me, Earl Lassiter—*fuck me!*"

She might just as well have kicked him in his aching balls, because the word hung ugly on the beauty of her mouth. But even if he was crippled, Earl might have gone right down on his knees and crawled to her, just so he could bury his face into the silken smoothness of her belly, so he could feel the golden roundness of her thighs against his cheek.

But somebody was coming, laughing and calling out from up the path, a babble of voices that came slamming into his head and rang echoing there. Shaking

like a pine sapling caught in a high wind, Earl reached
helplessly out to her, his mouth moving without saying anything.

Then he was gone, whipped around and running,
plunging through a hedge and falling, getting up to
run blindly on. Breath rasping in his throat, heart
clattering, he raced clear down to the highway and
broke through brush there. Standing in the road,
sweat pouring off him, he looked wildly right and left,
then trotted across the highway into trees where he
could work his way unseen back to the house.

Christ; it was still all lit up like some gigantic
whorehouse, most of the cars still nose to bumper
along the curved drive. Earl slipped along to the
toolshed and climbed quivering into his pickup. He
was gone in a moment, back wheels throwing gravel
and not giving a damn if it broke some Caddy's windshield, maybe even hoping it would.

Inside the house, Avery Coffield heard the roaring
motor, lifted his head, and grinned. Couple of hot-
pants kids eager to get off from the old folks so they
could hump in the back seat, he thought; it would be
good to be that young and horny again.

At his elbow, Lowenstein was saying something
about a give-and-take proposition, about labor pools
and water power, and that he knew the drought was
unusual, and if somebody had the foresight to build a
dam—

"Avery, you old bastard!" Sam Harvey's face was red
and his eyes didn't track. "Come on, boy; women are
all in the library, and it's time for some serious
drinkin'."

And Martin Nelson carried himself straight up, as
he always did when he was drunk; there was Jellico

busting a gut over something Burr Watson said. Good old boys, every one of them; they knew a party was for eating and drinking and, later on, a little nooky. Not like this Jew salesman or organizer-engineer, or whatever the hell he claimed to be. Down here, damnit, there was a time for hoorawing and a time for business, and folks had better sense than to mix them up.

"Ease off, boys," Avery said. "You're settin' a bad example for Mr. Lowenstein here, and the first one of you hollers out Beevo's is goin' to be in a whole world of trouble."

"*Me* down yonder at Beevo's?" Sam Harvey said. "Hellfire, boy—I'm too goddamn respectable to be caught at a nigger whorehouse."

Will Jellico let out a yip that made the kids jerk their heads around; they were jitterbugging out on the lawn, but Avery didn't see Jessica with them, nor the Lassiter boy. He didn't expect to see Elliot; Elliot would be dancing attendance upon his darling mama and the ladies—the older ladies.

"Get caught?" Jellico snorted. "Who'd be able to tote you off? Not the sheriff; hell, it'd take the whole damned state *po*lice to tote just your pocketbook, Sam; much less get your fingers out'n everybody else's."

Stiffly, calmly, Martin Nelson intoned, "Beevo's is a mighty good idea about now."

"Yeah," Sam Harvey said, eyes bulging. "Could be a mighty damned good idea; as daddy of the bride, I'd be doin' my bounden duty to see the groom knows what-for. Avery, far as I know, your boy ain't never been to Beevo's."

Avery's lips were getting numb, and the Jew was still at his sleeve. He felt more like sneaking off upstairs and lying down for a while; it had been like that of late. But they were all watching him and he had to say something. "Elliot's a quiet one, that's for sure."

"Ain't natural to be *that* quiet," Jellico said. "That boy needs some stumpjuice poured down him, and to get his wick dipped."

"Sure hate to have my little gal disappointed," Sam Harvey said. "Everybody knows what an old he-coon *you* are, Avery, but—"

"Goddamnit," Avery said, downing his bourbon, "you say Coffield, you say cocksman; there ain't no difference. I'll go get the boy, and Mr. Lowenstein"—he found the dark, too sober face at his side—"you get to ride with us. I mean, you come all the way down here to run a survey on Temple County, here's where you get to know it from the bottom up."

Will Jellico yipped again, and turned it into a full-throated Rebel yell. "Bottom up! Best goddamn way I know of lookin' at 'em, but belly up ain't bad, neither, and I'll whup ass on anybody says sideways ain't good, too."

Standing in the library door, Avery motioned to his son, and when Elliot dutifully trotted over whispered to him, "Your girl is out there dancin' with the Watson boy, and he's got a hand on her tit. Don't you give a good goddamn?"

Elliot said, "I—well, I—"

"Oh, shit," Avery said. "You ain't even started to get drunk. You been pourin' tea for your mama and the old ladies?"

"They're having coffee, Daddy, and I—"

Avery got him by the elbow. "You're comin' with me, boy." He practically dragged him across the lawn as the others fell in behind, and they all piled into Avery's car. Elliot sat pinched between him and Sam Harvey; the others gobbled and whooped in the back seat. Avery grinned into the windshield as the Caddy swerved off the highway and bounced along the creek road, its headlights stabbing the night. Mr. Ira Lowenstein might be some cramped back there, with the boys wallering all over him, but he'd bet a bushel the Jew wouldn't say a goddamn thing about it. His kind wouldn't; they were always good salesmen. Son of a bitch coming down here like he had something to give away, and all the time he wanted something from Temple County, more than the county wanted to give.

All that slick talk about setting up a pulpwood center here, a big mill; hell—there were mills in Bogalusa and Mobile, and the wood had been hauled there ever since folks had been cutting it. Pulpwood; Avery spun the wheel to avoid another car and made a face at the night rushing past his window. Pulpwood was for them that had to scratch for a living, like cutting railroad crossties used to be, a business for hardscrabble farmers trying to eke out a hand-to-mouth existence, for woods runners and niggers who couldn't make out any other way.

This was still cotton country, by God, and a few bad years didn't change that fact. Come high water or drought or goddamn Yankee infiltrators, this was cotton country and always would be. Wait until Mr. Lowenstein tried to get a toehold here; see if anybody would sell to him and his outfit. All he could pick up was little dabs of land that didn't amount to anything, and as for building a dam, the Lassiter place was the only one with any hill to it, where the Tchufuncta might be diverted and backed up. Ben Lassiter sell *his* land? That ornery bastard would rather trade his medals for cornmeal. Like medals meant something, and money didn't. Shit.

"Yonder it is!" Sam Harvey hollered, and Avery focused upon the ramshackle building with the parking lot discreetly around back. One big bulb hung over the sign with moths swooping around it, and a bat winging in every so often to pick off one, but any man with balls could have found it in the dark. Avery slewed gravel as he braked to a stop. When the others piled out, he clung to the wheel for a long, sweaty second. The crabmeat, he thought; his belly was getting old as the rest of him, and he ought to know better than to slosh bourbon over crabmeat and caviar and whatever the hell else he'd stuffed down.

Elliot stood beside the car, momentarily forgotten by the others as they hauled Lowenstein into Beevo's. He stood paralyzed in his fancy, tailored jacket until Avery climbed out and took him by the shoulder.

"You're goin' in there, boy. You're goin' to lose your cherry like a man. You'll get pissy-assed and fallin' down drunk for the first time in your starched and ironed life, and you'll put the meat to some black nooky, like you should have done years back. Goddamn if I understand how I ever let your mama make such a—"

"Don't you *dare*," Elliot hissed. "Don't you mention her name here, of all places."

"And don't *you* try to run off on me now," Avery said, "or I'll stomp a mudhole in your ass and walk it dry. Now git!" He flung Elliot at the door, and followed the boy into Beevo's, into sweaty smoke and a jukebox blaring, and the smell of raw white lightning. And that other smell, the one that flared a man's nostrils and made his crotch tingle—the faroff, perfumy, primitive odor of black whores.

There was room at the bar, and Avery pushed Elliot into it. Beevo's hairless head bobbed in greeting, his flat, quick eyes darting to Elliot, then crinkling into smile lines as the black welcomed his customers, the cream of Temple County society.

"Mist' Coffield, suh; purely a pleasure to see you here."

"Set out the Mason jars, boy," Avery told him, "and tell me about that new gal you got."

Beevo's blueblack face glistened; his shirt was yellow silk, open at a fat throat; his smile was wide and gold-toothed. "Beats all, Mist' Coffield, how you knows everything happenin' in this county. Just got her in a spell back, and she's purely somethin', I swear."

Conscious of Elliot's pale, tense face, Avery said, "Clean, you black bastard; she sure as hell better be clean."

"Why, suh! You ever know ol' Beevo's gals to be anything else? This 'un, now—she's special enough for your ownself; ain't but fifteen, and got sweet lil' hard knockers—"

Will Jellico hammered on the bar. "Knock her up, that's what. Knock her down, then knock her up— *whooie!*"

"She'll be for my boy here," Avery said, and took a long, hard swallow of corn that burned all the way down.

Beevo winked and nodded and leaned close, his elbows on the bar. "Maybe room seven?"

"That ain't a goddamn bit funny," Avery snapped.

Drawing back immediately, Beevo widened his wet smile and rubbed at his bald head. "Just in case, suh. Anything you say, Mist' Coffield."

Turning on Elliot, Avery said, "I say drink up, boy; swallow it down like a man. It'll put lead in your pencil."

Arm moving jerkily, Elliot drank the clear liquid

and choked. He held to the bar top and tugged his collar open; the tartan tie hung limply.

"That's the way," Avery said. "That's the goddamn way; have another—and Beevo, tell your new gal a horny young stud is just about to tear up her pea patch."

"Yessuh; gets her ready right now; she'll be proud to take on a Coffield, suh."

"Bet your ass," Sam Harvey said.

"And raise you six inches," Burr Watson laughed. "Hey there, Mr. Lowenstein—you got that much left after they clipped you?"

Lowenstein was flushed, his coat gone and sweat blotting through his shirt. "I do—do okay."

Hang in there, you son of a bitch, Avery thought; do all we ask, be one of the boys, so you can soften us up and sell us your city ideas. He looked at Elliot, and his eyes dared the boy to get sick and puke. If the kid had half the brass the Jew did—

Beevo was in the back door, rubbing his hands together, the gold smile stitched on. Avery took his son by the arm and pushed him that way. "Go get her, boy." He watched Elliot; it would be all right; it would work out. Avery had another drink, and another, only half listening to the others hoorawing Lowenstein, knowing they were setting him up for room seven, the one with the fake mirror in its wall. He thought that even if Lowenstein knew about it, the man would go ahead and perform for them. Part of the survey, part of marketing, part of making a horse's ass out of yourself in order to sell something.

Head buzzing, Avery wished the jukebox wasn't so loud, that the bunch of white trash over in the far corner would hold it down. He shouldn't have eaten the crab, he thought, and gulped another swallow of corn to ease his belly. Lowenstein? He didn't give a bird turd that Sam and Martin were steering the Jew out back to room seven. When Will and Burr laughed up to him, telling him to come on, Avery shook his head and drank some more, pushing his stomach up against the bar. The jukebox thumped and whined; some woods runner broke a glass; a car roared away outside.

Beevo was at his arm, sweating and trying hard to grin. "Mist' Coffield—that there was my truck. He— your boy took it. I ain't worried, suh; I knows you'll get it back to me in one piece. But—"

Avery hissed, "But what, goddamnit? And keep it down, hear?"

"It's Lucy, suh; the new gal. Your boy—well, he beat the shit outa her, Mist' Coffield. I mean, he near about tore *up* that gal, after he tied her down and stuffed a towel in her mouth. I swear, we had some mean 'uns in here before, but him—"

"I'll bring back your truck," Avery said, "or get you another, if he piles it up."

"Yessuh, I knows that, suh. It's just—well, that gal's bad hurt, and there's goin' to be a doctor, and she'll be outa action for maybe a month, and—"

Thrusting a hand into his pocket, Avery jerked out his billfold and emptied a sheaf of bills on the bar. "Take her to that nigger doctor, that Davison. And keep your mouth shut."

Beevo's fingers closed on the money, spirited it away. "Two other gals seen some of it, and the Yankee was just comin' outa room seven. Might be, it'll take more'n this, to keep it all real quiet. I mean, it ain't like he was natural; he was cryin' harder than she was, and callin' her sister and mama and beatin' away on her—"

Avery pushed away from the bar. "Beevo," he said,

"shut the fuck up. Close that big mouth and keep it closed. You think you're goin' to squeeze *me*, siphon money out of *me* like corn out of a still? You black son of a bitch, I got you under my heel, and all I got to do is stomp down. So I'm tellin' you flat out that gal *and* you better be out of this county by Monday. You hear me, nigger?"

Beevo swallowed, his smile gone. "But Mist' Cofield—that ain't much time. I'd have to sell out and move—it just ain't much time."

"Longer than it'd take for this whorehouse to burn down," Avery said. "A whole lot longer than it'd take for your balls to get cut off."

Beevo sidled back, passed one hand over his head, and nodded.

Avery drank from the Mason jar. The whiskey was bitter in his throat.

CHAPTER 5

Earl didn't know where he was going, just so he got away from The Shadows and Jessica's stark, taunting image. All that beautiful body just begging for it, that sweet feathery snatch hidden from him all these years, shining right out in the open, and horny Earl Lassiter had lit a shuck, cut and run away from her.

How come she kept saying do it there in the light, where they could get caught by anybody coming down the spring path? Somebody *had* been coming. And damnit, her saying *fuck* like she was no better than some two-bit whore; that wasn't right, either.

Between his thighs, his sack acted like it was a balloon. The stone ache; he'd heard men joke about it, but it wasn't all that damned funny. It hurt like all billy hell. He wasn't scared of Jessica, or not doing it right and having her laugh at him. It was the light, and people all over the place, and Jessica Coffield acting like she wanted to get caught doing it.

Wildly, the truck careened down a back road, and because he didn't have his mind on what he was doing, the Chevy spun out and threw dirt. Hands sweaty on the wheel, Earl tried to shake off his shame, tried not to feel less than a man. Driving slowly then, he realized he was in the Hollow, in bootleg country.

His lights found a battered GMC he recognized,

Billy Dee and Joe Blake's. They'd be off on their regular Saturday-night doings, out here for some corn whiskey before starting their real devilment. He didn't want to see them, and started to speed on past, when he caught sight of loose red hair. Earl cut his motor and killed the lights. In sudden, eye-blinking dark, he could hear katydids and the faroff call of a whippoorwill.

"Hey, Jolene—that you?"

"Hey, Earl. Coffields run you off?"

"Run myself off," he said. "Too rich for me, I reckon. Boys been gone long?"

"Long enough so the skeeters about to carry me off. They have to go clear over to Clark County for that stuff?"

Earl rubbed his hand across his lower belly. "Don't know who's sellin' it out here, and I ain't studyin' on findin' a still in the dark, where they don't know who I am."

"Billy Dee left most of a six pack here, but it's gone warm."

"We could cool it in the river," he said.

The GMC's door creaked open, and he could see the shadow of her getting out. "Just you and me? Them boys will be fit to be tied."

"Just until they get wall-eyed drunk," Earl said.

She came around the truck and climbed in beside him. "I don't like it when they're drunk." Jolene's perfume filled the cab, and bottles clinked on her lap. "I never did like 'em the way I like you, Earl. But you never gave me a chance."

"You got the chance," he said, and coasted the pickup away before turning on lights again. If Jolene didn't run off at the mouth, the Blakes would never know where she'd gone; they might figure she drank

their beer and left. Jolene Kobburn did about anything she damned well had a mind to; the trouble was,
she had a mind to do it with just about everybody.

They passed a beer bottle back and forth, and her
hand crawled around on his thigh. He wasn't scared,
and never had been. Jolene had better sense than to do
it in the light, and she was easier to talk with. When
he parked at the river, Earl felt loose and laughing,
and shucked out of his clothes almost quick as she did.
Weak moonlight spattered through the trees, and Jolene's skin was white in it, darting down the sand to
splash into dark water where she whooped and hollered.

Catching up with her, Earl wrestled her around and
she threw water into his face. She was kind of chunky
in his arms, but big-titted, and he didn't mind that she
kissed sloppy. It was all fine, just fine, and when she
broke loose to run up the bank, he galloped after her
with his pecker waving like a singletree.

He forgot the rubber saved for months in his wallet,
forgot it all but the gripping warmth of her soft
thighs, in the wet velvet depths of the thing that closed
around him so hungry and slick. Gasping, heaving up
and down and locking her legs around his back, Jolene
put it to him, and Earl gave her back lick for exciting
lick. He wanted to bellow like a bull, whinny like a
stud horse, because he was doing it, doing it at last,
and it was better than he'd ever dreamed.

"Love me," Jolene panted. "Love me, honey."

"Sure I love you," he answered, pounding away ex-
ultantly, and when the great, rolling explosion tore
him apart, he moaned, "Oh—oh I love you, Jessica."

She went still beneath him, and her legs dropped
away. "Get off me," she said. "You ain't a damn bit
better'n Billy Dee and Joe; all I'm good for is a quick

screw. All you care about is my ass. You don't give a damn about *me*."

"Jolene, I never said—"

Scrambling away from him, she flung on her clothes. Earl put on his pants, looked around for his shirt as she said, "I hear a car comin', and I hope it's them Blakes, ready to whip up on you."

He'd discovered his shoes by the time bobbing lights showed him the shirt, caught on a branch. "Get in, Jolene," he said. "I'll carry you home."

"They'll have whiskey," she said, propped against the pickup. "They call me by my right name, anyhow."

"Damnit, Jolene," Earl said. "That ain't a truck, it's a car. Get in and duck down on the seat."

"You think *I* give a shit who sees me? And I ain't hidin' account of you, Earl Lassiter."

Lights caught them, impaled them against the darkness like blinded moths in mid-flight. Shielding his eyes against glare, Earl murmured, "Oh migod, it's the sheriff; it's your daddy."

Deep and scratchy behind the wall of light, the voice said, "Over here, gal. And boy, you haul it outa here quick as you can."

Helplessly, Earl said, "Jolene—"

She was walking slumped into the lights; they outlined her legs through the thin skirt, showed the shoes she carried in one hand, glowed around her wet red hair with sand in it. Earl got into the pickup and keyed its ignition.

"Haul it!" Sheriff Kobburn ordered, and Earl turned around to go pretty quick past the police car. He couldn't see Jolene anymore, even when he looked back.

CHAPTER 6

Ira Lowenstein glanced at the newly painted church as he drove past in late-morning Sunday sunlight. Three churches white inside and out; two white outside, black within, and there'd never be a *shul* here. This single, dusty thoroughfare dividing a clutter of buildings was a place where time had been caught and held, many years ago. Some of the stores even had false fronts, and he was sure he'd seen an outhouse.

Head still throbbing from last night's partying, Ira drove the black Ford slowly, and ran through what he had learned of Temple County: population 16,403, and only a little over 5,000 were white; median income, $1,237.00; unemployed or underemployed: 29.2 percent—one hell of a labor pool.

Through the windshield he looked at closed stores—groceries, gas stations, garages with muddy tractors and beatup trucks waiting new life; combination jail and city hall, a hamburger joint, but no bar, no beer garden. Temple County was legally dry, kept that way by combined votes of bootleggers and churchgoers. So there was Beevo's. Ira rubbed one hand at his temple and shook his head, glancing across at what might be a clinic of sorts. There was something on its dry patch of lawn.

Oh, goddamn; it looked like the charred remains of

a burned cross. Was it possible the Klan was still alive here? That could mean trouble the company didn't want. Ira brought the Ford to a stop and stared. Sure as hell, somebody had burned a cross in front of the neat white office with the house in back—or halfway burned it; greenish rags had gone out, and the wood itself was tilted drunkenly, one arm seared through but the rest only browned. He looked at the office sign: *Calvin R. Davison, M.D.*

Driving on, Ira passed Coffield's Feed Store, and bumped over railroad tracks. Just beyond a long-closed passenger depot, empty flatcars waited for Monday-morning pulpwood. Above them and to the right stood the town's water tower, a pregnant, bulbous silver. He swung left on a gravel road and kept looking, crossing one loop of the redbrown river, pocked with cypress stumps and a few sandbars. A mile or so beyond here, he thought, where the hills rose on each side and the Tchufuncta had cut a deeper channel, would be the site for a dam.

Not far from the road, he caught sight of a low building with a rusted tin roof, a log house set farther back, and the first irrigation ditch Ira had seen around here. A mill, he thought, probably abandoned, its stovepipe sagging, a glimpse of an ancient sheet-metal boiler black with age. Cane mill, cotton gin, sawmill? Nothing else made sense for Temple County. Pulling over to the side of the road, Ira studied the lay of the land. It was too far from the river to have been a flour mill, and that irrigation ditch was edged with raw earth. There was an RFD mailbox at the turnoff, and Ira made a note of the name on it: *Lassiter.*

Backing into the lane, he pointed the Ford back to town; he'd seen enough. Time to go back to the rooming house where railroad men and drummers sometimes stayed over—and one hungover Jew. Coffield had said something about a meeting of the local club this evening, the Templars; maybe this Lassiter would be there; maybe people would stay sober enough to talk sensibly about bringing new, vital business into the area.

Ira grinned ruefully; if things didn't work out, maybe he could burn a Star of David on somebody's lawn.

"Just kids," Sheriff Floyd Kobburn said. "Couldn't be nobody else." He lounged against the door of his patrol car, where he'd made the nigger doctor come out to him. "Saturday-night hoorawin', that's all." He grinned, because the Yankee nigger was upset; behind him, the good-looking woman was more than that; she was scared through. But then, folks said she was from Georgia, not up north, and Georgia niggers had sense enough to know their place.

Davison said, "Aren't you going to check out the remains of that cross? The cloth on it looks new, from a party dress, looks like. Wasn't there a big party out at The Shadows last night? It seems somebody would remember an expensive dress like that."

Kobburn scratched his protruding belly and pushed back his cowboy hat. "You talkin' about the finest folks in the county, boy. They ain't got time to mess with the likes of you. Anyhow, we ain't got no police labs like in the movies," he rumbled, "and if'n we did, what am I goin' to charge some funnin' kids with—arson, maybe?" He didn't like being called out on a Sunday morning, especially with the bitter taste of Beevo's stump whiskey hanging sick in his throat. He'd rather be in the bed, or laying in wait for that son of a bitchin' Lassiter boy to come barreling down the highway in his pickup so he could arrest him for speeding, get him real good. That bitch Jolene, so much like her whoring mama; she was bound to get herself knocked up sooner or later. *Then* what the hell would he do with her?

"Then that's all you're going to do about it," Davison said, "pass it off as a joke, deny the existence of the Klan? Damn it, I came down here to do good, to bring some much-needed modern treatment to the disadvantaged—"

Kobburn pushed himself away from the car and hitched up his gunbelt. "You *see* anybody in bedsheets? Anybody shoot out your windows, threaten you with bodily harm? No? Then it just might be some of them there *dis-advantaged* folks that never asked you to come down here. Maybe some of 'em would just as soon you lit somewheres else. Ol' Doc Christopher been seein' to the needs of this county for a long time, includin' the *dis-advantaged*."

"All right," Davison said, "all right. I reported the fact that a threat was implied here, and I'll report the same to the state police."

Kobburn itched to slap a knot on the nigger's head, but this wasn't the time or place. Davison would screw up, take a baby from some black gal, or better yet, make one with some underage cropper wench, and Kobburn would come down on him like a tall pine. There was always a way, if a man waited and watched.

"You do that," he said. "You tell the highway patrol about nightriders and arson; you tell 'em I can't handle my own county."

The woman eased up and pulled at Davison's arm. Kobburn's eyes flicked over her, and he thought she'd made Beevo a good whore; she was light-skinned and smelled clean and had a little sense. A little burrhead, four, maybe five years old peered out from behind her, clinging to her skirt so it was pulled tight across her thigh.

"Calvin," she was murmuring, "Calvin, I asked you—"

"Better listen to your woman, boy," Kobburn said. "She's got more brains." He swung around and pulled open the car door so abruptly that Davison had to step back. He gunned the car motor and pulled away. When he looked into the mirror the nigger was still standing there, the burned-out cross behind him.

Probably them Blake boys, Kobburn thought; little bastards got into any devilment they could find. And into Jolene, too? Probably; that girl would screw a water moccasin, was somebody to hold its head. So much like her goddamned ma, it was a wonder she hadn't run off with somebody already, like his wife did. But damned if he was going to get stuck raising Jolene's kid, too. Be a heap better if he put her on a bus to New Orleans and sent her off to learn to type, or to beauty school, before her belly got big and she'd be hard put to name her bastard's daddy. He'd been putting it off for a long time, too goddamn long; folks were laughing at him behind his back account of Jolene.

It didn't worry him none, long as Avery Coffield backed him at the polls, but when word got to Lila Coffield, things might change. She'd been Lila Ruffington of Clark County, and wasn't one of them Ruffington women didn't walk like her ass was cake and she was scared to crack the icing. Prissy, every damned one of them.

Kobburn headed for home, then changed his mind and steered for the creek road and Beevo's place. Hadn't been for old Beevo, there wouldn't be a pretty

good kitty piled up over the years, enough to get Jolene out of town and keep her in school. Beevo was a
smart nigger, even though there'd been word of some
trouble out yonder last night.

The patrol car met a black Ford. Kobburn didn't
wave at the driver. It was that Jew boy tryin' to cozy
up to Coffield, and it was for sure he wouldn't be here
long. Nigger doctors and Jew boys; let one of them in,
and pretty soon they'd be all over the place, thick as
seed ticks in Johnson grass, and just as ready to suck
blood. Avery Coffield was only funning with him; he
wouldn't be around for long.

In daylight, Beevo's looked wore out and tacky, and
when Kobburn wheeled around back, his mouth all set
for some hair of the dog, he was surprised to see so
much activity. A couple of strange niggers were loading crates onto a flatbed truck. They went fencepost-
still at the sight of him. And there was old skinhead
Beevo himself, huffing and puffing.

"Hey, Beevo."

"Yessuh. Okay, boys—keep loadin'."

"What you up to, Beevo?"

"Gettin' out," Beevo said. "Mist' Coffield, he said
to, and I don't aim to leave much behind."

"Coffield down on you? How come?"

The black rubbed his sweaty head. "That youngun
of his'n. Boy ain't natural; out here to get his wick
dipped, and first I know, he's tearin' up my new lil'
who'."

Kobburn frowned. "And you played the fool, tried
to get money outa his daddy."

Beevo shrugged and looked at his truck. "This ain't
the only dry county in Mississippi."

"You got somebody else in mind?" Kobburn asked.
"Somebody can take your place?"

"Don't give a damn," Beevo said. "Gone is gone, like your money, sheriff."

"U-huh," Kobburn grunted, "like *your* money. There's this fella in New Orleans, a white man—"

"Sho'," Beevo said through his mouthful of gold, "what else?"

Every goddamn thing that could go wrong had done so with a vengeance. Avery's belly was bothering him more than usual, and Lila had turned on him with a cold fury she'd never shown before. Because of Elliot, Beevo was clearing out of the county, and it might take a spell to get somebody in to replace him; half the whores would scatter over into Clark County.

It was one thing for Elliot to beat hell out of a nigger gal because he couldn't face up to screwing her; it was something else for him to go running to his mama about it. More like one woman gossiping to another, Avery thought, and tightened his fist on a glass of milk laced with bourbon. Somehow, Elliot and Jess had gotten mixed up; she had the strength and brass, while the boy—Avery sipped at his drink and shook his head; couldn't rightly call Elliot a boy.

And now, Lila was making damned sure he stayed whatever the hell he was; the engagement with Mary Alice Harvey was being broken off, and Elliot was going off to school, too. Not that he was worth a good goddamn on the place, anyhow, but it didn't seem right for a man not to have *one* of his children to home.

Lassiter had; one off in Korea with the Marines, trying to be a big hero like his daddy, but Earl staying on the land and working it good. That was another thing, Avery thought: once Elliot was out of Temple County, maybe he couldn't be protected from the draft board anymore. Avery looked into the honey-brown milk; probably they wouldn't take him, any-how; psychiatrists had all kinds of tests that would show him up for what he was. Son of a bitch! How did it happen? Why?

If the boy married Mary Alice, folks might stop whispering about him and how he just hung around the house all day, helping his mama restore the old wing. Hell of a job for a man, but not to hear Lila tell it. Sensitive, she said; had to find his own way in his own time; shouldn't have his wife picked out for him. And what was wrong with marrying the banker's daughter? Sam Harvey was a good old boy, and if this drought kept up, it wouldn't hurt to have a bank in the family.

Besides, what was going to happen to the Coffield line? Ben Lassiter had two boys, both of them with balls. Jessica getting married wouldn't be the same; her younguns wouldn't be *Coffields*. His might be the last headstone in the family cemetery wearing the right name. If Lila hadn't been so stubborn about having children, turned frosty and so goddamn prissy that they'd had separate bedrooms for years—

And now, on top of it all, his belly kept warning him he'd better go down to New Orleans and see the doctor again. Business, folks thought; he wasn't going to have anybody figuring Avery Coffield was getting weak or something. So any other doctor was too damned close.

All the time, Ben Lassiter kept working his scrubby fields like a strong buck nigger, all those old holes punched in him in the war not bothering him a lick. Stubborn, ornery bastard with two boys, and one of them bred to the land, like he ought to be. It wasn't right; never had been right. Coffields had been here

long as Lassiters, and that statue in the town square of
Colonel Isaiah Lassiter just meant they'd been quality
back in the War between the States. They hadn't been
anything since, unless you counted Ben's crazy doings
in World War II, and it didn't take more than a wall-
eyed fool to get himself all shot up. But when they
both came home with the National Guard outfit Avery Coffield commanded, which one got the big welcome, highup colonel or lowrank sergeant? Shit.

The Lassiters never had two dimes to rub together,
and if it wasn't for all the publicity about Temple
County's very own "hero," Ben would never have been
invited into the Templars. That had opened the door
to more rednecks, men who'd scraped together a little
money by contracting pulpwood, men whose grand-
parents hadn't even been born here. It was a hell of a
note when family and tradition went out the window,
when a boy might just as well be a split-tail, and a
man's wife sassed him about it.

Gloomily, Avery Coffield finished his drink and sat
staring at his new swimming pool, its surface ruffled
only by the struggles of a lone grasshopper. Trapped,
it didn't have sense to know it, and just kept right on
kicking.

Earl Lassiter eased a tree limb away from the
mouth of his irrigation ditch. It was just a little pine
limb, nowhere big enough to stop flow from the river,
and he wondered how come the vegetable patch had
gotten only a trickle of water late yesterday. Nothing
else jammed the ditch that he could see, but he meant
to work his way back up it, to be sure.

He didn't feel good about last night; first the mess
with Jessica, then getting caught doing it by Jolene's
daddy. He felt sorry for Jolene, because she sure got

what-for when the sheriff carried her home. But Earl
felt grateful to her, too; he wasn't a cherry anymore,
and even if he wished it could have been different—
better, maybe—that couldn't be changed now. Both the
Blake boys would have put it to her, if she'd stayed
with them. Still, Jolene deserved some better than she
usually got. She didn't hurt anybody or make trouble,
and maybe—Earl squinted along the ditch bank—
maybe she was just lonesome.

Hunkering down, he looked at where something
square and heavy had left a mark in the soft ground,
and his eyes traced a narrow path through bent grass.
Earl stood up, and found he was on a direct line with
Avery Coffield's cotton gin, and beyond that, the big
house—and the swimming pool.

"Be damned," he said aloud, thinking old Avery
just couldn't wait, so he sneaked somebody over here
with a pump and line to steal our water. The water
didn't matter so much, but stealin' it did. He coulda
had his own ditches dug a long time back, or he
coulda *asked* us for help.

But Avery Coffield wouldn't ask for anything,
much less of Ben Lassiter, and the pool was mainly for
Jessica's good-bye party. Everybody knew her daddy
gave Jessica all she wanted, and it was hard to fault
the man for that. She was the kind that made any man
want to do things for her. And *to* her, Earl admitted,
shamed again because of the night before. Well, for
certain he wouldn't tell Ben about the water; it would
mean bad trouble, and come down to it, no real harm
had been done. It only pointed up just how far Avery
Coffield would go, how much his own rights meant to
him over those of his neighbors.

Trudging on up the slope, he could just about hear
the corn growing, and the green smell was good

around him. Passing through it, Earl went into the old
mill and took up his tools. Sundays, he could put in a
whole day working on the post peeler, and he had an
idea he wasn't too far off, now. It had taken him a
year to get the old donkey engine going, to take down
the ancient boiler, scrape it out, and put it back together. The belts were shabby and about worn
through, but they'd work for now.

Of course, once he had the peeler operating, he'd
switch from a wood burner to a gas engine; there was a
'46 Ford block down at Hale's Garage would do just
fine. Problem was, he was having a hard time getting
the blades set just right, and as he fiddled with them
now, wished for the hundredth time that he had special steel to work with, instead of discarded plow
blades.

When he looked up from tightening a bolt, Ellen
was standing there, his daddy's coat and tie hanging
over one arm.

"Sorry," he said. "Forgot 'em, I reckon."

"Have you a good time?"

"So-so; left early. I fit in about like a possum at a
hound dog convention."

Ellen's deep, calm eyes studied him. "It's how a
body thinks, not what he wears; how he does, not what
he's got."

"Tell the hound dogs that."

"Miss Jessica tree you, too?"

Earl put down the wrench. "Seems like you're doin'
some bird-doggin' yourself, Ellen."

Stroking his father's coat, she changed the subject.
"You put a heap of sweat into that thing there. You
gets it done, what's it goin' to mean?"

"Money, I reckon. Every sapling on them useless
hills can be turned into fifteen, twenty cents apiece,

maybe two bits. I get this thing whizzin' along, I can turn out maybe thirty posts an hour, and that ain't bad."

"And if it don't work?"

Earl moved around the long table, stooping to eye the alignment of his blades. "It'll work; it's got to."

"If it don't—"

He looked up at her. "I won't do like Alvah, if that's what you mean. I'll find somethin' else."

"That's good," she said softly. "It'd kill your daddy to lose both his boys."

"He wouldn't show it none," Earl said, and went on to stare thoughtfully at the hooks that would hold poles in place. The crank screw that would push them along the blades would be thrown in and out by a lever. It would work, he was certain.

"Ain't his way to show much," Ellen said, "but he feels, right enough. You—I mean, if you feel you have to go off on account of him and me—"

Picking up another wrench, Earl kept his eyes upon it. Four years now, that had been in her mind, like a red coal hidden by a pile of ashes, covered over but still burning. He said, "You and Pa make the same mistake; two pups out of the same litter, they ain't alike. Me and Alvah ain't, either."

He tried to blink it away from behind his eyes, but the picture came back: that night with Pa standing over Alvah, big fist cocked back for another blow, and Earl's brother sprawled on the floor, blood on his mouth; Ellen huddled in a corner, her nightgown about ripped off, one rounded, dark breast showing.

. . . *Ought to kill you,* Ben said. *You wasn't my own blood, I purely would.*

And Alvah, coming painfully to one knee, shaking his head: *Over a nigger?*

A woman; a damned fine woman. Get that through your head, boy.

Alvah, rubbing his mouth, eyes still glazed: *Only been one real woman in this house, and she got worked to death.*

When Pa reached over the mantel for the rifle, Earl came tumbling out of the loft, catching hold of the stock and hollering, *Pa! No, Pa!*

A long, stretched-out piece of time where everybody stood real still, not even breathing, and Pa saying at last, *Reckon you better git.*

Ellen, then, begging soft and tearful; *Please—please, Ben; he's your son, and he didn't mean—*

Hell he didn't, Pa said, and Alvah stumbled around stuffing clothes into a bag. Earl wanted to cry so bad his chest hurt, but his eyes stayed dry as his mouth. Then Alvah was gone, and he'd stayed gone these four years.

Now Earl said, "Alvah had his way of thinkin', and I got mine. You didn't have any place to light when Pa took you and your baby in; Pa didn't either, but he didn't know how he'd boxed himself in until you stayed here a spell. You been good for each other, and that's the way of it."

Holding the coat close to her, crushing it to her breasts, Ellen said, "If I wasn't b-black—"

"That's the way of it, too. What'd you say to me— it's how a body thinks, not what he wears? You got your skin to wear, and if you took the loan of somebody else's, it wouldn't fit you no more than Pa's coat does me."

A single crystal tear trembled on the ends of her charcoal lashes. Ellen might have tried to say something, but the words choked off. She turned and walked quickly out of the mill.

Earl looked after her, then back to his work, glad it had come out in the open, instead of festering in the dark. They could let it alone now. There were things a man couldn't fight, or run off from; you could pitch a squalling fit against the world because you weren't born to a plantation house and Jessica Coffield, but the world wouldn't pay you a nevermind. A man ought to make out what couldn't be changed and accept it, then get on up the hill.

There were plenty of hills in Korea, and Alvah was still alive in them, or they'd have gotten word by now, a telegram like when the Sikes boy was killed, and the Murchison brothers. The War Department even sent notice when somebody was wounded; a dozen or more Temple County families had received those. And if somebody got bad hit, like Junior Pritchart when he lost his leg, he got sent home. So Alvah must still be in one piece, over yonder in the rice paddies and hills.

Working at the crank screw, Earl wondered if combat was anything like hunting deer in the canebrakes, or rabbits in the brush. Alvah had grown up with a gun in his hands, just like Earl, because game was meat on the stove when times got lean. Only the game Alvah was hunting in Korea hunted him back.

He tried to concentrate on the post peeler, changing a blade angle here, tightening a belt there. He remembered that he hadn't seen about getting a price on the valve grinders in town; he'd been too full of Jessica Coffield to think about anything else. It hadn't been fair to Jolene, emptying all that need into her just because she was handy, but Earl didn't know what he could do to make it up to her. Sheriff Kobburn would purely have it in for him from here on, and that beer-gutted old bastard had a head that swiveled around like a hoot owl's, so he could see everywhere at once.

It would be a spell before Earl dared to approach Jolene, even to pass the time of day.

Laying the wrench aside, he went to stoke the furnace and wait for the boiler to build up a head of steam. It was a wonder nobody else had thought of peeling posts and shipping them off to the big cities, where folks would buy them to close in their yards. The shipping and marketing and all that remained to be worked out later, once the machine itself was done. He could go get banker Harvey then, show him the piles of neatly barked posts, and see could he swing a loan for whatever else he might need. Posts made more sense than grinding up all the saplings for pulp; they were worth more.

Sure, he pictured himself saying to the banker, sure they'll be treated, so they'll hold out for years; just takes a mix of creosote and diesel oil cooked into the wood in that tank yonder. That adds a mite to my cost, but once folks see their fenceposts won't rot out right away, they'll pass word around.

Watching the pressure gauge climb, Earl knew his peeler wouldn't knock pulpwood cutters out of business. It would take him a year to use up all the saplings on the Lassiter place, and after that he'd make his own deals for stumpage, buying it close by and paying a shade more than going rates. How long would it take to buy a new tractor, new pickup, put in Rainbird sprinklers instead of ditches? He had the time; once the peeler worked and his Pa saw it, they'd hire a cropper to help with the truck garden.

The shaker valve hissed steam, and Earl set his pole into position, worked the lever. Belts tightened, and slowly the pole rotated; slowly the blades bit and brown bark peeled away from white wood. He wanted to jump up and down, to holler it all out at once—how the bark was his fuel and there'd be no waste; how he'd cut and trimmed the old plowshares so they could be sharpened by loosening a couple of bolts, how *good* it all was. But he'd been disappointed before, so after the first clean post dropped off the table, he disengaged the belts and lifted another one into place. The piney smell, the steam and metal and oil smell, was all around him, sweeter than honeysuckle, richer than jasmine.

Shirt off now, worn-out pair of work gloves keeping pitch off his hands, Earl worked on, grinning in the heat, reveling in the noise. If only Alvah was here to help, to feed in poles, stack them, tote them to the tank for cooking. Wouldn't Alvah be some surprised, when he came home and saw how his baby brother made something out of nothing, a real bigod *mill* that went chug-a-*money*, chug-a-*money?*

If Alvah ever came home.

CHAPTER 7

He'd always liked New Orleans, at least the old parts. It had that flavor of antiquity, or continuity, of so many generations standing behind those now here. And there was so much to do, places to go and foods to sample, woman flesh to savor, too—damned little of which could be found in Temple County unless a man sneaked around.

But Avery didn't get the usual lift of holiday emotions when his plane touched down at the airport, and riding the taxi into town simply irritated him. Checking into his usual suite at the Monteleone Hotel on Royal Street, he had a Ramos fizz sent up, and called to confirm his appointment, halfway hoping it would be put off. Yes, Mr. Coffield, said the lush voice he remembered, the doctor will be waiting for you.

He sat on the bed and finished his drink, putting the voice to a mental picture of Dr. Rafferty's receptionist. Twice before, he'd noticed the woman, because she was the noticing kind. All that crisp white starchiness couldn't hide the richness of a fine thoroughbred body, high and full in the knockers, slim and lithe in the flanks. In fact, the nurse's getup called more attention to what she had, like special goodies hidden in plain tissue paper wrappings, and just aching to spill out.

And there was something familiar about the set of her graygreen eyes, something vaguely known in the way she carried herself so proudly, and if her honey-blond hair was worn long, instead of curled and swept up around her ears—

No, Avery thought; there wasn't that much resemblance between them. He sighed, put on his seersucker coat, and rode the elevator down to have the doorman signal him a cab.

The medical building was new, but the smells were old and sterile, just that hint of alcohol and disinfectants, gauze and pain. Two other patients were in the paneled waiting room, but the receptionist came from behind her desk to smile Avery in to the doctor.

"So nice to see you again, Mr. Coffield. You always seem to bring the great outdoors with you."

There *was* too much likeness, Avery thought, staring into the mischievous, dare-you directness of her eyes, and maybe that was why he'd never tried to put the make on Miss Tolliver before. She touched his shoulder before drifting back, and he felt the warmth of her slim fingers clear through to his skin.

Through the examinations, moving down the hall for more X rays and a GI series, he kept thinking about Miss Tolliver. How old was she—twenty-six, -seven? Dressed right, she could look much younger, but Avery had a hunch she'd been old as she was now while she was still in diapers. Some girls were born women, like Jessica; like this one.

Rafferty was efficient, with none of the old-man shakiness of Doc Christopher at home, with none of that I-slapped-your-ass-when-you-came-into-the-world, boy. He was all business, but when he looked at the lab reports and scanned the X rays, Avery could sense a hesitation, a certain reluctance. There was a *No*

Smoking sign in the office, but Avery lighted a small cigar and waited the man out.

"Well, now, Mr. Coffield," the doctor said, leaning back in his chair and making a steeple with his fingers. What the hell was that, Avery wondered, a church symbol, a prayer, eternity?

"Well, now—things have changed a bit since your last visit, and perhaps you should have returned sooner."

Avery flicked ash into the wastebasket. "I'm a man grown, Doctor, not some little old lady who has to have sorghum mixed with her medicine."

Dr. Rafferty moved his fingers apart and put his hands flat upon his desk. "All right, then—straight out. From all I can see, the carcinoma is inoperable."

Proud that his fingers didn't tremble the cigar, Avery said, "Guess you know the next question, too. And I reckon you always have to guess at the answer. How long have I got?"

"You're a direct man, Mr. Coffield, so I'll try to be. It will depend upon your strength, and perhaps your fortitude. A year, possibly two years, if you can take it. With chemotherapy, bed rest, sedatives—no more than two years, if that long."

Taking a drag on his cigar, Avery held fragrant smoke in his mouth, let it out when he said, "Thanks. It ain't much time to do all I have to, but I'll make out. All that treatment—it'll have to be at home, because with that kind of schedule, I can't be takin' trips to a hospital."

The doctor frowned, and Avery cut him off with another question, one that caused Rafferty's eyebrows to crawl up. "Your nurse out yonder, Miss Tolliver— she came from a good family, out of good blood?"

"Why—I suppose so," Rafferty answered. "Not one

of the old-line Creole families, of course, but early American, I think. A widow; her husband was killed in Korea, during the early fighting in 1950. Why do you ask?"

"No younguns?"

"No children, but—"

"Not barren, is she?"

Rafferty's frown deepened, his eyes squinting through rimless glasses. "Now why would you be interested in such—"

Avery stood up, and if his knees were shaky, he didn't show it. "Thanks, Doc; I appreciate all you've done. I'll see to the rest of it myself."

In the outer office, he waited until an old woman and a pimply-faced kid had been sent into examination rooms, then walked over to the desk. Miss Tolliver glanced at his cigar. "You didn't blow smoke in his face, did you? He hates that."

"No more smoke than he tried to blow up my butt, at first," Avery said. "You got a first name, Miss Tolliver?"

"Sandra," she said. "Sandy, if you like."

"Sandy, I got two propositions to make to you. One of 'em is immoral as all hell, and the other one is worth a whole lot of money. You want to hear any more?"

A corner of her ripe mouth lifted; her breasts lifted, too. She said, "Both sound interesting."

"Good," he said. "I'm at the Monteleone, and I'll make reservations for Antoine's. Seven o'clock in the lobby?"

She nodded. "You could have asked before, you know."

"Now I'm a man in a hurry."

"Not too hurried, I hope," she said, her laugh throaty and silken.

He clenched the cigar in strong teeth and strode out. In the hallway, Avery took out a handkerchief and patted sudden sweat from his cheeks, then buried the cigar in a container of sand because it tasted rancid and he didn't want any more of it. Funny; for years he'd been halfway decided on giving up smoking, and now there wasn't any sense to it.

Ira Lowenstein examined the crude machinery. "It makes sense," he said to the boy. "You've worked out a pretty good thing here, and from scratch. I can see where you're going to have some problems, but they're minor."

Earl Lassiter felt like he was smiling all over. "I never talked to nobody about my peeler before. I mean, my old man knows it's here, but he never showed interest."

"For somebody with no technical background," Lowenstein said, "you've done one hell of a job. Have you checked marketing possibilities, shipping, and labor costs per unit?"

He looked at the stack of freshly peeled posts, at others cooling in the big, welded vat. It was sweltering under the shed, and ought to be, with that antique furnace and boiler going, and bark smoldering in a pit under the cooking vat. But Ira was damned glad he'd come.

"No sir," Earl said. "Figured I'd see the banker about that, but I know my poles can go out on the flatcars, just like pulpwood. The L & N will be glad to tie on an extra car."

The Louisville and Nashville line would be happy to add a baby carriage or wheelbarrow, Ira thought;

since the line had stopped hauling passengers, it depended solely on whatever freight it could pick up along backwood spurs like this. Ideas were turning in his head, and again he blessed the opportunity given him when he had run into this gangly boy at the Templars Club in town. Those beefy, redneck bastards and their coarse jokes, their not so subtle needling, their concentration on whiskey and sex—and then there was this boy and his father, standing aside from the others.

Both had looked out of place as Ira felt, both a little shabby, but the drinkers paid a certain respect to the older man. Ira knew why, when he wandered around the clubroom and peered at old pictures along the walls, photos of Templar past presidents, or men who'd donated goodly amounts of money, and several framed news clippings about Temple County's own hero, Sergeant Ben Lassiter.

"Do you think the local banker will be interested?" Ira asked the boy now.

Earl shrugged. "Can't say as how Sam Harvey ever jumped into the water without measurin' how deep, testin' how cold, and lookin' around to see which way the wind was blowin'. And *then* he'd take quite a spell to decide which bathin' suit was right."

Ira laughed; he'd found it fairly easy to laugh with Ben Lassiter, too. The man didn't keep working on Ira's Jewishness, and although there was a leathery, closed-up aura about the man, he'd opened up when he found Ira had been infantry, too, and in a regular army outfit. They had the corner of the bar to themselves after that, Templars staring and shaking their heads, but not trying to crowd in on Ben Lassiter. Ira had the feeling that Ben was not the kind of man to crowd.

"You really know the people in this county," Ira

said, "growing up here. But have you thought beyond the post peeler to something else, something bigger?"

"Nah," Earl said, "be glad just to get my little old shirttail mill goin', maybe put in a couple more irrigation ditches."

"That's your water ditch then?" Ira asked. "The only one around here?"

"Not for long," Earl said. "This drought keeps up, folks'll come around to my way of thinkin'; leastwise, the little farmers will. Don't know about Avery Coffield and them other big cotton planters; take a heap of ditchin' for them."

Walking around the peeler, Ira inspected it from every angle, marveling at the ingenuity that turned plowshares into cutting knives, at the latent mechanical marvels in this boy's untrained hands. And the kid had a dim sense of marketing, also something that was yet only a stirring. Ira said, "Mr. Coffield seems intelligent and reasonably cooperative, more than the rest of them. Surely he'd accept any innovation that would save him money—or make more."

"Mr. Lowenstein," Earl said.

"Ira, please."

"Ira, then. Temple County folks take some knowin'. Take Avery Coffield, and my daddy, too, and all the rest of 'em. They do things like their daddies did, and their granddaddies before 'em. What's old and set, why—that's right and proper, and nobody ain't about to tell them no different."

Ira blinked. "But Coffield has been encouraging me to—"

"Hate to say this," Earl put in, "but I reckon you don't understand. They're just funnin' with you, Ira, hoorawin' among themselves about this—and you'll 'scuse me—this here Yankee Jew they got to use room seven at Beevo's, so they could watch through the fake mirror, and the like. They got more devilment studied out for you, but when the newness wears off, you bein' here ain't goin' to make a ripple. Now my old man, he ain't quite like that. Oh, he's solid set in some ways, but he used to tell me and my brother about this friend of his, a replacement from New Jersey named Lipshutz. Reckon he was kind of close to this Lipshutz, because he never got over the fella bein' killed the way he was, helpin' out my pa. But offhand, I'd say Ben Lassiter's about the only man in the county wouldn't devil you none."

Ira nodded. "And you."

"Me? I don't count for much—yet. Ain't been out in the world; ain't met different folks, but I figure if a man don't stomp on me personal, I won't go out of my way to stomp on him."

"I'll be damned," Ira said. "Out of the mouths of babes—no; I take that back. Out of what may be the new man down here, *homo superior southernis*. Listen, Ben—when I look at your invention, I don't just see a post peeler. I see a start, a beginning. I see right through the walls to that river where it runs between the hills, and water backing up behind a good dam, water to supply power for another mill, a far larger mill, another spur line coming in right behind it—"

Earl said, "You talkin' about a pulp mill, right here in the county?"

Excitedly, Ira said, "Sure, sure; and in a few more years, why not a complete paper mill, turning out newsprint, everything? The raw material's here, the labor and water and central location, all right here. Think of it, Earl."

"Never looked that far ahead," Earl said, wiping his

hands on a rag. "I'd be happy to just get out my
posts—"

"For a start," Ira said, "for a good start that will
soon turn into a minor sideline. Not one peeler, but
six or eight of them, with specially machined parts, a
pressurized cooker instead of that open vat, and men
trained to run them."

Earl looked at the rag he held, at the fire dying under his vat. "Got to be a catch to it. You're some kind
of salesman, a drummer—"

"In a way," Ira said, taking off his coat, "but I'm
really here to investigate, and if anything looks good
to me, advise my people to buy. If I'm selling anything, I guess it's progress."

"Buy what?" Earl asked. "My daddy's land for a
dam, for a big mill? I don't reckon he'd sell. His land
means just about everything to him."

"Then it's up to you. I can make *you* an offer, Earl.
A crash course in mechanical engineering, the whole
four years and a college degree if you want, or inten-
sified direction from our company specialists. I'm sure
you have other ideas in your head—"

"Yeah," Earl said quickly, "yes sir. There's this idea
I got about fixin' a machine to jerk a whole pine sapling out of the ground, root and all. Just cuttin' it off
wastes about twenty percent of the pulp left in the tap
root. I could make blades to chop the surface roots,
and—"

"That'll take knowhow," Ira said, "and you can get
that in Boston, all you need, all you want. It doesn't
have to be tomorrow, or next month; because I know
you want to get your pole-peeling business off the
ground first. But if you had the backing you need for
that, and people to take over after you left—"

Earl ran his hands over the crank screw, looked at the worn belts, and smelled fresh pine sap. "But it don't come free."

"We're businessmen," Ira said. "Nothing comes free, but I am making you a solid, honest offer—education and training, a good salary while you're studying, a piece of the action and stock options when you get back."

"And I got to put up my end of the trade," Earl said slowly, "a toehold in Temple County, the dam site. I got to convince my daddy to sell most of his land."

Ira Lowenstein opened his shirt collar more. "It's a fair trade, and a damned good offer. We'll pay far more than the land is worth."

"Pa never put a price on his land," Earl said. "He never had it in his head to sell so much as a square foot. He don't even let nobody walk across it, without his sayso."

"Then you'll have to make him see what all this means," Ira said. "You'll have to talk to him, because it will mean the difference in you being just another pretty good mechanic, or a topflight engineer."

CHAPTER 8

The food at Antoine's was always superb, and Avery tried to do it justice, especially the *pampano en papillote*, but he kept feeling the thing inside him. It was a thing only microscopes could see, but spreading every minute of every day, eating away at his guts as if he were a seven-course dinner and it was eager to get to dessert.

He wanted to scream at it, *You stupid bastard! Why don't you compromise? When I'm gone, so are you; most of me and all of you will get flushed down the drain after they scrape me out and pump that purple stuff into my veins, after they pack me wtih sawdust or whatever the hell they use after I'm gutted.*

Staring at his plate, he managed a wry grin. *Talk about eating yourself out of house and home.*

Old Caesar hovered anxiously nearby. "Anything wrong, Mr. Coffield?"

Avery shrugged at the pink-cheeked waiter, silver-headed but so damned healthy at what—seventy, seventy-five? Avery would never reach that age, anyhow. "No, Caesar," he said, "everything's perfect. But since I'm off my feed a little, we'll take some more wine, and you might double the brandy in my coffee later."

Sandy Tolliver was busily cleaning her plate. "Mine, too," she said.

She was a pleasure to watch, Avery thought; a hearty, appreciative eater, but one who'd probably never put on an extra pound. She enjoyed her wines, too. A zest for living, she had, a vibrancy and excitement; a damned fine-looking woman. She talked, but not too much, and not about kids and patterns and the next goddamned party, and which wife was on that week's shitlist. Sandy also knew how to listen.

When they'd finished *café royales*, he took her to a couple of Bourbon Street joints, where she matched him drink for drink and never wobbled. Avery got to feeling better, but knew a feeling of urgency, of hurry, and Sandy sensed it, felt it through the booze and smoke, over the pounding, gutbucket music.

Mouth tingling against his ear, she said, "Let's get the hell out of here."

Avery liked her straightforward attitude, and not having to play all the silly games. She knew what he needed and wanted it, too. He took her right up to the suite, and while he was calling room service for a bottle and setups, Sandy ducked into the bathroom. He had drinks mixed when she came out of the shower, all fresh and glowing and so damned *alive*. There was just a big, fluffy towel wrapped around that full, rounded body.

Over the rim of her glass, eyes dancing, she said, "Here's to that proposition you mentioned, the one that's immoral as all hell."

"And my other offer?" he said.

"Right now," Sandy answered, putting down her glass and dropping the towel away from her body as she sat cross-legged on the bed, "I'm only interested in the first one. Lie back, Avery; no—don't even take off your shoes. Let me do that for you; let me do it all for you, because I want to."

It wasn't only that she was beautiful, or that she seemed a riper, matured version of somebody long known; it was Sandy Tolliver's eagerness that started him feeling young and pushed the shadow off into a corner. And after that, when he was stripped and her hands were moving slowly, tantalizingly over him, it was the things she did to him, the way she took over. Deft and agile, hungry and unabashed, she was like no woman Avery had ever experienced. He'd known whores, a few of them white, and a couple of girls before he married Lila, and there'd been that half-starved woman in Italy in '44. But nothing like Sandy Tolliver, and maybe there had never been anyone like her, and he was suddenly angry that she had been kept from him so long, and now there was no time.

But she took away the anger with the folding of her rich breasts about his shaft, her graygreen eyes staring up over his belly and chest, into his own. Then there was only the top of her honeyblond head, the warm, soft enveloping that concentrated the entire world into just one place, that drew all time past and time future into this wildwet, shuddering moment.

"N-no!" Avery gasped. "No, damnit—I won't be any good for anything else if you keep on—"

She paid no attention, and he thought, she's going to do it; she's not even going to take away her mouth when it—oh damn, oh damndamndamn! Fingers dug into her hair, Avery tried to pull her off, tear her away, but she clung to him greedily, and then there was no use trying. He arched and groaned and gave himself up.

Chest pumping, the strength run out of him, he felt her hands going, roaming, cupping, caressing, finger-walking over his tender parts. Voice low and throaty, she said, "Oh, yes, you'll be good for everything else, lover. I'll make you good; you'll see."

Most of his life, Avery Coffield had been listening to preachers holler about being born again, but there in that hotel room, he learned its meaning. With this woman, he was everything—stud, lover, master, and slave. He was so damned young that all notions of right and wrong hadn't been stamped into him yet, and so strong that he could go on and on, making each time better than the last and accepting it all as his due, giving it all to her as her right.

Dawn was pinkgray around the curtains when Sandy turned on the radio, and music celebrated this spanking-new day. A drink balanced upon his bare chest, cigar in his hand, Avery thought that even a funeral dirge would have sounded like a triumphal march. She lay on her back beside him, the length of her body touching his own, as if she could not bear to have an inch between them.

"Don't you want to know about the other?" he asked.

Sandy touched the icy glass to each of her upright nipples before answering. "The other what?"

"What I said in the office."

"Only if it means I can stay right here with you."

Draining his glass, Avery put it on the bedside table. "It's something like that."

She finished her own drink and got rid of the glass so she could roll against him. Her nipples were cold from the glass, and rigid. "You don't have to do anything for me, you know. I'm not a whore, or a little girl whose seduction bothers your conscience."

"And you don't have to be sorry for an old man who ain't goin' to get much older."

Nuzzling into the base of his throat, Sandy said, "Sure, I read the lab reports. I was interested in you, but I don't make a habit of laying terminal patients out of charity. I'm sorry, yes, but selfish, too. I *wanted* you, Avery; I still do."

"I wish," he said, "oh damnit, I wish I could run off and marry you."

"Just running off would be okay," she said.

"Can't do that, either," he said, and lying there with the warmest, most honest woman he'd ever known, Avery told her of The Shadows, the land, the long, unbroken line of Coffields that stretched clear back to Revolutionary times, admitting that his only son was queer, and maybe things weren't going too well with the cotton.

Then, taking a deep breath, he brought it out: "I got to thinkin' about it when the doctor told me I'm finished. Goddamnit, that don't have to mean the Coffields are finished, too. We got this old family cemetery, and every damned Coffield in it would rattle his bones if it all stopped with me. Elliot ain't about to put a baby into a woman's belly, that's for certain. But I reckon I'm still man enough to do it myself. Only the boy's name—and it's *got* to be a boy—his name has to be Coffield."

He stopped and thought it through, this vague plan that had been forming in his head, in his soul. Elliot would shit a squealing worm, and Lila'd have a tizzy, but bigod they'd both have to take it, or he'd see they were both out on their asses.

"Sandy," he said, "I want you to marry my boy, but I'm the one to give you a baby."

Her head snapped up. *"What?"*

Quickly, he said, "Before we leave town, I'll deposit fifty thousand dollars in your bank, no strings, no taxes. I can still manage that much. And I'll rewrite my will, see that you get a full share of The Shadows, a trust fund, and another full share for your son."

"I'll just be damned," Sandy said, sitting up now, long legs curled under shapely buttocks.

Lifting himself to one elbow, Avery said, "I ain't kiddin'; I mean every word. Look—I asked Rafferty if you came from a good family, good blood. Now I don't care about that; I care about *you*, and you deserve a hell of a lot more than a paid-up apartment and a few weekends on the town. What we've done, what you showed me—and there just ain't that much time, goddamnit. I'm a dyin' man, and I got to squeeze every minute until it hollers calf rope."

"Hush," Sandy said. "Hush now, because I don't want to start pitying you. Let's lie back and close our eyes for a while. I'm a little tired and a little shaken up, and I'd like to dream on this."

Avery sighed and put his arms around her. "Never thought much about clocks before. Now there's a big one, tickin' away in my head, and I hate to waste time on sleep."

"I'll wake you up happy," Sandy promised.

Ben Lassiter put down his cup with a jar that spilled coffee onto the oilcloth. "Boy, you come at a man with somethin' like that, afore he's had time to get down his grits and eggs?"

Stubbornly, Earl set his jaw. "It's time," he said. "I thought on it all night."

Ben sat erect in the straightback chair. Down the table, little Marcie stopped eating, too. Ellen took a pan of biscuits from the oven of the wood stove. Ben said, "After you showed that Lowenstein your play pretty?"

"It ain't a toy," Earl said. "My post peeler works, and it's goin' to bring in more cash money than we could make in five years off vegetables."

"Cash money ain't the whole world."

"It's a goodly chunk of it," Earl insisted. "If we had it, I could go off to engineerin' school and be somebody."

"You a somebody now; you walk your own land."

"I walk *your* land, Pa. If it was mine, I'd do more than scratch dirt in it."

Ben made a fist on the tabletop. Marcie's big, liquid eyes shifted back and forth between the men. Her mother came over and put a steaming biscuit on her plate. "Eat," Ellen said.

"It'll be yours someday," Ben said.

"Time I'm wore to the bone and broke down like an ol' mule. Pa, it ain't like givin' it *all* away, givin' *any* of it away. There's good money waitin'."

"For my gulley, so water can back up over everything; so I can lose my house, where your granddaddy lived and died, and his daddy afore him? There ain't enough money for that."

Earl pushed aside his plate. He'd come this far and had to take it all the way now. He said, "In the olden days, just about this whole valley was Lassiter land, even that bottom land Avery Coffield owns now. All we're doin' is to sell a piece of what the Lassisters got left. Take the money and buy more, if you got a mind to. It'd just be gettin' back Lassiter land, tradin' one piece for another. And you know blame well the water won't come up to the house, or reach the mill site."

With a glance at her mother, little Marcie took her biscuit and slid off her chair. Ben held out his cup to Ellen, and she filled it with coffee. Funny, Earl thought; his old man wasn't staring at him eyeball to eyeball; it was like he was putting off his decision by not looking at Earl.

Grunting, Ben said, "You never smelled one of them damned pulp mills. It stinks for miles around. Smoke and noise and folks you don't even know, runnin' every whichaway like an anthill got kicked over. Boy, this land is good like it is, clean and proud; the work's honest, and you don't have to bend your neck to nobody."

"It ain't never been good for me like it is for you," Earl said. "I need my own jacket, a brand-new pickup insteada one hung together with spit and bailin' wire. I need to—to *know* things, Pa, more'n Temple County. And I mean to."

Ben's callused hands fisted on the oilcloth. "Your brother run off, and I don't know as how he done much for himself."

"You ran him off, Pa. You told him to git, and you know where he is, know he's tryin' to do like you done in the other war, get himself medals so Temple County will be proud of him; so you'll be proud of him. But we ain't talkin' about Alvah; we're talkin' about the Lassiters goin' to stay hard-dirt, raggedy-assed farmers not much better'n croppers, or are they goin' to *be* somebody."

Ben's face was hard. "You lettin' your mouth overload your ass, boy."

"Rather have it whipped, than hangin' outa my overalls." Earl glared back at his father, his own hands fisted.

Ellen put the old iron coffeepot between them and waved Marcie outside. "Ben, Earl, best you two mules back off some. You, Ben—you know I always kept my place, and maybe a nigger ain't got the right—"

"You ain't a nigger," Ben said sharply.

Propping her hands on the table, dark hands on white oilcloth, she said, "I'm black and your woman and I'm a nigger to everybody else in Temple County. But you *listen* to me. Lord knows me and Marcie are beholden to you for all you done, but I reckon I let that weigh too heavy on me. I ought to said somethin' about Alvah, not let you run off your own boy. He was young and full of risin' sap and needin' a woman, and to Alvah, there ain't no doubt I'm a nigger wench. He'd stayed, it all woulda worked out. He didn't mean to rape me, Ben; he was just so horny he couldn't stand it no more."

"Ellen—" Ben said.

She cut him off. "Now it don't make no nevermind; Alvah's gone, but Earl's right here, and if you don't aim to lose both your sons, I 'spect it's time you learned to *bend* your neck some. Earl's right, and you're wrong on this, and I've had my say." Skirt swishing, she hurried from the kitchen and out the back door, hands pressed tightly to her stomach.

Earl listened to wood popping softly in the stove, to a breath of wind that stroked along the house, the bright, unknowing laughter of Marcie in the front yard.

Ben said, "You want some more coffee?"

"Appreciate it," Earl said.

"That's a fine woman," Ben said, "finer'n anybody else can know. It ain't just she's young and pretty. After your ma died, it was like I was fallow ground, and every year I kind of weeded over some more, got drier and crustier. Ellen now, she come along, and afore I knew it, she had me hoed out real gentle and turned to the plow so I could feel the sun, so I could grow somethin' again. Land and a man that ain't put to good use just ain't worth a damn, neither of 'em."

Waiting, Earl stirred his coffee, the clink of the spoon loud in his ears, and after his pa rolled a Prince Albert and struck a match to it, he heard Ben say, "Alvah was wrong. I never worked your ma to death. She was always weak in the lungs."

"He knew that," Earl said. "He just had to hit you back a lick for knockin' him down."

Fragrant blue smoke wreathed Ben's lined, sunbrowned face, and he squinted through it. "Ellen said we was mules, but I reckon it's more like this here old bull and a young bull in the same pasture. Could be, the old feller whups the youngun a time or two, but the new bull, he wins in the end, because he's a heap younger."

"They don't have to butt heads," Earl said, "but bein' bulls, they don't know no better. Men are some smarter."

Ben looked directly at his son. "I ain't a mill hand."

"You do like you want," Earl said. "You always do."

"See to it, then," Ben said. "The lawyer doin's and the rest of it."

Earl's breath hung in his throat. "That—it's—I swear, Pa, you ain't goin' to be sorry."

Dragging on his cigarette, Ben said, "I made many a mistake in my life, but can't say as I'm sorry but for one of 'em. Tell me somethin', Earl. If I'd given you one, side of your head, would you've cut and run, or stood to me?"

Feeling his mouth twitch, Earl said, "I don't see as I'm bullish enough to stand to you, but while you was makin' a supper off me, I reckon I'da got in a bite or two, if I had to take a stick of stovewood to do it."

Ben laughed, leaning back and balancing his chair on its back legs. "Can't nobody fault you for bein' a Lassiter right enough. All right, see to your post peeler and dam and mill, boy." He held himself for a long second, then said, "No, that ain't right."

"What ain't right?" Earl asked, suddenly afraid.

"Callin' you *boy*," his father answered. "Seems like you just rared up on your hind legs like a man grown. Reckon you won't mind bein' called—son?"

"No," Earl said gruffly, "I won't mind that a'tall."

CHAPTER 9

Elliot met the woman, and it didn't really surprise him. What did shake him a little was her looking so much like Jessica; taller of course, and more mature, but still close enough to discomfit him. There was a difference though; Sandy Tolliver was so much more feminine, and he thought perhaps he might actually become friends with her. She wasn't a bitch like Jess.

He hadn't questioned his father when Avery called the school and said he was picking him up for a trip. Since that ugly scene in Beevo's, he'd been more afraid of his father than ever. But from the time the Caddy pulled up to his fraternity house at Southern Mississippi State, Elliot sensed a change in Avery. The man was more talkative, not so overbearing. He'd lost weight, Elliot noticed, and although Avery's face seemed a shade haggard, he seemed to boil inwardly with some new excitement. Still, Elliot sat over beside the door, keeping distance between them.

Then, when Sandy greeted Avery with such familiarity, Elliot knew there was something between them, and it didn't bother him. Slowly, and so long as it didn't mean a confrontation, Elliot was beginning to slough off his father's attitudes. He wished he could also push away the dominance.

"Go on out on the town," Avery said. "Hit the

Bourbon Street joints, boy; do you good. You and me, we're goin' to be comin' into town just about every weekend for a while."

Dismissed, Elliot had his first drink in the bar off the Monteleone lobby, checking his reflection in a blue mirror and admitting he looked every inch the well-dressed, elaborately casual, college man; more like a sophomore than a gauche freshman.

Strolling through the early-evening revelers, pairs and trios of male tourists with flushed faces and whiskey sparkle, Elliot found himself anticipating the night. It was evident his father didn't want to be bothered by anyone but the lovely Sandy Tolliver. Elliot imagined the young woman was very good at bothering a man. If only she didn't remind him so much of his sister.

A bar-walking stripper shook her sequined crotch in his face, and Elliot left half his drink to go somewhere else. One place had a good jazz pianist, and he listened with interest until a frowsy woman insisted upon him buying her a drink. He left there, also.

Down a side street, a dimly lighted club beckoned. Inside it was smoky and noisy, but more crowded, and Elliot had to squeeze himself into a corner of the bar. It was only after his second drink that he noticed there were only two women in the place. He ordered another manhattan and sipped while he congratulated himself upon how well he was doing in school.

His mother thought he should major in design and art, but midway through first semester he'd changed to political science, with a minor in psychology. Of course, he still carried the art courses, because he *was* talented in that field. But somehow the maneuverings and power structure of politics began to intrigue him, and he found a penchant for understanding motives and complications.

"Tulane?" a man's soft voice said beside him.

"I beg your pardon?"

"Tulane University? You have the look of a pre-med student, but I could be wrong. Loyola produces some outstanding lawyers, and you could be one of those, too."

The man was nice-looking, neatly groomed, and well-spoken, so Elliot said, "Oh, nothing quite so professional, and a much smaller school—Southern Miss."

"But a college man, anyhow, so I was partly right. Just visiting our city? Oh, my name is Terry."

"Hi, Terry," Elliot said, and gave his own name, and accepted another cocktail. The club didn't seem as loud, and the air became more breathable, and there was a goodness about the night. It was filled with intelligent understanding and a new closeness. He found himself talking more and drinking more.

So he wasn't too offended at the grotesque parody of two men dancing together. Half closing one eye to get them in better focus, Elliot watched for a moment before realizing it was neither grotesque nor parody. Terry's knowing, gentle hand was stroking his thigh; Terry's breath was warm upon his cheek.

"I have a little apartment close by," Terry murmured. "You want to, don't you?"

Elliot trembled upon a high, frightening escarpment. "I—I don't know; I've never—"

Far below the cliffs, smoky warm depths swirled and teased. It was cold where he stood; it had always been cold and lonely. He took the reaching step outward. "Yes," Elliot Coffield said, "I want to, very much."

* * *

Avery Coffield was filled with the wanting, no matter how often she drained it sweetly from him. The pills may slow you down, she'd warned, make you sleepy. But sleep was a sneak thief that stole precious time, and he seldom let it rob him. Lying there with his cheek pillowed upon her deeply haired mound, its marvelous shaping springy-feathery against his skin, Avery breathed the vital essence of her. The flavor of her was yet upon his tongue, spiced by urgent twistings and soft, frantic cries.

What a fool he had been; taking as gospel the hellfire and damnation preached by older boys: shoot, youngun—anybody knows a woman does somethin' like that, she ain't nothin' but a lowdown whore. Course, it's different with niggers. But a man, now—hooie! Was a man to get down there and put his *mouth* on it, well goddamn. Them ol' cartoon books, they're full of shit, drawed up just to make you get a hard on. Ain't nothin' like that in real life, less'n the feller's a *queer*. Might be different with niggers, but I ain't never heard one of them braggin' about lickin' a wench's pussy.

Sandy's hands were on his head, drawing him gently up the magnificence of her nude body, and Avery kissed along the honeyed rivulet of her golden sweat, resting most of his weight upon hands and knees.

"Lie on me," Sandy murmured. "I love to feel your weight on me."

"Ain't much as it was," he said, lips against a nipple, "but I don't miss my belly much."

"I love your belly, chubby or flat—and your hair, and your ear—"

"Hold up, Sandy; the spirit's willin', but this ol' flesh—"

"You're the strongest man I ever knew," she said,

"the kindest, most mannish man ever. All right, I'll mix us a drink."

Lolling upon the pillow, Avery watched the smooth rhythm of her buttocks, the rippling play of her long legs and thought that here was eternity. For him, it had to be, and maybe she'd been all of that to her husband, too. There was another unlucky son of a bitch had a short run before he got treed. Sandy never said much about him.

Sitting on the bed, she passed his drink and toasted him with her glass. "Elliot; did you tell him yet?"

"Pretty soon," Avery answered. "Few more times down here, so folks will get used to the idea of him seein' somebody in New Orleans, and I'll tell him."

"He seems a nice boy, but shy."

Whiskey and coke cooled the back of his throat. "If he was a *boy*, don't know as I'd let him near you. Hell, I'm even jealous of that chair you set in, at the office."

"That's good," Sandy purred. "But how will Elliot take it?"

"Any damned way I tell him. He don't get to pick, else he gets cut off at the pockets."

"And your wife?"

Avery studied the rim of his glass. "Lila's gonna accept it, way I put it to her."

"You never say much about your wife."

"You never said anything about your husband."

Emptying her glass, Sandy clinked its ice. "Frank was damned happy to do his internship in the Army, where the pay was good and they made him an officer. He was a captain when the Chinese overran the Second Infantry Division up in North Korea, near a village called Kunu-ri. He was killed there."

Avery waited awhile before asking, "Was he—was it this good for him and you?"

"Yes," Sandy almost whispered. "But he was gone so long, and there was the waiting and waiting, the goddamned waiting. When it was certain there was no mistake, and he wasn't coming back—" For a second Avery thought her eyes were misting up, but they were bright when she turned to smile at him. "Well, I'm very glad you came along, Avery Coffield. I was tired of doctors who smelled of pain and antiseptic, of flabby old men and pimply young men. Once there was even a cab driver, surprised as could be; he smelled, too."

Avery said, "I don't want to hear about 'em."

"You asked."

"I won't ask again."

She trailed a hand over his belly. "Do you want another drink?"

"I want you," he said. "Jesus; that's goin' to be the hardest part, not bein' able to want you like this."

"This," said the swarthy man who looked like a wedge stood on its narrow end, "this is a little bonus, Sheriff. Hundred extra every week in your envelope."

Floyd Kobburn ran stubby fingers over the sheaf of bills before tucking them into his pocket. "Man likes to know he's appreciated."

They were in the storeroom piled high with wooden cases where Beevo had used an upended box for his business. A small desk was in its place now. It was early Friday evening, before the farm boys and pulpwood cutters came in any numbers. Just in case, Kobburn had parked the patrol car on a side road and cut through the woods, glad the weather had cooled.

He nodded thanks when Dominic Scarpo poured

them both a drink of fancy bourbon. "Reckon them slot machines won't hurt nothin'."

"That's where the bonus comes from," Scarpo said. "They're takin' to 'em already. When they start the dam, there'll be more money around; then we'll try out a crap table."

"Well, now," Kobburn said, "crap tables is more like gamblin'." Funny, he thought, how this New Orleans Eye-talian just said flat out how it was going to be, instead of asking. He'd shown up in Temple County, him and two other ugly fellers, right after word was sent down to somebody Kobburn knew in the city. He hadn't expected white folks, though you might say dagos wasn't exactly white.

"More like money," Scarpo grunted. He sat in the only chair, so Kobburn had to prop his haunch against a box. "First the dam, then the mill, and a steady payroll. This asshole setup wouldn't be worth peanuts right now, if it wasn't for the alky."

That was something else, Kobburn thought; the bootlegging had gotten out of hand, organized, sort of, since Scarpo got here. It was getting hard to find halfway decent drinking whiskey, because most of it was being shipped out, and Kobburn didn't even know where. A good part of the nickels and dimes going into those slot machines came from straight out of stills off in the piney woods.

"Managed to hold the nigger whores together for you," Kobburn said. "Some of 'em wanted to follow old Beevo, but I told 'em they'd wear out their asses in jail."

"Two-dollar tricks," Scarpo said, rolling his wide, beefy shoulders. "The Saturday-night good old boys will pay ten bucks a throw for some classy white stuff."

Kobburn blinked at his empty glass, but Scarpo didn't reach for the bourbon bottle. He said, "Hold on, now. There ain't never been no white whores in this county, and onct word gets out there's nigger *and* white women here together—"

"What?" Scarpo barked. "What? The church people gonna march on me, run me outa the county? I wasn't sent up here for nickles and dimes, sport. What's good for me and my people, that's good for you, too. Keep it in mind, Sheriff."

Rubbing a hand over his face, Kobburn muttered, "It's got to be held down, that's all; kept real quiet like. And it'd be a heap better, was you to keep any white women separated from the niggers."

Scarpo's laugh sounded like two steel files rubbing together. "Different drinkin' fountains?"

Taking off his hat, Kobburn fanned himself with it. "Maybe a couple little trailers, like. Long as white women stay a *long* ways from nigger women."

Scarpo crossed thick arms across his chest. "And if one of the town bigshots wants one of each, at the same time? Somebody like Harvey or Watson or Jellico?"

"They wouldn't do that," Kobburn said. "They was born and raised here, and they wouldn't do that."

"If you'd make book on that," Scarpo said, getting up from the desk, "you better stay away from the crap table; you ain't a gambler."

"Oh," Kobburn said quickly, "I couldn't let nobody catch me here. Not me bein' sheriff."

The man's laugh grated on him, and Scarpo's hand was in the small of his back, pushing him for the store-room door. Kobburn's hand went to the envelope in his pocket, brushed it, then fell to hook a thumb in his black gunbelt. Outside on the gravel, he turned and pushed out his chest. "One thing, mister. Any decent white girl comes here with some skylarkin' boy, you run 'em right back out. That's somethin' folks just won't stand for—their daughters foolin' around no juke joint like this 'un. *I* couldn't help you none then."

"Man, man," Scrapo said, "that just scares the hell outa me."

Kobburn said, "Can't nobody make money, you get burned out."

Scarpo's expression changed; the heavy brows knotted. "Yeah," he said, "yeah. I'll see to it, Sheriff."

Feeling some better about things, Kobburn stood looking at the closed door for a spell, then strolled off toward the woods, holding in his belly. White whores at Beevo's; how about that? Maybe juicy young girls with the down still on them; classy stuff, the Eyetalian said, good lookin' enough for a man to pay ten dollars.

He got clear to his patrol car before Jolene somehow got herself mixed up with the idea of white whores. The little bitch had been staying home a lot, mooning around the house and playing records. Nigh onto six months and she was still dragging ass. Not yet, she kept saying, when he told her she ought to go off to school, study typing or maybe beauty-parlor work. At least, she wasn't knocked up, and that was a pure-D blessing, with an election coming up, and summer nearly done. Hell of a chance he'd have, even with Avery Coffield behind him, if Jolene looked like she swallowed a watermelon seed. First sign that gal was missing her period, and he'd ship her off to Mobile or somewhere right quick.

She had her mind set on that Lassiter boy, the one that was puttin' it to her out in the woods, and maybe that would be the answer. Who woulda thought that

skinny youngun could invent a thingamajig that
turned out money like the United States Government?
Half a dozen machines he had going out at the old
sawmill now, and that Yankee Jew backing him with
cash for trucks and the like. Everything in just a few
short months, or was it nearer to a year?

How long was it going to be, before that dam got
built? Folks kept talking about it, even though Avery
Coffield and the other planters kept trying to stop it.
Could be, it would never block off the Tchufuncta
River, time so many legal papers quit flying. But even
without the dam, Earl Lassiter had a good thing
going, and Jolene could do a heap worse than get herself married to him. It would purely take a load off
her daddy's mind.

Backing the patrol car, Kobburn eased it along the
dirt road, mindful of keeping it clean as he could. Mason didn't come around twice a week to wash it for
him anymore. Since that nigger went to work for the
Lassiter boy, he acted like he didn't need the four bits,
and Kobburn hadn't found another boy yet. He
would, though; first nigger got drunk and cut up another one, he'd get to work out his fine on the car.

He wondered again why the Eye-talian hadn't got
local niggers to help him, why Scarpo brought up the
other dagos. Maybe they worked cheap as niggers, and
maybe they bunched up the same way. Kobburn drove
to his house, parked, and got out to stretch. The smell
of side meat frying reached him, and he scratched his
belly. Jolene was showing her good side, right enough.
He'd tell her it was all right to see the Lassiter boy
again.

CHAPTER 10

Driving out of town toward The Shadows, Avery realized that Sandy had a buzz on, and couldn't fault her for it. She had a lot to face up to, and knew it, but he meant to make things easy on her as he could. Hanging around Will Jellico's law office hadn't done much to ease her tension, and to tell the truth, he'd gotten pretty griped at Will himself.

All that crap about how he couldn't afford to settle fifty thousand on the girl Elliot was going to marry, come Christmas vacation. Why, Avery, why? Boy's not even finished his first year at school. And Avery answered, why the hell not, since it's my business anyhow. Damnit, nobody knew better that things weren't like they ought to be; three poor crops in a row, Lila still pouring money into redoing that old wing of the house; cars for both younguns—and naturally, Jessica just had to get herself a fancy sports car. And college costs, and wages eating away at him because the hands had to be paid, getting the land ready for next year.

Sandy put a hand on his thigh, and he smiled around at her. Christ; would he even *be* here next year? Had to be, since Sandy hadn't caught yet, and that fretted hell out of him. Maybe that damned thing gnawing away inside him had gotten into his balls and made him less than a man.

"Not far now," he said to her. "Your new home, and your son's."

"If it wasn't for—oh, Avery; I'm scared. But I want the same thing: a home place, protection, a child. Our child."

"Your *boy*," he said, easing the Caddy around a curve. "Yours and Elliot's, far as the world knows."

"But facing your wife and children," she said. "I wish I had a drink."

"Me, too," he said. "We'll get some at the house, and I reckon I could use another pill."

Her hand tightened upon his thigh. "Is the pain bad?"

"Tryin' to be, but I won't let it. Look—don't you worry about Lila and the rest. I'll handle 'em."

Sandy pressed close to him. "Forcing me down their throats this way, they'll hate me."

"No more'n they hate me, but my mind's set to it, Sandy. There just ain't another way, and you don't know how much I appreciate what you're doin' for me, how proud I am. Never loved a woman like you; never even knew one like you."

"Avery—" Her lips were at his neck, her arm across his shoulders.

"We got to keep up appearances, for the niggers, anyhow. Lila dotes on that old wing of the house so much, she can move into it; Jess, too, when she's home. Elliot'll have to stay where he is, but he won't be home much either. We'll put on the biggest damned weddin' party this county ever saw."

"I wish it was for us," Sandy murmured, then straightened and sat away from him. "Oh! That's it— The Shadows?"

Pulling the car into the gravel drive, Avery looked to the columned front porch, and saw them there drawn up in a skirmish line, ready to do battle with him—Lila, Jessica, and Elliot. His wife and daughter were in front and close together, with Elliot hanging back some.

There wasn't going to be any trouble with him; he'd already been told and told good, and understood that it was his ass if he tried to weasel out of marrying Sandy Tolliver. Funny thing; after those weekends in New Orleans, the boy was easier to get along with, and even seemed to think hitching up was a pretty good idea.

But since his ma and sister had been at him, Avery didn't know. Elliot never laid claim to a backbone. Avery climbed out and went around to open the door for Sandy. Her hand was cold in his as he led her up the steps.

"This is Sandra Tolliver," he announced. "Elliot's fiancée, the woman he's goin' to marry come Christmastime. Lila, Jess—say hello to her." He waited, and they waited in silence, and Avery threw it in their faces: "Goddamnit! You howdy this lady or every goddamned one of you'll wish you had."

Jessica slammed her MG to a stop in front of the drugstore, where she'd had Ron Benning wait until that incredible affair at the house was over. When he came ambling out, big and shaggy in his football sweater, she wanted to hit him, simply because he was a man. Her knuckles were white on the steering wheel, and she was still trembling inside. The nerve of him; the goddamn, bare-faced *nerve*! Her father had picked one wife for Elliot, and when that didn't take, chose another one, and brought her home to make sure.

And Elliot, gutless as ever, simpering around this Tolliver woman as if it was his own idea. Lila might pretend to believe that, but Jessica never would, despite her brother's trips to New Orleans, because Avery had always been there at the same time, on "business."

"Sure," she grated, and Ron Benning hauled his bulk into the MG to say, "Huh?"

"Not you," she said, "just men in general. Christ, but I'm sick of them."

The woman was so pretty, in a cheap sort of way; a young widow, an RN—why the hell would she tie herself to a weakling like Elliot? Jessica frowned; did Sandra Tolliver have something wrong with her, the way Elliot had? She wondered if lesbians and male queers got together, and if so, what happened between them. It had to be the money, the land, she thought; The Shadows and its cotton fields and family cemetery—

"You gonna sit here all day?" Ron Benning asked.

The cemetery, Jessica thought; hell yes—that was it. Daddy and his fixation upon the Coffield line. If Elliot didn't get married, didn't produce a son, there'd be no Coffield name. Her lips twisted as she gunned the MG's motor and swung the car into a tire-squealing U-turn. Unless there was something she didn't know about, Elliot would have a rough time getting it up for his bride, but maybe the semen could be poked up her somehow.

She hit the brakes so suddenly that Benning had to grab to keep himself from going through the windshield. "Hey, Earl," she said. "How you doin', stranger?"

He stood awkwardly on the sidewalk, filled out in the shoulders a bit since last summer, his jeans oily and workshirt spotted, but he had the door open on a new Ford pickup.

"Howdy, Jessica. Good to see you home."

She draped an arm across Benning's shoulder. "Meet Ron Benning; he's Southern's star football player, the one who'll beat Ole Miss for us this year."

"Fullback," Benning said, and stuck out a paw.

Earl shook it briefly. "Howdy."

"I hear you're just doin' wonders with your old mill," Jessica went on. "Regular businessman now."

"Just gettin' started," Earl said, shifting his feet and looking uncomfortable.

Remembering what a scaredy-cat he'd been the night of her going-away party, she thought, and stared at him until he knew she wasn't ever going to forget it, either. Was he still a virgin? "I just thought of something. Elliot has a new fiancée, and you ought to come meet her. We'll have a swim party this evenin'—"

"Cold for swimmin'," Earl said, putting his hand back on his truck door.

"Oh, didn't you know? Daddy has the pool heated. *Anybody* can swim in the summer. But if you can't find anybody to bring—"

She saw him look at Ron, then his eyes reached for her own, not embarrassed or all that uncertain now. "We'd be proud to come over for a spell."

She wouldn't ask who the girl was; certainly not Mary Alice Harvey? But that would be delicious, wouldn't it, almost-wife meeting wife-to-be? That ought to curl her daddy's hair. "Why that's fine, Earl. We'll have a buffet table and all that, and you can tell me about your big success. I mean, it's not often a home-town boy makes good."

Abruptly, she swung the sports car away in a wake of dust. Earl still wanted her so badly that it showed in the tenseness of his body, the set of his mouth. If he was going around with Mary Alice, he wasn't a cherry now, but Mary Alice never did have a dime's worth of imagination. Once they were together, he could compare them and see how much he was missing.

"Nobody said nothin' about a swimming party," Ron grunted.

"I just did," Jessica said, "and my daddy's always just tickled to do whatever I want."

"You want," Lila Coffield hissed, "*you* want! It's always been whatever *you* want, and nobody else counts. I don't know how on earth you got poor Elliot to agree to this—this farce, but I certainly don't."

Avery had carried a glass into the old wing from the library bar, a big one. He took a swallow from it and said, "Elliot ain't marryin' you, though I expect he's been wantin' to all his life."

Lila paced the bedroom, austere in design, faithful to the restoration. "But that woman, and a widow. What do you know about her? I tell you, Avery, I won't stand for this!"

He leaned against a fireplace mantel and took another swallow. "You jealous of Sandy? She takin' your baby boy from you?"

"Why, I never—you have no right to speak to me this way, Avery! I am your wife, and—"

"Are you?" he said. "Have you ever been? They say a man gets old before he gets wise, and I reckon I'm about old as I'm ever goin' to be. So I know better now, Lila; I sure as hell know better. Just get it straight, *wife*—Elliot's marryin' her come December, and that's it. If you go whining around and make him feel guilty about desertin' his darlin' mama, I'll come down on you all like stink on shit. I stopped by Will Jellico's on the way home, and we talked about codicils and the like. I can legally cut off my childrun with a dollar apiece, and even though I can't do that

to you, and even though you'd keep right on support-
in' them, there's a way around that, too. It's all set for
me to sell out everything I own, every inch of land and
this house, to boot. And I promise you I'll spend every
goddamned dime before I die, if I have to throw it all
in the river. All you'll get your hands on is the insurance, and let's see if you can keep Elliot and Jess in
school on that. Hell, I might even stop payin' the pre-
miums."

White-faced, stunned, Lila stared at him. "You—
you'd go that far to hurt us?"

"Far as I have to," Avery said, "so don't get my back
up no more. Just do like you always done—smile and
sashay around and show off your nice house to your
nice friends. But after they're gone, this is your wing
of the house. You spend most of your time here, anyhow."

She put a hand to her face, as if she'd been slapped.
"And you will stay over there?"

"We been more'n a bedroom apart for a long time."

Backing away from him, Lila was shaking. "I see it
now. Oh yes, I can see this in all its ugliness, its perversion. And under my own roof—so sordid and shameful.
It's bad enough that you—you *animals* go slinking off
to that nigra crib, but to bring such a bitch under *my*
roof and m-marry her to *my* son, in order to carry on
your dirty, godless perversions—"

"Shut up," Avery said. "It's my roof or nobody's,
and Elliot is my son, too—or could have been, if you'd
ever weaned him."

Lila's back was against the wall, her fingers scratching at it beside her hips. "You have a son; you made
Jessica as much like you as you could, and ignored Elliot because he—he was sensitive and so ill as a child.

Don't blame me, Avery Coffield. Don't you dare blame it all on me!"

Avery finished his drink, but it didn't warm him much. "Blame don't matter now. You won't tear up the peapatch, either, because appearances mean so damned much to you. You'll go on just like before, seein' to it that the niggers don't gossip. Only, hold this in your mind, Lila—I never been so set on anything in my life, and anybody that gets in front of me will get stomped. That means Sandra Tolliver gets treated good as anybody in this house. You understand that—understand it real goddamned good."

Swaying, Lila used the wall to brace herself. She was hating him with her eyes, her soul, with every fiber of her tensed body. After Avery closed the bedroom door behind him and walked partway down the hall, he heard his wife break something fragile and expensive, heard the frustrated crash.

"He splashes a heap of water, doesn't he?" Jessica said. "You ought to see the way he chunks around other football players at school. Is Ron takin' up too much of the pool, Earl? You and Jolene haven't even got your feet wet."

Although she kept her voice sweet, Jessica was still mad clear through, and Earl Lassiter inviting the town punchboard didn't help things. And her daddy hadn't even looked at her new swimsuit; normally, he would have had something to say about how scanty it was, but he was clear across the pool, hanging around Elliot and that Tolliver woman. *Her* suit wasn't any more daring than Jessica's.

But that poor, chubby Jolene—Jessica stretched smooth legs on the chaise longue and flicked a glance at the tacky ruffles Jolene wore. The girl would be hog fat in a few years.

"I don't swim very good," Jolene said, hanging on to Earl's hand. "You go on, Earl. I'll see if Mr. Coffield will give me a drink."

Jessica's eyes taunted him, so Earl trotted to the edge of the pool and dove in, slicing the water cleanly. She watched both boys for a while, comparing the golden bulk of Ron Benning to the lean whiteness of Earl. Ron's summer tan had almost faded, but Earl's neck and arms had burned deeper, browner, a startling contrast to the rest of his skin. Laying that roundheels Jolene Kobburn; it would be a wonder if he didn't catch something.

Elliot laughed at the bar, and the sound irritated her. He never laughed with Daddy; it was always Daddy laughing at him. The woman had to do with it, Jessica thought, and her father seemed more interested in her than Elliot, half drunk so early in the evening, and carrying on like he was twenty years younger. No wonder her mother had retired to her room right after dinner with one of her sick headaches.

There went Jolene, waddling to the bar. Jessica pulled a robe around her, but left it hanging open. She forgot the boys in the pool and walked quickly.

"Daddy—you forgot our shaker."

He cocked his head at her. "Sure did, baby. Well, help yourself. Sandy here was tellin' us about the crazy stunts the hospital interns cut. Pour little Jolene a drink, too; she looks cold."

"I'll go put on somethin'," Jessica said, and left them, but he didn't even notice she was gone. When she looked back, he was laughing again.

Sweater and slacks, heels, and a jacket carried over one shoulder, perfume on her throat, a quick brushing of her long hair, and Jessica went downstairs again. Earl was standoffish, and Ron more interested in showing his muscles, and the rest of them were ignoring her, listening to Sandy Tolliver.

She caught Earl climbing from the pool; Ron was still lunging back and forth, throwing spray. Jessica said, "Take us out of here."

"Where?"

Impatiently, she shook her head. "I don't care; anywhere. We can all pile in your truck, take a ride."

"I'll ask Jolene."

Jessica ran a fingertip down his flat stomach, over the crotch of his trunks. "Just tell her."

But when they crowded into Earl's truck, Jolene wanted to go home. Pouty as Mary Alice Harvey, Jessica thought, but with even more cause; couldn't look pretty or think of anything to say. Maybe Jolene was good at what she did, and the lord knew she had enough practice, but when she was on her feet, she was out of place. So Earl didn't really have a reason to sulk; he was well rid of Miss Roundheels, and Jessica kept teasing him with her hand, sitting between him and Ron. She laughed into one face, then the other, and drew a leg along one of theirs.

"Where we goin'?" Earl asked. "You want to see my mill?"

"I've seen mills," Jessica said, "but I've never been to Beevo's."

Earl took his foot off the gas. "Are you out of your mind? *Beevo's*?"

"Why not? I hear a white man runs it now, and there's slot machines and just everything. Are you *scared* to take me there, Earl? And here I had the idea you were all grown up. Ron wouldn't be scared."

Ron rolled massive shoulders. "I'm not afraid of anything."

"See, Earl? If you don't carry me—"

"Scared's got nothin' to do with it," Earl said. "It just ain't right, that's all."

"You'd go with Jolene."

"No," he said, "I wouldn't."

"I bet you haven't been there yourself. Would they let you in?"

"If I wanted."

"Well there's the light," Jessica said, "and you just let Ron and me out, if you're so scared. We can catch a ride back."

She cut the ignition key and threw her leg across Earl's to stamp on the brake. When she pushed Ron out, Earl said something under his breath, but she was running toward Beevo's, toward noise and lights and people who'd pay plenty of attention to her, people who would be sure to tell her daddy.

Moving through smoke and whiskey smell, Jessica turned off conversation as heads turned, and she recognized some of the faces, startled, open-mouthed faces.

"We'll take a quart," she said to the man who bulged behind the bar. He looked at her, at Ron and Earl coming up beside her. The jukebox was loud. Then the bartender looked beyond her, past her, and the man there said, "Haul it on outa here."

She wheeled to face him. "My; you don't seem to be an improvement over Beevo. Are you related to him?"

"You can't stay here," he said. "Move."

Everybody was watching, and Jessica held her ground. "Our money's good as any; better than most. Why can't I—"

Shorter than Ron Benning, but seeming bigger, the

dark man jerked his thumb. "You give away what my girls sell."

Ron Benning rolled his shoulders and pushed between them. "Look, you—"

He went down so quickly that Jessica didn't understand why. But there was another man moving in on Earl, and the fat one had come from behind the bar with amazing speed. The dark man caught Jessica's wrist and started dragging her across the room toward the door.

"Earl!" she screamed. "Earl—"

But they were chopping at Earl, too. He fell against the bar and one of the men hit him low in the belly, the other in the head. Gasping and stumbling, she was pushed to the truck and flung into the front seat.

"Next time," the man said, "I pull down your drawers and paddle your ass in front of everbody. Vinnie, Fats—throw them kids in back. Drive, rich girl."

Jessica drove, biting her lips and refusing to cry.

CHAPTER 11

It was like still-hunting for fox squirrels, Earl thought; you dressed warm and dark, took a rifle and box of shells, and were in position before daylight. Because you were part of the scenery when dawn broke and the squirrels began to stir, you were accepted until the first shot. Then the waiting started again, but by the time the game had watered and found feed and holed up until afternoon, you were on your way home with a sackful of meat.

But Earl would never have gone hunting boogered up as he was. He hurt like hell, and the swelling in his balls would take days to go down. The blue lump along his cheekbone wasn't bad, and didn't affect his shooting eye. But he was packing another hurt, maybe worse than the others—Jessica.

Lying on his left side, snugged at the base of a loblolly pine and screened by a clump of bitterweeds, Earl strained to make out the buildings below, but they were fuzzy, dark within dark. Jessica had pushed this, not knowing or not caring how it ended, and he should have had better sense than to go with her, to take her to Beevo's. She was so mule-headed, and that football player kind of sneered, and—oh hell, Earl thought; that wasn't what bothered him now. He *had* gone into the juke joint with her and Benning, and gotten hell beat out of him account of it, and now he was lying out in the brush with his 30-30 because one thing just naturally followed the other.

It was Jessica parking his truck by her daddy's toolshed and running Benning inside the house; it was her squirming all over him in the dark, saying how sorry she was, and putting both his hands on her tits, kissing him and running her hotly reaching tongue into his mouth.

There was a special heat about Jessica then, all wiggly and hungry, and when he tried to tell her how it was, she bit his lip and took one of his hands to run it up under her skirt. Her thighs were strong and her thighs were wondrous soft, and the pulsing mound beneath tight silken panties just snugged his palm.

All his life, he'd wanted Jessica Coffield, with about as much chance of getting to her as that damned Indian spring had of turning into a waterfall. But when he pulled his mouth loose from hers, all he could gasp was, "Damnit, Jessica—don't you see I can't? They kicked me in the crotch and I hurt so bad I'm about to bust, and I *can't* do it to you now."

She'd stiffened and pushed his hand away. "You mean you won't. I swear, Earl, I'm beginnin' to think you and Elliot are both kind of funny."

That made him mad, and he told her to get on out of his truck, that if she thought he was funny as her brother, to go ask Jolene Kobburn. If a man was hurt, it wasn't his fault. Then she'd said that she'd find out if Ron Benning didn't get well quick, and Earl told her to go ahead, go ahead.

Just before he drove off, hunched up in the seat and grunting as he put in the clutch, Jessica stood there in the night and said, "You'll be back, Earl Lassiter; you'll always be back."

Not with his tail between his legs, he thought, and because he felt like a whipped hound, anyhow, made too much noise when he got to the mill. He forgot the new load of saplings and ran into them, knocking some into the water tank and rattling it like the hinges of hell. Even though the mill had spread some, he still kept his room in back, and got into it to turn on the light and peer at his face in the mirror, to drop his pants and gingerly touch his sack. It was already puffing up and turning funny colors. They had no call lighting into him thataway, when all he meant to do was carry Jessica out of the place; especially, they had no call kicking him in the nuts when he hadn't lifted a hand at them.

Then the door creaked and he looked up to see his pa barefoot, long-johns top and overalls with only one gallus hooked. "You all right, son?"

"I ain't drunk; just forgot those saplings."

Ben eyed him. "Get into a scuffle?"

"Got scuffled *on*, more like it. Them fellers at Beevo's jump salty right quick."

"You make trouble for 'em?"

"Damned fool enough to let Jessica Coffield talk me into takin' her inside, her and her college boy. It was that, or leavin' them to walk home, and I had the ride."

Ben came over and sat down on the cot. Embarrassed, Earl pulled up his pants. Ben said, "Nutted you, did they?"

"I'll get over it," Earl said.

"Cold water helps," his pa said, touched him on the shoulder, and left.

Now, with morning-dew chill on his face, Earl turned over onto his other side, able to make out the shape of Beevo's as the sky lightened. He wondered if

his brother was doing the same, yonder in Korea, or if
some enemy soldier was still-hunting Alvah. It would
be a whole lot better, going at it man to man, Earl
thought, without mixing tanks and airplanes and artillery into it. But war didn't seem to make good sense,
anyhow, fighting over a piece of land that wasn't your
own and you didn't want in the first place, tying into
somebody hadn't done wrong to you, some man you
didn't even know.

The folks down there in Beevo's were different;
they'd walloped him and kicked him without cause,
and he had to show them their mistake. Earl wiped
dampness from his rifle barrel with a kerchief, and
tested how he could lie on his belly without hurting. It
took some adjusting, but he could get a good sight on
the door. He waited a mite longer on the light before
squeezing off the first shot.

It took off the doorknob, and Earl jacked another
round into the chamber, levering the Winchester
deftly. One into every truck tire he could see, a couple
into the dark blue Chevy's tires, too. Turning attention to the rambling building, he began taking out
windowpanes, tasting gunsmoke, feeling the familiar
jar of the rifle against his shoulder.

The hollering started down there, and it sounded
like a handgun popped, so Earl slid down behind his
hump in the ground and went eeling over to his right,
some yards away. From there, he went to work on the
pair of new trailers this Scarpo had hauled in. Seemed
like the bullets went right on through them, but high,
in case girls were in them. They hadn't done anything
to him.

He stopped firing to change position again, and
somebody yelled inside Beevo's; a handgun popped
twice, and Earl caught a glimpse of a quick shadow

ducking out back around the truck. The sun was brighter now, and he could see the outside box the phone line led into; he put two bullets into it, and metal flew.

Another man scooted out the back and behind a trailer. Earl figured they'd take to the woods and try to come around on each side of him, and rolled over to reload.

He looked back quickly when a rifle sounded, a sharp, flat crack that made him want to pull in his head like a turtle. But no bullet snapped past him, or even whined high overhead. In Beevo's parking lot, a man yelped and went lickety-split back for the house. The long gun hammered again, and the man behind the trailer hunted himself a better hole. The shots were coming from piney woods near the creek, clear around the other side of the juke joint.

Earl grinned so wide it hurt his jaws, then settled down to taking out the rest of the windows, hearing his own shots echoed by the other rifle. It would take that Scarpo feller and his buddies a while to fix up the place; probably a lot of bottles busted inside, too; and for sure, some whores were peein' themselves so bad they might light out when the shooting quit and never come back.

It was enough, so he saved the last couple of rounds in his Winchester and took off through the brush, walking slow because hurrying pained him between the legs. The rifle barrel was warm, and the morning was fresh, all shiny. A man did what he had to, and the day always looked good.

At the mill, he put up his Winchester and washed, then went to the house for breakfast, trying not to limp. His pa was already at the table with a cup of coffee, and red-eye gravy was cooking. Earl sat down in his place and winked at little Marcie; the girl giggled and ducked her head.

Ben Lassiter said, "First thing they teach you in the infantry is watch your flanks."

"Yessir," Earl said, wondering if his pa stayed up all night, or slept so light he knew when Earl was walking out.

Ellen brought a mug of coffee and set it before Earl. She was trying to look stern, but a twinkle showed through. "Mules work better in harness when they both pullin'."

Ben Lassiter lifted grayish eyebrows. "Who in this world is talkin' about mules? The army quit usin' mules a long time back."

"Folks around here still use 'em," Ellen said, back at the stove, "and they cut a clean, deep furrow."

"I swear," Ben grunted, "this woman's got mules on the brain. Me and my son was discussin' military tactics, and we was just about to change the subject to mill machinery. You aimin' to work mules into that talk, too?"

Ellen served a platter of grits and eggs. "Talk what I know best," she said, "and I been around mules all my life. Seems I can't get away from 'em."

Dominic Scarpo lifted his head and peered around the corner of the bar. "Get away from the window, Vinnie. Them goddamned hillbillies could still be out there."

"*Figlia butana!*" Fats hissed from where he'd jammed his bulk behind the jukebox. "Them bastards coulda killed us all."

"If they meant to," Scarpo grunted, coming to his knees. "They were shootin' high, but damn!—look what they done to the bar."

"Knocked out tires on the truck and car both," Vinnie said, pistol in hand. "That second son of a bitch missed me an inch. Who'd figure these rednecks to set up a crossfire? And how come, huh? Tell me that—how come? Nobody else wants this joint."

Scarpo climbed up, head cocked to listen. He was shaken from his own near miss behind the trailer; he could swear the bullet had fanned his hair. "Call the sheriff, Fats."

Vinnie said, "Sheriff? We can handle this ourselves; we always do."

"On our own turf," Scarpo said. "What the hell we know about the woods? Moccasins out there, quicksand, all that crap—and a couple bastards in their own backyard that can crease a gnat's ass at three hundred yards. You wanna take off after 'em, go ahead. I'll say *addio* and send to New Orleans for another soldier, 'cause you ain't comin' back."

"Dom," Fats said, "the phone don't work."

"Shit," Scarpo said. "Vinnie, change the tires and go find the badge. You check on the girls, Fats, then haul it back and help clean up this mess."

"Ain't we gonna *do* nothing?" Vinnie asked.

"Yeah, we're gonna do like I said, at least until we find out the name of the game."

Some time later, Sheriff Floyd Kobburn climbed out of his car and whistled. "Looks like a war come this way."

Scarpo put aside a broom and waggled a thick finger. "Come on in back, but watch the glass. We just got it swept up, even with the girls workin'. Two of the black ones run out on us."

"Reckon who done it?" Kobburn pondered, pushing back his hat. "Too early in the day for just hoorawin'."

"We threw some kids outa here last night," Scarpo said. "A smartmouth girl with long, blond hair; sexy little piece; a Joe College type; a skinny country boy. Made the girl drive the pickup, a red Ford, new."

Kobburn found a box to prop his haunch against and whistled again. "Sounds like the Coffield gal makin' her kind of trouble, and I don't know no college boys, but that new red truck—yeah; the Lassiter boy. He ain't a troublemaker."

Scarpo poured two drinks. "He got caught in the middle, I guess."

"Your men put a hand to him?"

"Vinnie and Fats dropped 'em both."

Kobburn downed his whiskey and shook his head. "It'd be Earl Lassiter come callin', then."

"There was two of 'em; pinned us in a crossfire and stuck me with about a thousand dollars' damage."

"*Two* of 'em," Kobburn repeated. "With rifles, I 'spect. Ben Lassiter, too. Didn't mean to shoot you up, mister; if they did, I'd be callin' ol' Doc Christopher to make out coroner reports. They was just passin' word."

"What the hell does that mean?" Scarpo's face was darker.

Slowly, Kobburn said, "You all are new around here. There's some folks you can lay a hand to, and some you can't. Now, I know a man or two in this here county woulda come back last night, and come a-killin'. But Ben Lassiter and his youngun ain't that kind; they're hardshelled and almighty touchy, but they're fair enough. Reckon you have to see that your boys pull in their horns 'til they find out which end is up. A drunk woods runner takes a swipe at you, then you got call to turn him out, but even then, best not to use more'n one man on him. He won't fault you for that, and next time he comes back, he'll mind his manners. But he's bound to get his hackles up, if'n two, three fellers climbed him."

"Ain't this a bitch?" Scarpo drained his glass and refilled it. He didn't pass the bottle to the sheriff. "I don't believe I'm sittin' here listenin' to a lecture about rednecks from a redneck. Now you listen, sport—you're in my pocket, and I won't stand for any hillbillies shootin' up my place, scaring off my girls. So it's *your* turn to pass word; you tell those country sons of bitches that I—"

Kobburn leaned across the desk and took the bottle without asking. He said, "You must be a pretty smart feller, to get sent from New Orleans, smart enough to stay here and make a right good business. You made a wrong move and the Lassiters knocked some of your checkers off'n the board. But they're done with it, less'n you stir 'em up again, and that wouldn't be a'tall smart."

Scarpo took a deep breath and leaned back in his chair. A piece of shattered windowpane fell to the floor behind him. He nodded then. "Okay, okay, go tell 'em I'm done with it, too."

The sheriff grinned. "Guess it's my bounden duty to check out a shootin', but it ain't nobody's business to spread talk around. Them Lassiters are close-mouthed; won't nobody hear it from them. Yessir, close-mouthed as loggerhead turtles."

Swaggering a little, Kobburn hitched up his gunbelt and left the room. Fats came to lean against the door-frame; he was sweating.

Scarpo said, "You believe that? What the hell is a loggerhead turtle?"

Fats shrugged. "Beats me. What you want I should do about the missing girls?"

"More'll come in," Scarpo said. "There ain't never a shortage of whores. Go on cleanin' up the joint, and if you find any loggerhead turtles, be sure to sweep 'em out."

Blinking, Fats said, "You think a *turtle* would come in here?"

"What you want from me—blackeyed peas? How the hell do I know?" Scarpo said. "But I'm learning."

CHAPTER 12

Avery sat at the table, one hand atop it, one against his belly. It didn't seem important that the county commissioners were getting a better payoff from the man who took over Beevo's. Sam Harvey absorbed money like a sponge, anyhow, but Avery suspected Martin Nelson could use it. His Moss Hill wasn't doing any better than The Shadows, but Martin had his store to fall back on.

Sam kept looking at him. "You feelin' up to snuff, Avery?"

"I'll get by. Thing is, if it catches up to me, I got somebody in mind to fill my seat on this board."

Martin Nelson fiddled with an unlit cigar. "Will Jellico can do it real good; maybe Burr Watson."

Pushing his fist against his belly, Avery said, "I got my boy in mind."

They stared at him, and Sam said, "Well, now—ain't Elliot a mite young?"

"Coffields always been county commissioners," Avery said stubbornly, "and the boy's president of his class, doin' real good at political science and the like."

Martin Nelson rolled the cigar in his fingers. "He ain't votin' age yet, and you want us—"

"Damn right," Avery said, "and I don't want no ar-

gument about it. Since I took sick, I been doin' a heap
of thinkin', and writin' down a lot of things I remembered, puttin' them in a safe place—Beevo's payoffs,
some of them sharecropper deals at our stores, that
county road a half mile outa line so it could reach
your place, Martin. And you, Sam—the way your bank
picked up back land taxes without notifyin' anybody."

"Now hold on, Avery." Sam Harvey was red in the
face.

"That's what I'm doin'," Avery said, "holdin' on
with teeth and toenails, and I mean to keep hangin'
on until my grandson's born, and my boy's appointed
to fill my place on this board. Won't be long; they
been married six months and when a Coffield drives a
nail, it stays drove. Hell—you think I don't know how
you bastards been lettin' that Jew's company wheedle
you, how you been lettin' him pick up right of ways
and clearances and all that shit?"

Martin Nelson said slowly, "Times are changin', Avery, and what with the drought—"

"Goddamnit, both of you got plantations. Where
you think you'll get cotton hands, field hands, once
they got that stinkin' pulp mill in here? Sure, you got
machines, but you need men to run 'em, weighers,
pickers, hoers. Ain't a machine been made that can
chop weeds out'n cotton like a good nigger."

"Plenty of niggers be left," Sam said. "Buildin' that
dam and mill can't hire 'em all."

Avery made himself take the hand from his belly,
stood up and walked to the file cabinet where there
was always a bottle of bourbon. He drank right from
the bottle, and set his face against the burn. "What you
figure on payin' your hands?" he asked. "Same as now?
That Yankee outfit's goin' to raise wages, sure'n hell.

Tell you somethin' else—you'll see white men workin' right alongside niggers in that mill, both gettin' the same pay."

Martin shook his head. "Ain't never been that way in Temple County."

Avery mimicked the man: "Times are changin', and if this board don't keep a tight hold, there's liable to be a woods runner on it, or a preacher that'll come down on the sheriff to cut off bootleggin' and close Beevo's. For nigh onto a year that dago's been payin' off real good."

He took another swallow of whiskey and wiped his mouth. "That's one reason I want my boy here. He's changed a heap since he got married, and he's a Coffield to the bone. All that political stuff he's learnin' in college—you all may need it, afore long."

Sam Harvey doodled on a pad. "Was you to get down real sick, or—well, if you couldn't handle the job anymore, I reckon there wouldn't be no big to-do, was we to appoint Elliot to fill your chair. But you'd have to resign before next election, so he could be an incumbent. Will Jellico's goin' to be pissed off, and Burr—"

"I'll take care of 'em," Avery said. "I got enough on both to put 'em on the chain gang."

"Avery," Martin said, "I wish you wouldn't go on thataway. We're all friends here, all good ol' boys."

"And I know a good ol' lawyer boy in Jackson," Avery said. "Works for the state attorney general."

Sam Harvey nodded. "Soon as you're ready, Elliot's in."

"Thought he might be," Avery said. "Now let's us all have a snort in honor of my grandson."

Martin Nelson forced a grin. "Some months early, ain't you? And no guarantee it'll be a boy."

"First Coffield youngun is always a boy. You want to bet on it?"

"Not with them odds." Martin poured bourbon into a water glass. "Elliot done well by himself; that Sandy is a heap of woman, I'd say."

"And you'd be sayin' right," Avery agreed, but felt sorry for them, because they could never *really* know. He even felt sorry for Elliot.

But Elliot wasn't feeling sorry for himself. Driving home for spring vacation, he was quite content. Of course, it was a bother, having to keep his trysts in New Orleans secret, and to be very careful about playing around on campus. It wouldn't do for word to get out, not even a whisper. That could kill his political ambitions in the state, and practically get him lynched in Temple County.

He drove the conservative Buick carefully, glad he'd chosen it; a Ford or Chevy was just a bit tacky, but a dark Buick wasn't flashy; it kept him one of the crowd, but a small step up; just right. He'd been looking forward to getting home since his father told him about the county commissioner's slot. That would be a great help: youngest in the state, but a boy knows his way around, yessir; one of the Coffields, you know.

Watching green fields roll past his window, Elliot thought he'd enjoy seeing Mama, though she'd been cold since his marriage, and more so, since Sandy was pregnant. Someday, he might be able to explain it all to Mama, but not just yet. It was odd, but he didn't resent Sandy a bit. After all, if it hadn't been for his father's affair with her, Elliot might never have known what it was like with Terry—and a few others.

She would be a tremendous help to him when he ran for state senator; every back-home politician had a wife and kids on the speaker's platform. She was bright and very nearly beautiful, and would be a fine hostess. In the governor's mansion? Elliot wondered, and smiled into the windshield. One step at a time: break the ground, sow the seeds, cultivate the crop properly; his smile widened. Mustn't forget the manure; oh yes, plenty of highgrade horseshit. Voters thrived on it.

He was probably the only student at Southern with three distinct wardrobes—one kept at Terry's apartment for those special occasions, another right up to campus style, and a third to wear in Temple County. It was all being put to use, the image, the right profile, the in-depth studies of those who would be his constituents. A few more years and he would be a bigger man than his father had ever been, but in his own way; yes, in *Elliot* Coffield's individual fashion.

As the feed store's redbrick loomed ahead, and the familiar railroad tracks, the loading station, he found himself looking forward to a reunion with his "wife." Sandy was the only woman friend he had; all the rest were as bitchy as Jessica, except Mama, of course. Mama always understood, but he couldn't *talk* with her the way he did with Sandy, couldn't share. With Lila, it was always the house and that certain, smothering superiority. Sandy knew what he was, and accepted it without all the recriminations.

But it was becoming exceedingly difficult to stay neutral in a warring household, to remain the mediator when battle lines were so sharply drawn: his father and Sandy; Lila and Jessica. If it was only Jessica, he'd thoroughly enjoy cutting her up, which was something Sandy just didn't do. Waving at people in town, smiling and nodding, Elliot turned off on the road to home. If Jessica thought she was winning the battle, wait until Sandy's child was born. The baby would give him a firmer grip on The Shadows than she'd ever had, with all her shooting and horseback riding and evening drinks with their father. His smile was warm and genuine as he turned into the gravel drive.

A couple of miles down the road, Earl was grinning, too, because now the way was clear for him to go north. Not only was his peeler mill hard put to keep up with orders, but he had somebody to take his place, see to things while he was gone. His pa would never work inside and there was no use asking, especially since he'd bought that piece of land across the river. Pa would be around to take a look once in a while, and Ellen could handle the money. Ellen was good at figures, and with little Marcie going into first grade, she'd have the time. Didn't seem natural for her little girl to be old enough to read and write, but there it was.

The good part was Mason; he'd come over quietly from the Coffields and asked for a job without saying how come he left, and Earl never questioned him. Mason had hands about good as Earl's, when it came to machinery; he could kind of taste it when something was wrong, and get in and fix it. He'd worked at the Coffield cotton gin for longer than Earl had been born, and, when the gin wasn't running, did yard work and the like. Dan Mason was too good for scuffling around a yard; he belonged in a shop, and the others would work for him real good.

Be different, Earl thought, was any of his sixteen-man crew white, but a black didn't mind a black foreman. The pole haulers wouldn't care either, since it was the Lassiter mill. Earl felt good about it, and went to packing his new suitcases, knowing that there'd be grumbling, was folks to know the mill wasn't *all* Lassiter, that the Greater Atlantic Corporation had a finger in things, through Lowenstein.

Might be some fretting, Earl thought, but any bad-mouthing would soon turn itself off, because he was paying better than pulpwood buyers, and he'd bought the new stakebed from Burr Watson's lot instead of going up to Meridian for it. Bought a lot of other stuff in town, too, though it cost a mite more. Ira Lowenstein said that was how to do it, long as it didn't run into too much money, so as not to antagonize local merchants. Antagonize; that meant make somebody mad.

He'd needed GAC backing, anyhow, first for the good steel peelers and feeding screws he'd designed, then setting up contracts and carrying a payroll and for the cooking vats and generator—just about everything. It wouldn't be long before he'd need a loader, maybe see about his own equipment for cutting posts and bringing them in. Like Ira said, the less he had to pay out for services his own company could give him, the better.

Pulling a price tag off a sport jacket, Earl folded it carefully. Ira had been busy hereabouts, getting all the legal stuff seen to, teaching Earl about business methods. But it was time to learn a whole lot about things that counted even more—machinery, design, engineering. And Ira was going north with him, to help him get set up.

In a blue suit, Earl carried his suitcases from the room he'd insisted on keeping in the mill. Hefting them into the pickup, he looked up the path toward the house for his pa and didn't see him. Then, across the millyard, he saw Ben Lassiter coming slowly, kind of stooped over like he'd maybe turned real old overnight.

"Pa—what's the matter?"

Ben held out a yellow paper. "Mail truck come by; ol' Billy Smith give this to me personal."

Earl felt a chill. "Alvah?"

Ben nodded. "He ain't dead, though. Telegram says how the Defense Department regrets to inform me Corporal Alvah Lassiter has been severely wounded in action. Your ma, she kept the one that come on me, kept it in her scrapbook."

"Don't it say anything else—where he is, if he's comin' home?"

Ben shook his head. "Depends how bad he got hit, then if he *wants* to come home. Don't figure he does."

"Maybe he got it all out of his system, Pa; bummin' around and war and such. When you come down to it, home's home, and there ain't no other."

Folding the telegram, Ben put it in his shirt pocket. "To some; to you and me."

Earl put his hand on his daddy's shoulder. "I could put off this trip."

"No, son. Nothin' to do but wait, but if you hear from your brother, you might tell him he's welcome."

"I'll do that, Pa; I surely will. You drivin' me to town? I'm supposed to meet Ira, and he'll carry us to Meridian airport in his car."

"Reckon not," Ben said. "I'll set by the river for a spell. Mason can bring the truck back."

"Well then, you take care." Earl shifted his feet and looked down, looked up again. "He'll come home; I got a feelin'."

He watched his father plod up the rise and turned to climb into the pickup cab. It was funny how he'd never thought of his pa getting old, getting tired. In the rearview mirror, he saw Ellen come out of the house and take Ben's hand. Earl drove off, mixed up in his mind, wanting to stay but needing to go. Pa was right; he'd do no good just waiting here, for Alvah might never come. He'd lied about his feeling; he didn't have any, one way or another.

When he changed to Ira's car, he didn't tell the man about Alvah; that was family doings. They talked about Boston, and what all Earl was going to do up yonder, about the dam getting put in before he got back, how they meant to move the peelers to one side and pour slab for the pulp mill.

"It'll be good to be home for a while," Ira said, driving up the highway. "No offense, Earl, but I feel as if I'm in a foreign country down here."

"Reckon I'll feel the same up north," Earl said. "Dumb ol' country boy come to the city."

"Nobody will bother you," Ira said quickly. "The corporation has plans for you, and you're bright, the brightest I've seen in Temple County."

"Everybody ain't stupid down here," Earl said. "Stubborn maybe, but not all that stupid. They just got their ways."

Ira sighed. "I know; I'm thankful you're flexible, Earl. There are changes coming—not only here, but all over the South; New England woolen mills are moving to the Carolinas; whole sections of backward, undeveloped areas are being opened up. Incomes will rise."

"And Greater Atlantic Corporation gets its share," Earl said.

"Of course; if not us, then somebody else. You were our key in Temple County, then you turned out to be a mechanical genius, and the company is very interested in you. They'll take good care of you."

"I mean to see to that," Earl said softly, watching

the fields, seeing them greener this year. It was too early to tell if there'd be another drought; right now, it looked promising, but June could bake the land to a frazzle again. Would Jessica be home from school in June, hauling around some other athlete? He'd only caught a glimpse of her this spring vacation, and she'd howdied him sweet as anything, just to show off the pouty-looking swimming champion who'd replaced Ron Benning. Earl could swim the river good as anybody, but he never saw the sense of doing it faster than anybody else.

Pulling the car into the airport parking lot, Ira said, "I'll turn it in here and pick up another when I get back. We have a couple of hours to hang around, so I'll see to the baggage and check reservations. Since this isn't a dry county, we can have a beer in the lounge."

"Good enough," Earl said, not wanting to show he didn't know a damned thing about airports and putting down a tremble in his belly. He wandered over to the magazine racks and pretended interest. They called his name three times over the speaker before he realized it was him they were talking about.

He looked around, but didn't see Ira. The lady at a desk pushed a phone toward him and he said thank you, ma'am, then: "Hello?"

"Darling," she purred in his ear, "I'm at the Sunset Motel. It's real easy to find, right on the highway."

"Jessica," he mumbled. "Look now, I'm about to catch a plane, and—"

"I know, dear; that's why I'm here, why I'm waitin' so impatiently for you. It'll be a long, long time before we see each other again, and Earl—oh, Earl! I *do* need somebody to talk to. I'm so—so desperate. *Please*. It's room 201."

"I don't know," he said. "The airplane—"

"You won't fail me," she said with what sounded like a sob as she hung up.

Finding Ira in the lounge, he said, "I got to go somewhere."

"Now?" The man's dark brows arched.

"Be back right quick," Earl said. "Take me a taxi and be here by four; plane don't leave 'til four-thirty."

Ira Lowenstein frowned. "Is something wrong? Anything I can do?"

"Somethin' personal."

Ira said, "Everything's arranged in Boston; limo to pick us up, hotel reservations, a meeting tomorrow morning, everything."

"Don't aim to miss it," Earl said, and hurried out to find a cab. Jessica sounded like she was in trouble, and he thought of that mess at Beevo's; had she got mixed up in something like that again? Maybe it was her champion swimmer; maybe she got hurt. Somebody was bound to hurt Jessica Coffield sooner or later.

The cab driver grinned at him when Earl said Sunset Motel, and Earl didn't know how much he was supposed to tip when he got to the place, so he gave him a half dollar. The driver said thanks like it pained him.

Earl had never been to a motel, either, and felt like hidden eyes were watching him through every window, that somebody was about to come out and ask him what he was doing here. Then he went the wrong way for the 200s, and had to cross back over the court, the back of his neck warm. Before he could knock on the door of 201, it swung back and Jessica hissed, "Come in, quick!"

She had the shades pulled and it was dark, but a

radio was going. Blinking to focus his eyes, Earl said, "What's the matter?"

Then he saw she had on a black, lacy thing that didn't quite cover those smooth, golden thighs, saw that her breasts poked hard against material so thin he could make out the nipples. Jessica's hair spread over her shoulders and down her back, long and loose and fluffy. He could smell her perfume from where he stood, and it was hard not to stare at the bottom of her flat stomach, where the see-through lace kept calling attention to her mound.

Earl swallowed. "You said you was in trouble."

Her hips were rocking to the music, her hands passing over them. "I said I was desperate, and I am. You're desperate, too—always have been, where I'm concerned. Now here we are, shut off from the rest of the world, and there's a pint of bourbon on the table. Here we are, Earl Lassiter—and now you don't have any excuse; nobody'll walk in on us, and nobody kicked you, so if you're really a *man*, and not just some fraidy-cat country boy—"

His eyes followed her hands, watched them cup and offer the high globes of her breasts. His mouth was dry when he said, "I—how'd you know I was leavin' today?"

Heavy-lidded, her seagreen eyes beckoned him; her ripe mouth was full and damp. "*Are* you leavin'?"

"The plane—Boston—"

Moving close to him, she slid off his coat and her fingers worked swiftly, agilely at his shirt. He could feel the heat of her, breathe in the musk of her, and every touch of Jessica had been dreamed for so many years. Somehow he was on the bed with her, everything flung away from him, everything that would get in the way of their bodies. He couldn't stand anything between them. Oh god, but she felt marvelous, soft and firm, all silken and slidy, all hot and throbbing. Her mouth was honeysuckle and her breath sunwarmed magnolias, her tongue a quickwet butterfly.

His head was spinning and his heart tried to jump out between his ribs. Hard—he was so hard and aching—and her legs, Jessica's slim, wiggly legs—wet and burning to his touch between them. Then he was on her, blindly seeking, probing, upon her with her breasts flattened against his naked chest, her belly reaching up at his and pumping—oh lord, oh lord.

Jessica Coffield. He was *inside* Jessica Coffield, crammed to the root inside her, and she was moaning; she was clawing at his back and biting his throat and he couldn't hold out one damned second longer because it was too good.

"It's all right," she said. "It's just fine, because we're goin' to keep right on doin' it, over and over and over. Ahhh! Oh yes, baby—like that; just like that—"

She was the river in July, washing warmly over him and through him; she was summer wind rocking soft-green trees in rhythm, and moonlight silver on Cape Jasmine and mockingbirds celebrating starshot midnight. Soft and deep, snug and enfolding, flowing and gripping as if she meant never to let go, and he was a willing prisoner, caressing the magic of his caging. She was all the fairytale dreams of Jessica, and the wet, startled nights, and even though he held her so closely, it was hard to believe she was real.

Even when she made drinks for them, and sat on the side of the bed trailing her hair over his belly like scented netting, she was still the princess from the big white house, the tomboy on horseback, flirting but unreachable. He had to keep touching her all over, to make sure she was really there.

"You're very sweet," Jessica murmured, stroking her hair back and forth over him, "but you don't know a whole lot, and a blob like Jolene Kobburn can't teach you much. I'm goin' to show you, Earl."

He didn't know how to take that; it made him kind of mad and kind of excited. He said, "I got to catch the plane."

She got up and moved around the bed, and he couldn't take his eyes off the swing of her tail, the shape of her buttocks. *His* juice was in her, carried hotly within that perfect body. Jessica picked up the phone and made a call.

"There," she said, "that's fixed. Mr. Lowenstein can just wait on you to get to Boston; tomorrow, maybe. I just changed your reservation."

"But—" he said, and no more, because she closed his mouth with her own before moving her lips to his throat, his chest, his tender nipples. Her tongue was an electric prod, making him flinch and squirm, and he kept thinking that it wasn't right for her to be so experienced, so practiced, because in all his dreams, Jessica Coffield was only for him.

Then he just didn't give a damn about airplanes or Boston or Jessica not being dressed in flowing, gauzy white like a bride. He didn't give a damn about anything in the whole world, except here and now and feeling what was happening to him.

Softly through the warm, dimly through the complete letting go, her voice whispered, "You'll always be mine, Earl Lassiter. I can do anything I want to you, and you'll always be mine."

He couldn't answer, didn't want to, didn't have anything to say.

CHAPTER 13

"I don't give a damn if he's *green*," Sandy said. "He's a hell of a lot better than that doddering old wreck, and Avery needs him."

Lila didn't bother to hide her distaste. "You might allow Avery's *wife* to make such decisions. A nigra doctor—"

"Oh hell," Sandy said, "it only makes sense. Avery won't go to a hospital, doesn't even want me going when I'm due, so the only sensible answer is to care for him as best we can here, in his home, as he wants it."

Lila moved to the library bar and poured a drink. Sandy's hands knotted in her lap, then lifted to smooth the maternity dress over her huge stomach. Lila said, "He's stubborn as ever."

"He's *dying*." Sandy's fingers clutched her dress, twisted it. "And he's not having an easy time of it; can't you understand that?"

Drinking, Lila managed to smack her lips with a ladylike air, and looked archly at the other woman. "I understand he's gettin' his own way, just as always."

Grunting up from the couch, Sandy moved awkwardly to the door. "It's all right with me."

"It would be," Lila said sweetly. "What isn't?"

Sandy labored up the stairs and paused to pat at her hair before opening the door to Avery's suite. Dr. Davison was just putting away his things, and looked around as she came in. Avery's eyes were closed and a tube was in his arm; his drawn face was the shade of dirty ashes.

She whispered, "Any change?"

Davison shook his head. "He really ought to be in intensive care."

She moved closer, kept her voice low. "It wouldn't do any good and we both know it. As long as the barbiturates work—"

He gestured at her stomach. "You're a good nurse, but not in any shape to help him. Let me send somebody in and—" Davison stopped, brown forehead furrowing.

"Never mind them," Sandy said. "I'll take care of it."

"You're too close, you know."

"Not close enough." She gnawed at her lower lip. "He—I think he'd let go, if I have his—his grandson. Look; I know the pain killers aren't doing much; he just won't admit it, and it would be better if—if he—"

Davison took her hand between his fineboned brown ones. "Life and death; we try to make them conform to our needs, but they don't."

"I can induce labor," Sandy said.

And from the bed, Avery Coffield whispered, "And take a chance on losin' him? No, damnit—no."

She went to him. "Avery, can I do anything—"

"Don't fret about me. I'm makin' out just fine. How are you?"

Making a smile, Sandy said, "I'm okay. He's kicking a lot."

Avery struggled to focus his eyes on the doctor and nodded thanks. Davison bobbed his head in return and took his bag.

"Can't get used to that," Avery said after he was gone.

"He's very good," Sandy said.

"Some vets are, too," he mumbled, "but I ain't a horse, or a nigger."

"Don't be such a bastard."

One corner of his mouth lifted. "No sense changin' now; wouldn't fool nobody."

She touched his cheek, brushed her fingers gently over the pain-sweat there. "You've never been a bastard to me. Can I get you anything, do anything?" His face was so thin, the cheekbones prominent, eyes sunken.

"If you wasn't so big in the belly—"

Laughing, she said, "I do believe you'd try."

"Damn whistlin' I'd try, and do it, too." His smile faded. "You know, I been doin' a lot of thinkin', and most of it about you and our boy. But some about other things, other folks. You and Elliot hit it off pretty good, and I'm proud for that. Might need him, even though I got my will iron clad. They got to be good to you, else you can throw 'em out on their asses."

Avery coughed and his face went tight for a moment. "Trusteeship for my grandkid; dates all rigged to take effect after I'm gone so long. Course, was Jess to get knocked up by one of her *athletes*—" He grimaced but shook his head when Sandy reached for him. "But it don't seem likely. She don't do a damn thing without meanin' it. She ain't come home yet?"

"No," Sandy said, "she hasn't. Elliot's on the way, though."

"Like to see that gal married to somebody with balls enough to take a lighterd knot to her; takes a strong rein on a hardmouthed filly. Jess ever—ever talk to you about somebody special?"

"We don't talk much," Sandy said.

"Scrunch over here," Avery said, "and put your belly where I can lay my cheek to it. Yeah, that's it. Like to do a heap more, but—say! I felt him; I pure-D *felt* him kickin' his stall. I'd say if God's anywhere in this world, it's in a woman's belly. Lila now; she never let me do this. Claimed it wasn't seemly."

Sighing away from her bloated stomach, he said, "Might do me a kindness and get hold of ol' Ben Lassiter. Been thinkin' on him and his, thinkin' on makin' my peace with him. Not that I'm gettin' religion this late in the day, mind you—but just in case."

"I'll bring him," Sandy promised.

"Uh-uh; don't you go bumpin' over back roads. Send Dan Mason—damn; forgot Dan quit me. Whole covey of damned niggers quit me."

"I'll find someone right away," Sandy said.

"He's about the only one I want to see. Hell with Sam and Martin and the rest of them goddamn buzzards; said all I need to 'em, and they don't like it." His hand clenched around her forearm, without strength to it. "I just got to see Thomas Elliot Cof-field; that was my daddy's name, and it'll be his. Did I tell you that?"

"Yes," Sandy said, "you told me. Rest now, darling. I'll send for Ben Lassiter."

Closing his eyes, Avery said in a reedy whisper, "If he won't come, screw him, but see he's asked proper."

She watched him awhile, glad he could sleep even a few minutes. There was still amazing strength to him; lesser men would have given up long ago, and let the coma blanket them. She had seen it a dozen times before, but never like this, never with so much resistance. Sandy pressed her stomach, her full breasts, like paired jugs. "Hurry, Thomas Elliot Coffield," she whispered. "Hurry, damn you."

Shoeless foot propped on the pillow, Jessica stretched her leg and made a cute face. "I swear, Doctor, I just don't know how it happened. I was just on my way home from school, and now this. I mean, I was just gettin' out of my car to check the tire, and sort of twisted my ankle and it hurts *so* bad. Wasn't it lucky I was right in front of your clinic?"

Davison glanced at his nurse. "Yes, lucky," he said. "Miss Hockett, please remove the patient's stocking."

Jessica smiled. "I thought *you* were the doctor. Comin' from up north and all, surely you aren't scared to just examine me? An emergency and all?"

"It's a medical rule to have a nurse present—"

"Rules," Jessica said, putting her hands behind her head and leaning away so she could arch her back. "Some folks spend their whole lives makin' rules, and others just go along followin' those rules, meek as field mice. But some don't."

Jesus, Davison thought, but this one grabbed at a man's groin, just by being in the same room. And the way she was put together, slim but ripe, with jeweled parts so cunningly designed, and a certain clockwork inside that provocative body that went tick-tick-tick. She was a time bomb, he reminded himself, high explosive that could blow up in a man's face and destroy him. But Jesus, the way she was put together, and that hot, slidy look in her eyes—

He said, "There's that bandage to be changed, Miss Hockett, and the boy's eyes to be washed out."

"Doctor—" she protested, black eyes cutting hard at Jessica.

"Leave the door open," he said. "It'll be all right."

Golden skin was smooth and firm beneath his fingers as he probed the finely structured ankle. With an effort, he held back a quiver as his hand moved carefully up the rounded calf. "There's no swelling, and seems to be no damage."

"But it hurts," Jessica insisted. "I just know I can't walk on it." Her eyes taunted him, and her lips were damply red. "Maybe I'm hip-sprung, like a horse, and you ought to do a complete examination."

"No," he said quickly, "there's no need. I'll tape the ankle, and—"

Jessica said, "I hear you've been treatin' my daddy."

"Mr. Coffield? Yes."

She stretched languidly and ran her eyes over him inch by inch, lifting her skirt higher than necessary when he began to tape her ankle. "Then you can take this off at the house, when you're there. I suppose you're takin' care of Sandy, too."

Davison wanted to linger at the job, but didn't dare. Her perfume swam around him, and the heat of her could make him dizzy. "Mr. Coffield agreed to that; he wants her to have the baby at home."

When he stepped away from her, Jessica sat erect. "His home and my home; not hers."

"But as your brother's wife—"

She ignored that. "How near is she, and how near is Daddy? Come on; I know Daddy is dyin', or is it against medical *rules* to tell a member of the family?"

"I don't know what's holding him together," Davison said truthfully, "except a desire to see his grandchild. An amazing man, your father. Another man would have died a year or eighteen months ago. But his daughter-in-law didn't get pregnant for so long, and he's determined to see his grandchild. An amazing man."

Sliding off the table, Jessica straightened her clothing. "He used to be." Walking to the office door
with no sign of a limp, she smiled brightly back at
him. "See you later, Doctor. I really appreciate your—
attention."

After she was gone, the smell and feel of her stayed
in the office a long time.

It had been a long time, Ben Lassiter thought; he
hadn't set foot on Coffield land since before the war,
and then only a time or two when he was a towheaded
youngun. High-toned folks don't cotton to hard-dirt
farmers, Ben's daddy had said, but that big white
house and all them acres don't make them no more
quality than us, boy. We ain't croppers and we don't
owe nobody, and we walk our own land, same as them.

Still, Ben might have tried to be neighborly, except
it was hard to do, starting back when they both were
going to school. One boy with sheepskin-lined jacket
and shiny boots; the other trying not to shiver, and a
big hole in his shoe sole; one going home to dinner in
a car, and the other making do with cornbread, or biscuits plugged with sorghum molasses. Avery was the
natural leader; he was captain of any team, and didn't
pick Ben when he could.

Then, years later, there was the National Guard
company formed in Temple County, and Ben could
sure use the dab of money they paid for going to drill
one night a week in the high school gym. Then came
summer camp, and right after that, the war; and
wouldn't you know it? Lieutenant Avery Coffield,
and captain when the outfit was called to active duty,
getting more chickenshit as he went along, lording it
over the enlisted men like he was born to it.

Stopping the pickup in front of the porch, Ben got

out. Maybe Avery was born to be top dog; some was, and some wasn't. And some of them once on top slid clear to the bottom. Ben started to wipe his feet on the doormat, but quit and banged the heavy brass knocker instead. Echoes hadn't stopped sounding inside the house before the door swung back.

"Howdy, Buster," he said to the black face peeping out.

"Howdy, Mr. Lassiter. Come on in, suh. I'll carry you right on upstairs where Mist' Avery in the bed."

" 'Preciate it," Ben said, looking straight ahead as he followed Buster through the entrance hall and across a room near about big as his whole house. He couldn't help seeing big mirrors with gold around them, and fancy furniture; couldn't help feeling carpet deep and soft as spring grass under his feet.

Once the Lassiters had had a place like this, over across the Tchufuncta on a pretty rise, and to hear it secondhand from his grandpa, it had even been bigger and grander, before the Yankees burned it. Seemed like it took a family forever to get back on its feet, after the house went up in smoke and carpetbaggers stole most of the land. But bigod, the Lassiters never cropped for nobody else, nor took charity.

He wasn't prepared for the look of Avery Lassiter. He'd seen that waxy look on plenty of faces, but they were all dead. The room smelled of death, too, like it was hunkered down in a corner. Ben walked to the bed, hesitated, then took off his flop hat. It all came flooding back—aid stations and GIs with tubes in their arms like this; field hospitals stinking of blood and piss, the odor of rot all the antiseptics couldn't hide; still forms under sheets.

"Avery," he said.

Opening his eyes, Avery Coffield took a while to focus. "Ben; proud you come. Take a seat."

There was a straightback chair beside the bed. Ben sat in it, waiting. What did Avery want? Too late to block the dam; no good to try and talk Ben out of letting the pulp mill go in. But even on his deathbed, Avery Coffield was ornery enough to try and make things go his way.

Rolling his head to one side, Avery struggled to adjust a pillow under it. Ben didn't reach out to help, and pretty soon Avery got it set and said, "We been neighbors all our lives, and our daddies and granddaddies afore us."

"No," Ben said, "we just lived next to each other."

"All right," Avery sighed. "Man gets in my shape, he looks back a heap, because there ain't nothin' to look forward to. I ain't beggin' off for things I done in my life—'cept maybe a few, and they ain't enough to help my tally sheet none. But I reckon I'm sorry I rode you so hard in the army."

Ben nodded. "Rode me hard and put me away wet, like when you wouldn't give me no furlough to come see my wife when she was took real sick. Like bustin' me when I come back from bein' over the hill. There was other things, Avery."

Sucking for air, Avery said, "I know, I know, counted 'em all over in my head while I'm lyin' here. Goddamnit, I just figured out how come. I had the rank, but you—you were the soldier, Ben; it all came natural to you, and they all looked up to you. Specially"—he pulled for air again—"after we got into combat and there wasn't no way of keepin' you from bein' sergeant. You—you had the belly for fightin' and I didn't, and there's the truth of it."

Softening, Ben leaned forward on his chair. "Some take to it, that's all."

Avery's cough was a deep, racking sound. When he stopped, he said, "I envied you gettin' all those medals, envied you comin' home a sure enough hero. And— and—" The cough shook him again, and there was pink on his lips.

"Ease off, Avery," Ben said. "It's all behind."

Shaking his head weakly, Avery went on: "Then there was your two boys, and all I had was Elliot. Damnit, if I could have swapped Jess's guts for his, maybe he'da been what I wanted, what I needed. I was glad when your oldest run off, but when I'd see Earl sweatin' aside you in the field, so close to you and the land—I just didn't have no use for you, Ben Lassiter. You had somethin' I couldn't buy, and it stuck in my craw."

Ben said, "Can I get you somethin'?"

"Pour us a big goddamned drink of whiskey," Avery said, "if you got a mind to."

Finding the bottle, Ben splashed bourbon into water glasses. He had to hold one to Avery's mouth, and watched a little color creep into the man's thin, sagging face.

"Better tell you the rest," Avery murmured, eyes closed. "It's Jess. I got it fixed pretty good for Elliot, and there's goin' to be another Coffield to carry on the blood. But Jess—" His eyes came open with an effort. "Your boy is smart, Ben; he's smart and tough as whang leather, maybe tougher'n his pa. If you could see your way to—to kind of help get Earl together with my Jess—I know better'n to offer anything to the bargain; not to you or Earl, and lord knows there ain't all that much left, 'cept my land. But Earl could keep a tight rein on Jess; I know it. I been thinkin' on it—"

Ben waited; Avery's eyes were closed and he might have slipped off, but he pried them open again and motioned for more whiskey. Ben fed it to him and said, "If he gets time, a man makes his peace. I know how hard it was for you to admit wrongin' me, and I won't carry it against you no more. But Earl is a man grown, and if I was to gee-haw him, he'd balk in the traces."

"You could—you could maybe sweet-talk him some. Them two belong together, Ben. I'll talk to Jess, if you—"

"Avery Coffield," Ben said, "you're still an ornery son of a bitch, still atryin' to run things to suit you. You'll be makin' a trade with the devil for a good seat in hell."

The smile was faint as Avery whispered, "Got me one in the front row. And I ain't no more son of a bitch than you, but bigod, we always been our *own* sons of bitches."

"Can't promise nothin'," Ben said, "but I reckon I'll give it a try."

"All I can ask," Avery said. "Proud you come, Ben; proud you took a drink with me."

The woman came big-bellied into the room then, her eyes sick and worried. She went to the bed as Ben stood up. Leaning over Avery with her belly in the way, she touched his wrist.

"Thank you for coming, Mr. Lassiter," she said. "He's asleep now, but he wanted very much to talk with you."

"We talked, Miz Coffield," Ben said, seeing the pain in her eyes, the hurt that was linked to the dying man. "You—you take care of Avery's grandbaby, now."

"His—grand*son*," Sandy breathed.

"Yes'm," Ben said, put on his hat, and walked out.

CHAPTER 14

Alvah hung to the rails of the walker, rocking with the slow movement of the endless belt beneath his feet. His *foot*; that other thing was only equipment, like something you'd draw from the supply room. And where foam rubber cupped his stump just below the left knee, it hurt like hell, bringing out sweat upon his face.

"You shouldn't push it," the physiotherapist said. "That's enough now. Time for your ultraviolet and massage."

A cane now, skinny in his hand and nothing like the comfort of an M-1 rifle butt. Forget the M-1, he told himself, hobbling over to the spotless white table; forget the BAR and the Browning water-cooled and .45— all the tools of a man's trade. If it had been his hand blown off by that gook grenade, he could still find work somewhere: Africa, South America, wherever brushfire wars were being fought. But no; it had to be his fucking leg, and wouldn't nobody hire a man that couldn't run to save his ass.

"There now," she said, adjusting the open-end oven over his reddened stump. "I'll be back in a few minutes."

Alvah watched her trim little tail going bippity-bip in the blue- and white-striped dress. PT technicians were civilians, and this one was cuter than most, all fluffy light hair and a freckled grin and that tight little ass. Back home, they'd say she walked like two bobcats fighting under a sheet.

Feeling heat on his leg, he took a cigarette from his pajama pocket and snapped his lighter at it, then lay back and watched the smoke curl up. No sense watching Miss Rogers; she'd have to be psycho to make it with a cripple. Besides, he couldn't remember having a hard-on since leaving his leg over yonder on Ballbreaker Ridge. Not even a wet dream in all these months, but before that last patrol, him and old Lou Miller all shacked up with three little gook whores, *three* of them—

Ash dribbled onto his chest and Alvah brushed it away.

Miss Rogers said, "There's an ashtray. I'll take this hood away and start your rub now."

"Tell me," he said, "would a whole woman rub somethin' else on a man, even if he wasn't but part a man?"

Her freckled face was calm, the gray eyes steady. "I would; I have."

He grunted and kept still as she palmed wintergreen-alcohol-olive oil mix over his stump. "Guess you get used to crips, workin' on 'em all the time, or maybe you're queer for 'em."

She didn't flinch; her fingers moved over the flap they'd sewn around bone as she said, "I go out with amputees and other men. Perhaps I have more empathy for amputees than a woman who hasn't been close to them."

Nerves jumped in his leg, but Alvah kept his face stiff and his voice even: "When I can walk, go out with me?"

"No," she said, her fingers moving, kneading lightly, "because I can cope with hate or bewilderment or helplessness, but I ran out of pity a long time ago."

Deliberately, Alvah flicked his cigarette over the polished floor. "Reckon you'd be so goddamn chipper if you lost a tit?"

Miss Rogers drew a towel over his stump and leaned his crutches against the table. "Corporal, you're liable to stay lost, unless you learn to take a good look inside yourself."

Needing to shake her up, to make her ache a little, too, he said, "You get a charge outa makin' it with guys missin' *both* legs? How about basket cases? You can really play boss lady with those freaks."

She took a deep breath. "I was going to marry a Marine sergeant, but he was at the Chosin Reservoir, and he's still there. If he had come back a basket case—you're damned right, I would have gotten a charge out of him, because he'd still be whole inside. But you—"

Alvah watched her walk away and pulled a pajama leg down over his stub. How the hell was he supposed to know? Lou Miller would have said, you 'fay bastard, you got more mouth than sense, and Lou would have been right in a way. But she could *talk* about screwing somebody ought to be in a sideshow, because she didn't have to really do it.

Bigmouth mother, Lou Miller would say, and Alvah would come back with how come they issued a spade to a spade. Shit; what did Miss Tightass Rogers know? What did anybody know? If he'd realized his leg was gone, he wouldn't have let Lou tote him off that ridge. But the goddamn thing felt like it was still there, and even yet, Alvah's toes hurt. Ghost pain, the doctors called it, nerve ends signaling lies from empty switchboards.

Tucking crutches under his arms, Alvah left the false leg on the table. Miss Rogers could hang it up or stuff it. He moved clumsily out of PT and down a long, waxed corridor. Trust the fucking stateside medics to keep decks good and slippery, so any gimp could go skidding ass over end.

"I covered you," Ira Lowenstein said as the limo threaded deftly through more traffic than Earl had seen, "but I hope you realize I stuck out my neck to do it."

Running his hand over a soft leather seat arm, Earl said, "Couldn't see how just missin' one plane would hurt."

Ira sighed. "Because there's only one northbound plane a day out of that airport; because when company wheels are set in motion, it's not intelligent to slow them down. Earl, you never explained that sudden delay."

Earl looked out the window. This was the place of Old North Church, Bunker Hill, but all he saw was a lot of big, grimy buildings, cars going every whichaway. "Just somethin' personal."

Glancing sharply at him, Ira said, "A woman?"

Earl didn't answer, because she wasn't just a woman. Jessica was all women, and yet she was none of them. It made his belly itch to think of her, and he crossed his legs.

Ira said, "I know how important that can seem. But you should make a certain place for it, a certain time, at *your* convenience. It should never interfere with business."

In a nice kind of way, Earl was getting a lesson and realized it. He liked Ira, and not only because the man made everything possible. He couldn't understand tak-

ing insults and keeping still when it was time to rear
up on your hind legs, or the man's nervous, mule-
headed intensity, but he liked Ira anyway. How could
he explain Jessica to him, to anyone, to himself? He
wasn't about to try, so he said, "Sorry, Ira; didn't
mean to put you in a bind. I just kind of forgot airplanes and everything else."

Leaning back, briefcase on his thighs, Ira said, "I
can remember how it was, although sometimes my
wife can't. Brenda understands, but I've been gone a
long time."

"Didn't know you was married," Earl said. "You
never said. Look, if you ain't seen your wife this long,
I'd just as soon go to a hotel." *Motel*, he thought;
walls nobody could hear through and the door locked;
Jessica all naked and shining like somebody'd taken a
soft cloth to her. He'd like to rub all over her with a
piece of white velvet.

"We have a large apartment," Ira said, "and the
company thinks I should keep you under my wing,
since you're my protégé. When you're more familiar
with the operation, you'll have your own place."
Turning on the seat, he nodded at the window and
added with a note of pride, "We're coming into Bea-
con Hill. It wasn't so long ago that a Jew couldn't live
in this district."

It was the first time Ira had mentioned his religion,
Earl thought; it made him feel funny, the same way
seeing the limousine driver had. Somehow, Earl had
figured him to be black; in the movies, they were.

Ira said, "I've been eating grits and greens, catfish
and cornbread and God knows what else. Tonight, it's
matzoh balls and *tsemmis*; your turn to wonder what
the hell."

"I'll make out." Earl smiled.

Ira smiled, too. "I'm certain you will; yes, quite sure."

Jessica said yes, she was sure, goddamnit, and her mama said don't curse, dear. Jessica said oh hell, and went behind the bar to mix sidecars in the big silver shaker. Five . . . six . . . seven . . .

"But I just don't see how he could do it to his own family," Lila said.

Elliot leaned on the bar. "He's keeping it in the family, and Will Jellico says the will is airtight."

Banging the shaker down, Jessica said, "Sure, *you* don't give a damn; in fact, you're enjoying it. I'd like to knock that baby in the head."

"I'm sure you would," Elliot said, taking the shaker and pouring himself a drink.

"Just listen to us," Lila said. "Avery lying up there dyin', and that woman about to give birth to a—a—"

"Baby, Mama—heir?"

"You know very well what I mean, Elliot. Right under our own roof, and Avery on his deathbed, and we're talking about tryin' to break his last will and testament."

"*I'm* not," Elliott said, and Jessica's eyes were venomous.

Upstairs, Calvin Davison was busy, sweating, harried. The woman was straining, her pelvis convulsing, and in the other room a senile old doctor was bumbling about Avery Coffield; a white doctor with the shakes and thick glasses and thirty years behind the times. The other Mrs. Coffield insisted a white doctor be here. Maybe it would be better if Doc Christopher *did* screw up Coffield's life supports.

He glanced across at his nurse and said to the

woman writhing on the bed, "Push. That's it; that's the way—push."

Cupping the head in his hand, supporting the tiny back, he carefully passed the slippery weight to Miss Hockett, and saw to the umbilical cord. The baby cried as it was being cleaned, and on the pillow, Sandy Coffield's head rolled from side to side.

"You can rest now," he said.

"No," she mumbled, "no. Avery—"

"He's still alive," Davison said.

Sandy fought to sit up, and he held her down. "Be careful; you can tear—"

Her face was streaked, her eyes pleading. "If the baby's all right—"

"Fine, just fine."

"Then take us to him. Please, damnit. He's suffering so much."

"Miss Hockett," he said into the nurse's disapproval, "the wheelchair."

The baby cried until he was placed against Sandy's breasts. She kept drawing great gulps of air to keep herself awake and alert, and Davison felt a great deal of respect for her.

"Stay close," he told the nurse. "I'll push her in there. Watch the baby."

In Avery's room, Doc Christopher peered at the oxygen mask, creaked over to check the needle in his patient's arm, and rubbed at his back as he straightened. He'd helped them into this world, and there were times he ought to be helping them out. So many squalling younguns, most of them making it through diphtheria and whooping cough and snakebite before sulfa and penicillin. Just as many dying now, seemed like, but there were more of them.

Avery Coffield now; he'd seen Avery through influenza and a dose of clap and warned him about drinking so much, and what the hell did it count for right now? Avery had been at the end of his string months back, but tied a knot in it and hung on.

Too damned mean to go when he was called; always had him a head like a pine knot; no more to it than that. Some went whining and some hollering, but Avery wasn't fixing to pass until *he* decided, no matter about the pain tearing him up, turning his guts like new plowed ground. The nigra doctor might call it something else, lay the blame on his miracle drugs, the machines yonder, but it wasn't nothing but Avery Coffield setting in his heels.

Smart young feller, that nigra; busy as all getout in his ramshackle clinic and taking care of his folks right good. But how would he make out when the call came for Dr. Edward H. Christopher, and he was the only doctor in Temple County? Not many smart young fellers wanted to take up practice in the ass-end of nowhere. They went to the cities, into specialties, and got rich, stayed right on top of the latest research. They didn't get chickens and roasting ears put against their bills; they knew most of their patients as names in the book, as symptoms. They didn't birth them and have to bury them, and they didn't know yet that nothing changed and it didn't count for much, come down to it.

Doc Christopher wiggled his glasses around on his nose and reached over to the little wheel on the oxygen tank.

"Doctor," Davison said, pushing back the door and wheeling the chair close. "I'm sorry, but she thinks seeing his grandchild will help."

Christopher dropped his hand. "Can't hurt him

none." He moved slowly across the room, grateful for the chance to sit down.

"Avery?" Sandy said, and stronger: "Avery?"

He'd told her that his daddy died in this bed, and his granddaddy before him, and he'd be damned if he'd go to a hospital for it. Coffields got born under this roof, and Coffields died here, and maybe that's why he had been so scared overseas; he was too far from home, and they'd put him in foreign ground when he belonged out yonder in the family cemetery.

"Avery?"

His eyelids fluttered, and his voice was no more than dry leaves rustling. "Still here."

"Take off the mask?" she asked Davison.

"All right."

"My—the baby," Avery whispered.

"Right here, Avery. I'm holding him, and he's just beautiful, just fine. Thomas Elliot Coffield is just f-fine."

"It's a boy, Mr. Coffield," Davison said.

Avery's eyes trembled open, and his jaw hung slack, but they could make out his words. "Meant it to be," he said, and stopped breathing.

Davison caught up the oxygen mask, snapped an order to his nurse, and Doc Christopher pushed himself up from the chair to say, "Never mind, never mind. I'll do for him now. Tied off his belly button when he got here; reckon I can see him out proper."

"Yes," Davison said. "Yes, Doctor."

And Sandy lifted the baby as if Avery could see it, and said, "Oh damn, oh damn," before she started to cry.

CHAPTER 15

When he was buried, Jessica cried some because her daddy wouldn't have liked brown grass in the cemetery, and because Lila had smothered the casket in roses and Avery never gave a damn for them. Patting her eyes dry as Preacher Sanders droned on in the August heat and mosquito hawks flitted above the sunscorched crowd, Jessica saw Sandy making a pure fool of herself. The woman was loaded; she'd been at the bar all morning and might disgrace them all. As it was, folks kept peeping around at her and whispering among themselves; she was making more noise than the widow.

Aware that she looked good in black, Jessica had defiantly made a crimson slash of her mouth so she wouldn't look as washed out as her mother, or puffy-faced like Sandy. Keeping her head down, she watched Elliot for a while; he looked strong and wasn't; looked dignified and was gloating. Surely he knew better than anyone that the baby wasn't his; she couldn't picture Elliot bedding a woman. *His* child, hell. It was his half brother, and hers, and Jessica could never forgive her daddy for that.

It wouldn't have been so bad, if her daddy had let her in on it; bad enough, but she understood the value he placed on his name, on continuing to have Coffields buried out here. But to slip around, seeing that woman in New Orleans every weekend and playing like he was on business, all the while hinting it was Elliot that had the romantic interest!

All the time, he ignored Jessica. No more rides together on horseback, the sidecar ritual gone, no more straight-out talk; he was so wrapped up in that bitch Sandy that nobody else existed. And sinking most of The Shadows capital into a trust fund for his brat, giving Elliot control, dominance over Lila and her.

Across the cemetery, segregated by death as well as life, blacks gathered in a little bunch: Buster, Dan Mason, field hands whose names Jessica didn't know; that sassy maid Zora, Auntie Kate, who'd cooked for Avery most of his life, the yard boy. Elliot was their boss now, except Dan Mason; he'd quit The Shadows and gone to work in that tacky little mill of Earl Lassiter's. That Dr. Davison was there too, with his wife; prim-looking woman, Jessica thought.

But Elliot had to go back to school next month for more of his political foolishness; the absentee county commissioner. Without Avery behind him, he might not last long on the board, and he didn't know doodly about the land, about growing cotton. Jessica eyed Sandy again, holding that damned kid and sobbing. There was a way around Elliot; there just had to be.

At last it was over, and folks eddying around the family, saying how sorry they were, what a good man Avery was, and you all just holler if we can do anything to help, anything at all, hear; sorry, Lila; sorry, young Miz Coffield, Elliot; Jessica, I'm purely sorry. What the hell was old Ben Lassiter doing here?

"Here's Earl Lassiter, Miss Morgan. Earl, meet your secretary, Camille Morgan," Ira Lowenstein said.

"She'll show you around the office until I get back."

She was tall and black-headed and sleek; she had kind of slanty brown eyes and fair skin that glowed. Somehow, she reminded Earl of a well-turned machine part, but without looking hard. She put her hand in his slim and capable hand, saying, "Hi; please call me Cam. Mother had this thing for Greta Garbo when I was born."

"Cam," he said, "yeah," without the slightest idea what she was talking about; Greta Garbo? "Don't know what I need with a secretary, Cam."

Still holding his hand, she winked at him and lowered her voice. "Most executives really don't, but please don't tell anybody. Your office is down here, and if you can look busy in it, so can I. Let me say I'm happy to have a boss so young, someone not bald and paunchy and smelling of cigars."

She awed him some, and he almost said yes ma'am, but stopped himself and followed her into a small office. Cam Morgan moved like well-oiled machinery, too, and if her pale blue dress was simply cut and not nearly as sexy as things Jessica wore, she got the idea across just the same. Her perfume was different, flowery, and he watched closely as she showed him how to work the phone buttons.

"I have your number and address on file," she said. "Are there any personal numbers you'd like on my list?"

Earl shook his head. "Just Ira Lowenstein and his wife; only ones I know."

"Boston isn't an unfriendly city," Cam said, as Ira came to get him.

The engineering board room was big, with windows on two sides that overlooked the city eighteen floors below. Maps and charts and a blackboard were on one wall, a draftsman's tilted desk at another, a bookcase took up the rest of that wall; a long table, a dozen chairs around it. Earl said howdy to names he went over in his head and filed away: Patrick Neely, wearing a squeezed beet face; Dino Raineri, small and dark and quick; Victor Quinn, skinny as a marsh crane and about as gray, with the look of a high school principal. Earl put down Mr. Quinn as the boss.

"Sit, sit," Neely said. "So you're Ira's boy wonder."

"A wonder at any age," Ira said easily, "with calluses on his hands instead of his ass."

Uncomfortable, Earl tried not to wiggle around while Ira explained about the post peeler, and went into details about the dam, the production capacity of the pulp mill. He heard figures and forecasts and phrases he didn't understand, and wondered how Ira could keep it all in his head like that.

"Yes," Quinn said from behind big, rimless glasses, "we've read the reports, Ira, and appreciate the field work, the help this young man has been."

"Earl," Ira said, "please show them your next idea. Use the blackboard."

Stiffly at first, fretting about not knowing the terminology and not talking like the rest of them, Earl chalked a rough sketch. "This here is a tree puller, and it ain't figured out all the way, but down home I reckon the pulp cutters are losin' about twenty percent on every tree. We got a heap of pines, and even if they cut 'em off right next to the ground, they lose all that taproot."

Interested now, warming to his subject, he went on: "I see a machine like this here—a kind of scissors-grip knife blade that'll bite into the whole tree from opposite sides; then a tube shear made up like a snappin' turtle's jaws. The shear is jammed vertical into the ground until these plates stop it. Then the crane part just snatches up the whole tree, root and all. The ground roots get cut off."

Neely and Raineri were leaning forward. Quinn asked, "What do you propose to mount this tree harvester on?"

Earl said honestly, "Damned if I know; maybe a great big thing like a caterpillar tractor and a dragline put together. Thing is, once a pine tree's roots get jerked loose and that twenty percent of pulp gets saved—no bark on it, neither—it'll make the land a heap easier to replant. Replantin' ain't far off, if you mean to keep on makin' pulp, and this way, we don't leave no stumps behind."

"He can mount it on a prime mover," Neely said.

And Raineri added, "With the tubular shear clamshell hinged on a vertical lift."

Earl put down the chalk and dusted his hands. Ira Lowenstein smiled, and Quinn nodded, then got up to pour coffee from a silver pot. He said, "I was thirty years old with my own machine shop in Chicago. Because I was doing all right and had a couple of patents, I thought I knew it all. When I went to school with Greater Atlantic, I discovered there was very much more. Do you think you know it all, Mr. Lassiter?"

It was the first time anybody ever called him mister. Earl said, "No sir. I aim to know a whole lot more, everything there is, everything in all them books over yonder. I *need* to know so much it makes my head ache and my belly turn over."

Victor Quinn put out his birdlike hand. "Mr. Lassiter, welcome to Greater Atlantic."

* * *

The company was down in the slime of a rice paddy behind curving dikes, and the CP set up behind a big rock in a dry field; and there was Luke the Gook on top of Ballbreaker Ridge, his mortars staring down everybody's throat. Alvah stirred in his sleep, seeing it all again, smelling the shit, hearing the rushing whisper of mortar shells.

"Hey, redneck," Lou Miller said beside him in the muck, "think I got their observer spotted."

"So what? This whole goddamn outfit ain't goin' anywhere."

On his back now, helmet tucked against the dike, Lou got a smoke going, took two deep drags and passed it to Alvah. "Since you're always breakin' your ass to be a fuckin' *hee-ro*, the great white hope, I was thinkin' we take out that OP tonight."

"You take point," Alvah said. "You're tailormade for night work."

A mortar whistled in; its *crump!* geysered filthy water and mud. Lou said, "And *you* got to smear this concentrated gook crap on your face. How about that, Mr. Charlie? Maybe you better go barefoot, like a natural-born shit-kicker."

Alvah turned in his sleep, grunted when his stump bumped the padded side of the hutch over it. Lou Miller was damned good, and the kid—Johnny-something—was all right for a replacement, too. They went up the ridge without drawing fire and found the OP. The gooks were changing watches just then, a bitch of a thing to happen. That's when it hit the fan, everybody banging away at once, and that goddamned grenade knocking him down.

All the way down, Lou carried him, with gooks tearing up the slope around them and popping the night air like bullwhips. Johnny-something didn't make it, and when Alvah saw what had happened to his leg, Lou's belt twisted around a bloody stub below the knee, he wished to hell he was back there, too.

Shaking, sweating, Alvah came up in bed and fumbled for a cigarette. The flare of the match threw a circle of yellowpink light against his eyeballs. He stared into the dark a long time, hearing a man snore, another one groan softly, the night-watch nurse moving around her office. When he had to piss, he reached for crutches, then put them aside to strap on the leg. Quietly, cane feeling along the waxed floor, he made for the head.

"You came out ahead," Jessica said. "You and your so-called wife. But Mama and I got it where it doesn't show."

Elliot said calmly, "We're still a family, Jessica. And Sandy *is* my wife; Thomas Elliot *is* my son. Don't forget it again, and please keep your voice down. There are others in the house."

"Yes," Lila said. "Mind your manners, dear."

Jessica drank her sidecar, fingers tapping restlessly against the icy shaker. "Tell that to your daughter-in-law, Mama. When she comes to, that is. I swear, I thought she was goin' to pass out in the grave."

"D-don't," Lila said, face pained.

Whirling on her brother again, Jessica said, "Am I supposed to ask you for an allowance? May I please sir continue in school, or do you mean to put me out in the fields?"

"I suppose your major is drama," Elliot said. "You're so good at it."

"Please, children." Lila clung to the arms of her chair. "That nigra doctor is still upstairs. I *told* her it was too early to take out little Thomas Elliot, but she insisted. And she's certainly in no condition to care for him, and now you—you're fightin' like sharecropper younguns with your poor father just laid fresh in his grave—"

"Oh, stop it," Jessica said. "You never cared anything for him, and neither did Elliot. He—I—until he brought that tail-shakin' bitch home—stealin' my daddy from me, screwin' him down to a shadow. Killin' him—"

Elliot's slap was almost casual, but the force of it made her head ring. He said sharply, "You're hysterical. You're so upset by your father's death that you don't know what you're saying. And you'll never say it again, Jessica. Understand that—*never!* If you can't keep your emotions under control, I suggest you get the hell up those stairs and have that nigra doctor give you something to quiet your nerves. Right *now*, Jessica."

Hand to her burning face, eyes threatening to flood, Jessica ran from the library. When she reached the foot of the stairs, she put a hand on the mahogany banister to steady herself, then climbed slowly. Pausing outside her daddy's suite, she grimaced at Sandy lying disheveled across the bed, at the crib set up nearby. Davison was just closing his bag, and the baby was quiet.

He turned and saw her. "The child will sleep quite a while; nothing serious."

Jessica leaned against the doorframe. "The new master of The Shadows ordered me to get a sedative from you. It seems I'm hysterical, or about to go crazy or somethin'."

"Well," Davison said, "if you're really upset—"

"I'll take it down the hall," Jessica said. "In my room."

In the corridor, Davison hesitated, hands clamped upon his bag, watching the provocative roll of her hips beneath the clinging black dress. Jesus, if his own wife wasn't so crazy scared about moving back to the South, if Sarah could forget Georgia and remember how it was for them in Chicago, maybe he could keep his eyes off this teaser.

"Miss Coffield," he said, but she was already in her room, its door left open. He sure ought to walk downstairs and out of this house. Walk, hell; he should run. He took a step along the hall, then another.

He saw the white, wide bed, the pink coverlet, but not Jessica. Stepping into the room, inhaling the musky fragrance of her, he stiffened when the door closed behind him. "Wait a minute," he said as she slid around him and reached behind her back for a zipper. "You know and I know—damnit, your father just died and—"

Her breasts stood out in bold relief until she pulled the zipper and dipped her shoulders forward to wriggle from the dress. Her bra was black, her panties, too, but frilly with lace. She said, "Daddy died for me the day he brought that bitch home."

Unhooking the bra, she let it fall to the floor. "He used to come in here and tuck me into bed, that bed, and we'd talk. I mean really talk, even if I was little. But when she came, he didn't talk to me anymore." Her fingers hooked into the top of her panties.

Davison stared and tried to say something, anything.

Jessica stepped naked toward the bed, legs flashing, breasts high and full and tipped with vibrant pink. She said, "I'll bet you've had white women before, up north."

Lying on the bed, she hiked her hips to slide a pillow beneath them; a silken pelt of curly gold gleamed up at him, and she said huskily, "If you don't screw me, I mean to holler rape just as loud as I can. You know what they'll do to you, for tryin' to rape a white woman?"

"Damn," he breathed, "I think you would. I *know* you would. But your family's here, and they'll be wondering what I'm doing so long. There's no time for this—"

"You just better make time," Jessica said. "However long it takes." Her belly rippled and her hips swung back and forth, her thighs parted.

Davison went to her, ripping at his pants. Rage mixed with lust already had him hard and aching. This arrogant, spoiled girl had him; this gold and white bitch threatened every long, grinding hour of study and doing without and medical practice. Those mounded breasts were really twin barrels of a shotgun aimed at his profession; that seething, feathered mound was bait for a lynch rope.

Covering her without tenderness, knowing only a need to punish her and perhaps himself, Calvin Davison drove deeply into her twisting flesh. He pounded her, slammed into her, hammering while she bucked and rolled and fought him back fiercely. There was no beauty to it, only a blinding fury of conquest, only this savage striking of pelvis to pelvis and the wet slapping of their bellies.

It was animal-quick and feral, and when Jessica's moans grew louder, as she shuddered beneath him, Davison clamped a hand over her mouth. Her sharp teeth bit into his palm as she reached orgasm, and a spiteful heartbeat later, the marrow of him came boiling down his spine to skyrocket into her.

Gasping, they trembled together for a long moment before he took himself roughly from her and off the bed. A shorter moment, tucking his shirt and zipping his pants, and he was gone with his black bag held low before his groin.

Jessica rolled off the pillow and curled herself into a sweaty ball. He was bigger than any man she'd had, and maybe everybody was right when they whispered about black studs. She'd made him do it to her, forced him the way backwoods white trash forced little nigger girls. She reached for the pillow and hugged it to her breasts, rubbing her cheek into it.

Daddy went to Beevo's all the time, and knew what he was doing, because buying it was making them do it, too. It was better that way, better if they were scared.

Have that nigra doctor give you a sedative, Elliot said. She smiled against the rumpled pillow. He sure had; he'd flooded her with that special kind of sedative, and when she pressed her thighs together she could feel overflow sticky there.

Daddy did it all the time; ever since she could remember, he went down to Beevo's every Saturday night with his friends and bought any woman he liked.

Hugging the pillow closer, she hissed into it, "Why didn't you stay with them, instead of going to *her*? See, goddamnit—I paid you back. I screwed a nigger, too."

CHAPTER 16

It was rightly named The Shadows, Sandy thought as she poured another drink. The damned house echoed and brooded, hatred and suspicion lurking in every dark corner. But the silent thing that stalked the halls was worse; it was called loneliness.

Sitting on the bed, she looked over at the crib where Thomas Elliot slept; he slept a lot, so she couldn't be loving to him all the time. That left a lot of hours in the day and far more during the night. It was worse now than when she was a child, even worse than that terrible gap when Frank Tolliver was killed in Korea. It had taken her almost a year to find herself after that; she didn't know if she could bring Sandra Ascott Tolliver Coffield out of hiding this time, didn't know if she wanted to.

If she just had someone to talk to; Elliot was understanding when he was home, which wasn't often. When he wasn't at school, he was always involved in something political, traveling the lower part of the state. But at his best, Elliot had never been Avery, couldn't be. So she talked to her baby and to the maid Zora, and to Auntie Kate, who came up from the kitchen to "do for Mist' Avery's grandson." Late at night, Sandy talked to herself.

Jessica and Lila? Oh God, how she dreaded facing

them at mealtime, and lately Jessica had been appearing in the cemetery, too, silently accusing, hard-eyed. At the table, they talked around Sandy or through her, and never asked about the baby, never went up to see little Thomas Elliot. But they hadn't hidden the whiskey or locked it up, and Sandy was grateful for that much.

There was the radio and decent music from New Orleans, country songs out of Meridian, and Sandy kept it going around the clock. She also kept a bottle beside the bed so she could find it when she woke frightened in the dark, when the baby's cry brought her up shaking.

Almost, she wanted Avery back on his bed, suffering and shrunken; almost. But even before him, she hadn't been able to adjust to pain and death on the wards, taking each agony, each patient loss personally. It was easier being an office nurse, a receptionist. When she'd seen Avery Coffield the first time, she had hoped nothing serious was wrong with him. There was something prideful about him, a confidence and strength that had appealed to her. No, she did not regret Avery Coffield.

Lifting from the bed, she carried her glass to a dresser and refilled it from the bottle there. Blinking away tears, Sandy swallowed whiskey; their time together had been so damned short, so unfair, and near the end, too much like trying to care for her own father when he lay dying. Her mother had stayed drunk most of the time, during that last, awful time.

It didn't even look like home, Alvah thought, pulling the car off to the side of the road and resting his elbows on the steering wheel. How long had he been away? Two years on the road, two more in Korea, more than six months in the hospital; a lifetime. The old mill had been fixed up and expanded, the road widened, and trucks were moving around; noise and bustle. Hell, he might have known, because nothing stayed the same; blow down a Korean village and come back through a few months later, it'd be patched together, with maybe new shacks added. People changed, too; they lost parts of themselves.

Reaching down to knead sore thigh muscles, Alvah stretched his left leg. It worked well enough to get him here from the Coast, hurting some, but working okay, like a green replacement attached to an outfit of seasoned combat men. It screwed up once in a while, but the rest of the platoon pulled it into shape. Alvah smiled bitterly; some replacements didn't make it through the first firefight.

He kept looking up at the old house, and thought he saw a woman moving across the porch. Ellen still there? He'd sometimes wondered how long she'd last with Pa, after that crap he'd pulled with her. Ellen's baby ought to be what—five, six years old by now, and maybe she had one or two more. Wouldn't that be a bitch, half brothers or sisters that were bloods? Lou Miller would get a boot out of that. Hey, you 'fay bastard; not me, man; call me blood.

Alvah used the dash lighter to light a smoke. In Korea, you found out that gooks were yellowish and niggers were shades of black and brown, but all blood ran red. You found out that the Marine you trusted with your life was a man like anybody else and skin color was only camouflage. Hell, you even had to respect the chinks for coming head-on into a wall of machine-gun fire, and tip your helmet to some gooks for being the mean little shits they were. That didn't mean you didn't kill them quicker than cottonmouth moccasins and stomp in their heads to make sure they didn't crawl off to bite you some other day.

You'll hack it, Lou Miller said to him in the hospital, and don't let me hear no shit about takin' your end of the money from them gook jeeps we sold back to them. Hell, man, you got a better chance of gettin' it stateside on a hospital plane.

Always a hustler, Lou was, quick-fingered with cards, ever on the lookout to make a handful of Military Payment Certificates or a bucketful of gook *whan*. But what Lou didn't understand was that Alvah didn't know how to hustle, didn't know anything but busting his ass on a hard-dirt farm or busting somebody else's ass in combat. And who'd hire a one-legged strongarm man?

After collecting mustering-out pay from an office pinkie, and getting straight with the VA guy about the disability pension, and all that unemployment shit, that school information Alvah didn't need, he was a civilian again. What goddamn prospects, he asked the VA guy; what kind of school—one for crips? I'll just gimp into Temple County and see if there's any openings for a fire-team leader, maybe a machinegunner. And the old guy said kind of sadlike, you have your biggest war to fight yet, son, and that's with yourself.

So now he sat looking through the windshield of his Chevy, looking up at what used to be his own home like it was some kind of tactical problem and figuring how to flank it. Alvah wasn't sure why he'd come back; maybe just to get the feel of it again before taking off. Lou Miller wasn't back from gookland yet; Alvah had called the number in L.A. and got told no, real short. Things gettin' tight in L.A., man, Lou said at the hospital; whitey ain't welcome in my neighborhood, but I be happy to see you anyhow, you got no better sense.

No flanking this problem, Alvah told himself; he had to play Marine and make a frontal attack. He drove slowly past the mill and saw another big site marked out; this one would take in the old house itself and half the garden, too. How had anybody convinced his pa to let that happen?

He got out stiffly, holding to the car door until he got a grip on the cane, and looked up as his father came out onto the porch. Ben Lassiter hadn't changed much; a little stooped, some grayer, but he still looked hard as an oak stump.

"Well," Ben said, "you're on your feet, anyway."

Alvah slapped the cane against his left leg. "One foot."

"Beats lyin' on your back," Ben said, "or gettin' pulled around by a dog."

"About all it beats," Alvah said.

Ben said, "Come in and set."

Alvah was glad his pa didn't reach out to help him up the steps. He made them one at a time, using the cane for a brace, irritated at noise the mill made behind him. "See you got a business goin'."

"Earl's business; me and Ellen's lookin' after it 'til he gets back from Boston."

Familiar smells closed around him inside the house: cornbread, greens, piney wood in the stove; familiar furniture—hide-bottom chairs, oval picture of Grandpa, hand-tinted; quilting frame drawn up to the wooden ceiling. And Ellen at the stove, a little smile on her dark face, clean gingham dress. "Howdy, Alvah," she said. "Welcome home."

He said, "Howdy, Ellen," and eased down in the chair that had been his, and the coffee was good, the bluesweet odor of the old man's Prince Albert good, too. But tenseness was there, a waiting kind of thing nobody wanted to bring out.

Clearing his throat, Ben said, "Earl wants you to take over the peeler mill, and you can talk to him about what all else. We got a phone now."

Alvah sipped black coffee. "Little brother's come up in the world, seems like. What'll you do?"

"What I do best, work the land. Bought us that piece acrost the river, and you 'member that rise in the ground? Foundation poured for a new house." Ben cleared his throat again. "You don't see the mill, you could farm some."

"Never was much for the land," Alvah said and tasted his coffee.

Ellen brought the pot to the table. "Your daddy listened every day to the war news, and followed it close in the Meridian *Star*."

"Yeah," Alvah said, "but they won't build no other statue in the square, or hang no other newspaper stories on the wall at the Templars. I hear they got a statue of Benedict Arnold's leg somewhere up north, but I don't reckon anybody'll put up one to mine."

"You done all right," Ben said slowly. "You went and done your job and got back."

Fingers tightening on his cup, Alvah said, "Don't you ever wish you was back to it? I mean, how can a man settle down to scratchin' the dirt, after combat, after knowin' how—how—" The words wouldn't come because he couldn't string them together. How could you explain feeling so goddamn *alive* because you were kissing cousin to death? How to tell the savage joy running through you like good whiskey when you took an enemy position, the exultation hot as your smoking weapon when you cut down charging gooks?

It was like having a woman, and there was no way of telling that feeling to somebody never had one.

"Never held with war," Ben said. "Them medals come from gettin' my tail in a crack so I had to do somethin' to get it back out. Wasn't no youngun when I went in, and a heap older when I come out. Made up my mind the onliest way they'd get me to another war was if the enemy put his foot on Lassiter land."

"But the excitement," Alvah said, "the pure-D livin' of it—"

Rolling another cigarette, Ben said, "Doin' what you got to is one thing; likin' it is another."

Alvah sat still for a while, then pushed back his cup. "You and me never seen eye to eye, Pa."

Ellen said quickly, "It was the same with Earl, but they get along real good now."

Ben made a motion with a callused hand. "There's money comin' to you."

"Don't reckon I need it," Alvah said, getting up with help from his cane.

"This is still your house," Ben said.

Alvah's smile was twisted. "You're lettin' somebody tear it down. I'll make do on my own, look around for a spell, see some folks. Thanks for the coffee."

"Alvah," Ellen said, but he kept going, doing his best to walk steady.

Earl had been at his books steadily; now he sat back to rub his eyes and glance at his watch. An hour more, and it would be coming on Saturday morning. If he could hang on, he had the whole weekend to catch up. A little tired, he was still hungry in mind and body. Rising from the desk, he started for the kitchen to stir up something to eat. It was easy to feed his belly, but it seemed like his head had a hole in it, and the more knowledge he poured in, the more he needed. Most of it stuck, but there was so much more waiting to be digested.

He opened the refrigerator door—*fridge,* not icebox; that was part of the learning process also, not only schematics and geometry and all pertaining to engineering design, but how to talk like he wasn't fresh out of the woods. Things went better if you didn't stick out like a whiskey runner at a Baptist prayer meeting. Take in some culture, too, Ira Lowenstein advised; get the feel of art and the city, but especially the company.

Don't have time for those cocktail parties and such, Earl protested, and Ira said, they're business also; watch how much gets done at those gatherings, and you can't keep your nose in a book all the time. Don't you get enough schooling and on-job training during the day? And Earl said there just ain't—isn't—enough time. But by then, he figured he needed his own place, and Ira had helped him find it.

When the door buzzer sounded, Earl turned from the fridge with a carton of eggs in one hand. He still held them when he opened the door. She smiled at him, then at the eggs, and Cam Morgan said, "I have it on good authority that deli food is better, so I brought some."

He felt silly standing there with the box of eggs, wearing socks and his old jeans and a sweatshirt. Cam looked even better than she did at the office, if that was possible. "Mighty thoughtful of you," he said. "Come on in; I'm gettin' tired of my own cookin'."

"Ira thought you might be," she said, walking in with a shopping bag to pause and look around. "You haven't changed a thing; our tastes must be similar."

Earl blinked. "*You* furnished this place?"

Cam headed for the kitchen bar. "At company expense, naturally. Let's see now—whitefish, lox, cream cheese, bagels. . . ."

Looking for his shoes, Earl noticed she was efficient in the kitchen, too; no wasted movements, that precision machinery purring along smoothly. In the several months he'd known her, Cam Morgan never seemed to fumble anything, never looked sweaty or had a red nose. She seemed different in black velvet slacks that didn't expose her long, modeled legs but clung tightly over the hips, so he could see the sleek working of buttock muscles.

"Never mind your shoes," Cam said. "I'll just kick off mine, so we can curl up on the couch or sit on the floor and pretend it's a picnic."

"Pretty nice of you, to give up your weekend like this," he said, accepting a bagel. "Didn't expect a midnight picnic."

She cocked her head to one side, highboned face framed by curling black hair, slanty eyes dancing. "All study and no recess will get you all A's, or flip your wig. Can't let anything bad happen to my boss; I might get another one not nearly as interesting." Cross-legged on the carpet beside him, Cam poured white wine. "You are interesting, you know."

"Me? Just a woods runner without no—any—education." Did the wine taste flowery, or was it her perfume sneaking into the back of his throat, drifting up from the deep cleft of her breasts?

"The rough edges make you appealing," she said. "Challenging, I suppose. And education is as education does."

Cam saying the last part that way, reaching her eyes across to his, made him tingle. It had been a long time since Jessica, and when he bunched up nerve to call her long distance, Lila Coffield had answered saying she'd pass on the message, that this was a bad time, so soon after Avery passed on. He hadn't known Avery Coffield was dead. Pa used the new telephone about once a month, and then it was about the mill.

"You're sort of wild and more than a little sweet," Cam Morgan said, leaning so he could look down the front of her blouse and see she didn't need to wear anything to hold her up. "I find myself wishing I'm the first, but I sense I'm not."

He almost said the first what, but covered with a big swallow of wine, and when he put down the glass, her neatly shaped lips were very close, damp and shining. Earl kissed her and cupped the breasts she put into his hands, felt her leg sliding between his own. Without clumsiness, because Cam Morgan was never awkward, they were bared to each other on the carpet, and he was content to follow her lead, one lingering, adept move at a time. When it was just the right time and he entered her, Earl knew he'd been right in his first appraisal of Cam Morgan: she was wonderfully designed and well-oiled machinery, and he had always appreciated machinery.

"I can handle any damned machine," Alvah Lassiter said, "from a jeep to a tank, and you know it well as me."

Sheriff Kobburn leaned back against the fender of his patrol car and picked his teeth. "Ain't seen no tanks around here of late, and hellin' over them back roads in a pickup ain't gettin' a load where it's supposed to go. How come you askin' me about it, anyways?"

Alvah shifted his weight to his good leg. "Oh shit, man; reckon I know your business most good as them back roads. Figured it'd be a help to you, takin' me to that new guy runnin' Beevo's."

Kobburn grunted. "You don't know my business; ain't nobody does. And that Eye-talian at Beevo's—"

"I know those back roads," Alvah cut in. "Every cowpath between here and the state line; I know places a car can go, and where it can't, and I got ideas about a four-wheel drive that'll change that last part. If you don't carry me out to Beevo's, I'll go by myself."

Scratching his belly, Kobburn pushed away from the fender. "Get on in. That Eye-talian could use a good driver, and I 'spect it's the least I can do for another one of Temple County's war he-roes, 'specially one all crippled up."

"That's it," Alvah said. "That's the first and only time you put your mouth to me thataway. Do it again, and you'll be holdin' your guts in both hands like so many fresh chitlins."

Kobburn had already wedged his bulk under the wheel and his face went red as he turned. "Now looka here, boy—"

"Boy, your ass," Alvah said, "*boy* your fat civilian ass. In Korea, I killed twenty-one gooks that I know of; twenty-one poison-mean shits that'd hang you out to dry in a minute. You been totin' around that Magnum half your life, and you'd be lucky to drag it out without shootin' yourself in the foot. That'd be the fartherest goddamn thing you could hit, so don't you *boy* me. If I had both my legs blowed off, I'd still be able to open your belly like you growed a zipper on it."

Kobburn put the car into gear, a vein throbbing in his neck and sweat around his collar. Teeth clamped hard on a cigar butt, he drove out toward the creek road. This Lassiter youngun always had a wild streak to him, and going off to war had only made it worse. It was like carrying a coiled timber rattler on the seat beside him, one somebody had been poking at with a stick, and Mama Kobburn hadn't raised nobody's fool. Alvah Lassiter was all swole up with poison and just bound to let it out on somebody.

Clamping stained teeth around his cigar, Kobburn drove without saying nary a word, but an idea was working in the back of his head. Scarpo was so goddamn bossy, it'd serve him right to get this young rattler dumped in his lap, fangs and all. Might be they would cancel out each other, and that'd be just fine, too. There was always somebody waiting to take over Beevo's, and always another whiskey runner.

CHAPTER 17

Jessica came in from the fields grimy and sweaty, to head for the library bar and pour a big, icy drink. Reconsidering, she dumped half the whiskey and added more chaser. Exercise was good, they said; too much liquor was bad. Flopping in a chair, she put her feet up. She had never realized how hard her daddy worked, how many things had to be seen to, how many things went wrong.

Sipping her drink, she hoped the ditch network would be finished in a day or two, but oh damn, the cost. Even using cheap hand labor, irrigation was expensive. And that cotton gin, always breaking down. She'd barely got the spring bales shipped, and if the beatup machinery kept jamming, she'd be lucky to ship the fall picking, what little there was of it.

Already, they were talking in town about how taking water out of the Tchufuncta this side of the growing dam might be illegal, talking about filing water rights and such. That was something Avery Coffield never had to worry over. But Earl Lassiter and that Yankee Jew could just put out guards or something, if they meant to keep her from irrigating.

There was a twinge in her tummy as she drank. So far she'd been lucky; she didn't show, and it just seemed she'd put on a little weight. But the thing kept growing, and soon as she saw to the fall crop, she would have to do something. She still had some jewelry and a fur coat, still owned her little MG, and if Elliot paid any attention to The Shadows, she could keep them. But no; he was so goddamn wrapped up in running all over the state, joining Elks and Lions and the Masons and every other group he could find.

He could spend money on anything, but she had to haggle with second-rate field hands because the best went to work on that dam. Finishing her drink, Jessica thought the pulp mill would take more, when it went up. But how many could one mill hire? There'd always be niggers sidling around with hats in hand, ready to accept any kind of wage.

Lila came into the library, fanning herself. She was a bit haggard, but looked cool in white organdy. She took a little glass of chilled white wine at the bar and glanced disapproval at her daughter. "That sun is just *ruinin'* your skin.'"

"My hands, too," Jessica said, "but somebody has to keep this place together."

"It's not fittin' for a lady to be out yonder with the nigras. When your brother comes home—"

Banging her glass on a table, Jessica said, "*When* he comes home, it's only to touch base and sober up that bitch so he can carry her around and show what a fine family man he is. Some man! Elliot wouldn't get his pretty white hands dirty."

"Now, dear," Lila said, "he's goin' to be very important someday."

"And by then, all we'll have left of The Shadows will be this house and a couple of acres—if we're lucky."

Lila sipped her wine. "Oh, I'm sure things aren't

that bad. We women just don't have the head for business."

Jessica stood up, looked at the bar, and moved to the doorway instead. "You don't see what a bastard Elliot is because you just won't. No more restoration on the old wing, and he wouldn't send me back to school. I tell you and tell you that we can *lose* The Shadows, and do you listen? It's only *Elliot* and Mrs. *Elliot* Coffield and Thomas *Elliot* Coffield, and we don't matter, and I'm goddamn sick and tired of even hearing his name!"

Lila looked shocked. "I do declare, but you're soundin' more like your daddy every day. I must say it's not the least bit ladylike."

Jessica left her mother and headed for the stairs, the thing in her body nagging at her. She would have to do something about it soon; there wasn't much time.

"Wait," the scarecrow man in black intoned. "Wait, chillun; all in good time. But I say to you—I say to you—we been waitin' for two hundred years, and all it's got us is some more waitin'."

"Yeah," the congregation chanted. "Yeah, yeah."

Calvin Davison shifted on the pew; he could feel his wife fidgeting beside him. Sarah's face was pulled tight, and her full lower lip was caught in her teeth, but beyond her, little Peter was leaning forward raptly. He'd never been attentive in church before. Davison took Sarah's hand. It was sweaty; he patted her fingers and focused on the Reverend Lucien La-Beaux again. Had to give it to the man, he thought; not the usual visiting black preacher, but the kind of fire and brimstone he was expounding from the raw-pine pulpit might singe the church. No wonder the local minister looked uneasy; the Reverend Raymond

Brown had grown up under a load this firebrand never knew.

Still, Davison wondered, how much easier had it been in New Orleans? The weight was everywhere in the South, perhaps more precariously balanced in a small town, but waiting to come smashing down, anyhow.

LaBeaux lifted his arms and spread them, hung his head and became the crucifixion. The crowd was quiet. He snapped up his head and raised his arms high, supplicating. "But there is resurrection comin'. I say unto you—resurrection! Not quick as the good lord made it, oh no. We got no angel to roll aside our stone, but brothers and sisters, we're pushin' at it ourselves. We're nudgin' it, because nobody else is goin' to roll it aside for us. We have to do it ourselves. And I tell you, we're beginnin' to see a ray of light in the darkness! Oh yes, lord—there's a new dawn comin'!"

A heavy woman in the front row cried, "Hallelujah!" and somebody in back called out, "Lord, lord!"

Sarah tugged at Davison's hand and put her lips to his ear: "He's stirrin' them up so. Let's get out of here, Cal."

"You know we can't," he whispered back.

LaBeaux pointed his forefingers at the crowd, scowled over them, and cocked his thumbs. His voice dropped. "But one step at a time; you're lookin' straight at what would have stopped the chillun of Israel if they hadn't got away from ol' Pharaoh just one step at a time. It's how Moses got 'em across the wilderness and into the promised land, by puttin' one foot ahead of the other, slow and easy. I say unto you—*they* been promisin' and promisin', and *we* about to take that first step to collect."

Holding them on the point of his silence, LaBeaux dropped his aimed fingers and turned his palms upward. "Now, if Brother Brown will lead us in the hymn—"

Outside, Davison had to hurry after his wife as she dragged Peter toward their car. She had the door open when he caught her wrist. "What the hell is the matter with you?"

"What's the matter wtih *you*?" she demanded, pushing the boy into the back seat. "Did you know that—that troublemaker was goin' to say all that?"

Davison got in and started the motor. "No, I didn't, but what did he say that was so bad?"

Knotting her hands in her lap, Sarah said, "You really don't know. You've been here two years, and you really don't know."

"Sarah," he said gently, "you're not happy here, and I understand that. But I've explained time and again that these people need me more than they do in Chicago. The treatment up there isn't nearly good enough, but it's far better than no medical attention. The clinic—"

"The clinic!" she said fiercely. "Your work! What are you, some kind of Messiah, like that Creole nigger in the pulpit? In olden times, they nailed the Messiah to a cross, but here they won't spare your family—me; Peter. They'll nail us *all* to a tree and burn down your precious clinic. That cross on the lawn—you think that was a joke? That unburned cloth came from an expensive gown, not a rag. Are you stupid enough to think some scared nigger won't report every word he heard in that church today?"

Carefully, Davison said, "The word is black, Sarah; not nigger."

She turned in the seat, looking back at their son. "In Temple County, it's *nigger*. Don't you forget that, Peter; first time you do, you'll wind up like—like—" Sarah hid her face in her hands.

He drove quickly down the gravel street and pulled around to the front of the house. "Peter," he said, "your mother's upset. Go on in and make us some Koolaid; we'll be there in a minute." Then, to Sarah: "Don't tell that story to the boy."

Tear-stained, she faced him. "Maybe I ought to, so he can see how it is and not get mixed up in any civil rights nonsense. When I got out of Georgia, I thought I was free of this, but here it comes again. Peter should know his uncle got nailed to a tree and set fire to, because he beat up on a white man tryin' to rape me. Oh lord, oh my god—and me only thirteen years old, just a little older than our son now. And poor Ethan, screamin' his heart out, screamin' and screamin'—"

Davison took her in his arms and buried her face in his shoulder. "Don't, Sarah, don't. Peter is only six. And this is here. That was Georgia, and a long time ago. I know what it took for you to come here with me, and I'm very grateful. But you're letting a traumatic past affect the present. We haven't been bothered—"

"We will be," she said into his coat. "Oh migod, we sure will be, if anybody listens to that LaBeaux. Registerin' to vote—" Sarah lifted her face. "That scares 'em, Cal; it scares 'em crazy, because in this county there's more than twice as many of us, and a scared man, he'll purely *kill* you. He'll never, never *let* anybody register, and it's goin' to wash over onto everybody, not just those who try. This is no big city; this is a little bitty town, with one sheriff and a sometime deputy. You've seen *them*, but what you haven't seen is the look in crazy eyes, the hate in crazy eyes—in fire-light—migod, migod, in firelight—"

He caught her hands. "Easy now; easy. You're hysterical."

Don't get hysterical, Elliot told her; surely you're not an alcoholic, Sandy. You just drink a little too much, and you can do without it for a few hours. We have to make that Templar meeting tonight, and it really wouldn't do for you to get smashed there. Women are allowed only a few times a year, and it's important to me that you make friends with the other wives. You'd be surprised how many of them influence their husbands' votes.

I'll try, Sandy promised; a cold shower, fix my hair, that new dress you brought. It's a very nice dress, Elliot; you have good taste.

And because he was her only friend, her link with reality, Sandy made it—that night and whenever he wanted her beside him at some gathering. She'd lock her teeth and hold back the shaking and smile when she had to refuse creamed chicken. The half-pint bottle in her purse carried her through, if she only went to the ladies' room two or three times and used the breath mints.

Sometimes Elliot brought a friend, some bright and burly young man whose face and manner seemed interchangeable with the ones before. None ever swished, but the attachment was there for Sandy to see, if nobody else; Elliot was very careful that way. Anything to keep from being lonely, she thought, envying him at the same time she was being grateful for the chance to have a couple of cocktails while they were in another part of the room.

But she was too talky, pushing it, trying hard to be

friendly, and Sandy could feel the other women drawing back. She was a stranger among them, and would be, if she lived there another twenty years. There was a man or two, hinting, circling like cautious he-dogs smelling the possibility of heat but wary of a bite. Sandy couldn't handle them, didn't want to, and retreated behind her glass, or into the ladies' room with her small bottle.

She always hated to go home; even Thomas Elliot was alien to her now, his care practically taken over by the old black cook. His crying bothered her, so much like her own silent misery. Sandy was afraid to leave him and go to New Orleans, see a few friends; not in that house, with those two women hovering like sharp-beaked birds. Anything could happen. But Elliot didn't want her taking the child along, either. Every night Sandy listened to the shadows and felt them creeping ever closer and there was no way out.

"Figure that to get you out of traps the feds set?" Scarpo asked.

"Know it," Alvah answered. "They're watchin' for hot cars, and road-block 'em while they're bringin' up somebody behind you. But with this rig, if they get too close, I cut across country, right out through the woods."

Scarpo lounged behind his desk in the storeroom. "Easier to dump the load."

"No payoff there, for either of us."

Nodding, Scarpo knew he had a winner here, had known it when the sheriff dropped off the kid and he listened to the four-wheel-drive idea. A short-time winner, anyhow. He had the balls to be Sicilian, but not the shrewdness. Scarpo had seen guys like him before, hot to go, ready to take any chance, and they made

pretty good button men, hit men you could send anywhere and get the job done. But they never lasted.

"Okay," he said, "you get somebody to help fix the
truck like you said. Riggin' it with phony pulpwood is
good, and so's the idea of day runs. These other dum-
mies, they always wanta make it night, when the feds
are watchin' closer. You can move into one of the cabins, but that comes outa your end. If you get next to
one of the broads, it's on her off time." He put elbows
on the desk and leaned forward. "When that goddamn
Kobburn said your name, said Lassiter, I didn't know
what the hell. I mean, I'm still findin' bullet holes."

Alvah said, "Sheriff mentioned that. They won't be
back."

"Not to see you?"

"Uh-uh. Pick any cabin?"

Shrugging, Scarpo said, "What's different about
'em?" And thought, that's how it is—the kid's family
don't want nothing to do with him, and this Lassiter
don't give a damn. Gimpy, pissed at the world, a loner
looking for a way to prove himself, make his bones.
He'd do okay until his luck ran out, and New Orleans
was pushing for more alky. With this crip, they'd get
it.

Using his cane, Alvah went to his Chevy and pulled
it behind a cabin, dragging in the duffel bag and toilet kit, all he had. One room, shower and toilet, radio;
no TV like some of the big motels, but Beevo's didn't
cater to tourists and what the hell was there to see in
Temple County?

Scarpo was a hard-ass and a businessman, but he
didn't say anything about the leg, and he was paying
to rig the GMC pickup like Alvah wanted. They'd put
in the front drive, but chop it so the truck wouldn't
have such a high center of gravity. Twelve inches

clearance was normal, but that stuck the rig way up in the air, so it could flip at high speeds. Eight inches would clear anything in the woods but a stump, and it would handle a lot better. Dual carbs, fuel injection, high-speed rear end—they'd play billy hell catching Alvah Lassiter with a load. He'd put ass in all their faces.

Thinking who he'd get to help him work on the truck—Billy Dee Blake, probably—Alvah dropped onto the sagging bed and propped his leg. So Pa and Earl had shot up the place, put Scarpo and his boys to cover like rabbits. Ben was always set on a hair trigger, and it looked like Earl was getting sand in his craw. And big, fat ambition to go with it. Talking Pa into letting a dam get built, into tearing down the house, setting up that post-peeler business and going into cahoots with some big company to get a pulp mill in; it looked like his baby brother was on the road to being another Avery Coffield, big man in the county.

The kid still had both his legs, and Pa still had his black woman in the house. Funny that didn't bother him now, even though Ellen looked better than ever. Maybe being with Lou Miller in that gook whorehouse had had a lot to do with it. Korean women weren't black *or* white, and sharing them with old Lou brought the spade bastard closer, even.

But he still remembered Pa ready to kill him over Ellen, Pa making his pick between them. Well, Alvah Lassiter made his pick, too. He was on his own, and meant to stay that way.

CHAPTER 18

There was another woman at Cam Morgan's desk, and she didn't look as if she belonged in an office. She was regally tall, an ashblonde with high cheekbones and cool green eyes in a fashion model's face.

"Mornin'," Earl said. "Miss Morgan sick?"

Even her smile was cool. "I'm Stacey Haslitt, Mr. Lassiter. Miss Morgan has been transferred."

He blinked at her. Transferred? Nobody said anything to him about that, not even Cam when she kissed him goodbye. "Get my home, please," he said, and swung into his office.

The phone rang and rang, and finally Earl hung up. He was reaching for the intercom when Ira Lowenstein walked in. "Quite a lady out there," Ira said.

"But not my lady," Earl said. "Where is she, and why did Cam—"

Ira moved across to the small bar and poured coffee. "Your office got bigger and so did Cam's. She took you far as she could, Earl. Stacey Haslitt can take you farther. She's old Boston family, knows a lot of people, very conversant with the theater and art."

Rocking back in his chair, Earl said, "You tryin' to tell me that Cam—I mean, I was just a job for her, an assignment?"

"Something like that," Ira admitted. "She's a company woman, looking to her own future within the structure. A pyramid climber, if you like. In a giant corporation, you either climb, or stay there in the base where everybody else climbs over you and leaves a lot of footprints."

"Damn it," Earl said, "Cam and me—"

Ira blew his coffee, sipped it. "A time and a place, remember? It was the company's choice, *and* hers. I'm sure you'll find Stacey a suitable replacement."

Whipping out of his chair, Earl stalked to the window and stared through it. "You use people like spare parts, like they're interchangeable?"

"We change them," Ira said, "you, me, Victor Quinn, people much higher up. You know how you're always making design changes on your tree puller for more efficiency, better operation?"

To grimy rooftops, to the busy streets far below, Earl said, "I also believe in durability."

"Sometimes, yes; sometimes a planned obsolescence."

Earl turned from the window. "We're talkin' about *people,* not machine parts."

"Cam Morgan isn't on the scrap pile," Ira said. "As Pat Neely's assistant, she's taken a big jump in the structure."

"All right, Ira," Earl said. "I'm just an ol' country boy, but I'm learnin'." And when Ira left, he thought yeah, sure as hell he was learning. Cam Morgan had been sent to grind off some of his rough edges, to be his sex life, and to feed information into him as computers were programed.

Push the button and Earl Lassiter does this; put in a new tape and he does that. Climb the pyramid, Ira said, or get footprints stomped all up your back. And outside was Stacey Haslitt, who knew about theater and art and the right people; she probably had a master's degree in English, too. Show the Mississippi redneck how to talk better and give him something to talk about besides pulpwood and engineering. Cam had been picking his clothes for some time, getting him used to the city, making sure all his buttons worked. Now Stacey would continue his education—indoctrination, Earl realized. All that sweetness in bed, that naturalness, the glad, warm giving of Cam Morgan—

"Oh shit," Earl said, as his phone buzzed, then, "Yes?"

Stacey Haslitt's smooth voice said, "A Miss Coffield; will you take the call?"

Fingers squeezing into the phone, Earl said, "Yes, of course. Jessica?"

Such a different voice, the same husky, sensual quality that always skipped up and down his spine. "Earl, darlin'; it's so good to hear you."

"Where are you, Jessica?"

"Right here in this terrible town, at the airport. When I called, they kept puttin' me off, shufflin' me around—" There was something else in her talk, Earl thought, a desperation unlike Jessica.

He gave his address, promised to meet her at his apartment within the hour. "I'll call the doorman and have you let in. Is there somethin' wrong, Jessica?"

"Kind of," she said, and hesitated. "Earl—"

"Yes?"

"Nothin'; I'll see you soon. You'll be there?"

"Sure," he said, and when she said goodbye, he held the phone awhile.

Buzzing Ira, he said he'd be gone for the day, and cut off the man without explanation. Of course, Stacey murmured, she would see to the doorman and have a company car waiting on the street, but if Mr. Quinn called?

He was already passing through the outer office when he answered: "Tell him whatever you please," and thought of adding, stuff that in your computer. But seeing Jessica was more on his mind than shaking up the cultured Miss Haslitt, so he hurried on.

At the apartment, he fumbled the key twice before opening the door. If he hadn't seen her head over the back of his leather recliner, he'd have known she was in the room anyhow. Faint but tingling, an eddy of Jessica Coffield's special perfume reached him as the golden head turned.

Dropping his attaché case on a table, he went around in front of her, hands reaching out. Jessica didn't get up and flow into his arms, and he saw why.

"Earl," she said, "I knew you wouldn't fail me. You never do."

She was Jessica and she wasn't; the slim body was bloated, grotesque; her face was puffy. She was pregnant, so big that her time must be pretty close, and he didn't know what the hell to say.

"I'm not askin' you to marry me," she said, "and I hate to ask for anything else, but I just have to. Since Daddy died, Elliot's been actin' like nobody else counts. I—I sold my car and jewels, but it's not enough. You know how Temple County is, and I *couldn't* stay around there so folks could point their fingers at me—"

Awkwardly, he stepped back. "Can I get you somethin'—a drink, coffee?"

She shook her head. "I used up most of my money hidin' out, so nobody would know. Then I came to see you, when I couldn't think of anything else to do."

Earl poured himself a strong drink. The motel in

Meridian, the missed plane; his mind counted back, and it was just about right. He said, "If you won't ask me to marry you, I'll ask you to marry me."

Jessica flared at him. "What the hell will that solve, Earl Lassiter? Everybody'll know, anyhow, and you're doin' so well here—"

"I can go home any time," he said.

"No; there's so much goin' on down there, Elliot bein' so mean and all; then there's the trouble comin'—"

"Trouble?" Earl wasn't tracking; all he could see was Jessica's swollen belly and his baby in it.

"With the nigras and with that pulp mill buildin'. I swear, it's hard enough to keep field hands as it is, but what with all the talk—"

"Jessica, why won't you marry me?"

For a moment, the old flirtatious Jessica broke through as she tilted her head and gazed up at him through lowered lashes. "I didn't say I wouldn't *ever*; it's just that right now, it wouldn't work out."

Swallowing whiskey, Earl said, "But isn't it too late to do anything about the—the baby?"

"Way too late, silly. I wouldn't do that to your child, anyhow. But until I get things settled with Elliot and that woman he's married to, it's best we keep the baby a secret."

He didn't know how he felt—guilty, scared, mad at himself, sorry for her. A baby; damn, a baby; his and Jessica Coffield's. "How are you—we—goin' to keep that kind of secret? I mean, isn't your mama lookin' for you, and you have to go home sometime, and—"

Leaning forward, the backs of her hands on her knees so that her palms seemed to be supplicating, she said, "I have it figured out. I can have the baby in Meridian, under another name, but I have to turn him over to somebody right away, some nice family who'll take care of him until the time is right. Earl, if I could get The Shadows workin' again the way it used to, I wouldn't have to bother you with this."

"It's right you came to me," he said. "I'll check with Ira—he's kind of my boss here—and see how my account is. I know the post peelers are makin' money, and I haven't spent much of what they're payin' me up here—"

Jessica said, "It won't take much, and just until I can get back to The Shadows. Enough to pay for takin' care of the—of our baby."

Earl frowned at his empty whiskey glass. "You didn't even tell your mama?"

"Nobody," Jessica said. "You're makin' so much of yourself up here, and when you come back home, you'll truly be a *somebody*. I'm proud of you for that, Earl Lassiter, right proud. I always knew you'd be more than a hard-dirt farmer, knew it right from the start. So I don't want to mess up anything for you—for us."

She was still beautiful, he thought, and would be again. His pa said some women got prettier after they birthed, and there was Ellen for an example. And she was Jessica Coffield; it would take a whole lot to change that.

Jessica said softly, "You know, I always kind of pictured you and me at The Shadows, livin' the good life, the way it ought to be lived. All this nigra trouble will simmer down, and everything will be just like it always was, only this time for you and me, Earl."

The Shadows, Earl thought; Lassiter land and Coffield land joined, producing as it could and should; The Shadows and Jessica. In the back of his head, maybe he had always known what he wanted, but now it was within reach.

Ben Lassiter reached for another hot biscuit. "Ellen," he said, "ain't no use gettin' riled. What other folks does is their business, not ours."

"I don't know," she said. "So much doin' in town, but they don't talk much to me. It's like lines gettin' drawn, but I ain't on either side."

"You feel you got to choose a side?"

Ellen spooned sugar into her coffee. "There's Marcie, Ben. I worry for her goin' to school."

"Could be that's all there is to it," Ben said, "just talk."

"Not this time. It scares me bad."

Wiping his mouth, Ben said, "Scares you *I* might pick a side, and you got it figured which way I'll light."

"You're white, Ben."

"I don't think on it when I'm with you and Marcie."

"*She* has to think on it every day; the younguns pick at her, and lord knows what'll happen do they get the schools integrated."

"Don't reckon that'll happen in our time."

Toying with her spoon, Ellen said, "Suppose it does? If they try it—oh lord, lord."

Ben said, "I'll see to Marcie. Damn it, these black strangers easin' around town, talkin' up trouble—and there's just as many white troublemakers. Better off was they to let things be."

"It's past time for lettin' it be," Ellen said quietly. "I'd be proud to see Marcie in a good school, a sure enough school. But God knows I don't want to see her hurt none."

Ben pushed back his plate and rolled a cigarette, scratched a wooden match to it. "Marcie can be sent off somewhere 'til it blows over."

Biting her lip, Ellen said, "Don't figure it'll blow over. They—some are bad-mouthin' me, callin' me Aunt Jemima and the like. And Ben, I ain't certain it ought to pass on by."

"You been listenin' to that New Orleans preacher. Damn it, he ain't one of ours."

"Maybe none of us are yours." Ellen's voice dropped to a whisper.

"That ain't what I meant," Ben said, "and you know it."

"Reckon I know you better'n anybody else, but you got some deep places nobody ever reached into, Ben Lassiter, not even your ownself. If it comes to killin', are you certain sure where you stand?"

He moved from the table, stood for a long moment, then walked out onto the front porch. All around him, the wood was new and fragrant, the view strange to him after so long in the old house. The company Earl was tied to, they'd thrown up this new place in a big hurry, but he couldn't fault its construction. Like they jumped in sudden to work on the mill, the dam; like they were in a godawful hurry to get it all done at once. A screen of loblolly pines kept him from seeing the big mill going up, and that was good. Down the hill, he caught a flash of sunlight on water where the dam backed it up. Before long, mudcats would be growing in there big as olden times.

Damnit, Ellen figured she knew him clean down to the marrow, and could be she was right. She might be treeing the wrong he-coon, too. Take a youngun and grow him up so he had niggers for friends but couldn't bring them in the house, and it was like high wind bending a sapling. If the wind kept blowing, the sapling stayed bent over, twisting itself against niggers and Jews and Italians and Catholics and anybody else didn't belong in the same grove; even the Methodists had a place off to one side.

Then along came a lull, and a man named Lipshutz, a bigod man and soldier any way you looked at him. And along came Ellen Nash, good a woman as God ever waddled a gut into, and a sweet little burr-headed gal called Marcie.

Maybe then, the twisted-around pine found out that oaks and cypress and sweetgum trees had their own right to sun and water.

Walking the length of his new porch, Ben sat in one of the hide-bottom chairs toted up from the old place, tilting its back against the wall so he could prop his feet on the railing. His grandpa made those chairs with his own hands, and they were solid as the day they got pegged together. Lord knows how many cowhide bottoms had been replaced, but in time they all fitted easy to the shape of a man's ass.

All right; so pine trees and sweetgums didn't cross; the seeds didn't mix, so that much was against nature. But put a jack to a mare, and you got a mule smarter and stronger than his dam or sire—only mules couldn't make mules; they were sterile. Did that mean nature never meant for mules to exist, and it was only man's messing around that bred them?

Ellen and Marcie both was smart as any white women hadn't got a good education, and had a heap better common sense than some Ben could name. Where the hell did those young, ornery niggers get off, calling her Aunt Jemima and poking at little Marcie? There was colored folks, and there was flat-out niggers; there was whites and there was white trash.

Maybe what Ellen didn't understand was if it came down to it, Ben Lassiter stood for himself, *his* rights, *his* land, and his own folks. If that meant straddling the fence, so be it, and any black, any white tried to push him off better give his soul to God, because his ass belonged to Ben Lassiter.

Alvah Lassiter cruised the purring car down a back road, feeling every bump from the heavy-duty overload springs because he was running empty. His fish poles poked out the back window, and there was a bait bucket on the floor, pretty good camouflage if he needed it. Ol' pus-gut Kobburn was in on the alky running, so the local law didn't lay for Alvah, but Scarpo'd had word that feds were starting to nose around. There'd been a brush with some just outside Gulfport, but he'd put tailpipe in their faces for a stretch, then lost them by taking off across country with the four-wheel drive.

Now he was feeling pretty good; speed and the challenge did that to him, made him come alive again. He was looking forward to getting back to his shack at Beevo's and tying one on. Driving slow and easy, he shifted weight from his false leg and wondered just how much money Scarpo was making from the alky. He'd picked up some information already, enough to make him know why bootleg whiskey wasn't all that profitable anymore, but straight alcohol was.

Woods runners with stills hid back in the piney brush had a good thing going now. They retailed Mason jars of bustskull to the locals, but the bulk of their output went to Scarpo. Alcohol that rated about 190 proof wholesaled for four bucks a gallon; colored, "aged" and flavored, and cut a dozen times, it poured over bars for forty cents a shot, twenty-eight shots to the fifth. The profit ran about a thousand percent, over and above protection money and operating costs. Of course, the feds got screwed out of their taxes, around $11.40 a gallon.

Drifting the car around a curve in the gravel road, Alvah remembered something Scarpo had let slip, something about the big picture with combined output of 190 proof maybe topping fifty to a hundred *million* gallons a year. That was a hell of a lot of money, and Scarpo's end of it was only a pimple.

Alvah didn't really give a rat's ass how many were getting rich on hauls like his, all over the country. He was doing okay, and he had an idea that trying to make himself bigger would probably get him dead. Guys who ran operations that widespread didn't screw around.

That was the only bug, he thought—screwing around; *not* screwing around. It still wouldn't work for him, although he tried a couple of times with the whores. That grenade might as well have blown off his balls, too, but there were times when he got falling-down drunk and dreamed of the gook whorehouse and the fun there with three slant-eyed dolls and ol' Lou Miller. That's when he stained the bed in his sleep, and maybe it meant he was getting better, but he couldn't do a damned thing about it when he was awake.

Coming up on Beevo's from the creek road, Alvah eased the car into a storage shed, climbed out, and pulled a sliding wall of phony soft-drinks cases across the opening. Limping a little, he went to the back door and let himself in.

Scarpo looked up from his desk. "Quick run."

"Got quick for a spell outside Gulfport," Alvah

said, taking the stuffed envelope from his hip pocket, "but I lost 'em."

"You push it too goddamn much. You *like* them feds on your ass."

"Mindin' my own business, just cruisin' when they picked me up. Next run, I'll change over to the pickup, and I reckon it's time we repaint 'em both and switch the plates."

Leafing through a sheaf of bills, Scarpo nodded, then dropped them into his desk drawer. When he looked up at Alvah, his eyes were black marbles. "This bullshit everybody's talkin'—crosses and fire and all that. Local hillbilly like you oughta know how solid it is."

Alvah helped himself to a drink from Scarpo's desk bottle. "Afraid it'll hurt business? Damned right, if it blows up. Be a lot of corn whiskey sold, but more give away, and won't nobody be hangin' around here to dance and hooraw with whores."

"And the stills?"

Alvah shrugged. "Boys'll be too busy slippin' around with guns to work their stills. If things get real mean, nobody will stir around after dark, unless they're up to devilment."

Scarpo spread thick, hairy hands on his desktop. "That Creole nigger preacher, that LaBeaux. Suppose he didn't make it outa New Orleans no more?"

"Might help," Alvah answered, "might not. He got 'em all stirred up, and it looks like they won't settle down. If it ain't LaBeaux, it'll be somebody else. Lot of strange spades in the county now."

"Shit," Scarpo said. "If it ain't one thing, it's another fuckin' problem. Why the hell don't the jigs play this civil rights game somewhere else, some big town? How come they got to do it here, in *my* territory?"

Putting down the whiskey glass, Alvah said, "Maybe it won't be any skin off our asses. The whites need some place to meet and tell each other how mean they are and what all they're goin' to do to the next uppity nigger. Might even be a jump in business."

"Alky is the business," Scarpo said. "This goddamn joint is peanuts. You think you're the only runner I got? Hell, there's six more pickup points in this county, and four across the line. People in New Orleans ain't gonna' like—" He broke off and lifted a stubby finger at Alvah. "See what you can do, hometown boy; talk to them dumb bastards on both sides."

Alvah braced his bum leg and moved away from the desk. "I'm a driver, that's all. If not here, somewhere else. You talk to 'em."

Outside, he tried not to limp as he crossed to his cabin, but slipped in the gravel and banged his shoulder against one of the whore's trailers. She came around the corner and caught his elbow, helped him to catch his balance. He started to curse her for it, but looked into soft dark eyes instead. Staring, he could feel a sudden warmth low down in his belly.

CHAPTER 19

It wasn't that she'd changed the apartment decor to a bunch of whites and pale blues, that the furniture was so much glass he walked easy for fear of breaking it or his neck. The right touch for intimate gatherings, Stacey Haslitt said: cozy but sophisticated. What bothered Earl was the way she had a manicured, highly polished fingernail in damned near every aspect of his life. Stage plays he didn't understand, and art galleries that were worse, and gentle, constant correction of his speech, but all the time standing sort of to one side, aloof and unapproachable. It made him wonder how she'd look with her hair mussed or her dress rumpled. Stacey was just too damned perfect.

He'd been busy as a cottontail in a room full of bobcats, which might be the reason Stacey had never deigned to grace his bed. Even in production, the tree puller developed bugs, and he was always down in the plant, or retesting in the field. Earl liked that, because he didn't feel right unless he could get his hands dirty once in a while.

And they were feeding him progress reports on the pulp mill, statistics of projected production and supplies that made him dizzy. He was beginning to get a hold on the abstracts, but it was harder than working with solid, honest machinery. Between cram classes on

aspects of engineering he'd never imagined, there was
the worry about Jessica and their child. Now he was
sorry he'd let her go like that, and hadn't heard a
word from her since. His pa said she hadn't been seen
around town, but that didn't mean she wasn't holed
up out at The Shadows, the baby already born.

If he'd argued with her, tried to make her stay in
Boston, Jessica would have got her back up, anyhow.
When she got an idea in that beautiful head, she was
stubborn as old Avery Coffield himself, and *he'd* been
the big daddy of all hammerheads. Earl admitted she
was right about not screwing things up here, and they
both knew how Temple County gossips would roll the
scandal around in their spiteful mouths, chewing it
over and over until all the juice was gone . . . Miss
Uppity Coffield, got herself in trouble and no better
for her, acting like she's too good for plain folks . . .
bound to happen, just like I said, aswitching herself
around without a lick of shame . . . reckon who the
daddy is? . . . Expect it could be just about *anybody*,
spoiled rotten like she was by her daddy, never going
to church, tomboying around in the woods with lord
knows who . . . I tell you, if she was my youngun,
she'd 've got herself switched right good. . . .

Jessica could have called, could have written, Earl
thought, just to let him know she was all right, to say
boy or girl. It would be like her to punish him some,
then come bouncing in all bright and shiny, like she'd
seen him just yesterday. There was only one of her, for
certain.

He opened a book on calculus, and balanced gingerly upon the edge of a hard, squared-off couch. On
the glass table, it seemed the book was hanging in mid-
air, and it made him uncomfortable to let go of it. It
was like the future with Jessica, silken and lovely as

silvered dandelion seeds carried along summer wind. They were fun to chase and hard to catch, and when you did get one in your hand, it crumpled at the touch.

Earl looked up as the door swung open, and Stacey moved gracefully inside with the key in her hand. Outside, there was a windy spatter of rain, but it had only dared to brush her coat, not ruffle her sleek hair.

He didn't say howdy; she didn't like that word. He watched her hang the coat in the closet, nod at him as if he was one of her subjects she happened to notice, and thought, damned if her hairdo didn't look like a rich, golden crown, her dress simple yet glittering as a coronation gown.

"You've forgotten," she said.

"What?"

"The concert; Boston Pops Orchestra. You won't have time to dress, and you certainly can't go like that."

"Hell with it," Earl said. "When I get into that tux, it feels like I've been starched too much and ironed 'til I'm singed."

Stacey moved to the corner bar and posed upon a stool, one long leg out, the other foot tucked under the rung. Light played along the length of nylon. "You look quite presentable in formal dress."

"Just one of so many damned penguins. Ain't— isn't—there any country music in this town, pure-D ol' hillbilly music?"

"I wouldn't know," Stacey said. "I don't imagine it would appeal to me."

Earl slammed his book shut. "What *does* appeal to you, Stacey? I mean, besides force-feeding culture to an uneducated redneck like the precision-built corporation part you are? I wonder if you ever squished mud between your toes or popped muscadines in your mouth right off the vine, without washin' 'em first."

She lifted a delicate eyebrow. "What is a muscadine?"

"A wild grape," he said, "a goddamn grape that swells up all ripe and rich and sweet, and the juice runs down your chin when you bite into it. Go on, Stacey—go sit prim and prissy while you listen to fiddles they don't call fiddles and guys bangin' cymbals and pretend it don't—doesn't—hurt your ears. I'd just as soon study calculus."

Turning upon the barstool and presenting a pale ivory back to him, Stacey reached for white wine. "I can't recall ever going barefoot, and I prefer grapes this way."

The dress was open clear down her spine, Earl saw, but its front came up around her neck, which only accented the uptilted thrust of her breasts. He got up and went over to her. Stacey's perfume was light, a scent like some unpollinated hothouse flower. He said, "Do you get a zero on your report card for not hauling me off to the concert?"

Her profile was a serene cameo. "Really, Earl."

"Yes, goddamnit," he said, "really." The barstool got in his way and he spun it aside to bury his face into the vee of her neck and shoulder. She felt warm, anyway, and sat motionless until he moved his mouth up her throat to her carefully outlined mouth.

Did Stacey Haslitt struggle then, or was she responding? He didn't care, because no doubt her assignment made provisions for such variables—Section III, Subtitle A: (Subject Deviation from the Norm). He needed to mess her up, to crack that varnished exterior and see if warmth was hidden beneath it.

She tried to pant something against his teeth, but

his tongue choked it back into the sweet cavern of her mouth, and when Stacey's lean body wriggled against him, Earl scooped her up and carried her into the bedroom. As he dropped her across the bed, her green eyes were wide, that perfect mouth smeared. She'd already lost one shoe, and he flipped off the other to yank down her nylons. Her legs were long and twisting and translucent white; Stacey's hands tried ineffectually to straighten her gown, but he jerked it roughly up and ripped away see-through panties.

Her mound was full and heavily furred, throbbing in the cup of his left hand. Her mouth went soft beneath his, and his right hand fitted wonderfully around one firm buttock. "Yeah," he hissed between her parted lips, "really, really—" and went between those burnished thighs to probe the secret place of Stacey Haslitt.

Corporation woman, precisioned cog in that gigantic machine, never missing a tick; never had mud between her toes. . . . Not *like,* Earl—*as* . . . *do* watch your verb usage, Earl . . . dropping your "g's" can be charmingly provincial, but somewhat grating . . . not that tie; and not bourbon; people in these circles prefer scotch. . . .

But inside, she was slick and juicy as an ordinary snatch, and when he wrapped his fingers into her hair, when he pounded himself savagely into her glossy belly, the sounds of Stacey were half cry, half gasp. He used her violently, flinging her legs about, pausing to tear her evening gown down the middle so he could flatten her pointed breasts against his chest, then slamming up her again and again with a fury that rattled the bed.

When he came, she was shuddering against him, the length of her body jerking without control. Stacey's eyes were glazed open, her bruised mouth slack and her hair all undone, tangled. Propped upon his hands, still buried within her tremulous sheath, Earl stared down into the pale face for a long moment before feeling guilty. He had never acted like a stud horse before, and in the draining of whatever it had been—raw lust, frustration, anger—he knew a selfishness that didn't sit right with him.

He rolled off her to stride naked into the other room and pour a drink, wishing it was bourbon; goddamned scotch tasted like iodine. He poured it out and drank wine from the bottle.

From the bedroom, she said, "You son of a bitch. You redneck son of a bitch, come back here."

Earl waited until she said please.

"If that pleases you," the social worker said, "but even in these, well, strange circumstances, Mrs. Coffield—"

"You know damned well I'm not married," Jessica said, "and since I'm payin' my way right down the line, I don't care what you or anybody in the hospital thinks. It's what I want, and I want it done right."

The social worker pursed her unlipsticked mouth. "You must admit the situation is, shall we say—unusual. I do have a family ready to take the child soon as it can be released."

Jessica moved her head on the pillow. She was groggy, and felt as if dull pinking shears had been used in her crotch; her leaky breasts ached, but she wasn't studying on feeding the baby that way. "Just so his birth certificate is registered. I named him and made sure his footprint was taken. The rest is up to you, and maybe only a few folks in Jackson ever heard of the Coffields of Temple County, but you can bet they're the *right* political folks. The checks'll be steady, too."

"Very well," the social worker said primly. "I can hardly blame you for not wanting to see the—your child, but—"

"I saw him," Jessica said and sucked water through a glass tube. "I don't have to hold him."

"I suppose not," the social worker said, "so when the doctor—"

Jessica turned her back and snuggled into the pillow until the woman went away on squeaky rubber soles. It was over, the ugly ripping and antiseptic taste and the doctor looking like he wanted to puke; it was done and behind her now and nothing like it would ever happen again. Now she was safe and the pain, the distortion of her body, meant nothing. She would be beautiful again, firm and desirable as if it had never happened. It *had* happened and she was glad, but some people were going to be damned sorry.

"It's the sorriest thing I ever heard," Sam Harvey said, from his big chair in the bank's private office. "They just ain't smart enough to vote, in the first place, and in the second place, there's just too damned many of 'em. Hell, how many of 'em own their own land? And all the rest'll be raisin' taxes for *us*."

"Goddamn Yankees," Martin Nelson said. "Took nigh a hundred years to pry 'em outa here, and here they come back, stickin' their noses into other folks' business."

Burr Watson shifted uncomfortably. "It's me mostly caught a'tween a rock and a hard place, since *I* got to keep 'em from registerin'."

Sam Harvey swiveled in his chair, his eyes touching them all in turn. The bank was closed, and this meeting was being held in private. Maybe, he thought, he should have posted one of the deputies out in the alley, just to make sure no nigger was sneaking up to put his ear to the back door. He reckoned they didn't have the stomach for that yet, but these days there wasn't any telling, what with all the outside trouble-makers coming into Temple County.

He said, "Sheriff Kobburn will be there to back you up, Burr. That's why we give him two full-time deputies and another patrol car."

They glanced at Kobburn and C.J. Franklin. Kobburn pushed his hat back from his forehead and grinned around the stump of a cigar. "Got me two good boys—C.J. Franklin here and ol' Luther Travers. You all knowed both of 'em all their lives. Ain't *no* niggers, outside or garden grown, gonna run over us."

Burr Watson squirmed on his chair and patted jowled cheeks with a red bandanna. "Thing I'd like to be certain on is what the governor'll do, if we was to need National Guard troops in here. I mean, all them federal regulations and such, and I swear I seen two fellas claimed to be salesmen the other day, only I figure 'em to be federal men come asnoopin'."

"I been talkin' to the governor," Sam Harvey said. "He's just as much man as any man in the south, and you can bet on that." For a second or two, Sam found himself missing Avery Coffield, dead and buried a year. Avery knew how to get to folks high up, and although the boy Elliot was comin' along right good, it'd take him a spell to fill his daddy's shoes. "But," he went on, "the governor expects us to handle our own troubles 'less'n it comes right down to it. We done already voted Floyd Kobburn authority to raise all the volunteer help he needs, and Floyd—this here means more to you than the rest of us. They got us more'n two to one, and if we let 'em to the polls, how long you figure it'll be afore they elect themselves a nigger sheriff?"

Kobburn laced fingers over his belly. "I'm fixin' to come down on every nigger even looks cross-eyed, come down on him like a tall pine. And I aim to start knockin' heads on them city niggers, run them uppity black bastards outa my county with their tails atween their hind legs."

Martin Nelson made a bridge of his fingers and peered over it at Sam. "How come the other commissioner ain't here? Reckon we ain't all that important to Elliot Coffield no more?"

Elliot took the glass from Sandy's hand and she said, "Don't; I need a drink."

"You need to be reminded who you are," he said. "It was embarrassing to have people pretend to ignore your crude behavior."

"I—I didn't mean to," Sandy said. "I really tried to stay away from the bar, but there were so many people shoving drinks in my face, so many sweaty old men ogling my cleavage—"

"You've had plenty of experience at that, dear."

Sandy flinched. "It wasn't like—you don't understand—Elliot, I'm going paranoid in this house, only going out when you want me beside you. Your mother, and now that Jessica is back—it's too much. Why can't I take little Thomas Elliot to New Orleans and get an apartment? You don't need me as anything but a—showpiece. Please, may I have my drink now?"

He shoved it at her. "When you're at The Shadows, I don't give a damn how much you drink, but forget about New Orleans or anywhere else with *our* son. A wife and children are prerequisites for my campaign, and I expect Thomas Elliot to be seen on the platform with us soon. A babe in arms is good photo copy. Understand that clearly, Sandy."

Draining her glass, she said, "You're not listening to me. Nobody listens, and only you even *talk* to me. I can't stand it anymore, Elliot. I can't, and I won't. It's so miserable, so lonely—and what if I dropped him on the platform, or fell, or—"

He slapped her, and she almost fell off the stool, grabbing at the bartop. Elliot slapped her again, a full-handed blow that made her ears buzz and tears spring into her eyes.

"That's what if," he said calmly. "When I want my family with me for publicity, you'll be there, and you *will* be sober, or I'll beat you into sobriety. Now go drink yourself to sleep and dream on it, Mrs. Cofield."

Sandy wobbled off the stool and started around the bar, hand outstretched for a bottle. She watched her fingers tremble, and balled them into a fist. Arms across her stomach then, she turned away and walked unsteadily from the library.

From the patio, a young man entered. He was dressed conservatively, unobtrusively; his bronze hair was wavy but carefully short. He touched it as he walked to the bar and took the seat Sandy left. He said to Elliot, "I love it when you're so masterful."

Elliot poured drinks. "She's becoming a liability. Do you think I'd be a more sympathetic figure if my poor wife was so ill she had to be confined to a sanitarium?"

Mark Manley smiled, teeth white and even. "Especially if you struggled on bravely under the weight of misfortune, even appearing sometimes with your young son and apologizing for not being able to find a baby-sitter. It would endear you to the housewives."

"So long as it doesn't damage my image as a down-home boy out to do good for the deserving po' folks and keep the niggers in their place," Elliot said.

Sipping his drink, Mark said, "Elliot, you are just delicious."

CHAPTER 20

Alvah didn't know who she was, but if she wasn't a whore, she wouldn't be hanging around Beevo's. If she didn't carry black blood, there wouldn't be all that blueblack hair, a deeper than gold cast to her skin, and a certain fullness to her mouth.

When she spoke, her voice was throaty, lifting softly furred from somewhere deep beneath eye-catching breasts. "Sorry if I goofed. I thought you were fallin'. Can you tell me where I can find Mr. Beevo?"

Damn, Alvah thought; no woman had been able to do this to him since he lost his leg, but this one made him feel like a kid with a dollar in one hand and his primed pecker in the other, goggling at his first whore. "Ain't no Beevo," he mumbled. "Scarpo runs this joint, but what do you want here?"

The suggestion of a smile dallied about the corners of her mouth, a mouth full and ripe as mayhaw fruit. "I need a job waitin' tables."

She was dressed a shade too neatly, and there were far places in the sound of her, an echo not quite Mississippi. Tall as Alvah, long legged and slim, she stood proudly. He said, "Waitin' table is somethin' the girls do between tricks. You applyin' to be a whore?"

Something moved in her brown eyes, and she guarded it with a dropping of long, sooty lashes.

"You're pretty direct," she said. "A pimp would be sweet-talkin' me."

"You been there, then," Alvah said. Damned if her eyes didn't turn up a mite at the corners, like she was part gook, too.

"I'd better go see the man," she murmured.

He couldn't help it. "Wait; that ain't for you. Those drunks will mess you around and degrade you, and Scarpo won't let you keep all that much money, anyhow."

For a moment, the shield dropped from her eyes. "Thanks, but there are reasons, and well, like they say, it's liable to get hungry out if I don't do something soon."

Her arm was silken warm beneath his hand and Alvah trembled, breath hanging in his tightened throat. "Look," he said, "I'm a gimp, a goddamn crip, and if that don't turn your stomach—"

The woman's eyes searched his own. "We're all crippled in some way."

Afraid to let her go, he said, "I don't need philosophy any more'n I need pity."

"What *are* you lookin' for?"

"You," he said, "since I left my leg on the side of a stinkin' Korean mountain. I'm offerin' you a chance to stay out of Beevo's."

"You live here?"

Alvah nodded. "I'm one of Scarpo's alky runners. I won't be home all the time, but nobody'll mess with you when I'm not."

Still face, smooth promise of a face, she kept watching him. "I don't even know who you are, what you are."

"Whatever it is, it's better than you're goin' to find

in one of them goddamn cribs, and I'll see you're better off."

"Just one thing for starters," she said. "Why do you want a nigger to shack up with you? You can buy one for a few dollars a throw."

"I can't buy what I need from anybody, for any money," Alvah said. "I ain't been a man since that damned grenade, but here you come, all mornin' fresh and kind of sparkly, and your eyes turn up at the ends, and goddamnit—you're too good for this lousy joint. Somethin' else—yeah, I noticed you got a touch of the tarbrush, but that ain't what does it. I don't know what the hell does it. All I know is I'm scared to let you get away. Please don't go away."

"You're a strange man," she said. "Do you live in one of those cabins?"

Dropping his hand from her, Alvah said, "Yeah, and I'm sorry I hung on to your arm like that; just couldn't turn you loose."

She said, "You won't own me, you know, and I'll need to wait on tables."

"But they'll grab and pinch and make rotten jokes—all right; I'll fix it so you don't have to take anything else. Will you come with me now, right now?"

"All right," she said, and her just walking next to him made him tingle. She walked with slim back erect, in pride like a Korean woman, but without that splay-footed shuffle. This woman's stride was long and easy, her legs graceful as the flight of barn swallows.

He resented the tumble of the cabin, the smell and cheapness of it. Christ; what he needed was a gunny sergeant to kick his ass and make him police up this mess. "It looks like hell," Alvah said, sweeping rumpled clothes from the bed so she could sit. "Never fig-

ured anybody else comin' in here, and wasn't interested in doin' for myself. Can I get you a drink?"

"Maybe a beer," she said. "You haven't asked my
name; don't you care?"

"Sure; sure I care. But it won't make no difference."
Alvah brought two cold ones from the tiny fridge and
opened them. "I'm Alvah Lassiter, and you can call
me anything you like."

"Betty Jean," she said, accepting the icy can, sitting
on the bed back-straight but not stiffly. "Betty Jean
Parks." She sipped beer and tilted her head up at him,
hair a midnight waterfall down her back. "Alvah; is it
biblical?"

"Damned if I know." His throat was dry and the
suds didn't ease its ache, or still the jumping in his
belly. "Never been one for church, but if this is what
Holy Rollers feel when they go to jerkin' and hollerin', I been missin' out."

"Me?"

He nodded, wondering what the hell he was doing,
just standing there running off at the mouth, when he
wanted her so much he hurt all over. But she made
him awkward, made him shy as a youngun hadn't
popped his cherry, and Alvah thought maybe it was a
whole lot like that first scarey time. Could be, he
wouldn't be any good after so long without it, and she
might back off when she saw the phony leg, looked at
the reddened, flaccid stump.

"I wasn't woofin' you," he said. "About no woman,
I mean." And to hide his uncertainty, readying himself
for anger just in case, he propped against the table to
snatch off his pants. If she was shocked or sick, he'd
best know it right off. "Take a good look at this goddamned stub. Ain't many women would touch the crip
it's hung to, and it makes *me* itch where I can't scratch

to even rattle these buckles. Took weeks before I could make myself rub the hurt out of this ugly meat."

Betty Jean said slowly, "I know worse cripples; they're all around us, Alvah. So you can't shock me, although I'll admit I'm a little frightened, and it has nothin' to do with your leg."

She would run now, he thought; she'd shuck him and go whore for Scarpo and there would never be another like her. But she flowed up and removed her crisp cotton dress without fumbling, in a special, exciting dignity. Her bra and panties were simple, white, and a pulse hammered in Alvah's throat as Betty Jean leaned forward with hands behind her back to uncup her breasts. The hammering came near to strangling him when she swivel-hipped from the panties.

Beautiful all over; shiny all over like she had been buffed with the softest cloths; even her dark nipples reflected light while her blackmoss mound gathered faceted jewels of it. Chin up, mouth damp, and her eyes gone all smoky, Betty Jean waited for him. When he hopped to her, she helped him balance with the fitting of her body against him, arms around his waist.

Then they were together on the bed, and the fierce desperation within him caught her up. Her mouth was wildfire and her nipples drilled into his chest; her legs were sleek golden grippings, and Alvah shuddered as he plunged himself into her. Heaving, clenching her tightly to him, he fought the onrush of the deluge, but was powerless to stop it and was swept over and under by the torrent.

"It is all right," she gasped in his ear. "It's just fine, because we're goin' to be here a long, long time."

She was right; he was not shamed, but turned strong by her understanding, by the sweetsoft drawing within her nest, and even her sweat was precious. Again, Alvah moved inside her, his hands searching gently over the wonder of her body as the reborn part of him probed into the woman-core.

Betty Jean rode with him, rocked beneath him, surprised by this rare tenderness so interwoven by frantic celebration. Her aroused flesh rioted with Alvah Lassiter, even as some part of her sensed the threatening storm and her mind struggled in foamings of guilt and doubt and the warm bubbles of being truly, truly needed.

It was only after he lay softened beside her that she could bring herself into focus. She had been sidetracked so easily, for all her determination, by this hurt man who reeked of trouble and violence. Head pillowed upon his arm, Betty Jean thought she might have seized upon any excuse to avoid turning tricks for rednecks in that cruddy juke joint. So much for dedication, but so long as she could carry on her mission, this was better. She could work there, yassuh the 'fays and suffer their hands upon her, but she'd only have to screw this one while she listened. A protector of sorts would be handy.

"You're mighty handy with your mouth, preacher," Sarah Davison said, "but I wonder how far back you'll be when they start shootin'."

"Sarah," Calvin protested, "Please—"

"Sister," Reverend LaBeaux said, "I am ready for the ultimate sacrifice, but we don't see it coming to that."

"*I'm* not ready to look a shotgun in the mouth," Sarah hissed, "and my child isn't, either. This is Temple County, not the big city, and you've seen the law here. In the city, there's white law and black law, but here it's just Sheriff Kobburn."

Calvin Davison reached for his wife's hand, but she pulled back. "No," she said, "I'm fixin' to have my say, talkin' for me and others with sense enough not to get killed. Don't you all see them watchin' us, *feel* the hate out there? You're so damned starry-eyed you're blind to what can happen, what *will* happen if you don't get out of here and let us lead our own lives, let us *save* our lives."

Davison caught her arm then, drew her back into the chair. "Sarah, Sarah—"

"It's all right, brother," LaBeaux said from the front of the clinic's waiting room. "We have lived with fear for centuries, and it's not easy to come from the dark into the light. But we must move now; we must leave the shadows and face the sun of a new day, for thank the Lord, we are not alone. Sister Davison—you speak of your child; maybe he won't ever have to be afraid."

"No," she said, "because he'll be dead."

Davison stroked her hand and glanced at the local preacher for support, but the Reverend Brown's lined face was thoughtful and he remained silent.

LaBeaux stood tall and straight, his head thrown back. "We are strong, children; we have the strength of the Lord, and I say unto you: we will not retreat, we will not falter, and we shall overcome, because our cause is just."

Just another get-together of burrheads, Sheriff Kobburn thought, but he wasn't sure if that troublemaking city nigger was inside the clinic. He'd have to get on Deputy Franklin for not keeping better tabs on the New Orleans preacher, but ol' C.J. had more than likely been eying the nigger doctor's wench, and a man couldn't hardly fault him for that. That gal was bound to be a fine piece of ass, and there ought to be a way of getting to her.

Sighing, Kobburn eased around in the shadow of a chinaberry tree, and around him, the chirr of locusts went silent until he stood still again. He chewed the butt of a gone-out cigar and wondered if he could make it to the lighted window, then figured the hell with it. Too hot to chase coons tonight, and they'd be easier to pick off one at a time.

He remembered what the county commissioners said about a black sheriff getting elected in Temple County, was all the niggers given a chance to scratch a ballot. The idea made him bite down hard on his cigar; that'd be the sorriest day Mississippi ever saw, since the carpetbaggers came in. Wasn't much difference now—Yankee agitators and outside niggers brought in to stir up trouble and crowd white folks into a corner.

They'd play old billy hell doing that in *his* county. Kobburn leaned against the tree and scratched his belly. The commissioners already had a new jail going up, and he'd talked them into sending clear to Mobile for some mean police dogs. Listening, he heard a woman's voice raised, with fear wrote plain in it. Sarah Davison, he thought, showing a mite of sense. He took the cigar from his mouth and licked his lips.

But hearing her made him somehow think of his daughter off in New Orleans and going to school for typing and such. Hadn't been long, and Jolene wrote sometimes, mostly when she wanted money, and he was happy to oblige. Anything to keep her out of town and spreading her legs for every horny woods runner who looked at her twice. It was a fair wonder she wasn't knocked up yet.

The money didn't bother him none, what with a

steady payoff from Scarpo and a few little side deals with bootleggers, and his deputies wouldn't never miss the ten percent he held out of their paychecks. Them old boys had never had more than a couple of dimes to rattle before he hired them, and they mighta took the jobs for no pay, just to get the chance to bust heads.

Inside the building, they started to sing, and Kobburn grunted in disgust as he moved off. They hollered and clapped and carried on with nigger hymns like they'd get some good out of it. Hallelujah, you black bastards, he said to himself, and figured he ought to start leaning on old Preacher Brown afore long. That one had been a good nigger up to now, knowed his place and stayed in it, but he was mighty nigh to stepping in shit, and Kobburn would let him know.

Down the street and around the corner, the patrol car waited. Climbing into it, Kobburn checked the sawed-off shotgun in its door clamps and grinned. If the coons really started trouble here, he was ready, and it might be a good thing all around—thin out the burrheads some, and maybe get him some more deputies and a radio dispatcher, instead of having to call in all the way up through the state police, like he did now. When he got them mean dogs and cattle prods and some tear gas, wasn't nothing the state troopers could show him about handling his own county. He gunned the car and squealed its tires, pulling away.

From the alley, they watched him pull out, and one of them said softly, "He bird doggin' the preacher right close."

The other shrugged. "Don't make no nevermind; we slip the preacher in and out like we please. Goin' over to Clark County tomorrow, he is."

"Ain't frettin' none on LaBeaux; he take care of hisself, but Brother Brown—"

"Gettin' old, I reckon; not spry like he used to be. Better stay close to him, I 'spect."

"Tabbo," one man said, "you easy in your mind about all this?"

"Easy as I know how. They so used to talkin' around us and through us, don't pay no attention to their maids and yard boys and field hands. Ain't no way we don't know what's happenin' soon as they do."

The other man sighed and scratched a match to a handrolled cigarette. Its light flared briefly around a lined brown face, and the alley was dark again. "That sheriff, he a mean ol' bastard."

"Meaner'n a cottonmouth with a stomped tail," Tabbo agreed, "but like the preacher say, better us ol' knotheads get bit so the younguns don't have to."

"Don't know," the other said and pulled on his cigarette. "Just don't know if we can keep the younguns out of it. I just prayin' we can."

"Amen," Tabbo said. "Amen to that."

The morning was dew-fresh and bright. Reverend LaBeaux spread the road map on his knees as the car rolled west, and followed its progress with a fingertip. He was heavy with a country breakfast and hoped there wouldn't be an equally fattening dinner waiting him in Clark County. He tended more to the Creole custom of coffee and croissants for breakfast, a light seafood dinner, and making up for any lack at supper.

"All Indian names, I suppose," he said to the driver. "Hard on the tongue, brother—Tchufuncta, Hiwannie, now this Bouguefalaya River we have to cross into the next county."

"Never studied on 'em," the driver said. "Growed

up with 'em and just never studied on 'em. 'Nother car goin' to carry you around over yonder?"

"We think it's best," LaBeaux said. "Best, brother, for local blacks and different cars to haul me and the message."

"Reckon," the driver said. "Same thing, keepin' to back roads. This 'un ain't much, but it'll get us to the river bridge."

LaBeaux looked back at his map; Clark County, Jones County, Jasper County, then back to New Orleans. He loved planting these seeds, but it was tiring. He who sowed also had to rest.

"Yonder's the bridge," the driver said. "Big ol' hill past it, then we—"

LaBeaux saw the loaded long truck come barreling down the hill, its trailer heaped with pine logs swaying and threatening to jackknife, a plume of red dust boiling behind.

"Plumb fool," the driver said. "If'n he don't swing it off on the other road—"

LaBeaux felt the rattle of the old wooden bridge beneath them, and knew the light–shadow, light–shadow of its rusted iron framework passing. The oncoming truck didn't attempt the side road, and he saw the red, leering face of its driver through a cracked and dusty windshield. The road map crumpled in his hands when the truck roared onto the bridge, its trailer fishtailing.

"Great God!" cried his driver.

The trailer caught them, sledged their car with a rending of metal and splintering of glass and flipping it sideways. It crashed through a guard rail and whirled over and over before it hit the dank brown waters of the Bouguefalaya River.

BOOK II
1956

CHAPTER 21

She drove one of the trucks, a light pickup whose dusty blue offset her coloring, and although Jessica knew she looked better in an MG with her hair flagged by the wind, she had to make do. So she wore skintight jeans and an open-necked shirt that showed off her tanned throat and gave interesting glimpses of sunbrowned cleft. Her boots were tiny and tailored, and she thought she had just the right casual, touseled look. Her figure was better than ever. Hard work kept her slim and taut, and she had flat out refused to let her breasts sag, feeding that kid.

There were makeup and perfumes in the overnight bag; her two best dresses—one of them a slinky gown—frilly underwear, and a madly sensuous nightie. It should be enough to get the job done; she had no time for extended games.

Had it only been five years since the full weight of The Shadows had fallen upon her shoulders? It seemed longer, for it had been a downhill slide all the way and now she was getting desperate. The house itself needed repairs, roofing, foundations, paint, and plumbing, not any more frivolous restoration. She was a year behind at the feed store, and sure she'd get turned down for seed and fertilizer this spring, unless she paid something.

As if she didn't have enough trouble, the nigger problem was getting bigger all the time, and that stinking pulp mill was drawing off water needed for her own irrigation. All Will Jellico had to offer was lawyer talk about prior rights and such, as if the river didn't belong to everyone, as it always had.

Damn Earl Lassiter and that mill; if he hadn't piddled around with his post machine and talked his daddy into selling off land for the site, none of this would be happening. Thinking on it, she could look back and just about pinpoint the nigger trouble to that time, when old Ben Lassiter and his wench started paying more money for peeler wood, and hiring Dan Mason away from the fields to work for them.

A body would think they'd have more sense, but what could you expect from white trash that lived openly with a nigger wench, and took care of her bastard kid? There'd always been bad blood between her daddy and Ben Lassiter, and she could understand why.

Jessica drove faster toward Gulfport, because thinking of her daddy always brought Sandy into it, Sandy and her squalling brat. Who would think the woman could last so long, pouring down whiskey like it was well water, day after day? Oh, she got sick and stopped eating, and went on crying jags, but whenever Elliot came home, she straightened up and began to look better, act almost human.

Glaring into the windshield, Jessica frowned. Elliot and that woman, one as bitchy as the other; Elliot so goddamned important as a state senator, always running off, not caring about The Shadows or his mother or anything except his selfish career and his parade of prettyboy lovers. *Elliot.*

She forced herself to relax, to think of the secret hold she had on her darling brother. It always made her feel better, even if she wasn't hard up enough to use it on him yet. When she did—Jessica smiled and lifted a hand to her hair.

Maneuvering the pickup through the traffic of Pass Christian, Jessica drove onto the bridge to Gulfport, glancing only briefly at gray salt waters lapping the pilings. Ron Benning had been surprised when she called him, but said sure, sure, he'd be right happy to see her. Of course he would; he'd panted after her long enough back then, and the couple of quickies they'd had had made him think he was the greatest ever. He wasn't any girl's greatest lover, that was sure, but he was eager and obedient as a puppy dog, and his family had money.

That's what the world was patched together with—money; blood lines and tradition and a fine name didn't mean doodly squat anymore, only the cash. Damnit, her daddy's word had been good as gold anywhere in the state, but his word and power got buried with him. They looked on Elliot Coffield as Avery's heir, and said how it was wonderful Elliot was making it up so high on his own; so young, too.

Jessica lost her good mood again. That slick, conniving son of a bitch could do something to help, but every dime he got his soft hands on went right back out for future favors. Goddamn; if he ever got to be governor of the state, he wouldn't even stop there. He'd swish his way right on toward the White House.

Her laugh was bitter. It would do the Yankees good to have a downhome fairy running things up yonder, pay them back for all the dirt they'd done the South. But Elliot had about as much chance of that as a wiggle worm crossing the chicken yard, only nobody would dare tell him so. He was so damned bitchy.

Driving into Gulfport, she turned off the bay highway and angled inland, remembering the way from her college years, going over in her mind what it was she meant to do—beginning with a sultry *Ron, Darling.* . . .

"Hey, ol' man!" the towheaded youngun hollered, skipping back out of reach. "Hey, now—you better watch who you kickin' at! My daddy'll bust you good."

For a second, Ben Lassiter wished he had his gun, then knew it was better he didn't; he'd probably kill two, three of the little bastards. "Go git your daddy," he said. "I wish to hell you would; I wish *all* you little turds'd bring your daddies to me, but I know goddamn well they won't come."

He watched them circling, hissing among themselves like so many greasy little copperheads. If he made another move, they'd be gone lickety-split down some snakehole, and he was too damned old to run them down and stomp on them. Ben said, "Come on here,

Marcie. They ain't goin' to hurt you, not now and not ever."

Big-eyed, sad-eyed, and teary, her new dress with dirt on it, she came shaking to stand in his shadow, and that made him madder at her tormentors. Jesus Christ! And her only eleven years old. He roared at them, "I know you, Willie—you, too, Bart Lovelace! You carry my word to your folks—I hear about you devilin' this girl again, I ain't just goin' to kick *your* asses, I'm comin' for your daddies'. Hear me good now."

Bart went pale and whirled to scuttle off; Willie puckered up like he was going to bawl; another boy Ben didn't know set his jaw and sauntered away in no big hurry. When he got to the bend in the road, he cupped hands around his mouth to holler, "Ain't nobody scared of a *nigger lover!*"

Trembling near bad as Marcie, Ben took her books under one arm and held her hand. That little shitass needed his neck wrung; none of them Lovelaces had ever been worth shooting; nest of goddamn woods runners and bootleggers, cross-breeding among themselves until nobody knowed who was blood kin to who, and didn't give a damn nohow. No more real guts than a tumblebug, none of them, but just the same, next time Ben went to town, he would be toting a pistol. Didn't take guts to gun a man in the back.

Marcie trudged silently beside him, her pigtailed head higher than his elbow now, and he wanted to comfort her, but there wasn't a word of truth to anything he might say. So he said, "They hurt you, girl?"

Face held down, she shook her head. "Thowed dirt on me, is all."

Ben made a rasping sound in his throat. "Didn't do

to use all them bad words in front of you, but it's about all they understand."

"Heard 'em before," she said. "Hear 'em all the time."

They cut through the back of the mill yard and were just about to the far fence when the brightly painted loader came buzzing up and stopped in rolling dust. Big and black, Dan Mason climbed down and nodded to them. "Saw it from back yonder, soon's the school bus let them mean younguns off. Glad you got there, Mr. Lassiter; nothin' I coulda done but holler at 'em. Hey there, Marcie; sorry I was a mite late today."

"Happen more'n once, did it?" Ben asked.

"Most times, she cuts off through the woods and they don't get at her."

Ben let the child's hand go and took out his can of Prince Albert, shook tobacco into creased paper, and offered the can to Mason. The other man said, " 'Preciate it," and rolled his own smoke, then held a match for both cigarettes.

"Go long home now, Marcie," Ben said, and waited until she had crossed the walking bridge before turning to Dan Mason. "She never said, and I figured what with her walkin' from her school and them younguns ridin' from theirs—she never said, Dan."

"Salty lil' gal," Mason said. "Schools bein' apart, whites ridin' and blacks walkin', it don't make no nevermind, Mr. Lassiter; not these days. They got to keep peckin' at her and all the others."

"Hell," Ben said, "ain't none of it her fault."

"They'll peck her head bloody just the same."

"Be damned if'n they will. I'll carry her to school and carry her home."

Mason let slow smoke curl out of his mouth. "Can't do it for every black child."

"Don't mean to do it for *every* one, just my own, and don't wall your eyes at me, Dan Mason. Marcie's as much my youngun as if'n I sired her my ownself."

"Yessuh," Mason said, "and that makes it harder on her, I reckon; she got a lil' help, and they don't cotton to that."

"Son of a bitch," Ben said, "they better cotton to it. *I* ain't one to be settin' fire to crosses, and I ain't carryin' no signs, neither. I'm my own man on my own land, and *both* goddamn sides'll do well to leave me and mine alone."

"Mr. Lassiter," Dan Mason said, pinching out the cigarette spark and scuffing it on the ground with the toe of a workboot, "it don't seem like there's no middle ground no more."

Ben looked across the river at the screen of pines that hid his house. "You know, in my war, Hitler didn't go rollin' into Switzerland like he did them other countries. He coulda took it, but what with the layout of the mountains and every man there ready and able to fight, he'da lost so damned many men and machines he would of come out behind, anyhow. Switzerland stayed neutral."

Mason nodded. "Fact is, you a man by yourself, and yonder ain't no mountain. That lil' gal got to come down every blessed day for school."

"Dan," Ben said, "I'm beholden for what you're sayin', but I don't bother nobody and stand to myself."

He walked across the mill yard and through the little gate; the hanging bridge swayed beneath him as he crossed the Tchufuncta and moved into the pines. It was cooler there in green shade, where years of fallen brown needles made a deep bed.

* * *

Calvin Davison rolled away from his wife. Beside him now, Sarah lay still, the length of her fine body uncovered. She might as well have been a cadaver on a dissecting table. Sitting up, Davison switched on the bedlamp and reached for a cigarette. Sarah stirred and pulled up the quilt.

"You might as well hide it," he said.

"What do you want from me, Calvin?"

Naked back to her, he said, "What we had once—understanding, excitement, giving. Not—this."

Staring at the ceiling, she said, "Understandin' works both ways, like logic. I don't feel the way I did in Chicago; I can't. I'm too scared."

"Oh my God; here we go again. What's really happened here in all this time? A few brawls, legal maneuvering to keep blacks from registering to vote, a lot of bluster. That frightens you out of being a woman?"

"And Reverend LaBeaux?"

"That was a long time ago, Sarah. Besides, state police said it was an accident."

"White police, white accident. His driver was only eighteen years old."

Davison drew on his cigarette, the memory of sleek, whitegold thighs tugging at him, the image of a searing, gasping girl-woman bucking savagely beneath him in a mansion bedroom. "That back road into Clark County has always been bad, and that particular hill—"

"Dead Man's Hill," Sarah said, "for half-drunk rednecks wheelin' beatup old log trucks down it. Damn it, you're talkin' just like Kobburn's parrot."

"And you're talking like an hysterical, obsessed woman. Did I say *woman*?"

She was quiet while he hunched upon the side of the bed, the taste of tobacco dry in his mouth, the taste of her more arid. Then Sarah said, "I'm leavin' you, Calvin, and takin' Peter with me."

Stubbing out his cigarette with a furious twist, he turned to stare down at her. "Sarah, don't you see you're overreacting? Some racial memory, that traumatic childhood experience—"

"And now that Yankee nigger doctor—you know the one keeps his place so good?—now he's suddenly a shrink. Save that jargon for your field-hand patients, *Doctor*. You're damned right I'm obsessed, but with living, with seeing my son grow up."

Sarah jerked up from her pillow, quilt falling from bare breasts. "You think you know whitey, know Mr. Charley? Like hell you do; they put up with you because you're handy for emergencies until they can get a white doctor in here."

"One's on the way; young one just finished interning at Charity Hospital in New Orleans. It'll take him fifty years to replace old Doc Christopher."

"And a thousand years for them to accept us as people, as human beings. I'm still leavin' you."

"One step at a time," Davison said. "They've allowed a few to register, tame ones, but it's a start. And Sarah—I won't let you go, not with Peter."

"You can't stop me."

"I can," he said, "and I will." He lurched off the bed and into the kitchen for the bottle of scotch. Hell of a thing, he thought, drinking this late at night when he faced an early morning.

Sitting at the breakfast bar, he thought of ways to stop her, of what life would be like without his son. Peter was a good boy, solid and intelligent, perhaps bright enough for medical school, if his mother didn't cripple his ambition with her paranoia. He wondered if she would accept sending Peter off to boarding

school in the North. He wasn't rich, but with the overflow of black patients and their slowly rising wages, he
could afford a good school, and he had to admit Peter
was too sharp for the second-rate education the boy
was getting down here.

Damnit; why couldn't Sarah understand that what
he was doing was vitally important, that this horde of
suffering, ignored, inarticulate people *needed* him? At
first she'd seemed to grasp it, had helped out at the
clinic. Now she hid in the house and went out only to
hover protectively around the boy.

If Sarah would agree to the schooling, maybe it
wouldn't be right to keep her behind, but better if she
didn't smother the kid for a while. Later, if she still
felt the need, she could make frequent visits, or even
move up to be near him. But Davison had a hunch
she'd never come back, that she'd twist the boy into
her own fearful mold. For the good of all concerned,
she should stay a while longer in Temple County.

"Temple County," Ira Lowenstein repeated.
"That's where you came from, remember? I know it's
been a long time, but what was that cliché about taking a boy out of the country?"

"You surprised me, that's all," Earl said. "There's
that project in New Hampshire, and the Canadian
franchise for post peelers—"

Ira leaned back in a leather chair. "You're needed
down there, and nobody else is so eminently quali-
fied."

"The mill is a top producer," Earl said, wondering
why he didn't feel any thrill of anticipation.

"It may not be, if things continue like this. The people in the penthouse feel it's time you flew home and
took over the mill."

"As an engineer-administrator, or a politician?"

Ira smiled. "All that and pourer of oil upon troubled waters, too. Oily, politician—a redundancy?"

Propping elbows upon his desk, Earl said, "I get a duty call from Pa now and then, letters from Ellen. She mentions my brother, but Pa doesn't. I think I'd like to see Alvah, and—" He changed the subject. "Of course, I go as a team captain?"

"Some of the staff will remain, part will be transferred, and yes—you'll have a few specialists from the home office. I should think you'd be happy to get back to hog jowls and grits; a few more years hanging around the kosher deli, and we'd have a convert."

Earl grinned back at his friend. "Never get this old country *goy* to handle Yiddish. Took me long enough to speak Yankee without an interpreter."

"Oi vey," Ira said, rolling his eyes. "Old country *goy*? That's terrible, Earl." Sobering then, he leaned forward. "Anything you want, everything you need, within reason. This Mississippi beachhead is important, and there's a large investment involved. Whatever you have to do, to keep the mill rolling, to hold on to our contracts."

"I figured that, and since I hold most individual shares of the stock, it's important to me, too."

"That kind of *chutzpah*, I didn't have to teach you," Ira said. "They're still flinching upstairs at the deal you demanded when the company needed another few acres."

"And the water rights," Earl reminded, *"and* the tree-puller patents; considering it is a package deal, I wasn't out of line."

"Just out on a limb. Victor Quinn might have sawed it off."

Earl opened the middle drawer of his desk. "Then

I'd have gone home a long time back—to start my own company."

"What else?" Ira said. "Look, do you want anybody special with you?"

Glancing at the outer office door, Earl said, "Someone like Miss Farelli, or Cam or Stacey or Monica or any of those other cute names? I've forgotten most of them, Ira. They all did their lovely bit in punching my computer tapes, and in a way, I suppose I'm grateful to them. But no; I'll do my own programing from here on. I'm certain Francesca Farelli will have a new executive in here, and in my apartment, within days."

"Hours," Ira said, "if it matters."

"It doesn't. A place and a time, you said; to which I add—and a cause."

"You'll find one again, Earl."

Earl began sifting papers, stacking some atop the desk. "If it matters. Do I know the people going with me?"

"All but one, I think." Ira ran through a short list of names, then added, "There's Barbara Dexter; Ph.D. in political science, minors in psychology and sociology. A brain; high school in three years, a B.A. the same, then onward and upward."

"My watchdog."

"*Dog* doesn't fit Miss Dexter in any category. Earl—" Ira looked down, then up. "I'll miss you, I really will."

"And you, Ira," Earl said, "and Brenda, *and* her cooking."

"Like a younger brother," Ira said. "Not a protégé or points made upstairs because you worked out so well, but like my own family."

Yes, Earl said, and thank you, and cut it short because goodbyes still hurt a little and he owed so damned much to Ira Lowenstein. And to the man's choice in women? Buzzing for Francesca, Earl gave her instructions, picked up his briefcase, kissed her lightly, and headed for his apartment to pack.

A younger brother, Ira had said. And there was this maimed older brother Earl Lassiter hadn't seen in so many years. He wondered if Alvah cared.

CHAPTER 22

Fumbling, trying not to make noise, Sandy made it halfway across the living room in the dark before lights came on and struck at her. She put a hand to her eyes and swayed.

"Look at you," Lila Coffield said. "Just *look* at you, a complete mess."

Sandy blinked and groped for the stair rail for support. She dropped one shoe and almost lost her balance when she picked it up. "Lila, I—I'm just going to bed; please—"

"Where," Lila said, approaching like an avenging conscience, "is your skirt?"

"Skirt? I d-don't know—must have dropped it. Got-got my slip on, though." Shoving herself up the stairs, gone dizzy and with her eyes blurring, Sandy tried to leave it all behind her, the confused night, that somewhere motel, and especially Lila.

But the other woman followed her all the way to her suite, a vulture hovering in a black robe, ready to peck at Sandy's eyes and strip the meat from her bones. "Where have you been, out draggin' the Coffield name in the mud again?"

Dropping onto the bed, Sandy tried to hold onto the world so she wouldn't fall off. "Let me alone, Lila."

"I never thought I would see the day," Lila said,

"when anyone from The Shadows would be out actin'
like a common tramp. My son's wife—"

"Wife," Sandy said bitterly, "*wife;* that'd be funny,
if it wasn't so damned sickening. I've never been a wife
to Elliot."

Lila pursed her lips, crossed her arms over a shrunk-
en bosom. "Even if it's in name only, and lord knows,
no man in his right mind would go to bed with a
drunken woman who conducts herself as you do; no
decent man, anyhow—but you should have at least a
shred of decency left. Think of your child, of Elliot."

Sandy didn't catch all of it. She was too smashed.
She couldn't even remember the name of the man
who'd taken her to the motel, couldn't recall his face.
She knew only that he was a man and she had needed
him, needed someone. How had she driven home?

"Man," she mumbled, "a man. I don't give a damn
if he's decent, just that he's male. Elliot wouldn't
know about that, and maybe you wouldn't, either."
But Sandy thought of Avery Coffield and how he had
bedded this juiceless woman. She started to cry, big,
fat tears that rolled soundlessly down her cheeks. "Oh
Christ, I miss being loved."

Fluttering her black wings, Lila circled the bed.
"Love? What would a woman like you know about
love and respect? You're only concerned with animal
lust."

"Go away," Sandy muttered, putting her face into
her hands.

"Lust," Lila intoned, "wanton debauchery; I won't
have such perversion in my house!"

Sandy dropped her hands and focused hazily upon
the woman's contorted face. "Perversion? You want to
hear about perversion and deviation, Mrs. Coffield?
What are you, blind to the sweet, pretty men your fag

son brings home? Do you think they're really campaign assistants? Would you like to know what they do to each other?"

"You just hush up!" Lila said fiercely. "You're a wicked, sinful slut. Don't you dare put that corrupt mouth to my son's good name. You're unfit to be a Coffield, a wife, or a mother."

Sandy's tears kept flowing into the corners of her mouth. "My—my baby; my poor little baby boy. Gonna go to him, take him outa this lousy, spook-filled house. Thomas Elliot—gonna find him and take him—"

Lila's spiteful laugh was a cackle. "You can't even get off the bed, you drunken bitch, you cheap, whorin' bitch. And you'll never, *never* get your hands on my grandson. I mean to see to that, if it takes my dyin' breath."

By the time Sandy got her eyes cleared, Lila was gone. She went off the bed to her knees, tried to stagger up, and crawled to the bathroom. Holding to the toilet, she retched until she was so weak her head rolled loosely on her neck. Sinking back, she put her cheek against cool floor tile and curled slowly into a miserable ball. There was the taste of blood in her mouth, and she was so sick.

"Of course, I'm tired of putting on this redneck accent," Elliot said to his secretary, "but in Temple County it's vital to the packaging, Mark. You should understand that."

Mark Manley brushed at Elliot's sleeve, reached lightly to straighten his tie. "I understand; it just bothers me to hear you sounding like an ignorant hillbilly."

Patting the man's cheek, Elliot moved away, picked

up his briefcase. "I think you're bothered because of Toby, but you shouldn't be."

Sighing, Mark said, "I suppose I ought to be used to it by now. I keep telling myself you need these passing fancies, but you'll always come home to me."

"I always have," Elliot said. "Do you have the memos?"

"Right here, but what if they bring up your wife? It's becoming common knowledge, you know."

Opening the hotel-room door and stepping out into the hall, Elliot said, "You still haven't grasped our back country ways. One of the things never mentioned to a man is what his wife does, unless it's very good— and I *don't* mean how good a lay she is."

Mark followed him to the elevator. "Still, I'm afraid she's becoming more liability than asset."

"That's what my mother says. She's been on my back about Sandy's latest disgraceful episode, and she may be right. I don't care how many horny clods she picks up, but she isn't discreet, and her affairs are getting too close to home."

They got into the elevator and Mark pushed the "Down" button. Elliot said, "She'll have to be hospitalized for some exotic illness, and be certain the staff never mentions a sanitarium. Also, I want total legal control over Thomas Elliot; set the wheels in motion, today. It shouldn't be difficult to have her declared incapable or unfit. But again, use our friends in the press to keep it quiet."

At the lobby, Mark waited until Elliot stepped out, smiling and nodding to everyone in the state capitol building. He walked a step behind, marveling at the names Elliot remembered, the homey little touches with doorman and taxi starter. When Elliot talked with the little people, or in public, he was hearty and outgoing, his speech coarsened, heavily larded with downhome euphemisms that caused Mark to shudder inwardly.

On the way to the airport, Mark said, low-voiced, "This secret meeting with that fellow Scarpo—"

"To fatten the piggy bank," Elliot answered. "That's after I soothe the Temple County commissioners, promise them their sacred status quo, tut-tut about registry of nigras and convince them to keep the token voters. If there's any real violence down there, it could mean federal troops, and we don't want that. But neither do we want unbridled registering of blacks; there are just too many of them. The happy medium, Mark dear; the compromise."

"I don't understand about this Scarpo. He's already contributing quite a bit."

"And he'll kick in with more," Elliot said. "He has a good thing going. It would be simple for me to shut him down, and he knows it."

"That could weaken your power base with the commissioners, since he's paying them also—and that Neanderthal sheriff."

"Plenty to go around," Elliot assured him, "and you know very well it takes a tremendous amount of money to lay the groundwork for a place on the ticket as lieutenant governor. Then there's the pulp mill; ah yes—the pulp mill; I've been saving it until it turned ripe, and I think it's ready to be picked."

When the cab stopped, he left payment and the baggage to Mark, and was happy to chat with the ticket clerk, to exchange toothpaste smiles with a stewardess. On the plane, he closed his eyes and thought about the mill; so many regulations he could put against it, so much red tape and restriction, and they had to pay off to avoid all that. Or pack up and get out of the state. And really, those people had nowhere else to go.

She had nowhere else to go, and she was hurting. She ached from the beating her pimp had given her, although it was two or three days ago, but the other pain was worse. Jolene Kobburn dug into her purse and used Kleenex to wipe at her nose. She still had two bags hidden in the purse lining with her kit, but they were the last, and she didn't know when she'd find another connection. So she had to tough it out awhile longer.

He was home because the patrol car was in the driveway. Jolene chewed gum rapidly, sucking out its sweetness, even if the movement made her jaws ache. Jimmy Lee shouldn't't'a beat her up like that; all she'd held out on him was enough for a couple of bags, and she had that much coming from her daddy's check. Jolene tugged at her dress and went across the screen porch to tap lightly on the door. At her daddy's "Yeah?" her belly went all tight and jumpy, but she walked inside, anyway.

He was on the sagging couch, sock feet propped on the coffee table, belly hanging over his pants and out of a stained undershirt. The TV was on, and a fan moved warm air around the room. Sheriff Kobburn had a can of beer in one hairy hand and a cigar in his mouth.

"Goddamn," he said, "if it ain't the bad penny."

Jolene looked at her feet. "I—I come home for a spell, Daddy."

"In the middle of school?" Kobburn took a drink of beer. "Like you been five years to school."

"Well," she said, and put down her cheap cardboard suitcase.

Kobburn grunted. "Can you type a single goddamn line?"

"I tried," Jolene said. "I really t-tried."

"Sure you did, but it's a whole lot easier spreadin' your legs. Figured that wasn't no typewriter whupped up on you."

Dabbing at her nose with a Kleenex, Jolene said, "I could keep house for you."

"Shit," he said. "You and your ma put together couldn't keep nothin' but a whorehouse, and I ain't sure about that. You'd go broke givin' it away for free."

Jolene sniffed and scratched one arm and tried to look at him, but her eyes slid away. "I just don't have no place else."

Kobburn flung his empty beer can across the room and Jolene flinched at its crash. He said, "I 'spect you better hunt you one, then; crawl under a goddamn log or somethin'. Give you and your ma a roof over your head and clothes on your back, put food into your mouth, and what the hell did it get me? Go on, you bitch; shag-ass outa here just like she done. I don't want you in my house or in my county, hear me?"

Picking up her suitcase, Jolene turned and shuffled through the screen door. It bumped behind her and she stood uncertainly on the porch, then walked slowly to the street and up the block. Crossing over, she walked another block, changing hands with suitcase and purse until she got to Bubba Smith's gas station.

His goldtoothed grin was unshaven as he wiped greasy hands on a rag. "Hey, Jolene; when'd you get back?"

She straightened up and fluffed at her hair. "Do me a favor, Bubba."

"Sure, honey—long's you do me one back. We missed you around here, and that's a fact."

"Carry me out to Beevo's?"

"Clear out yonder? Look, you want a drink, I got some corn mixes right good with a cold dope."

"Reckon I can use some of that," Jolene said, going past the pumps and into the office with a provocative roll of her hips. Inside, she stood close to the man, her breasts touching him. "And I reckon you can use some of this. We had us some high old times, Bubba."

He pinched one nipple and grinned around her to paw in the Coca Cola chest. "Damned if'n we didn't. Guess I can get ol' Estis to hold down the station 'til I come back."

She stood waiting until he ducked into the back and sneaked corn whiskey into their bottles. Jolene drank greedily, welcoming the bite of the stuff, hoping it would do her some good but all the time knowing better.

"Hey, Jolene," Bubba said, "looks like your daddy didn't 'zactly welcome you back to town."

"You got some more of this stumpjuice? You mean these here bruises? Yeah, I guess you could say the sheriff tried to hurt me some, but he didn't reach where it counts." She touched herself low on the belly, made a slow circle over her mound with a fingertip.

"Whooie!" Bubba said. "*I* kin sure as hell reach it. Hold on while I call ol' Estis and get the bottle. Tote your stuff over to my pickup, and pretty soon— whooie!—be just like old times."

Jolene put her suitcase in the pickup bed, climbed into its cab, and held her knees together, fingers digging into her purse handle. She took her lower lip between her teeth to stop it from trembling.

* * *

He'd actually trembled, Jessica Coffield thought, or maybe it was more of a flinch. It was hard to tell on Ron Benning, with his new layer of fat. And *she* was the one who should be flinching, or kicking on the parquet floor while she squalled out her frustration.

But her smile was guileless as she touched hands ever so briefly with Mrs. Ron Benning. "Victoria," she said, "how nice to meet you. Ron should have told me."

"Yes," Victoria said, small eyes wary behind gold-rimmed glasses, "I thought he'd sent invitations to all his old friends."

Jessica tossed her head and laughed. "It's been so long, I imagine Ron forgot me."

He moved uneasily to the bar in the huge, shadowed living room. In another few years, he would waddle, Jessica thought, if the vulture he'd married didn't devour him before then. Clearing his throat, Ron said, "Drinks all around, I reckon?"

"Darling," Victoria said, "you know I never indulge in the middle of the day."

Adam Benning's hearty voice boomed across the room. "Damned if I don't; indulge every chance I get." He turned to his son. "Make 'em big 'uns, Ronnie boy, while I try to figure out how you could forget such a beautiful young lady. Hell, I only met her once when you brought her home on spring vacation, but I knew her the second she walked in."

Victoria swiveled her head. "Brought her here?"

"Quick visit, hon," Ron said quickly. "We were in the same class, and her brother—good ol' Elliot—"

Jessica took her drink. "Good ol' Elliot said stop by to see you when I'm in Gulfport. He's gettin' to be a power in the state, you know." Turning her head slightly, she winked at Adam Benning over the rim of her glass.

"Glad he did, right glad he did," Adam Benning said. "Been hearin' good things about young Coffield; yessir, good things. Got his finger on the pulse of the public. Just got himself another vote, if you got time to stay to dinner."

Victoria said, "Ron, dear; you *do* remember the Hamiltons. Sorry, Daddy Benning, but we do have a previous engagement."

All bones and brass, Jessica thought; the woman carried a stinger that made Ron hop when she said frog. "I'll make time, Mr. Benning," she said, "just so you won't be lonesome."

He cocked a bushy gray eyebrow at her. "Elliot Coffield would be a heap smarter if he put you on the platform with him."

"Daddy Benning," Victoria said.

"Yeah, Vicky, yeah; have fun with the Hamiltons, y'hear?"

Ron emptied his glass and said, "Come on, honey. Ah, Jessica—it was sure good seein' you again."

"Congratulations," Jessica said, and twinkled secretly at Adam.

Victoria said, "Miss Coffield, Daddy Benning; oh come *on*, Ronnie."

The big door banged, and Adam Benning said, "Freshen that up a mite?"

Jessica said, "Daddy—*Daddy* Benning?"

He laughed with her. "Never did cotton to that woman, and I just marked down Ron as a damned fool twice over."

Tasting her new drink, Jessica stretched her legs and watched his eyes follow them. She said, "There was never anything serious between us. Mr. Benning—

Adam—if you feel kind of compromised by my stayin' for dinner, well—"

"Vicky put an edge on her knife soon as she laid eyes on you, and honed it some more when I asked. Hell with her. If an old widower like me can't ask a girl young enough to be his daughter to dinner—"

"I wouldn't say old," Jessica said, arching her back a little. "Distinguished would be a better word. How long ago did your wife pass away?"

"Ten long years," Adam said, "but come to think on it, Wanda reminded me a whole lot of Vicky."

"And you've lived here in this big house all by yourself."

His wink was conspiratorial. "Not exactly alone *all* the time."

Tossing down the rest of her highball, Jessica stood up and stretched like a cat, smoothly and lithely. "If I could freshen up a little bit?"

"Sure, sure," Adam said. "I'll have the maid show you where, and tell cook to make dinner somethin' real, *real* special."

A big bluff man, but without the strength of her own daddy, she thought; not as good-looking, either. But this house was almost big as The Shadows, and right on the edge of town. She ran both hands over her hips and peered at him through her lashes. "You've already made this a special day, Adam."

CHAPTER 23

Calvin Davison had the big coffeepot on, and the clinic waiting room was filled with expectant black faces. Reverend Brown was there, uncomfortable as usual, but Sarah Davison wasn't. There were a couple of men he'd never seen in town, strangers who were letting their hair frizz out. And there was Betty Jean.

It was difficult not to watch that woman, because she had a glow about her, a shining quality beyond her obvious sensual beauty. Her skin was the lightest in the room, but there was no denying her blackness. The strangers lounged beside her on folding chairs, casually arrogant, sure of themselves. They were young, Davison thought, with a new wisdom in their hard eyes.

Reverend Brown stood up behind the coffee table and rapped diffidently for attention. When the buzz of conversation stopped, he said, "Well now, brothers and sisters, we'll open this meetin' with a prayer, and—"

One of the strangers stood up, too. "Just pass on that shit, preacher; let's get to the point."

Brown blinked and rubbed his chin. "Well now, brother, it's been customary for us to—"

"You uncles don't even know what *brother* means," the newcomer said. "And you're doing just what the 'fays want—praying for help instead of getting it on to help yourself. It's *doing* time, old man, and anybody waits around for a white angel to come swinging a sword against white men is a fool."

The reverend frowned. "Who are you, young man?"

"Call me Zip, and my brother here is Abe, which ain't our white Christian names, but they'll do. Before you start in singing 'The Blood of the Lamb,' lemme introduce a real sister—Betty Jean."

"Now wait a minute," Brown said. "Nobody knows you all, but I can smell trouble on you, boy, and that woman—"

"Boy?" Zip said, hands braced on narrow hips. "Boy? Hell, you even use Mr. Charley's words. Back off, uncle, and listen to our sister. You're about to learn something."

Brown looked for help to Davison, but Davison was watching the girl.

"First," Betty Jean said clearly, "we mean to stop any finking. The 'fays don't know what's happenin' unless some fink tells them, so if there's any Oreo here, anybody who's black on the outside, white inside, he'd do well to split right now, because it's goin' to be rough on him when we find out—and we *will* find out."

"Now look here," the preacher said, "you all don't come from around here, and nobody give you the right to mess in our business."

"This is *every* black's business," Betty Jean said, "and that's why we're here, as a cadre to get things rollin'. What have you done since Reverend LaBeaux was murdered, except pull in your necks? You allowed a dedicated man to go down, without a struggle to honor his memory."

"We got some folks registered," Brown muttered.

"Token niggers," Betty Jean said scornfully. "Tame

niggers that'll mark ballots like they're told. If there's to be any power, any justice in Temple County, every eligible voter has to be able to go to the polls."

"They ain't goin' to allow that," Brown said.

"We'll make them," Betty Jean answered, "force them."

The preacher shook his head. "You're talkin' big trouble, bad trouble that these folks don't need or want. You can light outa here when it starts, but *we* got to live here."

"Trouble will bring troops," she said, "and that's what we want, to take the so-called law out of that sheriff's hands. When enough blacks register and vote, we can put in our own officials, get some dignity and justice."

"You keep on sayin' *we*," Brown said, sweating now. "I'm talkin' about *us,* not you. I heard where you live, what you do. Can't no daughter of Babylon tell good folks what to do."

Zip and Abe moved together, a quick coiling, but Betty Jean stopped them with a motion of her hand. "Old man," she said, "in your eyes I'm a sinner. In my eyes, *you're* the biggest sinner, because I'm only sellin' my body for a cause; you're sellin' out your entire race. And your cause won't stack up next to mine. All you want is no trouble, so you can stand up there in the pulpit and have all the brothers look up to you. What you want is to go on kissin' the white man's ass so he won't kick yours."

"Right on," Zip said.

"Yes," Betty Jean said, "I came to do a job, and the best way I can do it is listen in on the 'fays, find out their plans, and the best place to do that is around their whorehouse. Yes, I live with one 'fay so I don't have to screw a hundred of them. And I can tell you every damned move they're goin' to make; I can tell you they're runnin' scared, because they can see the handwriting on the wall."

She paused for breath, and Davison thought, My God, how magnificent she is. She said then, "We have a white lawyer comin' out from the Coast soon, and a black lawyer drivin' in from Jackson. Abe here is a damned good photographer with press credentials, and there'll be more help. A certain man—"

Betty Jean let that hang, and Davison said, surprising himself, "The photographer means you're expecting violence, and want it in the press."

Luminous, oblique eyes fell on him, searched him. "That's right, Doctor. Violence is inevitable, and we use it, *use* it against them by spreading pictures in every liberal paper, hit the magazines and television. Then we get federal troops."

"You'd start trouble, to get that kind of publicity?"

Her eyes were attaching themselves to his soul as Betty Jean said softly, "If we have to."

Jessica meant to make this night a fantastic one for Adam Benning, one he would never be able to wipe from his mind or cleanse from his blood. At dinner he had ogled her cleavage, for she'd worn the sexy gown and leaned forward often, hanging on to his words of wisdom about the construction business. It had made him money before he retired—ha, ha, very young, of course.

Of course, she purred, and gave him a brush of thigh, a whiff of perfume, and told him what a smooth dancer he was. Adam Benning smoked very expensive cigars and drank excellent bourbon; his dead wife had filled the mansion with good antiques. He would feel right at home in The Shadows, she thought.

But when he reached for her, Jessica said, "The servants, Adam."

His face was red. "They don't live in."

"You're so wise," she said. "Sit back, darlin'—right there on the settee; that's right. Now be a good boy, be patient; let little Jessica do it all for you."

With that, she stood away from him and slowly, tantalizingly, peeled the gown over her head to show him she wore nothing beneath it, that she was nude but for net nylon stockings and spikeheeled shoes. Swaying from side to side, she teased hands over her body, cupping and presenting her breasts to him, rolling her hips and trembling the flatness of her smooth belly.

"Goddamn," Adam Benning breathed. "Never saw nothin' like that before."

Dipping gracefully to her knees before him, Jessica began to undress him, exciting herself when she saw he wasn't all that flabby. Twirling fingers into the gray-black matting of his chest, she nipped his throat, busied her other hand at his pants. When she had him stripped, Jessica pushed him back upon the couch and climbed above him, knees spread, rubbing and sweetly torturing him.

When he pawed up for her, she plunged over him, took him fiercely into her body and tried to devour him. Then Jessica forced herself to slow, to become loving with every tick-tock of her hips, each seesawing of her pelvis. Adam came violently, moaning because she had ringed his hairy nipple with sharp teeth, and she continued to work at him until he softened.

Face paled and breathing heavily, he lay drained upon his back. But when she slipped to the carpet again, Adam's eyelids fluttered and he rolled grunting

upon his side. Delicately, passionately, she brought
him back to life, using all she knew to make him more
of a man than he had ever been. He got a hand into
her flowing hair and groaned. Jessica closed her eyes.

Migod, migod, Adam Benning thought dizzily; no
white woman had ever done anything like this to him.
She was so fiery, so beautiful, and young, young. The
taste of her was caught in his throat, and the slick feel
of her burned into every pore; migod—she was melting
his backbone, drawing it out of him, exploding it out
of him—

And when he could see again, she was watching him
with the damnedest look in those green eyes. "Daddy,"
she murmured, "Daddy Benning."

"Sounds different when you say it," he sighed.
"Damn; I might as well stay right here the rest of the
night, because I ain't sure I can climb the stairs to
bed."

Jessica petted him, stroked him, spread the silken
netting of her hair across his stomach. "You're very
strong, Adam. You can do anything you want to, everything you want to—especially with me."

Forcing himself to one elbow, he stared down at her
beauty. "You—you don't have to go right back home,
do you?"

"I'll stay as long as you want me," she said against
his groin, and thought, just as long as it takes.

What would it take, Ben Lassiter wondered, to
show this bunch of goddamn knotheads what they
were doing? It was early in the night, but half the
Templars were already mean drunk, and the other
half just plain mean.

He didn't come in here often, but it was about the
only place he could pen up most of them together.

There was banker Harvey, and Martin Nelson and Burr Watson; along with Will Jellico, they were the big dogs in the county. That Coffield kid was bigger, but he wasn't around much anymore. And old beer-belly Kobburn himself, with one of his white-trash deputies.

There'd been a time when only them with money would gather in the club, when hard-dirt farmers were barred. Now the doors were open to damned near anybody, and that wasn't a good sign. Storekeepers and such had something to lose, did they think on it; them others didn't.

Picking up his beer, he moved along the bar next to Sam Harvey. "Hey, Sam."

"Hey, Ben." And no more; no how you doing, how's the mill coming, none of that, just a stretched-out waiting that Ben sensed.

Ben said, "Might try to talk some sense into this bunch, Sam; they go to burnin' crosses and such, the county'll be a mess."

Sam Harvey polished his glasses with a white handkerchief. "Folks around here think for themselves, Ben; you know that."

"Most don't think a'tall, and *you* know that."

Jukebox music thumped loud around them, and voices babbled hoarsely; back in the corner of the room, somebody let loose with a Rebel yell. Sam Harvey said, "Seems like you kind of lost touch with your own kind, Ben."

Feeling the anger rising, Ben cooled it with a swallow of beer. Martin Nelson came up on the other side of him, and started talking to Sam across him, like Ben Lassiter wasn't there.

He pulled out from between them and carried his glass over to where Will Jellico was talking to a couple of raggedy pulpwood cutters with the smell of resin still on them. When Will saw him coming, he put his back to Ben.

Ben put down his glass and went to the jukebox to yank its plug. They looked at him then, tight, closed-up faces staring at him like he was a stranger, like him and his family hadn't settled this goddamned part of the country.

He said, "Any man can't see changes comin' is a damned fool; you try to stop 'em, and you won't be no more'n crawdads rarin' up at a railroad train. You mule-headed sons of bitches do what you want, then—but I'm tellin' you plain—don't be doin' it to me and mine."

Walking slow and proud, he was halfway to the door when Billy Dee Blake said from behind the bar, "Reckon when a man hunkers down with a bitch dog, he's bound to come up with fleas."

Ben stiffened, but kept on walking, needing to get outside into air he could breathe. And Billy Dee Blake said, "Might cause him to lose his balls, too."

In the foyer, Ben stopped and reached up for the framed news clippings calling him hero, for the fancy scrolls that said how proud Temple County was of their native son. He tore them from the walls and smashed them against the floor in a splintering of glass and a spray of wooden splinters. Then he went out into the street and turned blindly down the sidewalk.

That's where they caught him because he wasn't paying attention. Something hard slammed alongside his head and drove him into the brick wall; somebody kicked him in the back and knocked him to his knees.

There was fog in his head, and he barely heard somebody holler that he was a nigger-loving son of a

bitch. Instinct made him roll to keep from getting
stomped, and he pawed out to catch an ankle and jerk
it. Blows landed on him as the man fell, kicks and fists
and a stick.

"Not too much!" somebody snorted. "Just enough to
let the bastard know he better shut that fuckin' mill,
and not open it 'til the niggers get some sense. You
hear me, Lassiter? Tell your niggers they ain't gettin'
no paychecks 'til they stop wantin' to vote. You hear
me, you goddamn nigger lover?"

The Lovelaces, Ben thought; some of those wildass
freejacks from across the river. They'd been laying for
him since he kicked one of their younguns in the ass
for tormenting Marcie.

"Shake him," one of them said. "Piss on him to
wake him up and be sure he gets the message."

He was sitting against the wall, tasting blood in his
mouth, his head ringing like a cowbell. They slapped
his face and one got him by the jaws, shaking his head,
bumping it against the bricks.

Ben snapped his face around and locked his teeth
into a thick thumb, grinding down hard as the man
squalled like a stuck hog and tried to pull loose. It
gave Ben time to put a hand into his shirt for his pistol, and he unclamped his teeth as the man he bit stag-
gered back and tried to kick Ben's head off.

The .45 bucked in his fist, loud as the cannon in the
square they shot off on the Fourth of July.

"Oh shit!" one of the Lovelaces hollered, and a
flung bottle shattered against the wall next to Ben's
head.

He got to one knee and wiped blood out of his eyes.
They were scattering like a covey of spooked quail,
but he drew down on the nearest running man and cut
a leg out from under him. The son of a bitch wiggled

around in the middle of the street like a snake with a
broken back, hollering and carrying on.

Ben propped his back against the wall and got to his
feet, the big automatic locked steady in his right hand.
He was standing like that when the doors of the Templar Club flung open and men came yelling outside,
only to fan out when they saw him and the downed
Lovelace. They scattered themselves wide, then stood
still.

Sheriff Kobburn and Deputy Travers hesitated. Nobody moved toward the wounded man. Then Kobburn hitched up his gunbelt and took a couple of easy
steps toward Ben. "Ben—"

"That's far enough," Ben said. "Five, six of them
Lovelaces jumped me, and I ain't killed one of 'em—
yet. That ain't sayin' I won't, or any other son of a
bitch lays hand to me."

"Now look here, Ben—" Kobburn was careful to
keep his hands away from his sides.

"*You* look," Ben said loud through split lips. "You
ain't takin' my gun for defendin' myself. I'm goin'
home to my own land, to my boy's mill, and so help
me God, any belly-crawlin' bastard so much as sets
foot on Lassiter land is goin' to get hisself buried
there. You bunch of pot-lickin' hound dogs hear that?
You, Sam Harvey? You, Martin Nelson, Will Jellico,
Burr Watson? You bigod *better* hear me good, because
if I have to kill one of your hired hands, I'm acomin'
for you next. And you, Sheriff—you pus-gutted sack of
hogshit, don't even let me lay eyes on *you* again."

CHAPTER 24

Betty Jean opened beer for them both. "Can't understand why you're so pissed. I mean, you don't ever see or talk to your old man, but you've been primed for trouble since you heard about him gettin' whipped in town."

Alvah swallowed half his beer at a gulp, and moved his stump to an easier position on the pillow. "He didn't get whipped; take more'n five Lovelaces to do that. But the idea of them goddamn freejacks gangin' up on him—"

"Freejacks," Betty Jean said.

"Oh hell, I ain't meanin' *you*. Lovelaces would be just as sneakin' mean was they lily white. Didn't mean you that time, either."

"Just mixed bloods in general, right?"

Finishing his beer, Alvah reached for a smoke. "Get off my back, Betty Jean. Some things just slip out of a man account of habit, because of how he was raised. I don't give a good goddamn who mixes with who, long's they don't stomp on *my* toes. I'm here with you, and that oughta prove somethin'."

She moved across the room with that particular feline grace. "Only that you needed a black woman to make you a man again. Why not a white woman, Alvah?"

"Shit," he said, "your skin's whiter'n mine, and I don't know why I couldn't make it with anybody else, at first. The shrinks didn't know, so how the hell am I supposed to? I know you're too damned educated to be a whore, and I know you've been on my ass for weeks. You lookin' to find another home, move across the way to one of them cribs?"

"When I am," she said, "*if* I am, I'll tell you."

Pulling on his cigarette, Alvah said, "I'm pissed because they jumped my pa, and it don't make a difference if we don't see eye to eye. Thing is, he's my close blood, and maybe that's somethin' nobody who ain't from a place like Temple County can understand."

"I think you're just lookin' for an excuse," Betty Jean murmured. "You never got over playin' soldier boy."

"Marine, damnit! *Marine*." He stared at her bared breasts, the golden shine of her. "It was a heap better than runnin' alky, a better job than whorin'. Takes a special kind to be a good Marine."

She tugged a half slip over her slim hips, long legs flashing. "Takes somebody with a taste for blood, but then, Korea was a white man's war, against colored people."

He sat up straight. "What the hell you talkin' about? You callin' gooks colored? That's the damnedest thing I ever heard, and if you think we didn't have black Marines—listen; I'll tell you about a black Marine saved my ass. He was one of the best, you hear me, the *best*. That hardnosed spade son of a bitch killed gooks better'n anybody in the outfit, and if you was to tell *him* he was fightin' some kind of race war, and on the wrong side, he'd've kicked your ass right up between your ears."

"Maybe he was just a handy Uncle Tom," she said, "a good Oreo."

Alvah swung his stump off the bed. "Don't put your mouth on Lou that way. Don't ever put your mouth on him like that. He was his own man and a damned good one."

"Because he happened to save your life?"

"Because he was *Lou,* goddamnit! I loved that spade bastard better'n my own brother."

"But he was always a spade bastard, a *spade* son of a bitch."

Slamming his fist against the bed, Alvah said, "All your fancy education ain't taught you shit about men. To him, I was a redneck bastard, a 'fay son of a bitch, but couldn't nobody else call us that. We cared about each other."

Betty Jean pulled on a silky blouse that outlined her breasts. "And the war's over for both of you, and you care in retrospect, but it's all over. Did you ever write him, try to call him when you got back?"

Alvah hesitated. "I didn't write because I was scared to get my letter back, scared to know he got killed in some stinkin' rice paddy. And I only knew he came from L.A., nothin' else." He stared hard at her as she sat to put on highheel shoes. "It ain't over, like you say. A thing like that, it's never over. Where the hell you goin'?"

"To town," she said.

He bent to find his prosthetic and fasten it on. "You're mixin' in things don't concern you, and you'll get your tail in a crack."

"*All* my people concern me," she said. "Not just one, and not because they're close blood, like you and your father. What do you care, anyhow? You have a run tonight."

"If I want it," he said. "I don't have to take it."

"Sure, you do," she said. "You can drive fast and take more chances and show what a wild, don't-care man you are, so you wouldn't miss a run. No more than you'd miss an excuse to attack the people who jumped your father. I think you need to keep proving you have balls, that you don't really care about anybody—not me or your father or the glorified image you carry of your Marine buddy, your token black friend, that Lou."

Alvah's jaws ached. "Ol' Lou Miller would have stepped over a dozen just like you, to lay one honest gook whore. 'Scuse me all to hell—a *colored* person, only with slanty eyes and just a dab of hair on her pussy. Colored person my ass; you know what the gooks call blacks? *Gahk-jaengi*. It's their word for nigger."

She swung the door back and paused. "Make your alky run; hunt trouble with the freejacks; do what you have to. Just allow me the same privilege."

Betty Jean closed the door on his set face and walked to the used pickup he'd bought. Lou Miller, she thought; Louis Miller, black Marine. She got into the cab and started the motor. No; it couldn't be.

Alvah showered and shaved, nicking his face twice. Why the hell couldn't she stay home and do whatever other shackmates did; why'd she have to stir into trouble? Christ, the only thing they had in common was screwing. She didn't understand him, and he sure as hell couldn't figure her out. All that crap about being responsible for all her people, for everybody with a drop of black blood. It was bad enough carrying the weight of your own kin, so how could you spread yourself so thin and cover the whole goddamned world?

Dressing, Alvah knew he had other things to think about, and went to the bureau to take his pistol from the drawer. No goddamn iron, Scarpo said; you get nailed with a load, our lawyers fix it, so don't go leaning on no cops, especially the feds. But Scarpo wasn't Temple County, and those fucking Lovelaces were. He jacked the slide on the .45 and put the hammer on half cock. Kobburn knew better, too; the sheriff was getting too big for his britches. No matter what Ben Lassiter did at home, it was no business of the law, and that big-bellied son of a bitch trying to arrest Pa when it was the Lovelaces who'd started it—

He slid the Colt into his waistband so his sport shirt hid it. The night's load was waiting in the woods behind Beevo's, so Alvah walked slowly to the hiding place, limping only a little bit. When he got behind the wheel, he felt better, like he'd had a shot of good booze, like he'd just come off a successful patrol, all keyed up and good, good.

Outside of State Line, a black car tried to cut him off, and Alvah figured screw it, he wasn't fixing to bounce off across the fields for just one carload of Treasury agents, so he put the heavy steel bumper into them and spun out the car, slammed it into a red dirt bank. It wobbled there for a second, then turned turtle slowly, and in his rearview mirror, he could see the wheels spinning in the air, for all the world like a loggerhead turned on its back and trying to set itself straight again.

He whistled all the way to Gulfport then, with half a hard-on, and made the drop, collected the payoff. Coming back by a different route, he was wishing somebody else would try to roadblock him, and the .45 felt solid against his belly. When he hid the truck and gimped into Scarpo's back room, he stopped and looked hard at the woman standing by the desk.

"Hey there, Alvah," Jolene Kobburn said.

"I'll just be damned," he said. "That you, Jolene?" Scarpo leaned back. "You know this broad?"

"Sure; everybody knows Jolene."

"She wants a job."

Alvah blinked. The sheriff's daughter, turning tricks at Beevo's, and ol' pus-gut getting a rake-off? Man oh man, what a kick in the ass for Kobburn. He said, "You certain on that, Jolene?"

"Hell, yes," she said, and he noticed her hands were shaking pretty bad. "I mean, I got a lot of friends around here."

Scarpo eyed Alvah. "How you think Kobburn will take it?"

"He's got no choice," Alvah said. "He's gettin' to act like he's runnin' things around here, greedier all the time. This'll take him down a peg. You want that, Jolene?"

"Damned right," she said, and dabbed a kerchief at her nose. "He won't come hangin' around here no more'n he has to, once he knows, and the son of a bitch throwed me out."

Nodding, Scarpo said, "Move into Trailer Four. We'll settle your cut later."

She hesitated in the doorway, suitcase in one hand, purse in the other. "Yeah, thanks. Alvah, much obliged, and you come see me."

"First thing, Jolene," he promised. When she was gone, he said, "She'll bring business, all right, if only so folks can laugh at Kobburn."

"She's hooked," Scarpo said, "a junkie. No problem controllin' her. Not like you. I heard about a fed car gettin' rolled."

"They got in my way."

"Nobody wasted," Scarpo said, "so it ain't too bad, but you coulda outrun 'em."

"Saved your load. Here." Alvah passed the brown envelope. "It don't matter how."

"Somethin' else—that nigger broad leadin' meetings at the clinic. These hillbillies see her there, see her here—"

"I'll handle Betty Jean."

"You do that."

"Scarpo," Alvah said, "I do my job. Just don't fuck with me."

Scarpo poured himself a drink of good bourbon after the door slammed. A crazy; he knew the signs; a wild hair in a whole damned county full of crazies. Like a mob of old mustaches and their vendettas, the blood feuds, the touchiness, everybody trying to prove his balls were bigger than the other guy's. Not a business head in the bunch.

Most of the old mustaches were gone now, and their Sicilian ways with them. Hardly anybody wasted a guy for personal reasons anymore; if somebody got burned, it was business, not emotional. But these hillbillies— Sighing, he drank his whiskey and wished the family would call him from New Orleans, tell him to come back.

"Coming home," Earl Lassiter said, "I didn't realize it would feel this way. I see places I know, and they look changed."

"Thomas Wolfe said you can never go home again." Barbara Dexter crossed perfect legs and glanced casually out the Cadillac window.

"Wolfe didn't live in the South. We always come home, if only to get buried on our own land."

Barbara looked down at the polished nails of her left hand. "And ye shall know the measure of a man by his acres."

"Something like that. Land is more important down here, and not only because the area is primarily agricultural; it goes deeper than that."

"Tribal boundaries," she suggested.

Earl watched the outskirts of Meridian slide past. Who ever thought he'd be returning like this, in a convoy of Greater Atlantic Corporation luxury cars, with a brittle and lovely Ph.D. on the plush seat beside him? Returning to trouble, to family, possibly to Jessica Coffield.

How was Pa, Ellen, little Marcie? Was the town the same, the woods still full of canecutter rabbits, catfish striking in the muddy river? And Alvah—Earl frowned; it was going to be odd, seeing his brother crippled, meeting him like a stranger when he wasn't supposed to be. So many important things and people sanded down smaller by the separation and the years, other things taking their place, and looming larger, maybe because they were new or set in different perspective.

"And tribal taboos," he said. "More than your sociology courses ever mentioned. They have to be respected, Barbara."

"Very clear," she said in that precise voice, "set in black and white."

He glanced at her, at the cameo profile of her smooth, strong face. "Shades of gray, variables. It's not all race. We—these people—get along well with individual blacks, but resent them collectively. Up north, the reverse is true."

"Yes, professor."

A little harder, he said, "The mill is *my* baby, and

I'm on home ground. Your degrees don't mean a damned thing here and theories are only that—theories. You're very good, or you wouldn't be here, but you're my walking computer, an adviser, nothing more. Forget that and you'll be back in Boston with a tightly rolled sheepskin stuffed up your ass."

She looked at him then, really looked. "Yes," she said, "I can understand why the company sent you—now. I don't often make mistakes, Earl. But the boy wonder, the homespun genius, meteoric rise within the company—so I was wrong. You're tough, and I can accept that."

"We'll get along then," Earl said and put a hand upon her nyloned knee. She didn't move it away, and he hadn't expected her to. Cam, Stacey, Francesca; now it was Barbara, beautiful, brainy, and ambitious, higher echelon, top-of-the-line programer. He wondered if the company had it all laid out for both of them: four bedrooms and pool, 2.4 children, apartment in Boston, servants a careful ethnic cross section, latest abstract prints on textured walls.

There was Quitman ahead, twenty miles down from Meridian, and he was surprised to see a motel, garishly neoned; tourist traffic must have picked up considerably. It would be handy for the new staff, for Barbara and himself; there would be no welcome for them in Temple County, no place to stay. Company housing would come later, he thought, an insular community slowly expanding invisible fences until all Temple County was walled in, without ever quite realizing how it happened. But Meridian would have the nearest airport for a long, long time.

Another few miles, and he began picking out landmarks—a giant live oak, starting point for many a coonhunt; the meandering creek; highway bridge across the Tchufuncta River, then the flag atop the U.S. post office, mailtime meeting place for howdying your neighbors.

Earl leaned toward the driver. "Next right, and on down the gravel road." He'd forgotten it was black-topped until the car rolled smoothly along it. It might have been better to slip into town—somewhat difficult with a woman who looked like a movie star and half a dozen Boston-tailored experts at something-or-other— but the company wanted a show of opulent determination, a convoy of Cadillacs. Impress them, Lassiter.

He did. Earl saw heads turning, mouths gaping; he didn't see a hand lifted in friendly greeting. There had been changes in Temple County other than blacktop and the smell of pulp. But when Earl thumbed a window button and windgrass odors, sundust odors, whipped against his face, he knew them and knew Thomas Wolfe was a liar. He had come home.

Up ahead, he saw for the first time the reality of his pulp mill, stacks tall against a brassy sky, sentinels at the border of his tribal land. Beyond them, a battalion of greenblack pines marking the river, and unseen behind the guardian line, waited his pa's new home.

"Something there," the driver said, slowing. "Pickets, and the gate's closed."

"Stop by them," Earl said, and shucked his coat as he climbed out.

Six men rested on signs reading "Yankees Go Home"; "Nigger Lovers"; "Shut It or Shoot It"; "Temple County's Not Black." They eyed him, eyed the Cadillacs.

Earl said, "Howdy, Joe Blake; Roy Lovelace—Shep, Unk—you all. Didn't know there was a union here."

"Well now," Joe Blake said, "if it ain't the runt of

the Lassiter litter. If'n it's too cold up north for you, it's too damned hot down here."

"Joe," Earl said, "seems to me that you're standing on my land." He looked up at the stacks and saw no smoke from them, looked across the cyclone fence and saw no lights in the mill, no workers moving about the big yard.

Joe Blake nudged Roy Lovelace and spat a glob of tobacco juice into the dirt near Earl's shoe. "You meanin' to move us?"

"I can give you first lick and make you holler calf rope any day of the week," Earl said, "and you know it. But I see the pack of you waitin'. Now *you* better see those black cars behind me, while I tell you my folks are not totin' signs. We're comin' through, and if you don't have any more sense than to stand in the way, there's goin' to be a whole lot of tore-up ass around here."

He put his back to them and got into the car. "Move it," he said.

They parted sullenly, seeing only intent men in dark suits, not calling his bluff. From some vantage point inside the mill, someone pushed a button. The big gates swung wide, and the cars passed through. As they neared the office, Barbara Dexter breathed, "I said you were tough; now I wonder if you're reverting to type. Your language slipped gears. For a moment, I thought you were going to get down in the dirt with them."

"If I had to," Earl said, "you're damned right."

CHAPTER 25

Oh Christ; oh good lord. The black thing hung threat-ening and chill sweat drenched her face, but the worst was not being able to wipe it away. No; the worst was vibration tearing apart her guts, twisting them. Oh God, Sandy Coffield prayed, make them give me just *one* drink. It wouldn't hurt them to give me just one drink.

The ambulance bounced sickeningly and Sandy retched. The nurse paid no attention. Sandy strained against the straps, jerked at the canvas jacket binding her arms to her body. If they'd just give her a drink, she wouldn't be so sick. Her mouth was dry, so damned dry, and her throat—

"P-please—" she groaned.

"Take it easy," the nurse said. "It's not far now."

They didn't understand. Nobody knew what it was like. Sweat puddled in her eyes, and she shook her head to clear them, but the sudden movement made her sick again. Her stomach heaved, but nothing came up, only a terrible bitterness that caught in her throat. Oh God, oh my God.

"Help me," she said. "Goddamn you—*help* me!"

Fat and placid in starched white, the nurse said, "Don't carry on so, dearie. I can't give you a sedative until doctor checks you out."

The ambulance swayed. Sandy closed her eyes and tried to pray, tried to think, but nothing was coming out right. Her mind skipped here, jumped there, like a frightened rabbit; around and around and around.

Jesus Christ, I know I haven't been good, but I haven't been all that bad, either . . . I never hurt anybody if I could help it . . . bad mother; I've been a sinful mother, not taking care of my son, but if You'll just help me now, I'll make it up to him, make it up to You. . . .

Making deals with God. How do you make a deal like that? What the hell have you got to offer? . . . Sick, so gaddamned sick, and that fat bitch doesn't care . . . hurt; belly hurts and my head and I'm shaking and if I don't hold on, hold on, I'm going to fly apart. . . .

"Ohhh!"

"Take it easy, dearie," the nurse said.

I wish I was dead . . . so easy to be dead, she thought wildly. Then: I'm not an alcoholic . . . I just drink too much. I could stop if I wanted, any time I wanted . . . only there's nothing to do and nowhere to go and God, you know how much I loved him.

Why won't that bitch give me a drink? I know she's got a bottle somewhere . . . medical alcohol, maybe . . . the straight, 190-proof stuff . . . I know I'm not an alcoholic, because I never had delirium tremens, never saw bugs crawling on my skin or anything like that. . . .

The bitch had a radio turned on . . . I'm dying and she's listening to music. Never liked that spooky symphonic music, all bass chords and thundering cadenzas that echo inside my head and make me lonely, make me want to cry and cry and cry. . . .

"Turn—turn off that damned radio."

"Dearie," the nurse said, "there's no radio in here."
Oh Christ; help me.

Jessica slapped the quirt against her boot. "You
could at least help me, Adam. See to the irrigation, try
to find us some more field hands, do something besides lie around with a glass in your hand all day."

Adam Benning stretched and grinned. "Told you,
honey; I'm a construction man. Don't know a damned
thing about dirt farmin'."

She strode past him to the library bar, poured a
short drink, and dropped an ice cube in it. Through
the window, she saw her mother piddling around in
the flower garden. Lila looked old, had aged percepti-
bly since Jessica came home as Mrs. Adam Benning.
But he's so old, Lila said; older than I am. And Jessica
said, he's young enough, and he's got money, Mama.

What a joke that was. Jessica's lips twisted bitterly
as the bourbon went down. Adam had some money,
but not nearly enough. The house in Gulfport had
been mortgaged to its chimneys, and brought very little. If it hadn't been for the antique furnishings,
Adam Benning would have come broke to The Shadows with her. The old bastard was glad enough to
move in, and should be.

It had only taken her a sweaty, frantic week to get
Adam to ask for marriage. Ask? He begged with his
tongue hanging out, and only rightly so. She'd used
every practiced, wildly erotic trick she knew to get it
up for him and turn back the calendar. He was kept
so busy screwing he could think about nothing else,
and he was stupid enough to think it could go on forever.

There'd been some good to that week, she remembered. Cutting down that high-toned bitch, not even

letting chubby Ron see his darling daddy—that had been enjoyable.

But after the hurried trip to a justice of the peace, and an orchid somewhat wilted, and back home to The Shadows, Adam Benning turned out to be the screwer, not the screwee.

Now what money he had was just about used up: the new tractor, rebuilding the cotton gin, paying off the feed stores. And now Jessica didn't know what the hell she was going to do. She clicked the ice cube against her teeth. At least, that bitch Sandy was off their hands. Elliot had finally smartened up and had her taken away to a sanitarium. If he'd only do the same with the bastard child he claimed as his own—

"Honey," Adam said, "you might bring me another julep."

"And I might not," she said. "You were hangin' around town today while I was sweatin' in the fields. Couldn't you find just two or three nigras to work for us?"

He sighed, put down his empty glass, and laced fingers across a belly that was thickening. "They're all too jumpy, them you can find. Hidin' out, mostly, waitin'."

"For what—somebody to feed them for nothin'?"

"Just waitin', seems like. Lot of talk about registerin' to vote, but that'll never happen."

Jessica dumped another finger of whiskey into her glass. "The mill; did you go out to the mill and line up some construction?"

"Trouble out yonder, too; pickets stoppin' the niggers from workin'. The Templars figured cuttin' them off at the pockets would bring 'em back into line. Storekeepers shuttin' down on credit, too. The niggers'll come to work when they get hungry." Adam grunted as he sat up on the longue. "Word is, them Yankees aim to start up the mill again, though. Some fella came in with a bunch of company guards, brought 'em in Cadillacs; they had sawed-off shotguns, and maybe a machinegun. This Lassiter fella said—"

Jessica spun on the barstool to face him. "Lassiter— Earl Lassiter?"

Adam nodded. "That's what they said; Temple County boy went north and got himself Yankeefied. The Templars don't cotton to him a bit, 'cause there's that mess with his daddy and his daddy's nigger wench."

"Earl Lassiter," Jessica murmured. She frowned; Earl had given her no trouble about supporting the child over the years, had in fact been generous. Would he want to see the boy? She couldn't allow that. It wasn't time for anyone to see him, but the moment could be getting close, forced upon her by events she couldn't control, by Elliot Coffield's selfishness.

Her frown smoothed into a smile. Elliot's position was a little weaker, although he was all set to milk public sympathy for his "sick" wife. And now Earl was back home. Jessica stared into the bar mirror. She'd have to do something about her hair, take care of her nails, find a good dress. Earl was at the mill, a highly profitable operation until the trouble started, and he might be just the one to get it going again. He'd always been kind of muley—except with her. And now he had the power of a giant corporation behind him.

It was strange that Earl should have risen so high, coming off a hardscrabble farm with only a high school education. But not so strange that their paths would soon cross again; he had always been handy when she wanted him. And Jessica wanted him. Now.

*   *   *

"Good to have you home, son," Ben Lassiter said. "New house don't rightly feel like home yet, but it will."

"Looks real nice, Pa," Earl said, shaking his father's hand. "This is Barbara Dexter. Barbara, my father— and Ellen Nash, and the young lady peeping around behind her is Marcie."

"Hello," Barbara said, no flicker of her gray eyes betraying shock or even surprise at seeing blacks.

Earl moved then to take Ellen's hand and hold it. "You're not a day older, Ellen."

"You're some heavier," she said, "and bleached out. Come on in the house. Marcie, fix the ice tea."

The furniture was the same, every piece of it familiar, not quite fitting into the new house, but Earl was glad it had been kept. He saw the rifle standing against the doorframe instead of hanging over the mantle with the others. His own 30-30 hung there, dustless and oiled.

"You see Alvah much?"

Ben was rolling a cigarette. "No more'n Ellen wrote you. Goes his own way. You like ice tea, Miss Dexter?"

"Thank you," Barbara said, sitting erect but at ease.

"Have to look him up," Earl said. "We could use him at the mill."

"Don't reckon he'll come," Ben said. "Asked him when he first come back. He's doin' like he wants. Seen men in the other war come home like Alvah; seems like they got so wound up by combat they couldn't hardly live no other way."

Earl said, "Where can I find him?"

"Beevo's," Ben said, and changed the subject. "You welcome to stay here, son."

"Beholden to you, but I better get my staff set up, and stay close to them."

"Well." Ben stubbed out his Prince Albert in a coffee-can lid. "S'pose I show Miss Dexter around the place some?"

Earl nodded to Barbara, understanding that his pa wanted him to talk with Ellen alone, and wondered why. In a moment Ellen said, "He means you to say goodbye to Marcie. Sendin' her off to my cousin in Jackson."

Earl watched the dark, shapely face, the liquid eyes he so well remembered; he saw a faint touch of gray in Ellen's cropped hair. "Things that bad?"

"Bad enough; whole county's down on him account of her and me. He ain't their hero no more. They whupped him some in town a spell back."

"Who?"

She rubbed her hands together. "He wants you to know, he tell you. It was afore they shut the mill down. They been pickin' at Marcie, too."

Putting down his glass of tea, Earl said, "And you're not going away with her?"

"My place is with him; always has been."

"Do you all need any money?"

Ellen shook her head. "Got more'n we can spend, thanks to you." She didn't look directly at him. "Won't do no good to argue him off his land, Earl. He ain't studyin' on runnin'."

"No," Earl said, "I reckon not." He stood up and ambled into the kitchen. There was the same old table, shaped by his great-grandpa, scarred and stained by generations of Lassiters. And there sat Marcie, pig-tailed head bent over her schoolbooks.

He said, "You'll come back soon, Marcie. Things'll change."

"Time I be an old lady," she said.

Sitting beside her, Earl touched her hand. "Way before then. It's already changing, Marcie; it's just having a hard time getting started."

She put oldwise eyes upon him. "I wouldn't run, neither, was I full growed. When I am, I be back."

"That's good," he said. "We'll need you. Well—take care, hear?" What the hell did he mean by that—don't get stomped, don't get hit in the head by a rock, try not to get killed?

"I take care," she said, and when he turned to go, added, "Missed you when you gone, Earl; miss you again, I 'spect."

"Me, too," Earl said. "I didn't know how much until just now."

In the living room again, he said, "When?"

"Got his mind set on the Greyhound tomorrow," Ellen answered.

"I'll be there."

"He don't want that."

Earl looked toward the front porch, heard Barbara's musical laughter. "I'll be handy then. Nobody will bother Ben Lassiter in broad daylight."

"Nary other time, head-on."

"Well," he said, and went outside to stand a minute beside his pa before saying evening to him and taking Barbara's hand to guide her across the swinging bridge. The click of her heels was loud in slowly gathering twilight, and down the river a whippoorwill mournfully celebrated the passing of day.

"Just passin' the time of day, Sheriff," Alvah said, sitting in Kobburn's own chair outside the jailhouse, tilted back on its hind legs and with his false foot propped on the whittled railing. "Man can't lay around Beevo's all the time."

Kobburn's jowled face was suspicious. He pushed

back his sweatstained hat, showing a line of white where sun didn't reach. "I ain't got time to mess with you, but I'll give you this much to chew on. I come out'n the Templars *after* them Lovelaces jumped Ben; didn't have nothin' to do with it."

"Didn't get after 'em, neither," Alvah said. When he lowered his leg, the switchblade snapped open in his fist, a long, lean blade he used to peel a splinter from the railing.

Kobburn's eyes followed it. "Your pa, he had that automatic on me."

"Wonder how come," Alvah mused, and sliced another raw piece of wood. "But that ain't here nor there, Sheriff. Why, if I thought *you* had anything to do with it"—the knife leaped from Alvah's right hand to his left and back again—"but course, you knowed better."

Kobburn started to hitch up his gunbelt, then changed his mind and kept his hands close to beefy thighs. Alvah grinned and said, "Just come visitin', like I said. Can't lay around with Beevo's whores all the time, even if one of 'em's a pretty fair piece of ass. Little ol' red-headed gal with a wiggle to her I remembered from afore. Sure felt funny, tho'—payin' for ass I used to get for free."

"You—" A vein swelled in Kobburn's neck. "You—"

Alvah balanced the switchblade upon his palm, his eyes wicked, his grin wolfish. "Worth every dime, she is; learned her a bunch of new tricks while she was gone, looks like. She can get a man on the floor and make him hit every corner of the room without missin' a lick. Good as any nigger thataway."

Kobburn's hands twitched and his belly trembled; sweat broke out along his jowls, clinging to unshaven stubble there.

"Come on," Alvah whispered, and the whispering made it worse, more deadly.

The sheriff took a shaky step backward. "I—you got no call on me, Alvah."

Still very softly, Alvah said, "I just give you a call on me, you son of a bitch. If you ain't got the belly for it here, you know where to find me." Then he got up and deliberately put his back to Kobburn, limping over to his truck.

When the Ford roared off, Kobburn sat heavily in his chair and dabbed at his face with a bandanna. That son of a bitch was crazy, flat out of his head. It had been *that* close, and he still felt the chill on the back of his neck. When he got settled better, he stared down the street after the truck and muttered, "Yeah—I know where to find you, all right."

CHAPTER 26

After a long talk with Dan Mason, who hadn't let the pickets scare him off, Earl left two Caddys parked openly in the mill yard and used the other as a shuttle to the motel in Quitman. He and his staff took a wing there, and he was only mildly surprised when Barbara Dexter got a room of her own; he hadn't read her as bowing to convention, but perhaps it was just as well.

Meeting with his men, he gave them a rundown of what he expected and what they could expect. They were good men and solid, but there were tense faces among them when they left. Then he called Barbara on the house phone.

She surprised him again; her robe was severe and simple, and she wore no makeup. Still, she looked pretty damned good. He said, "Sorry; I know everyone's a bit tired, but there's not a lot of time to waste. Drink?"

Barbara took the chair at the tiny table, ballpoint poised over a notebook. He poured martinis and sat on the bed. "If the company is shutting me out of any plans, I'd like to know it now."

Drink untouched, she angled her head at him, high cheekbones, full lower lip, disconcerting gray eyes. "How would I know that?"

"No games, Barbara. I've learned corporate struc-

ture pretty well—the watchbirds, right hand–left hand.
But if I stumble over some maneuver I don't know
about, it could cause a foul-up all the way around."

Picking up her glass, she crossed excellent legs, the
robe falling back to expose creamy thigh. "The company's moving at the state level; it shouldn't concern
us here."

"Politically? I thought so. But this is the hot spot;
what happens here influences the state, possibly the
entire South." He eyed her, this cool, sharp woman.
"You're filled in on me."

"I know you shrewdly took stock options, that your
patent royalties and real estate moves gave you control
over the mill. So you have a free hand."

"Yeah," Earl said, "and my neck out a country mile.
If we're stopped here, the company puts on a Band-
Aid and goes elsewhere, while I'm hung out to dry."

Barbara tasted her drink and shrugged; the movement rolled enticingly unsupported breasts. "A risk of
pyramid climbing. But what's the problem? Racial un-
rest—and about time, too; it brings labor troubles, but
nothing like union interference. That'll come later."

Earl sighed. "I'm the design man, the mechanical
engineer; you're the social structurist. But here you'll
be working with wheels within cogs that aren't easily
reached. Money is the oil that keeps all parts moving
without friction, right? Only in Temple County, no
amount of golden grease can make cogs function, once
they're pushed out of line. What we're up against is
the first tremors of an earthquake, rumbles of up-
heaval that threaten a tradition-bound, rigidly pat-
terned way of life. Emotions don't mesh smoothly;
they can't be neatly labeled and computerized."

"*I'm* supposed to be the sociologist," Barbara said.

It was Earl's turn to shrug. "Just trying to show the

variables. I understand this country, these people, because I am them. Scratch me and you find a typical Temple County redneck."

"Yes," she said, "and no. Your father isn't typical, neither is his mistress. There must be others. And don't underestimate that golden grease, Earl."

He got off the bed and poured another martini; Barbara shook her head. He said then, "We are a bloody people. Quick and deadly violence is always just under our skin. Logic and intelligence have nothing to do with it. Do you realize that honest-to-god feuds are still going on throughout the South, that the Civil War was only yesterday, that loyalties and poisonous hates are handed down from father to son to grandson? Christ, there are entire families here that have never been out of Temple County and have no desire to leave it. We may wear the same faces as people in Boston or San Francisco, but the bone and blood behind those masks are different, believe me."

Barbara recrossed her legs carelessly. No, he thought; never carelessly. This woman was diamond-beautiful and diamond-hard. It made her no less desirable, and she would be incredibly efficient in bed. There was a restlessness in him, a bubbling up of Temple County and red-dirt Lassiter land, reawakened smells of river mist and sweet corn unfolding to blistering sun. "Okay," he said, "end of lecture. Come here."

She raised an eyebrow. "What?"

"All programing and no poontang makes Jack a frustrated company man. That's another local euphemism; it means—"

"I know what it means," Barbara said, "and forget it. I'm worth what the company pays me, I never had to fuck my way up the ladder. I only work for you, Earl—not *on* you."

"Well," he said.

"Good night," she said.

And he could only stare at the empty room after she had gone and say to himself, yeah—good night.

Night hung warm and cloaking around Floyd Kobburn as he leaned against the chinaberry tree, the one with its deeper shadow. They'd been squabbling for weeks now, and he'd figured it about right. The wench was scared shitless, helped along every time she peeped around and saw him or one of his boys watching her. And today, here it came—the note written in long, easy strokes like her legs: *Please, I need your help. My husband won't allow me to leave town with my son.*

So he trotted the little nigger back with the answer, and the fancy high-yellow wench was just about to fall in his lap. Kobburn licked his lips and rubbed sweaty hands down his thighs. Deputy Luther Travis had one patrol car down the street, watching over both cars at the same time. The Davison kid would go with Luther, while Sarah and her high tits, her wiggly ass and good sense now—she'd ride with him.

Yonder she came, toting a couple of grips, the little bastard right behind, not so little now, growing and skinnying out. He moved out to intercept her, and Sarah gasped.

"Easy," he hissed. "Gimme them bags and hurry. Templars got this place staked out good."

She protested weakly when he shoved the youngun ahead, but Luther had him in the car before she could react. Holding back a laugh, he whispered, "In case we get roadblocked, want your kid to get through, don't you? Two chances, thisaway."

Sarah nodded and trembled into the car beside him. Damn; he could taste her fear, smell it through her perfume, and it made him feel right good, turned him horny as a boar coon. They were out of town and a mile toward the Clark County line when she said, "I brought the money."

"He won't miss it none," Kobburn said. "Makes a heap off white folks now that ol' Doc Christopher passed on, and near as much from the niggers." From the corner of his eye, he watched in the dash light, saw her kind of folding up on herself, knotting her hands tight to keep them from shaking.

"I—I appreciate what you're doin', Sheriff," Sarah said. "Wouldn't ask it of you, but there's no other way, and with all the trouble, and Calvin refusin' to let us go—oh my lord, I can't stand to see my boy hurt, Sheriff. I just can't stand that."

"You a right smart gal," Kobburn said, turning off the main road behind the other car. "You Georgia niggers still got some sense. Now a Yankee nigger like your old man—"

She shrank more, face down, shoulders trembling. Good long legs, he thought; wrap clear around a man's back, and them hard tits'd bore holes in his chest. He took his right hand off the wheel and reached. Sarah flinched back and put an envelope in his hand. He stuffed it into the seat cushion without looking at it; she knew better than to trifle with him.

Up ahead, taillights went on, and Kobburn slowed, touched his own brakes. They were around the bend in the creek road, and when both cars cut their lights, night came busting down like a black quilt thrown over them all. He could hear her breathing hard, panting.

"Oh no," she said, "oh, no—no. My boy—"

"Stays up yonder all quiet like, less'n you holler and get his head busted."

Drawn into a ball against the door, Sarah said, "Y-you have the money, all of it."

"Got you, too," Kobburn grunted. "Now get your black ass out on the ground and spread your legs."

He put down the blanket when she stumbled from the car, wishing he could turn his light full on her and see every hair. She stood quivering, not making a move, so he flung her down and reached up her dress to tear off her drawers and get a good hold where she was softest.

He ripped her bra, too; flung her dress up over her head because he never kissed a nigger in his life and wasn't fixing to start now. Kobburn had what he wanted, the hot, shaky feel of her tits, the slick, smooth belly with its deep fur piled down low. Mounting her, he shoved it deep, the way niggers liked it, and her shaking was better than getting screwed back. He pounded her hard, making her groan, hammering white meat up her until he puffed and let it all go.

The bitch lay still when he rolled off her, but he wasn't through with her by a damn sight. It took him a while to get it up again, but when he did, he gave her what-for every way he knew how. After that, Kobburn took a Mason jar of good corn over to the other car and let Luther have his innings with the woman. The youngun whimpered a time or two, but shut right up when Kobburn told him he'd get his goddamn head knocked off.

Feeling pretty good, he went back to his own car.

The wench was still lying spraddled on the ground.
He had to slap her up to get the names he wanted.
When he switched on his lights, Luther shoved the
youngun out, and they left the niggers to walk it on
into Clark County. Kobburn knew damned well they
wouldn't be back. The deep sound of the patrol car's
motor made him feel the same way, like purring.

Purring at idle, the Greyhound engine fumed the
street behind. Over at Bubba's gas station there was a
crowd, larger than the one at the Busy Bee Cafe and
bus stop. Somebody said there he is, and several people
avoided looking directly at Ben Lassiter when he got
out of his truck. They saw him anyway, and Ben
heard the hiss that ran through them when he lifted
down little Marcie, a shocked ripple that grew when
he offered Ellen his arm.

Be *damn*, somebody else said, but when Ben looked
at him, the man took to studying the bus schedule fly-
specked and dusty on the wall. Ben's 30-30 carbine was
slung over his right shoulder, and he kept one thumb
in the leather loop, so Marcie and her mother had to
carry the bags. They put them down on the sidewalk
next to the bus while Ben gave the driver ticket money
with his left hand. The driver stowed the suitcases.

Ellen was dressed up right nice, he thought, wearing
her new hat and fresh-washed gingham. Marcie was
dolled up, too, big eyes downcast. She stood looking at
the toes of her patent-leather shoes while three white
men and a black woman got on the bus. The black woman went down the aisle and sat all the way in back, on
the long seat across the axle, where diesel fumes rose
thickest.

"You got everything, child?" Ben asked, knowing
full well she did.

"Yes," Marcie said quietly, then looked up and held out her arms to her mother.

Quickly, Ellen stooped and hugged her, and as quickly stepped back, eyes darting from side to side under lowered lids. She didn't say anything; she had said it all at home.

Ben took the small dark hand in his own, and helped Marcie to the first scuffed metal step. Her lip quivered and he thought, be damn to every last one of them. Deliberately, he leaned down and kissed the child's cheek. "Take care, honey."

Whispers darted across the street like so many Blue Racers, like so many blacksnakes S-whipping for the tall grass, and over at Bubba's one exploded in a *Son of a bitch! Kissin' a nigger, right out in front of God and everybody else!*

Coiling and snapping at each other, the whispers fed upon themselves, spreading along the street and into every store, each building, growing stronger and more fearless as they traveled.

Ben ignored them, waving to the thin black face in the rear window until the Jackson-bound bus was clear out of sight. Beside him, he could feel Ellen rigid and just about not breathing, but he stood there a spell longer, just for spite. When he did move her toward their pickup, Ben took his time, dawdling some, thumb still hooked in his rifle sling.

Bigod! the hissing spat, *bigod, this time he done went too goddamn far.*

He handed Ellen up into the seat and closed the door, then walked easy around to the driver side. With one foot up, he spat a wad into the street, making a noise of it to show them he didn't give a popcorn fart what they thought, how much they chittered low among themselves like a pack of barn rats.

Thin echoes rolled up and down Temple city: *Kissed a nigger right out—much as claimed the black bastard for his own.*

Propping an elbow on the truck door, Ben shook out Prince Albert into a paper and rolled a cigarette, his eyes flicking them like the popper on a whip.

"Ben," Ellen said softly from inside the truck.

He thumbnailed a match, used it, blew a slow roll of smoke and snapped the match, dropping it into the dust.

"Ben," Ellen said.

Lassiter, that's who! That goddamn nigger-lovin' Ben Lassiter, ashowin' off his black whore afore all the decent folks in this town.

He unslung the carbine with a deft flip, and for a split second, the whispering stopped. Down toward the railroad tracks, a dog barked, every yap hanging loud and clear in the tight air. Ben passed the 30-30 across to Ellen and got into the truck.

It started up again: *Rubbin' the whole town's nose in it; struttin' her like he's proud of the bitch—reckon them Lassiters got a touch of the tarbrush?*

Keying the ignition, Ben drifted his eyes over all the near faces, and only some of them turned aside. Others stared back at him.

Maybe he figures he can lord it over everybody, with both his younguns to home—three goddamn Lassiters to watch, all to once—

Ain't but three of 'em—and the nigger.

No, ain't fixin' to forget the nigger.

Ben drove off, turned the corner, and headed for home.

"You coulda drove her up to Quitman and put her on the bus there," Ellen said.

"Man makes a stand where he has to," Ben said. "Couldn't give 'em the satisfaction."

"No," Ellen said, and looked back only once over her shoulder. "I reckon you couldn't, and stay Ben Lassiter."

CHAPTER 27

Elliot adjusted his linen jacket, glanced into the mirror, and said to Jessica, "God, I'm glad you rid the house of that clod for a few days. You ought to keep him in Gulfport. How could you marry him?"

"Because I needed him, damn it," Jessica said. "*You* won't lift a finger for The Shadows. I might ask why you keep Mark Manley around; somebody's bound to get curious, you know."

"Because," Elliot said, "in a certain way, I need Mark, too. But you wouldn't understand; you never actually needed anybody in your life, only what you could wring out of them."

Lila Coffield tilted her head birdlike. "Please, children."

"I'd like to wring something out of you," Jessica said. "Your neck, for instance. Damn it, I've used up what little money Adam had, and if The Shadows is to be kept goin'—"

Elliot picked up the silver shaker atop the bar. "Five—six—seven—wasn't that it, darling?"

"You bastard," Jessica said.

Lila said, "Children, if you're goin' to talk filthy—"

"You might as well understand," Elliot said, pouring his drink, "so long as the house and a couple of acres of grounds remain for public display, I simply don't give a damn about all that costly land. In fact, I've been seriously considering selling off most of it."

Jessica snapped upright, fist clenched around an empty glass. "You wouldn't dare!"

Elliot sipped and carefully placed his glass upon the bar. "I could and would and damned well might. Suddenly, there's a lot of money being poured into Sam Dustin's campaign—full-page newspaper ads, TV and radio spots, sound trucks, the works. I don't know where he's getting that kind of support, but I do know he has a solid political base in Natchez, and it's spreading statewide, unless I can counteract it—with more money."

"You always need more money," Jessica said.

"And so do you."

"I have a good cause," Jessica said. "The Shadows, Daddy's dream, the Coffields—"

"Bullshit," Elliot said. "My cause is better—me."

Lila rose and pulled her skirts about her. She was much thinner now, her face peaked, eyes sunken behind glasses she could no longer do without. She said, "I cannot remain here and listen to such obscenity."

They ignored her, glaring at each other. Jessica said, "You try to sell one inch of this land, and I'll stop you, Elliot; I swear I'll stop you."

His smile was icy. "Oh? Just how do you propose to do that, my dear? I suppose you can cause some minor legal delays, but I assure you, they can be surmounted by giving you major interest in the house. Don't forget my son; dear old Dad left *him* control of The Shadows, and as I'm Thomas Elliot's legal guardian—"

"Your son," Jessica said bitterly. "That's a laugh."

"To each his own," Elliot said. "Can old Adam Benning actually get it up?"

"I can make any *man* get it up," Jessica said. "Can you?"

Elliot toyed with his drink. "The things you don't know—"

"I'll stop you," Jessica cut in. "Not one goddamn inch of Shadows land, Elliot. If you can't squeeze Earl Lassiter's mill for your campaign contributions, don't even *try* to put this place on the market."

"Oh, for Christ's sake, go check the kitchen. Since Mama's gotten the vapors again, no telling what Auntie Kate is messing up in there. You wouldn't want to disappoint your lover who was, lover to be, would you? And darling, do something with your hair; you look absolutely provincial."

Jessica stood up. "You'd do well to rehearse your country-boy routine, or Earl may get interested in *your* hair."

Elliot smiled again. "Do you think so?"

She flounced from the library and slammed back the kitchen door.

Calvin Davison stared at the mess, at Sarah's things tossed about, the partially emptied closet. She hadn't, she wouldn't; not without saying something to him, leaving a note, some clue to where she'd gone.

His belly went tight; whirling, he lunged for Peter's bedroom. The boy was gone. Davison crumpled onto the narrow bed, hands clenching and unclenching. Damnit, she didn't have to take the boy. If she was so damned hysterical, if all their years together meant nothing to her, still she might have left Peter.

Where could she be heading? Not back to Georgia, not anywhere in Mississippi. Chicago, then? Sarah would need money for the trip, more to get established up there again.

Feeling as if arthritis had locked his knees, Davison got up and returned to his bedroom. The checkbook was gone, and he was glad. He'd know where she was by canceled checks, at least the city, and any competent detective could take it from there.

The smell of her was in the room, and the rumpled bed made him ache, so he went down the connecting hall into the clinic and snapped on a light. Sarah had picked her moment well; he'd been out at the African Baptist Church for a rights meeting because people were getting edgy about gathering at the clinic now. That gave her time to spirit his son away, and she hadn't taken the car, knowing he could have her picked up.

How, then—the bus? Too late for a bus run, so someone had helped her. Davison kicked at a waste can and dropped into his desk chair. Then he saw the bottom drawer pried open, and the steel box with its lid battered loose. She had stolen the movement money, every sweatstained dollar contributed by blacks who couldn't really afford to give anything away.

Aloud he said, "Damn you, Sarah. Damn you for being paranoid and stealing my son, this money. For that, I'll find you and take Peter away from you, but if you think you'll make me give up my practice here, the movement, you're out of your mind."

Putting his face into his hands, he rocked in the swivel chair. He should have gotten treatment for her, but the nearest black psychiatrist was in New Orleans; a white one practiced in Jackson but Davison could just see him accepting a Negro patient. More damn white and black, black and white. Somewhere, somehow, there had to be a middle ground.

* * *

"Stompin' on home territory again, huh, boy?" Elliot said, pumping Earl's hand. "Must feel pretty good,
bein' back where you belong, and looka what you
brought with you."

Taken aback, Earl said, "Elliot Coffield, Barbara
Dexter." He looked beyond the foyer, searching for
Jessica.

"Come on in and make yourself to home," Elliot
said, "but I'm givin' fair warnin', I mean to run off
with this beautiful woman." He led them into the living room. "Pure-D shame that Mama's feelin' poorly;
know she'd be right happy to see you. But Jess'll be
down in two shakes. Bourbon and branch water
okay?"

Earl stood uncertainly just inside the library, thinking that Avery Coffield ought to be towering behind
the bar, big laugh booming forth as he maneuvered
people into doing things his way. Elliot was a damned
pale copy.

Barbara said quietly, "Is he for real?"

He was proud of her polish, the poised, finely
molded body, the facile mind always working behind
dovegray eyes. Barbara's hair was short but attrac-
tively shaped, its deep bronze waves throwing off light
when she turned her head. She wore a soft blue dress
that caressed her every movement, and Earl figured,
sooner or later, woman. "I remember Elliot as being
more precise. Maybe this is his political face."

"Ain't no strangers at The Shadows," Elliot called
from the bar. "Come get your poison."

Barbara preceding him, Earl had gotten only halfway across the room when he heard the rhythmic click
of heels and stopped to turn and see Jessica.

She stopped, too, one foot out, chin up and proud.
She was more lovely than ever, more mature, a hon-

eyed ripeness to her that had a warm, musky smell to it. Not the scared, child-swollen girl she'd been at that meeting in Boston—how long ago—four years or better? Jessica seemed to have more depth to her, an extra richness of body and a more settled mind. She was more than special; she was Jessica. Like sunkissed mayhaws whose golden inner richness swelled against smooth scarlet rind, and your mouth went wet anticipating the bursting taste against your tongue.

"Earl—you look delicious."

"So do you."

Jessica laughed, that throaty, fluted melody he knew so well. "Do I? I could just kill Elliot for carryin' you off in here and spoilin' my entrance. I meant to come down the stairs like an oldtimey southern belle and—" Her eyes caught Barbara. "Oh; is *that* the associate you said you were bringin'?"

Her hand was small and sturdy in his own; her full breast brushed his upper arm. Earl introduced the women and watched the undisguised lancing of Jessica's seagreen eyes, the surprising lack of reaction of Barbara's. Jessica pivoted him aside anyway, chattering about old days and old friends, closing out Barbara and Elliot. She'd always had this trick of making you feel alone with her, Earl remembered; it was a good one.

Dinner was served by an awkward black girl Earl didn't know, and by Auntie Kate. He said hello to her and the old woman just bobbed her head in return, and didn't come out of the kitchen again. Despite his preoccupation with Jessica and Elliot's stock of country jokes, Earl ate hugely, savoring each near-forgotten flavor.

"Never get nothin' like that up yonder, I reckon,"

Elliot said over chicory coffee and deep-dish peach cobbler.

"Oh for God's sake, Elliot," Jessica said suddenly, "why don't you stop that good ol' boy talk?"

His smile seemed genuine. "But I'm so good at it. I even had Earl fooled, I think?"

"Sounded like your daddy," Earl said, and Jessica clattered her coffee cup.

"Daddy never had any real political aspirations," Elliot said. "He was content behind the scenes, while I find it more exciting to participate, to lead. If the ladies will pardon us, I'll call upon an ancient tradition of retiring to the library for cigars—although I can't smoke the damned things. Jessica, please show Barbara around the gardens, possibly the Indian spring."

Outside in the twilight, Jessica said, "You care for flowers, Miss Dexter?"

"I've never seen gardenias growing like this. So many overwhelm me."

Jessica moved along a flagstoned walk. "They're Cape Jasmines, and I can't imagine you bein' overwhelmed by anything. You look so efficient. I mean, down here ladies don't get to be executive assistants; we leave that to the men."

Barbara strolled easily, lithely. "I'm more efficient than most men."

"Do they like that?"

A jeweled hummingbird lifted from a cluster of pink oleander and whirred off home. Barbara said, "Does Earl Lassiter like it, you mean. He appreciates my work, my specialization."

"The Indian spring's down yonder," Jessica said. "Must take a lot of experience to be a—specialist. As I recall, Earl was always just a little bit square."

The path sloped downward and Barbara moved

quickly along it, stepping in front of Jessica. "Put away your knife, little girl. It's not sharp enough to use on me."

"*Whatever* are you talkin' about, Miss Dexter? I was just bein' neighborly."

"You were just being bitchy, and I don't have to take it. I don't have to tell you I know Earl only as a co-worker, either, and you probably won't believe me."

Jessica started to move around the other woman. "You're so right; I don't." She flinched when Barbara's hands clamped painfully around her arms just above the elbows, and tried to jerk angrily away. The coiling fingers bit deeper.

Barbara said, "Behind that sweet, innocent face, you're a nasty little girl, nothing more. If I wanted to fuck Earl, I would. I don't; I haven't."

"You—" Jessica struggled, lifted a knee that Barbara took calmly on one hip. "Let me go, you Yankee bitch!"

"Better," Barbara said, "more like your real self." She shook the hell out of Jessica, popping the golden head painfully back and forth so hard that Jessica couldn't get out a scream without rattling her teeth together. When she at last let go, Jessica collapsed, skirts spread, too shocked to cry, too mad to curse. She stared up at Barbara Dexter.

Swallowing then, she hissed, "I never want to see you at The Shadows again. You hear me?"

Barbara Dexter smoothed her dress. "Oh but you will, dear; you certainly will."

And not that much later, Barbara sat beside Earl in the Cadillac as it muttered along the road to Quitman. He said into the windshield, "The son of a bitch means to shake me down. Needs money to become

lieutenant governor, and laid it all out for me—how
badly he can screw up the mill, regulate its operation
and load us with taxes until we can't move. He even
showed me a copy of a bill ready to go into the senate
hopper; it'll strangle us."

"How much does he have in mind?" Barbara asked.

"Hundred thousand."

"Too much," she said. "It will be twice, three times
that when he decides to become governor. The mill is
jobs, and jobs are votes. He should see that."

"Not black votes. No such animal. Elliot could be
behind those pickets, behind the shutdown. He was always a sneaky little bastard. Damn! He's got us over a
barrel, though; a few more weeks shutdown can cost
more than his bribe."

Barbara crossed her legs. "I think there's a way out.
You were never close to Elliot Coffield, were you? Not
as you were with his sister."

He glanced at her and back to the road. "Not jealousy from you. No, dirt farmers and landed gentry
don't mix. Jessica was—different."

"Then you haven't really noticed."

"Noticed what?"

She pushed in the lighter, took a corktip from her
purse. "Elliot is queer."

Earl was quiet for a while. Then: "Just might be.
There was a girl he was supposed to marry—Mary Alice Harvey; he didn't. Then his daddy brought him
and his bride back from New Orleans, a woman nobody in Temple County had ever seen—Sandy something. But they had a baby."

"If that means anything," Barbara said. "In Boston,
they had me start a file on State Senator Coffield. His
wife is in a sanitarium, drying out, but her alcoholism
is well covered up. He's hardly ever home, and no

woman's name has been linked with his. Besides that, I'm—just pretty certain he's homosexual."

"That could tear him up," Earl said, "destroy him, if it could somehow be proved, but that'll be very difficult—"

Barbara's laugh was thin, metallic. "Not as difficult as you might think. There are always indiscretions, momentary lapses, discarded lovers willing to get revenge. The company can trace every move Senator Coffield has made over the past few years, run down every conceivable witness, buy hotel registers, set up pictures. Oh yes, the company can do all that and more."

Earl bumped the hell out of his hand against the steering wheel. "Then get on it tomorrow. No, bigod—get on it tonight. Call Boston and set the wheels turning. I'll stall Elliot, tell him we're considering making a deal. Goddamned Coffields; they never change."

"Not even Jessica?"

"I told you; Jessica is different."

Barbara Dexter looked out the window at the night. "If you say so."

CHAPTER 28

Alvah said, "You drink beer now? Cold one in the ice-box."

"Why not?" Earl said, and helped himself, noticing the woman's clothing, the neatness of the cabin. "Good to see you, boy."

"Oughta seen all of me; regular piss-cutter in Korea, I was."

Sitting in the only chair, Earl said, "I wrote every other week."

"Yeah," Alvah said, folding his emptied beer can in one hand and rattling it into a wastebasket.

"Alvah, I don't know what the hell it is with you, and never did. We used to be kind of close."

"Before I tried to screw Ellen and the old man threw me out." Squinting, Alvah said, "Can't say I rightly know you now, all dressed up and talkin' like big city. Recognize me without my leg?"

"Come on, now. We went different ways for a while, but we're home again, and I need your help."

As if he hadn't heard, Alvah said, "Little brother, you shoulda seen Korea, but you never made it, did you? Never mind; I'da racked up a score good as Pa's, if that fuckin' gook didn't blow off my leg."

"Pa didn't set himself up for his sons to match,"

Earl said. "There's a good job for you at the mill. I need somebody to handle security, and I thought—"

Hurling himself from the bed and balancing on his good foot, Alvah hopped to the small refrigerator and got another can of beer. His stump waved as he hopped back. "Thought you'd lay some money on a crip. Shit, you been gone so long you got no idea what's goin' on."

"All right, tell me."

"Pa didn't say nothin' to you about them bastard Lovelaces whippin' him around, about Kobburn tryin' to arrest *him* for it? How about Pa standin' up to the whole goddamn town yesterday, when he put Marcie on the bus and kissed her?"

Earl pulled in a deep breath. "No, he didn't say."

Pulling savagely at his beer, Alvah wiped his mouth and said, "And you talk about security for the damned mill. I don't give a shit about that mill, about your money. I got enough to get by. But what're you meanin' to do about security for Pa?"

"He won't hide," Earl said. "You know that."

"More the reason. He rubbed Temple County's face in it, and they're liable to get him for that."

"Liable not," Earl said. "Pa's always been respected around here."

"They run him outa the Templars, ganged up on him in the street, *afore* he strutted Ellen and the gal. Respect, my ass."

Earl said, "I'm meeting with the county commissioners this evening. I'll lay it out for them, hit them in the cashbox if they mess with Pa. Mean to, anyhow."

Bending his beer can, Alvah scored a hit on the basket again. "When we were little, you had as much sand as any youngun. Lose your balls up north?"

"Goddamnit," Earl said, "why don't you grow up?

All your life, you figured the best way to solve a problem was bust it in the head. If you couldn't do that, you cut and run."

"Just from Pa. Couldn't bust him in the head."

"Can't rattle every gourd in the county, either. Alvah, Alvah—the whole world gets older, gets bloodied up, gets a little smarter as it goes; things change, people adjust to those changes or get plowed under. There are ways to maneuver, to plan around obstacles—"

"Sound like some office general, tellin' us grunts up front how to fight a war. Maneuver, plan—and throw all Korea away, so other gooks can start chunkin' shit someplace else."

"We're not talking about war," Earl said.

"Ain't we, little brother? Okay, you talk to Sam Harvey and his ass-kissers, talk to Pus-gut Kobburn. *I'll* see to security for Pa."

"You never had to look far for an excuse," Earl said.

"Damnit!" Alvah hollered, and the door opened just then.

Betty Jean's eyes were bright as she stepped into the cabin, but the excitement in them faded when she saw Earl. "Oh," she said, "I saw that big Caddy outside and thought—"

Alvah said, "This here is Betty Jean, and gal—this's my baby brother, boss man of that pulp mill. You shook up, boy? You and Pa lived with one most your life, so why not me?"

"One what?" Betty Jean asked.

"Nigra, colored; oh, 'scuse me—now it's black."

Earl stood up. "If you change your mind, Alvah, you can reach me. Miss, my brother was never diplomatic, and I apologize for him."

"Goddamnit," Alvah yelled. "Go on, haul your 4-F

civilian ass out of here. Nobody apologizes for me, you hear—*nobody*!"

You have to help yourself, the psychiatrist said, and Sandy was beginning to believe him. Especially since the people from Alcoholics Anonymous had lured her into a meeting and she found what sense they made. Dr. Westbrook was pretty good, not at all like shrinks she'd seen in public hospitals.

She drank coffee from a paper cup and smiled wryly. Nurse Sandra Tolliver had never, never imagined she would be on the receiving end of psychiatric treatment, and she was thankful this doctor put no faith in shock treatment. Shuddering, she remembered vividly how patients had contorted under shock therapy, how blank they had been for long spaces afterward.

AA seemed to have the answers, she thought, glancing at heavily meshed windows without resentment now. Admit you're a drunk, then make a choice: either go on being a drunk, or do something about it.

If only someone had come to visit, she thought, it might be easier, and God, she felt guilty about her son. Closing her eyes, she tried to put his face together feature by feature, and trembled when she couldn't. No good worrying over anything you can't do something about right now, AA said. Make amends if and when you can.

What could she tell Thomas Elliot, and was he old enough to halfway understand? Elliot—he'd done the right thing, locking her away. Those messy nights in Meridian, or wherever the blackouts hit her, neglecting her son, crawling lower and lower in order to punish herself.

Opening her eyes, she took more coffee. Punish me

for what, she thought, taking money to marry a man I loved and having his baby? Staying in Avery's home surrounded by hate because I didn't have the guts to get out on my own, afraid to lose the last vestige of him? But ignoring his child, our child, and not giving love because I didn't get any?

Easy, Sandy told herself, easy does it. What had the last AA speaker said—you'll find sympathy only in the dictionary, right after shit and sweat. One day at a time, they said; anybody can go twenty-four hours without a drink, and all you do is put one day after another.

So she'd stopped taking paraldehyde, and if she didn't sleep all night, that was all right. And she could handle the delayed shakes, slow the squirrel-cage spinning of her mind. Maybe before long, Dr. Westbrook would move her onto the open ward, and after that, she might go home and start making amends to those she had hurt, begin a life of her own, be what she wanted to be, a person, a mother, a woman.

"I'm my own woman, damnit," Betty Jean said fiercely. "Not anybody's nigger."

"Didn't say nigger," Alvah said.

"The hell you didn't. What's with you and this sexual-racial thing, man? Can't you make it with a 'fay?"

He was strapping on his leg. "Yeah; made it with Jolene."

"A whore," Betty Jean said. "I mean find a woman you don't pay; are you scared of that?"

"Got a woman," Alvah said. Then, eyes boring into hers: "Who'd you think that big Caddy belonged to, the hotshot leader you all are waitin' for?"

Betty Jean narrowed her eyes. "Who said that?"

"You ain't the only one with an ear to the ground. Hell, you think I don't know why you hang around Beevo's? But if this guy's a hardnose spade, remember what happened to that New Orleans preacher, that LaBeaux."

"We'll never forget that," she murmured.

"He was only a sample. You act like you mean to run over folks, and pretty soon, anywhere you look, there's goin' to be a black body."

Betty Jean said, "Fear and ignorance; violence and poverty; those have always been your weapons."

"Not mine." Alvah stood up, tested the leg.

"Yours; you accept it, condone it. You never forget I'm black, do you?"

He looked at her. "You ever forget I'm white?"

She went to the refrigerator, put her back to him. "You don't have a run tonight; where are you goin'?"

"Yonder and back. Could tell you that leader oughtn't show his ass in a Caddy, but you won't listen; I could say meet a different place every time, but you're deaf."

"Oh shit," Betty Jean said, "like *you* listen to rational advice."

"Well now," he drawled, "can't rightly expect no redneck 'fay to have good sense. All we got in our heads is fear and ignorance, violence and—what was the rest of it?"

She slapped the refrigerator door hard with her open hand, and Alvah limped out to find his hot truck and sit in it a moment, looking up at a blood-colored sundown.

Ought to be home come sundown for sure, Dan Mason thought as he stood on the front porch of Ben Lassiter's house. Ellen and her man worked their fields like they had to or go hungry, even if it wasn't so any more. But only croppers sweated from can't-see to can't-see and got home at dark.

Dan took a porch chair and put hands on his knees, looking out yonder where he couldn't make out the peapatch. Wasn't a light on in the house, and yonder was the pickup, so they hadn't gone anywhere. Wouldn't be smart to traipse off somewhere, after what Ben did in town, and couldn't nobody fault Ben Lassiter for being a fool, unless it was over Ellen and Marcie.

Wouldn't hurt more folks to be that kind of fool, Dan thought, white or black folks. Ben's youngun, now—had a way of his own to him, too; right smart boy, nothing like his brother. Bright to know he couldn't right off make old Dan Mason mill foreman over white men, and skiddling around that by naming him assistant, so's he could handle the blacks. If those wall-eyed niggers ever came back to work like they ought. Mr. Earl wasn't about to let nothing happen at the mill. There was Ben's hardness in him, as well.

Where *were* Ben and Ellen? Dan scratched a match and went into the kitchen to find a light. When he flashed it around, he saw Ben's rifle gone from the mantel, saw Earl's 30-30 still there. Hand sweaty on the flashlight, Dan went outside and down the steps, moved along the path to the fields, swinging the spot from side to side. Every once in a while he hollered out who he was. It wouldn't do to come up on Ben in the dark.

The peapatch, and yonder lay their full sacks; they'd been through here, picking. Dan moved on to the corn, but it wasn't ready yet, and he found greens and cabbage beyond.

The circle of light danced nervously along the irrigation ditch folks had hoorawed Ben for putting in, went reaching out to where melons squatted like big green Easter eggs among snaky vines.

Busted open red and seedy, a watermelon bounced light back at Dan, and he felt his teeth setting together hard. Forcing himself to go on, he eased between the mounds and sucked breath when he saw them.

She was flat on her back, arms flung out. The light wobbled over Ellen's staring eyes, her open mouth. It reached to touch Ben Lassiter, one hand to his belly and drawed up into a ball, facedown, the other hand stretched to rest on Ellen's fingers. Past him, Dan Mason saw the straw hat, the slow and hurting crawl marks left in soft, sandy earth where Ben had dragged himself after he was hit in the back, hauling himself along a line of his own blood so's he could put his hand on his woman's dead hand.

Dan Mason rocked back and forth, snapping off the flashlight so he wouldn't have to look. It didn't do much good; he could make them out plain against his eyeballs in the dark.

"Lord God," he said. "Oh my lord God in heaven. Both of 'em shot down in they own fields, shot in the back. Have mercy on 'em, lord God—mercy on us all, 'cause this is same as throwin' gun shells in the fireplace."

Then Dan told himself, hush, nigger; you ain't been to church in a month of Sundays, and God ain't studying you nohow. But Dan didn't know where else to turn; nobody else this side of hell could help.

"Help me, you help yourself," Sheriff Kobburn told Scarpo, but the Eye-talian didn't seem to put much weight to it. "That Alvah's agoin' to bring the roof down on everybody, actin' the fool. Them federal men been around askin' me questions and not happy with the answers. I got this feelin', and that nigger wench stayin' with Alvah Lassiter don't make it no better. She's mixed up with that nigger doctor and the preacher, holdin' prayer meetings that ain't no such. I got me a scared nigger tells me she's a *agitator*."

Scarpo grunted. "What the hell you want me to do? I drop Alvah, he takes five thousand bucks worth of hot-rod truck, starts runnin' alky as an independent, cuts into my business."

"You stand for that?"

Leaning back behind his desk, Scarpo said, "Thought you told me guys in this county don't lean on the Lassiters. I ain't forgot all them bullets they put into my place, into the cars. They could put some into me and my boys next time, into you, too."

Kobburn scratched his belly. "Times has changed some. Ol' Ben tore his britches when he strutted his nigger whore and kissed her bastard youngun out in plain sight. Folks don't care what happens to them Lassiters now."

"That keep Lassiters from cowboyin' up my place? Now that nigger Alvah's screwin' is different."

"Seems like N'Awlins might be interested in all this hooraw," Kobburn said, " 'specially since it's goin' to cost 'em money."

"Even if you knew who to reach in New Orleans," Scarpo said, "I'd string you up by your balls if you put out word. I handle my own problems here, you got that?"

Kobburn said, "Still and all—" and shut up when he heard the squall of the siren. C.J. Franklin was on duty in town, and damn well supposed to stay there. Jowls shaking, the sheriff waddled to the door and flung it open; damned fool ought to know better than to come sirening out to Beevo's while folks was drinking and whoring. It scared hell out of them.

Red flasher whirling, siren dying to a low wail, the patrol car skidded to a halt in a shower of gravel, and Deputy Franklin piled out running. "Sheriff—"

"I hear you," Kobburn said, "and everybody else in the county, too. Goddamnit, what couldn't wait 'til I come back to town?"

Franklin was panting. "That Mason nigger works at the mill—called in and said Ben Lassiter and his wench're both dead, shot dead in the field. Told him not to touch nothin', 'specially the body, and swore I'd skin his black ass if'n he messed up footprints we could put the bloodhounds to—"

"Shut up!" Kobburn bellowed. "Shut the hell up, right now. Jump back into that car and hightail it to the office, and don't turn on that damn si-reen, neither. Put this in a towsack and sit on it, you hear? Don't run off at the mouth to nobody. Don't say *nothin'*."

Franklin swallowed. "Yeah, but—"

"*Hop!*" Kobburn said, hitched up his gunbelt, then snatched back his hands as if the buckle had been just pulled out of a hot fire.

Behind him Scarpo said, "What's up?"

Kobburn turned around slowly. "That roof I was talkin' about? It just now fell in."

CHAPTER 29

In the church rectory, Betty Jean looked at the circle of intent faces, trying to read them, trying to peel off layers of oppression so she could reach them. This was the local core of the movement, uncertain men and one other woman, a newcomer among them now, a square and blocky man beginning to gray. The others had seemed surprised when Dan Mason joined them, but accepted him gladly. Committing himself this late could mean he was a fink, Betty Jean thought. They could really use a leader; this bunch only halfway listened to a mere woman. What they desperately needed was Louis X.

"Sister," Reverend Brown said, "you keep talkin' trouble and blood. We pray it don't come to that."

"It will," she insisted, "and you all know it. You *know* they're not goin' to let anybody else register; they have their tame niggers sayin' yassuh-yassuh and votin' as they're told. They don't want any more, won't have the rest of us exercising our constitutional rights. Yes—it'll come to blood and violence."

A seamy-faced farmer said quietly, "On *us*; on our families and chillun."

"Somebody has to pay the price of freedom. Damnit, there's more of us, a lot more."

Calvin Davison said, "They have the police, the

guns, all the power, but there are logical men among them; there must be those who don't want killing any more than we do."

"Amen, brother," the reverend said, "for violence begets violence."

Betty Jean stalked the room, gesturing, her eyes flashing. "They come down on us if we do anything or not. It's past time we beget trouble on our own, so at least we accomplish *somethin'*. If a cur's goin' to be whipped anyhow, he might as well get in a bite."

She was magnificent, Davison thought, a golden tigress stalking the cage and raging at its confinement. So different from Sarah and her consuming fears. He watched the gleam of that rich mouth, the heaving of pert breasts, and knew a stirring within himself.

Sarah had been gone forever. At first he hoped she might come back, reconsider, see that what they'd had in the beginning was worth salvaging. It had been good, though sometimes they'd had to struggle along on what she brought home. Black models didn't make much back then; maybe they still didn't, but neither did interns.

When she left in the night, he sent telegrams to their old place, to her mother, wrote several letters a week. Once, just once, he got her on the phone and wished he hadn't. Sarah's voice had been like so much broken glass, cutting back at him, hurting as she'd been hurt, blaming him.

Rape; rape by two officers of the law while Peter sat under guard in a patrol car; white men taking turns on his wife after she'd given them money to see her safely away. Goddamn; if he'd ever carried doubts about being part of the rights movement, he had none now.

And if anybody should be calling for blood, it ought

to be him standing there demanding vengeance. But that wouldn't change anything, wouldn't return Sarah unfucked, wouldn't bring back their son—*her* son now. Another trauma had been smashed atop that earlier one of Sarah's, and she could never be the same.

Maybe he *was* to blame for staying on here, for not fleeing with his family. Christ; he was no saint, no visionary. He was just a doctor, trying his damnedest to do what he knew best, to help in his own way. You didn't cure a disease by killing the patient.

". . . might as well get in a bite," Betty Jean was saying, and he brought her into focus again, his belly tightening, all the long suppressed need surging through him.

Reverend Brown said, "Cur is a dog, and sometimes a dog is a bitch."

She whirled on him. "Still thumpin' your white man's Bible, preacher? Still shuckin' the people with the white man's Jesus? I told you why I was out there with a 'fay, to learn all I could. Well, I've done that. They're itchy about me now, so I'll play Mary Magdalene for you, preacher man, and see if you can be forgivin', too. Not that I give a damn, old man."

Dan Mason shifted his bulk in a chair. "Leave the child alone, Reverend. She doin' a job, like all us better be doin'."

The preacher said, "Dan, never thought I'd hear you eggin' on trouble."

"Never thought ever to see what I did," Dan said. "White man killed dead standin' up for what he believed in—a black woman and a little black youngun— and hisself, I reckon. Time for me to act the man, too."

A younger man said, "'Fays wastin' 'fays. Just so they don't run outa each other."

"Boy," Dan Mason said, "you fixin' to let your mouth overload your ass—'scusin' myself to the preacher and ladies. Only color Ben Lassiter had was *man*, and if'n you mighty lucky, you be as good someday."

Reverend Brown said, "Now, now, gentmun; what's frettin' me is they find some way to put the blame on us for them killin's."

"That'll be difficult," Davison said. "The whole county knows about Lassiter's trouble with the Lovelaces and the sheriff."

"Make no nevermind," Brown said. "They ain't lookin' for sense, just blame."

His wife brought in coffee, and the meeting broke up into eddying groups. Davison watched Betty Jean for a while, and moved over to her. "If you're leaving your cabin, you'll need a place to stay."

Dark eyes felt behind his own. "At least until *he* gets here. I can't understand what's holdin' him up."

"There's the clinic," Davison suggested. "My wife used to help there but she's gone. I'd very much like to talk more with you."

He had been calculated and weighed; Betty Jean smiled and said, "All right," holding out her hand for him to take.

"You can have a cookie," Auntie Kate said to Thomas Elliot, "and won't nobody slap your hand, child."

He retreated with an oatmeal cookie to climb the kitchen stool and sit there like a small, serious Buddha. "How come Miz Lila slaps my hand and you don't?"

"She got her ways, I got mine." Auntie Kate kneaded biscuit dough, whitening her black, wrinkled arms to the elbow with flour.

Thomas Elliot munched his cookie. "Mama comin' home soon?"

"Ain't you got no more to do than pester me?"

"I guess you're the onliest one answers me."

Auntie Kate frowned and pounded the dough. "Ain't your fault, child."

"Must be. Daddy just says hello sometimes, and Mama gets too drunk and then she's sorry and squeezes me too hard. Miz Jessica hates me, I can tell; Miz Lila, too."

"I say ain't your doin' and it ain't," Auntie Kate said harshly.

Thomas Elliot licked crumbs from his fingers. "Mr. Benning, now—he talks to me once in a while, but he's gone now, like Mama."

Auntie Kate looked away from the child because she had to. Poor, lonesome little scudder hadn't known a speck of love in his life, talking about Mr. Benning like he could have been a daddy, and that was a far piece from being so.

She remembered the set-to Miss Jessica and her husband had before he lit out for Gulfport; them cussing each other up one side and down the other, with her saying how he'd used her just to get him a young wife and a place to stay. And him going on about having to sell his big house and making his son and daughter-in-law mad, just to be with her.

Here in the kitchen, Auntie Kate heard words that made her ears burn, words she wouldn't say again just in her head. They went at each other like two lickered up niggers on a Saturday night cutting; Miz Jessica hollering she didn't know he was a pauper, and him yelling back she wasn't no better, and selling her—well, her body, to boot, just to get her a man she could shake down. Hadn't been pretty a'tall, and here was this poor youngun looking for somebody just to remember he was alive.

Closing her eyes, Auntie Kate held them shut for a spell, opening them to say, "Git you a handful of cookies and carry 'em to my cabin; tell my Sally play with you some."

He climbed down from the perch, sturdy and solemn. "Too little for Sally, she's seven. But she likes oatmeal cookies."

Auntie Kate looked after him and thought, he never got the chance to be a boy; walks like he's carrying a heavy load; walks like a little old man.

"Any time, darlin'," Jessica breathed into the phone. "I realize how very busy you are, but if your—assistant can set you free for just a little while—oh. Yes, Earl; I'm *so* sorry, and I shouldn't have intruded upon your grief. If there's anything I can do, anything at all—yes, of course. I'll call you later."

When she hung up, Elliot said, "Disgustingly bad timing, dear, but then you could never control your hots."

"*My* hots are normal."

"To you. Are they normal to our dear mama?"

"Go to hell," Jessica said. "I thought Earl might need comforting, that's all. His daddy shot down like that, and all."

Elliot studied his polished fingernails. "Logically speaking, that might be the best thing that's happened in this county for some time. It should put a lid on the nigra march to the courthouse next month. A graphic example of what happens when the boat is rocked, when traditions are flaunted."

"You're mighty smug," Jessica said. "What if the nigras *do* get registered? There goes Senator Coffield, Governor Coffield, Dogcatcher Coffield."

"*If* they somehow manage to pass literacy tests, if they pay the poll tax, if they can enter a voting booth without trepidation, then I'll worry about them. Until that halcyon day, my only preoccupation is with campaign expenses, and I do think that little problem has been solved."

Jessica said, "By Earl, you think."

"By the bottomless coffers of the Greater Atlantic Corporation, dear, their outpouring funneled through the so-called Lassiter pulp mill. Earl Lassiter is simply a mechanic who will prime the pump as he is instructed."

"Don't be so damned sure of that, *dear*. The Lassiters have always done things their own stubborn way, and even if Earl has been up north a long time, he still has that streak of mule in him."

Elliot patted his hair. "Because he didn't fall all over you? Miss Dexter is a lovely, polished—"

"I don't want to hear about that bitch," Jessica snapped, "and you think you're so goddamned smart about Earl, but you're not. I'm the only one in Temple County who really knows him."

"Not in the biblical sense, darling. There's Miss Dexter."

Jessica made two small, hard fists.

Kobburn punched a fat fist into the palm of his other hand. "You sure about that, Luther?"

"Sure's I'm standin' here. Catfish and mud turtles been at him, so I can't tell which one it is, but he got that yeller-lookin' skin all them Lovelaces has. Two lil' niggers seen him hung up on a log in the river and come arunnin'."

"Get hold of that nigger doctor," Kobburn said. "He's coroner 'til we can get one from Quitman."

"Started, ain't it?" Deputy Luther Travers asked. "Reckon state troopers be called in?"

"Not in *my* county, damnit; less'n I purely can't help it."

Luther rubbed his narrow chin. "I dunno; three killin's this quick—"

"You don't know shit from Shinola," Kobburn said. "Go do like I told you."

Then he leaned back in his chair and tried to figure out things. No way of finding who done in Ben and his wench; could have been most anybody in the county, and Floyd Kobburn's mama didn't raise no fools. He wasn't studying on traipsing around Lovelace country and all them white-lightning stills.

Have to check up on Earl, for sure; be easier than pulling Alvah's string; that crazy bastard had him a permanent case of the red ass.

Alvah most likely done it, caught a Lovelace off to himself and stuck that switchblade to him, or blowed a hole through him, knocked him in the head with a limb, howsomever. Wouldn't be the last Lovelace got his toes turned up, neither, if'n one of them didn't draw a bead on Alvah first. Whole passel of Lovelaces in the piney woods, and shirttail kin to boot.

But the Lassiters had family over to Clark County, cousins and the like. If they come into this, it could go on for years and for certain sure bring in state police. Nobody wanted that, except maybe niggers who didn't know no damned better.

Scarpo, Kobburn thought; that Eye-talian had much to lose as anybody hereabouts; more, even. Scarpo was near about slick as he was ornery and would turn off

Alvah afore everything got slap out of hand. Trouble was, there'd still be Earl.

Earl said no, he didn't want company and left Barbara Dexter at the house to walk along the river. He sat awhile and watched brown water move along slow and easy, looked down the bank to that slough where he used to put out sethooks with Pa when high water came every spring. Lot of big old mudcats got hauled out of that slough, fish that Ellen would dress out and fillet to roll in cornmeal and fry crispy outside in hog fat.

He figured it would be best to have Pa buried back across the Tchufuncta, in land he'd walked most of his life. Grandpa and Grandma were there, and Ma as well. He didn't reckon Ma would mind if Ellen was put down on the other side of Pa. Preacher McVay from the Baptist church would hem and haw at it, though, and the Methodist minister wouldn't even come if he knew.

The black preacher then. Pa might like that, since he hadn't set foot in a church door since Ma died, anyway. Yes, having the words said over him and Ellen by a black preacher would tickle Pa's funny bone, give him a last spit in the eye of Temple County.

Picking up a stick, Earl tossed it in the river and watched it turn slow in the current, this way and that. Stay close behind your dog, boy, Pa said; never let him follow a coon into the river, because that old coon will scuffle up on the hound's head and shove him under until he drowns. Coon gets by in water good as he does on land; might say it's his element.

And where was your element, Ben Lassiter? This mumbling old river, these mossy trees, that hard-dirt land over yonder. Not Europe or hero in the Templar

Club; wanting no more from life than to work the land and stay quiet with a good woman. Was it too much to ask?

Earl stood up, hands shoved into hip pockets. No, Ben Lassiter had never asked for anything—not credit at the store, not a man's hand to help, not a woman's forgiveness. If he couldn't do for himself, he went without and thought it no more than right for his children to do the same. Man walks his own land ain't beholden to nobody, Pa said; if a man don't beg a favor, he don't owe one.

Wind came whispering down the river, and if you drew it in deep, you could smell winter in it. Scuppernong grapes were turning yellow in the brush, and muscadines' purple hides about to split with ripeness. A few more weeks and first frost would whiten the ground in early morning. Then farmers would whet their butcher knives and their women would get out the scrapers and stone crocks and take to boiling water in big castiron pots outside in the cool, for it would be hog-killing time.

Barbara Dexter sat in the new house amid its old, worn furniture and wondered at the social mores that called for an undertaker to care for a white man, but a black granny woman to dress a black. She could smell the resiny pine of new coffins placed upon the front porch. There were no flowers yet; perhaps there wouldn't be.

She felt for Earl Lassiter, knew his hurt because she had been as close to her own father; not to her mother, that whiney, soft woman whose only litany was one of complaints. Her father had been strong and dominant, a pattern to follow, and if there was a touch of aggression in his dealings, it was only the spinoff of power.

Her mother called it cruelty, not accepting it as discipline.

There had been a coffin in the Dexter living room, polished gray and muted silver, and banks of lillies. There had been a respectful gathering of friends and business acquaintances, and her mother sniveling in a corner, accepting the homage as her own due. Nobody understood why Barbara slapped her mother and left that house forever.

Crossing her arms over her breasts, she pressed down until she knew pain. There were so many gelatin women, shivering, giving way at a touch, and few women with any real core to them. Perhaps there were none, the hint of steel an imitation—or just a come-on.

Restless, she moved onto the porch and saw him coming slowly up from the river, coatless and collar open, hands in his back pockets like a farmer carried them, his head bent. Was he tough enough to withstand this personal loss and still think clearly? Could he put the company's future above his personal feelings and understand that future was linked with his own? He was young, he was romantic, and Barbara suspected some of the company's careful programing had not taken. Greater Atlantic had plans for this man, but if he couldn't fit into those plans, there would always be someone else.

"Earl," she said when he came closer.

He lifted his head. "Walkin' over here's not the same as the old place. I guess he was happy here, though. I couldn't have made him move if he didn't want to."

Truthfully she said, "I liked him. I didn't know him long, but I liked him."

"It was that way with Pa; you did or you didn't, and nothing in between. I'll call the black preacher and lay it on for tomorrow. The way the county felt about him lately—there won't be any people."

"Not even your brother?"

Earl's jaws tightened. "Reckon he'll be paying his respects in his own way."

"I can find him, if you like."

"No. This is family. What you can do is get on the phone and shake up the company, tell them I want to know everything usable on Elliot Coffield damned quick. Monday morning the mill opens, if I have to run it by myself."

CHAPTER 30

"Shed your coats," Earl told his gathered staff. "Here's where you start adapting. All right—Abbot and O'Keefe, Engineering; Giorgio and Willoughby, Production and Supply; Blanski, Sales. Those are your areas of responsibility, gentlemen, although you may well find yourselves wearing several hats. Labor, PR, and Community Relations is Dexter's province. Smithson there has been doing a good job with Personnel, as is our bookkeeper, Pope. That's why they're still with us. Now, when pickets closed this mill, we lost one foreman. We'll replace him soon as possible."

Smithson nodded. "White man."

"Of course."

Barbara Dexter asked, "Is that necessary?"

"Yes," Earl said, and passed on. "We're going ten percent over prevailing wages, and here's a hot one for you, Smithson—wages are the same for black and white."

Smithson whistled softly. "Thing is, I'm not sure where we're gettin' labor. Just a few hung around when the pickets showed up, and they tried to stay out of sight."

"We'll get workers," Earl promised, "if I have to bring them in from Clark County. Production—your headache right now is supply. If the cutters are afraid

to bring in their loads, we're up the creek. Ten percent boost on delivery there, also. I understand there
are blacks hauling on their own these days, and when
the others feel that pinch, we'll see more trucks."

"All right," Barbara said, "technically we're in business, but nothing is really happening. Until you can
bring in outside labor, which the community will resent even more—"

Earl looked out the second-floor window and
smiled. "Here comes a crew now. Dan Mason is bringing them in. That's our black foreman, gentlemen,
and it seems he means to do a little more than his
share. Talk over your problems and solutions; I'm
going down to meet him."

Thank you, Dan, he said to himself as he descended
the stairs, and again for coming to Pa and Ellen's funeral. Maybe you'll take on a burden I'm not up to
yet; maybe you can tell Marcie her mother was murdered.

"Dan."

"Mr. Earl, these are mostly my own folks, and some
of 'em don't know one end from t'other, but I'll learn
'em."

"I know you will. Sign them in and put them to
work, and Dan—I have to be gone for a while. It's a
hell of a time to leave the mill, to leave you and your
people out on a limb, but—"

Dan Mason nodded. "Little Marcie, ain't it? You go
ahead on. We be hangin' and rattlin' here; time we
learned to do for ourself, I reckon. Far as we can go,
that is."

In the office they said, call the school, send someone
else to her guardians with word; so much depends on
you being here every minute—and Earl said, no, it's up
to me to do this, nobody else. So they backed off and

booked him a charter flight out of Meridian for Jackson. He didn't even change clothes before piling into the limo and telling Fernandez to stomp on it.

During the short flight, Earl tried to string words together, tried to make them sound as if everything would be all right. He knew damned well it wasn't, that nothing would ever make it right.

She knew something was wrong; he could tell by Marcie's watchfulness, the way she stood with her feet braced, as if expecting a blow. Her guardians, foster parents, whatever you wanted to call them, felt it, also. With no more than howdy and come right in, the Thompsons left Earl and Marcie alone in a small, neat living room.

"You've grown," Earl said.

"Didn't come clear over here to tell me that." Her eyes were bigger than he remembered, stretched in their watching, waiting.

"Marcie," he said, "you're just about sister to me; you know that." Oh Christ! How did you tell a girl her mother has been murdered? "I'm hoping we'll always be close."

She crossed her arms over her stomach and hunched forward. "It's Mama, ain't it? She bad off sick?"

He wanted to hold her, but she was braced against that. Marcie had never been one for cuddling, even to her mother. He said, "Marcie, she's dead, and Pa is dead."

The girl quivered and pulled her arms tighter. "Killed."

"They were together," he said, wishing she would cry, wishing he could. "At least they were together."

"Killed," she repeated and locked teeth into her lower lip to keep it from trembling. Earl saw her take a deep breath. "Reckon you be needin' somebody to come do for you."

"No," he said quickly, "no, Marcie. There's trouble down there, and there'll be a lot more—bad trouble that takes folks like Ellen and Ben."

"They—" Marcie's throat clogged and she started over. "They hurt much?"

Earl shook his head. "It was fast."

"Goddamn 'em," Marcie said, and lost control over tears. They welled from her eyes and spilled, tortured silver tracks down dark velvet. "Goddamn 'em, Earl."

Now the barrier dissolved, and he kneeled to take her in his arms and know the vibrations of her thin body. Marcie smelled of soap in her starchy dress; he held her until the shaking stopped. "You'll be all right. Stay here and go to school, make Pa and Ellen proud of you. You like the Thompsons?"

Her head bobbed against his shoulder, her voice muffled. "Like 'em fine. Like home better."

"Home will always be there for you," he said, "but not now, Marcie. Things are happening in Temple County, something that already made a move in Georgia and Alabama and Louisiana. It'll spread up here quick enough, and when it does, I'll send you north to boarding school. You're all the family I have left; I have to know you're safe."

She lifted her face. "Got your brother."

"Not even him. Alvah's not dead, but he might as well be."

Marcie's mouth trembled and she put a hand to her eyes. "Where you put her down, my mama?"

"In the old cemetery, right next to Pa."

"That's good," she said. "Mama wouldn't like it off by herself in the nigger graveyard." She backed from him, crossed her arms again, waited.

Earl said, "Maybe when you come home, there won't be different places for different colors. This thing happening, that's what it's all about. But right now it's dangerous and more folks will get hurt before everybody sees the right of it."

Gravely, she studied him, one leftover tear clinging to charcoal lashes. "Like they chunked rocks at us when we went to the white school?"

"Something like that."

"Had to keep goin', show 'em we wasn't scared. After a spell, they kept on hollerin' nigger, but they quit chunkin' rocks."

"I hope it's like that, too," Earl said.

She raised her chin. "When Ben put me on the bus, he kissed me."

"I know," Earl said. "He wanted you safe. Promise me you'll take care of yourself here, that you won't get homesick and come running."

Marcie watched him stand up and said, "Does the best I can."

He made her a grin and touched her damp cheek.

Quiet in the taxi, withdrawn in the plane, he held it all back, but once in the limo he slammed the seat with his fist until the driver turned around. "Something?" Fernandez asked.

"Everything," Earl said, "every goddamned thing I can think of."

When they drove into the mill yard, the new workers were circled up around Dan Mason and the foreman was talking, waving his hands.

"Something else," Earl said.

The driver said, "Understand somebody got shot at. You were too browned off for me to tell you."

Banging shut the car door, Earl walked into the crowd as it seemed on the point of breaking up. Dan

Mason said, "Anybody gets hurt, reckon we has to tote our own guns."

They both looked up at the sound of motors, and the crowd of blacks shifted, loosened its circle. Earl walked to the two dusty, battered pickups, tensed for trouble and thinking of his rifle over the mantelpiece.

The trucks stopped; three men in each front seat, three more in each bed, all carrying rifles. They looked alike in straw hats, faded shirts, and gallus overalls, looked alike in their washed-out blue eyes and lean faces, yellowbrown straggly hair.

The man driving the first truck was older, hunched in the shoulders, time- and work-worn. He said, "You'd be one of the Lassiter younguns, I 'spect."

"Earl."

"We be Hobbs from Clark County; some kin to your ma, some to your pa."

"Uncle Duane," Earl said. "Proud to see you all, but the funeral was two days back."

Duane Hobbs crawled stiffly from the truck and leaned back against the fender to stretch. "Some didn't rightly see payin' respect to Ben's wench."

"Your sayso," Earl said. "Mine to do how Pa would have wanted his burying."

"Ain't denyin' it," Hobbs said, propping his rifle against the fender. "Howsomever Ben did, it didn't give nobody call to kill him. So we come to stay a spell, bein' blood kin."

Earl said, "Appreciate that, Uncle Duane, but Pa didn't want a war."

"Way I hear, it's done started."

"My brother Alvah," Earl said, "but I figure if Pa was alive, he'd say rub their noses in it by keeping this mill goin', hit the banker and storekeepers and sheriff where they'll holler calf rope—in the money boxes. I'll need help to do that."

"Lovelaces was in on it, word is," Hobbs said, and rolled a chew of tobacco to his other cheek. Behind him, younger men sat dusty, watchful, silent. "Blakes, too; Kobburn."

"They're in on closin' down this mill, for sure. Scared off our help, except for what Dan Mason brought yonder. I'd be proud to pay good wages for work, if you all want it, but I know nobody can buy your guns. I'm not about to try."

Hobbs grunted. "Crops is in and it ain't hog-killin' time yet. Where you mean to bed us down?"

Earl reached for the man's hand. "Good to have you, Uncle; can't tell you how good."

"Lord, no," Jessica said into the phone. "I won't have you back here, Adam; Elliot doesn't *want* you at The Shadows. Yes, damnit—that's the way it stands. Don't argue with me. If you dare contest the divorce, I'll claim you're impotent. *Impotent*, I said. That means you can't get it up. And naturally, what with my brother bein' state senator and runnin' for lieutenant governor—what's that, Adam? Well, I never—screw you, too!"

She felt a hundred pounds lighter when she hung up the phone. Adam Benning was off her back, and when the divorce came through—as it certainly, swiftly would—the way would be clear for Earl. Jessica leaned back on the settee and smiled. When they were younger, Earl Lassiter had dreamed of The Shadows, hungered when he so much as looked at the great white house and what it stood for. He never said as much, but she had known; oh yes.

One by one, the obstacles were falling away. Sandy was where she belonged, in a crazy house; Adam in Gulfport to stay; even old Ben Lassiter and his wench were removed from the scene. There was Lila, of course—pottering about the house and taking to her bed at the slightest excuse, but Mama was no trouble.

Elliot and the boy he claimed as his own, Thomas Elliot; the insulting Yankee bitch, Barbara Dexter—only Elliot was in a position to be dangerous, and she had the cure for him, if she had to shove it down his throat.

But there was no reason Elliot should object; a family tie-in with the Lassiter mill certainly would help him politically. Thomas Elliot would be packed off to school pretty soon, and then Jessica could get rid of that sassy Auntie Kate. New money, new relationships; new machinery for tractors that were always breaking down, more irrigation pumps, a modern cotton gin. The nigras would come back when their foolishness was done with, and The Shadows would be bigger than ever.

Smiling, Jessica left the couch and went upstairs to dress. Poor Earl needed comfort in his time of mourning, someone to soothe him, tend to him, in his great loss.

"Ain't no great loss," Kobburn said. "Best Alvah's gone, and you can use both my deputies for runs on their off time, if'n you want."

Scarpo said, "See them other hillbillies know he ain't here. Don't want 'em nosin' around with guns."

"Be happy to. Now about my deputies—"

"Forget it; got enough runners. Just you see this vendetta don't get in their way."

Kobburn frowned. "Vendetta?"

"Feud, whatever the hell you call it."

"If'n Alvah Lassiter got spooked off, won't be no feud. Earl don't act like much man."

"For a big fatass," Scarpo said, "you jump to conclusions pretty quick. Sicilians got a sayin'—vengeance is a dish that tastes better cold. And don't ask me what a Sicilian is, just keep your eye on that kid that put so many holes in my place. Goddamn if I understand you people."

The phone rang and he picked it up, said *yeah*, listened a minute, and said *yeah* again, then hung up. "Your deputy. Says one of my cars is off the road and burnin'; runner didn't get out. Whole damn load of alky gone."

Kobburn put his hat on, took it off again. "You got any Lovelaces drivin' for you?"

Blinking, Scarpo said, "Yeah, why?"

"I 'spect you're one short. Alvah Lassiter ain't left the county." All of a sudden, Kobburn didn't feel very good.

"It's good to have someone to talk with," Davison said, not admitting he was nervous, that her very presence did something strange to him. "And if you don't mind sleeping in my son's bedroom, or if you prefer the clinic sofa, but that's kind of sagging—"

Betty Jean smiled at him. "Stay cool, Doc; no need to be embarrassed. I don't have a reputation to uphold."

He poured her coffee cup too full. "And no loose ends to tie up?"

"The man I was livin' with, the *white* man? We don't owe each other nothing. Does that bother you, Doc—that I screwed a 'fay? He wasn't the first. I had to turn tricks to get through San Francisco State, and 'fays dig us nigger gals."

Davison said thoughtfully, "It wasn't easy for me in medical school, either. If I was a woman, there were times I would have done the same thing. I'm a doctor, Betty Jean, not a judge."

She laughed, and blotted spilled coffee with a paper napkin. "Okay, I won't give you a bad time. I get pretty damned tired bein' on the defensive so much. We also serve who only lay and hate."

"The movement is practically your life, isn't it?"

Betty Jean tossed her wealth of hair. "It *is* my life, man. A cheap hustler with a shaky curette fixed it so I can't have kids, so all those little blacks out there are mine, in a way. They don't have to whore for 'fays, and I mean to teach them that."

Davison burned his mouth on the coffee and winced. He was acutely conscious of her perfume, put off balance by her honesty. "I agree, but not with your methods. There are other paths to the same objective."

"Straight out is the only way, Doc. Right on, or we never get it done." Her liquid eyes fixed him. "Why did your wife cut out?"

"Sarah was afraid."

"And you're not?"

"I am," Davison said, "but I'm here."

"Put down that cup," Betty Jean said. "I just made up my mind where I'm goin' to sleep."

She was silken against him in bed, hard-nippled and strong in the thighs, all dark fires racing. He was numb, but somehow more alive than he had been in years, every inch of him ultrasensitive, every alerted hair on his body sending frantic erotic signals. Cupping her, driving into her squirming, encompassing flesh, Davison gave up to the tender furnace of her.

For the first time since Jessica Coffield had commanded him to lay her, he was freed from the image of
white thighs and a golden mound.

For this woman was golden also, and did not fight
to conquer him, but met him with only a matching
hunger, a need as deep. Her buttocks rolled in his
hands, and her belly heaved beneath his, reaching and
twisting. She rode the foaming crest with him, moaned
with him, and locked her teeth gently into his throat,
raked his plunging back with her nails just hard
enough.

"That was good," she said when they lay side by
side. "It's been too long since I made it with a black
man."

"Too long since I made it with anyone," he said,
content to know the length of her body against his, for
now content to simply look at her in wonder.

"Do you know what you're sayin'?" Sam Harvey
asked. "You come in here threatenin' county commissioners like you mean to ride roughshod over us all.
Why, I knowed you when you wasn't high as a hoe
handle, Earl, and now you—"

Earl said, "No threats—gentlemen; a presentation of
facts, no more. Let me clarify them. One—the Lassiter
mill pumps a lot of money into Temple County. If
there is no payroll, *you* get hurt, and I can always buy
equipment and supplies in Meridian, not here. I imagine you're all feeling the pinch a bit already. I assure
you, it will get worse."

"Now look here," Martin Nelson said, "we didn't do
nothin' to you. It was some of them woods runners
actin' on their own."

"With your tacit approval," Earl said. "Two—I now
have guards patrolling mill property and eager to ride

shotgun on pulpwood trucks. They're all named
Hobbs, my kinfolk from Clark County. If by some
chance they're not enough, I'll call on the state police
and ask the governor for troops."

Elliot Coffield toyed with a silver cigarette case.
"The governor might not cotton to that, Earl."

"Any politician is amenable to money. Haven't you
found that to be so, Elliot?"

"Not," Elliot said calmly, "less'n he can buy votes
with it, and niggers don't vote. That's all the boys are
doin', keepin' niggers from the polls so they don't take
over the whole county, run over everybody, rape white
women—"

"Oh hell," Earl said, "save that crap for speeches. I
don't give a damn what the good ol' boys have in their
peanut brains, but they're interfering with me personally. So here's my third point—Lassiter mill is here to
stay, if it means opening a company store to undercut
yours, Nelson, and yours, Burr Watson. If it means
building barracks and bringing in workers from outside the county, and throwing my support behind this
civil rights movement, I'll do it. Lassiter land has always been Lassiter land, and that, by God, is that."

"Hold on," Burr Watson said, "about that store—"

But Earl was halfway out the door, and Elliot said,
"The boy's some upset about his daddy and don't
mean all he says. I'll see he don't get help from the
capitol, and you can count on it."

"Ain't the capitol frets me," Burr Watson said. "It's
a company store."

"He'll need licenses, transportation permits, all that
stuff has to be passed on at county and state level,"
Elliot said. "Reckon he can get it all?"

Will Jellico spoke up. "You all heard him. Support
the niggers, he said right out. Rubbed off on him,

bein' raised up around that nigger wench of his pa's. Well, if Earl Lassiter is another nigger lover, he just might find out he ain't got no mill to worry over. We got along afore it was built, and we can get by if it burns down."

"Now, Will," Elliot said, "we're all friends here and it won't go no farther'n this room, but it wouldn't do to talk like that nowheres else. Earl ain't about to get his niggers to the polls, and as for losin' the mill—no, it won't hurt your law practice none, but Sam Harvey's bank is spread a mite thin, and Martin Nelson's been buyin' up more land, and lookit ol' Burr yonder, squirmin' over that expansion to his store."

Leaning forward confidentially, Elliot said, "Just you all take care no white trash pesters the mill, and leave ol' Earl to me. For all his big talk, he flat knows I got him by the short hairs."

He had two drinks with them, and patted everybody on the back, but when Elliot left the meeting room, he wasn't smiling. The death of Ben Lassiter must have left Earl slightly off center. Surely he would soon recover his senses, or Greater Atlantic Corporation would pull him out and send in someone rational. It was only good business.

But when Elliot got into his car, he was still frowning.

CHAPTER 31

The doctor said, "Do *you* think you're ready to go home, Mrs. Coffield?"

Sandy hesitated. "I'm not sure, but do I have a choice? I mean, my husband committed me."

"This isn't a state institution. You can leave any time, but of course we'll notify your family."

"I—I'd like to make another AA meeting first."

He tapped a pencil upon a notebook, a younger man crisp and interested, black-rimmed glasses, sideburns a bit long. Looking down at her folder, the doctor said, "Your family situation hasn't changed. Can you handle that?"

"I have to," Sandy said.

"That's a good start." The doctor smiled. "When you're ready, Mrs. Coffield, you can be released any time."

Sandy went back to her room, admitting she was just a little scared. Jessica was out there, claws bared, and Lila, and Elliot. But there was also her son, Avery's son, and if she owed anything to the world, it was to be a mother to the boy. Staying sober, she could do that. One day at a time, she reminded herself. Sitting on her bed, she looked out through windows that weren't barred, at sunblue sky and green grass; out there any shadows were of her own making.

* * *

Crouched in the darkness of the cave, Alvah Lassiter
cocked his head, listened for a moment, then reached
for his pa's old 30-30. It was far from being an M-1
rifle, but it felt good, felt right in his hands, stock
hand-worn and slick, well balanced. It had been as
much a part of Pa as his arm.

Down by the slough, the truck was well camou-
flaged and just back from an independent run to
Gulfport. Scarpo's connection there didn't know he
was buying direct from Alvah, and there'd be no next
time with him. There'd be other wholesalers, and he'd
get around to them after he was done in Temple
County.

Slipping off the safety, he raised the carbine and
swept its front sight slowly over the brush.

"Alvah—hey, Alvah!"

He lowered the gun. Trust Earl to remember their
special hideout from the old days, and come snooping
to find him here. "You by yourself?"

"Yeah."

"Come in," Alvah called, "but don't leave a trail."

In jeans and workshirt and boots, Earl looked more
like he used to, a kid glad to be off in the woods when
chores were done. Alvah could never see him as a
dressed-up businessman.

Panting a little, Earl ducked into the cave and said,
"Figured you'd be here."

"So you found me, so what. Don't need anything;
plenty of chow, bedroll, the creek for water. Plenty of
ammo, too."

Earl peered into the darkness. Birds had used the
cave and their white smears were everywhere; so were
bat droppings.

"For how long, Alvah?"

"Long enough. Kobburn ain't fixin' to come after

me, and I reckon the Lovelaces are buttoned up pretty tight about now."

Earl hunkered down. "Give it up then."

"Ain't finished yet. There's ol' Kobburn himself, and the Blakes; they gave Pa a bad time, all of 'em."

"If you leave now, I can get you out of the country; anywhere you want to go."

Alvah shook his head. "I'm not charged with anything, and if I am, they'll play hell provin' it. You ought to see this is somethin' has to be done."

"Bullshit," Earl said. "You were never close to Pa. This is an excuse for you to get back at the whole world for losing your leg. Okay; you've drawn your blood. Let it go at that."

"When I'm ready, goddamnit. Go on back to your big mill, stink up the county, blacktop over Pa's grave when you spread out. You don't give a shit, but I do."

"I care," Earl said quietly. "Not only for Pa, but for Ellen."

"Care a heap more for bein' a big man, bigger'n Avery Coffield ever was. Always stuck in your craw, just a hard-dirt farmer with you tongue hangin' out after *Miss* Jessica and her big white house."

"And what the hell do *you* want, Alvah? Pa's medals, his respect? It's too late for his love."

Alvah said, "Don't come back here no more."

Earl stood up. "No need to. Somebody else will find you, and I'm sorry."

"Fuck you! Don't be sorry for *me*. No son of a bitch has to feel sorry for me."

Earl stooped and left the cave to walk slowly for the brush. Alvah went outside and looked after him. "Earl," he called, "you hear what happened to the gal I was shackin' with, that Betty Jean?"

Turning, Earl said, "Moved in with the doctor."

"Just wanted to know; don't bother me none."

"Well now," Earl said, "be particular, you hear?" And when Alvah didn't answer, moved away through the woods, careful not to leave tracks. A briar bush tugged at his sleeve and he unhooked the thorns so the branch wouldn't bend and leave a sign.

No sign of Earl yet, Jessica thought, and stamped back into the house for the third time. She'd left messages at the motel in Quitman, and at the mill. Of course, that Barbara bitch probably destroyed those. Once she'd answered the phone herself, and just the sound of that assured Yankee voice made Jessica want to spit, so she hung up without saying anything.

Thinking about it, Jessica could still feel the grip of the woman's fingers on her arms, strong as a man. Shaking her as if she was an unruly child, the very idea. Barbara Dexter would get her comeuppance, no matter what. The slut had no hold on Earl Lassiter that Jessica couldn't break, and it wouldn't take long to send her running back to Yankeeland.

In the library, Jessica paused at the bar but passed on to stare out the garden window at the swimming pool. That thing hadn't been filled in years, and she could see cracks in the tile, leaves blown into the bottom and not raked out. Daddy had been proud of that pool, the only one in the county, but there were other things falling apart, more important repairs to be made.

Where was Earl? Here it was near about dark, and he hadn't the common courtesy to return her call. She glanced at the phone and nibbled her lip; no sense acting like she was throwing herself at him. He would come, she was certain.

The time was right, and the setting, here in this
house that had always awed Earl, the perfect background for her. Lately, with Elliot taken to hanging
around so much, him and the other pretty boy, she'd
been bothered about having The Shadows to herself.
But Elliot got a call from the capitol, one that made
him priss himself off in a hurry, and she'd just as soon
he stayed away.

Elliot's "son"—she couldn't bear to think of him as
her half brother—was shunted off to Auntie Kate's
shack for the night, and her mama might as well be,
hiding behind her closed door, so the house was Jessica's alone. As it ought to be, she thought; as The Shadows would be.

She was dressed in gauzy blue, an off-the-shoulder
dress that did things for her tan and the way her hair
spilled down her back. The Cape Jasmines were nearly
gone, so she'd used a perfume like their heady scent,
and upstairs in what used to be her daddy's room, scarlet satin sheets on the bed, ordered clear from Califor-
nia. A decanter of brandy waited beside that alluring
bed, and candles to be lighted, old dance records on
the hi-fi. Where was Earl?

There. She caught the sound of a car in the drive,
and fluffed at her hair with both hands, so happy
she'd never nursed that little bastard and proud of
how her breasts stood out firm and high. Jessica
waited a decent time before answering the bell.

"Why Earl honey—so nice of you to come." She
went tippytoe and kissed him lightly upon the cheek.
"Come right on in."

She thought he looked almost as if he belonged,
gray linen suit and soft casual shoes, but she would
have chosen a different tie for him.

"Why the hurry-up call, Jessica?"

"Hurry up? I never said that; just thought you might drop by, if you could take time from your busy schedule for an old friend. But never mind, you're here and I've got sidecars just about ready in the library."

Girlishly, she took his hand and skipped ahead, tugging him, bending low so he could see she still didn't have to wear a bra—only sometimes. "You remember my goin'-away, swimmin'-pool party? Six shakes . . . seven—that's it, the perfect sidecar. You like it? My, you look businesslike in that suit. At my party, you carried an old jacket over one arm 'cause you were scared to wear it, and down there by the Indian spring—I swear, Earl; you've come a long, long way since way back then. But I always knew you would."

"Did you, Jessica? I didn't."

"Oh pish; you low-rated yourself way too much, but a woman can tell, if she's real interested."

He sat across from her on a barstool. "I haven't met your husband."

"And you won't. I'm gettin' a divorce. You were gone so long and—let's don't talk about it, darlin'. I'm here and you're back home at last. Earl, you have every right to shame me if you want, but please don't make me beg."

"Not you," he said, and she knew she'd struck exactly the right note, "not ever Jessica Coffield begging for anything. What do you want, Jessica?"

Coming around the bar, she turned his stool so she could move in between his spread knees, so she could put her mound right up against his crotch and her nipples to his chest. "Just you, darlin'," she breathed. "That's all I ever wanted."

She met his mouth avidly, squirming to him, and

when their tongues met, she could already feel him going stiff, rising quickly. Earl's hands felt over her straining body with that right mixture of awe and urgency, so she pulled away her mouth and stared into his eyes.

"Come upstairs with me," she said, pulse beating in her throat, "to my daddy's suite; it's all ready for the new master of The Shadows."

Face into her breasts and holding her so tightly she could hardly breathe, he carried her up the stairs while Jessica hoped he could see where he was going. "There, darlin'—that's the door." If Mama so much as whined out into the hall, Jessica would scratch out her eyes. "Course, my daddy never slept on sheets like those; they're just for you and me."

He put her gently upon them and she lay for a second watching him take off his clothes. Was it possible for a man's thing to grow? She didn't remember Earl being that big, but possibly she had him confused with somebody else. Lithely, she wriggled from her dress and let it drift to the floor.

"You're so beautiful," Earl said like a high schooler might, and there was something of the wanting-scared-to look upon his face that he'd worn the night he ran away from her at the Indian spring. Not again, she thought; not after she'd taught him so much in that Meridian motel room. And her spirits soared because Barbara Dexter couldn't be all that much.

"You're beautiful, too," Jessica said. That night at the spring, she'd commanded him to fuck her, saying it right out; now she knew him better. She said, "Please, honey—make love to me."

Once she had shown him how, but he surprised her by his deftness, and Jessica lunged upward, her belly rolling ecstatically when her thighs closed convulsively about his head. Dizzy, gasping, she fell back and felt him enter her strongly, penetratingly. The sheet was tickly-slidy beneath her buttocks, against her knees when she rolled atop him, along her ribs when he turned her again.

"Yes, yes, oh *yes!*" she panted. "Oh honey, oh darlin'—take me any way you want, every way you want—ahhh! Earl, *Earl!*"

And he did, more dominating, powerfully selfish, rolling her this way and that and making her reach orgasm again and again. But she weakened only for a little while, and by the time he turned onto his back, she began nipping her way down his belly. Every curling of her tongue was another strand in the cord that bound him to her forever; every shudder of his arching body was another sign of his total surrender.

When he lay drained, Jessica remembered to light the candles and turn on the hi-fi, and as music he must remember filled the room, she poured brandy. "You're all women and just one," he murmured. "Jessica Coffield is unique."

"I should hope so," she said, legs curled beneath her nude body and sitting snuggled to him.

There was noise in the hallway. Jessica tried to ignore it. A door slammed, and she thought, if Mama is poking around out yonder, I'll boil her in oil.

"Somebody else home?" Earl asked. "I don't want to see Elliot."

"Just my mama, and she's so poorly she seldom leaves her bed."

"You'd better go see," he said, and Jessica said, "Oh, damn!"

Top sheet pulled around her, she went to the door and cracked it. "Thomas Elliot—what the hell are you doin' here?"

"Come back for my fire engine," the boy said too loudly. "You seen my red fire engine, Miz Jessica?"

"*Get*," she whispered fiercely. "Take yourself back to the shack fast as you can, hear me?"

"Yes'm."

Jessica closed the door and found Earl sitting up, his legs over the side of the bed, holding his brandy snifter. He said, "Is that him, Jessica? Our boy?"

The glow was gone, all the bloom rubbed off by that little bastard. She got herself more brandy and let the sheet fall but Earl wasn't watching her body; he was searching her eyes. "No," she said. "Our child is still where I had to put him, well cared for and beyond reach of Temple County gossip."

"Then who was that?"

She sat on the bed. "I guess you'll find out, anyhow. That was my dear, lovin' daddy's bastard child, sired from New Orleans trash that Elliot *calls* his wife. My queer brother married her because it was good for his political career, and my sweet daddy kept her right here in this house, in this very bed, damn him. It like to killed poor Mama, but he had his own way as always."

"And the woman, the boy's mother," Earl said.

Jessica swallowed brandy. She'd take the hide off that catch colt for spoiling the evening. "Hopeless alcoholic, although I never would have thought she had a smidgen of conscience. Elliot had sense enough to put her away." She leaned over him. "Earl—"

He reached for the bottle. "I've put our baby back in my mind for years and pretended it didn't bother me."

"You supported him just fine," Jessica said quickly. "And this certainly isn't the time to drag a helpless child down here, what with the nigras threatenin' to take over the county, and folks killin' each other. You have enough troubles."

"I'd like to see him," Earl said. "Maybe it has to do with my pa's death, seein' him put down next to his pa and grandpa. It's not right the boy doesn't know his family."

Jessica leaned against him, but he didn't notice. She said then, "Soon as the trouble is straightened out, I'll bring him down here. Oh darlin', I've shielded him, protected him from ugliness so long, and I know it's just goin' to be terribly upsettin' for him. But you're right, of course. He should know his daddy and be proud of him, only I swear—I don't know how we're goin' to explain him. Maybe we could adopt the child, or play like we did, and then—"

"Jessica," Earl said, and she realized he wasn't going to spend the night, "I don't give a damn what Temple County thinks or says. That's something you should accept."

"Of course," she answered, wondering just what the hell she was going to do.

CHAPTER 32

Reverend Brown nervously eyed the three men in his rectory. "You got the wrong church; this here is Holiness Baptist, and I reckon you want Africa Baptist. It's out in the country."

He'd been out back watering the rose bushes when the long white car pulled up, just about sundown. Even with all the road dust and parked in the shadows of the big live oak, that car stuck out so much it made him jumpy. So did the men dressed all in black, wearing funny flat hats, especially the tall one that looked like he hadn't got his hair cut for months.

That one said, "You the preacher for both, ain't you?"

Brown bobbed his head, rubbed his hands. "That's right, brother, ever since ol' Reverend Kentson went to his glory. Hard to get a regular minister in here, so I just fill in, like. Leastways 'til somebody gets the call."

One of the men made a noise that wasn't exactly a laugh. "Gets the call."

The tall one said, "We make you jumpy, brother? That's good. All the brothers here been asleep too long; need some jumpin' up."

Brown was fascinated by that bushy hair. Negroes in Africa must have looked like that before they got civilized. "You—you must be the one that gal keeps talkin' about, some kinda leader."

One of them said sharply, "Not some kind of anything, old man—*the* leader. You never heard of Louis X?"

"Cool it, Abdullah; you and Gemal take the car out to the country church. Won't be hard to find, and nearest brothers put you up."

They snapped to like soldiers, lean and mean-looking in their black jackets, saying yessir and stalking outside; Reverend Brown would just as soon the leader hightailed it with them. They all carried the smell of real trouble.

"Now," Louis X said, "you and me and some coffee, brother. Tell me about our sister, Betty Jean."

Moving to the rickety gas stove, Brown put on the pot. "*Your* sister maybe."

"To all blacks," the tall man said. "Keep that in mind."

Uneasily, Brown fumbled around for coffee mugs. "She lived in sin with that wild Lassiter boy, then bold as brass, moved in with—"

Louis X said, "Lassiter—*Alvah* Lassiter?"

"That's him, craziest white boy in the county, got folks runnin' scared, hidin' in the woods, scared to sleep in they own beds. When all the trouble started, that Betty Jean gal moved in with the doctor and never bothered to hide it, what they're adoin'. Sodom and Gomorrah, that's what this town is comin' to; folks livin' openly in sin, carryin' on—"

Because the man's hard eyes stuck him like black icicles, Reverend Brown stopped talking. What kind of crazy name was Louis X, anyway, and how come he didn't clip his hair, sleep with his head in the top of a woman's stocking, like everybody else?

"Preacher," Louis X said evenly, "there ain't but one sin these days, and that's what the 'fays do to blacks, holdin' 'em in bondage, keepin' us slaves. Nothin' else counts. You preach on anything from your pulpit, preach long and hard on that."

Brown swallowed coffee that was too hot. "I do that, and they come down on me like ugly on a ape."

"You do that," Louis X said, "or you don't preach at all. We loaded for 'em, man. Before morning, be a whole bunch of FBI around this town, followin' me like I mean 'em to; be newspapermen and a TV crew. Anything these rednecks bastards try, it goes out all over the country."

The coffee tasted bitter, and Reverend Brown put down his cup. "Won't do me and my flock no good, does we get ourselfs killed."

Louis X said, "Bound to be casualties in war, man; like the books say, it's a calculated risk."

"Look here—these are *my* churches, and my folks, and even if I want to see our people get the vote bad as anybody else, I get marked down as some kind of agitator, and—"

"Hear me good," the tall man said. "You got no choice, man. You say what I tell you, or get your hat. The new order is here, old man, and we don't dig no Uncle Toms fuckin' it around. Now—where do I sleep? Got us a big day tomorrow."

Gone cold at the back of his neck, Reverend Brown pointed to the door of his dead wife's room. His hand was shaking.

His handsome face mottled and gone ugly with anger, Elliot Coffield stormed into the library and headed straight for the bar. He downed straight bourbon and kicked the bar, kicked it again.

Jessica said, "Daddy thought a heap of that bar. I hope you break your foot."

He spun on her, mouth working. "Shut up, you bitch; just shut up!"

"What's the matter," she asked, "did your country-boy image slip and catch you speakin' passable English?"

"Don't fuck with me, Jessica; don't even try to get cute. Do you know—" Elliot spun on the stool and poured more whiskey, drank it down. "Have you any idea what your lover did to me? That white trash son of a bitch—and *you* helped him, didn't you? *Didn't you?*"

She uncurled slim legs and stood up. "I don't give a damn if you pop a blood vessel or drop dead with a seizure, but if you mean for me to understand what the hell you're talkin' about, try makin' a little sense."

Squeezing the whiskey glass so hard his knuckles turned white, Elliot said, "He's blackmailing me; *me!* Let a hardscrabble dirt farmer rise above his station, and he gets uppity as any nigger with five dollars in his pocket. That bastard."

Jessica had never seen her brother so furious, and for a moment wondered if there was any way Earl Lassiter could use the information she'd given him about Thomas Elliot. Thinking hard, she could see no possibility; Elliot was Sandy's husband; the boy was legally their child, and anything else was unproven—and libelous—conjecture. She would deny everything.

"Settle down, Elliot; how can he blackmail you, for what?"

Elliot's mouth trembled, and she thought he was going to cry. "I'm so close, so *close* and this—Jessica, the gubernatorial candidate called me in. Old Bannerman could hardly talk, he was so shaken; acted as if he didn't even want to touch me with a long pole, but from all he said, he has no choice, either. Too late to drop me from the campaign, and I got the impression he isn't allowed to, anyhow. But he made it damned clear that I have to carry more than my end, that the party won't contribute another dime."

She said, "I thought you hit the jackpot with the Lassiter mill, and the corporation behind it." Jessica felt a sudden twinge of worry.

"Private detectives," Elliot went on, tight-voiced, "swarms of them; New Orleans, Baton Rouge, Gulf-port, Jackson—everywhere I so much as stopped over-night. Motel registers, affidavits from desk clerks, license numbers; they even bribed and threatened some people—"

"Men," Jessica said, "pretty young men; ex-lovers who turned you in. Now they can prove you're queer. You're out of politics, Elliot. Once that information hits the newspapers—"

"It won't," he said quickly. "I've been given to understand that. Oh lord—even poor Mark; somehow they got pictures of Mark Manley and me. It will simply *destroy* Mark."

Jessica went behind the bar and took a stiff drink. "Poor Mark, hell; you're in the crapper and you worry about another swish?"

Elliot's eyes were red, as if he hadn't slept all night. "You wouldn't understand; you never *try* to understand. All you ever cared about is yourself, and oh yes—for dear Daddy, the hots you had for him."

"You disgustin' little shit," Jessica said. "I'll be so glad to see you as just another goddamn fairy who had to leave the state. No more bigshot senator, no more walkin' all over me."

Acidly, Elliot smiled. "You're wrong, you round-heeled slut. Earl Lassiter blocked me from easy financing, but I can still get money for my campaign, more than enough. And how I do it will make you wet the panties you drop for any horny white trash."

Jessica stiffened. "You won't sell off any of The Shadows."

"Won't I? Can't I?" Elliot smirked. "All that bottom land you've been working like a common field hand; I don't need it anymore. All I need is a base in Temple County, the traditional manor house, and that's all I mean to keep. The rest of it goes; I can get a good price from Sam Harvey, since his land adjoins The Shadows on the east. Maybe that bastard Lassiter would be interested; he'll have to move this way sooner or later."

"No," Jessica said, then more strongly: "No!"

"We've been through all this," Elliot said. "Control of The Shadows is mine, one way or another. I don't mean to sell the house, and couldn't if I wanted, so long as Mama is alive. But you don't have a damned thing to say about it, Jessica. After I'm governor—"

She laughed. "Governor? You won't even be the governor's errand boy. I told you before, not an inch of Coffield land goes."

"You're so tiresome. What can you do—peddle that story about Avery screwing his son's wife? Spread it around that I'm a homosexual? Sour grapes, my dear, and everyone in Temple County knows what *you* are. Nobody would believe you."

Mechanically, she reached for the silver shaker and mixed ingredients into it, added ice, capped it. "They'll believe photostats."

He stared at her. "You don't have copies of that stuff Earl raked up."

"I don't need that," she said, calmly as she could.

Five . . . six . . . seven . . . the perfect sidecar. Jessica uncapped the shaker and poured. "I have something just as damaging, perhaps more so."

Elliot got off the stool. "You should have taken lessons from Daddy; he never bluffed. Perhaps if you'd watched how he operated, instead of daydreaming about him mounting you—"

"You—you goddamned simperin' *queer*! I'm not bluffin'; I can nail your girly hide to the wall, and I sure as hell will, if you make a single move to sell my land."

He lifted an eyebrow. "Really; I was under the impression it's my land, and my son's."

Jessica's lips curled. "And you're under the impression that your so-called son is the *only* Thomas Elliot Coffield."

Now Elliot's eyes widened. "What do you mean?"

"I mean," she said, savoring the taste of each word, "that there's another Thomas Elliot Coffield, tucked away safely where you can never find him. Oh, he's a little younger than the other one, than Daddy's sullen little bastard, but that really won't make any difference when his identity is known, when even his very name becomes public."

"This is some kind of trick, and I swear—"

Showing her teeth at him, Jessica said, "Try to swear out of the fact that the second Thomas Elliot Coffield is *black*, just as shiny black a little nigger as ever you saw."

Speechlessly, Elliot lifted his hands to the bar and hung on. "That—that doesn't mean anything—just a name—"

"A name on a birth certificate, duly recorded, attested to; born in Jackson General Hospital and witnessed by ever so many shocked white folks. It won't do you any good to tamper with the records, either; the originals are in a safety deposit box under another name. My, you should have seen how that doctor and those nurses looked at me, like I had some kind of contagious, terrible disease."

Elliot swayed. *"You?"*

"Sure; I had to have somethin' put back to keep you from destroyin' The Shadows. So I put by my nigger baby, with my own name on the birth certificate, right along with the pickaninny's footprint. You see, Elliot, I *did* know a little about how Daddy operated. He never let a thing stand in the way of what he wanted, anything he had to have, and neither will I."

"My s-sister and a—a nigger child—"

"The senator's sister; the lieutenant governor's sister—nigger lover with a little nigger bastard all this time. My, but you're goin' to look almighty silly. The Templars, the Klan, and all your hardshelled Christian voters—"

He swung hard, and the slap landed high on her cheek with enough force to spin her from behind the bar and drive her into a heap on the floor.

Gibbering, his eyes wild, Elliot plunged after her, tried to kick her in the head as Jessica rolled away in panic. She screamed when his foot struck her hip, and scuttled off on hands and knees. He flung the silver shaker at her; it crashed against the wall, splattering ice and a darkwet stain. Jessica screamed again.

"Stay away from me, Elliot! Damn you, stay away! If somethin' happens to me, everybody'll know—it'll be in all the papers, on TV—*Elliot!*"

"Elliot!" Lila Coffield echoed from the archway. "Whatever are you—"

"Mama," Jessica whimpered, "Mama, he's gone crazy."

Pale and drawn, a feathery wrapper hanging loosely about her frame, Lila said, "Now you all stop this squabblin' immediately. I will not have it; you hear, children?"

Elliot ignored her, stood trembling. "I'll find him, Jessica. I'll get rid of him and every incriminating paper in existence. And when that's done, I'll get rid of *you*."

Close to her mother, Jessica got shakily up and faced him. "You can't. I fixed you good, real good. You can just get your politics money somewhere else, anywhere else, because you're not about to sell off The Shadows."

Lila clutched her dressing gown closer. "Whatever are you talkin' about, child? Your brother wouldn't sell our home, wouldn't even consider it."

He was still panting, his hair tousled. "You sneaky, cunning bitch. You planned this a long time ago, right after Daddy died."

"I had to. You never cared about the land, the way Daddy did, the way I do. You'd do anything to be governor, even go to Washington, well—I'll do whatever *I* have to, so The Shadows goes on."

Elliot rubbed a hand across his face. "So you went out and found a nigger stud and deliberately got pregnant by him, then went away and dropped your black bastard and hid him—just for a weapon to use against me."

Lila Coffield put a hand against the archway. "You—Jessica—I don't understand what your brother's sayin'."

Elliot said viciously, "It's simple, Mama dear. Your sweet white daughter got herself knocked up by a sweaty, stinking buck, and whelped a nigger baby.

Then she named it Coffield, Mama—Thomas Elliot *Coffield*."

"You—you didn't, Jessica? This is a horrible dirty joke; you d-didn't—couldn't—"

"Cry all you want," Jessica said to her brother. "It won't change anything. You've taken the last money away from The Shadows, out of the fields and equipment so you can play big man all over the state. And dear brother—if any accident happens to me, it all comes out. I didn't miss a trick."

"No," he said, "I would imagine you're adept at turning tricks."

"Jessica! Elliot!" Lila's voice was a shriek. "Is this true—are you—my baby girl, my son—you—you—"

She swayed, tried to catch herself, and almost fell. When they didn't answer her, Lila turned slowly and wavered through the living room. They heard the screen door bang shut after her.

"I'll kill you," Elliot said.

"No you won't; you'd be killin' yourself, too. You'll survive, Elliot; you'll find a way to keep on and you'll get by. It just won't be as easy."

Shoulders hunched, he went back to the bar. "Where did Mama go?"

"The garden, probably. When she's not in her room, she putters around the garden."

"Better go get her," Elliot said.

Jessica rubbed her bruised hip. "You're supposed to be the man of the house. *You* go get her."

CHAPTER 33

She got off the bus carrying a little overnight bag, looking lost and uncertain. Sandy took a couple of steps toward the gas station and its phone, saw the loafers staring, and turned back. The bank, she thought; she could call from the bank and they'd send a car for her. Maybe; not if Lila and Jessica were home alone. Then she'd have to hire someone to drive her out to The Shadows.

Face up to things, she told herself, hesitating before the gilt-lettered window of the bank, smelling Temple County dust and feeling eyes crawling over her, sensing whispers. Beyond the window, a woman with hair drawn into a bun stared at her, and Sandy flinched at the rattle of a bicycle passing behind her. Forty miles to Meridian and an AA meeting; forty miles from any kind of help.

It's all there inside yourself, they'd told her; the strength is there, and when you need to get pumped up a little, we're within reach. Sandy gnawed her lips, shifted the small bag from hand to hand. No AA meeting in the daytime, anyhow; no member in this narrowminded, hidebound town. She was on her own.

The man came out of the bank, worn jeans, open work shirt, boots, an intense but open face. He stalked across the cracked sidewalk to a pickup and yanked open its door. Then he looked at her standing there and said, "Need any help?"

"I—" Sandy said, "I—was going inside to phone, have someone come and get me."

"Sam Harvey'll probably charge you a dollar and a half to use his phone. I'll be glad to drop you somewhere—if you're not afraid to be seen with me."

Sandy glanced through the window; the woman was still staring at her. She turned back and said, "Why should I be afraid?"

"You must be new in town," he said, and she liked the set of his shoulders, the stubborn look of him; he reminded her of somebody.

"I've—been away," Sandy said. "If it's no bother, I'd appreciate a lift to The Shadows. Do you know where that is?"

"Oh yes," he said. "I'm going right past it. My name is Earl Lassiter, so if you'd rather wait for another ride—"

"The Lassiter mill," Sandy said. She moved to the truck and climbed in to slide across the seat. "I'm grateful, Mr. Lassiter. I'm Sandra Coffield; Elliot's wife."

"I'll be damned," he said. "Everybody in the county will chew this over with supper. If you don't mind, I don't."

"They've been talking about me for a long time," Sandy said. "I should be used to it."

Driving along the main street, he said, "But you're not?"

"No." She looked away and felt dark eyes searching her, weighing her.

Earl said, "If you stay, you grow a callus." Turning left onto the back highway, he said, "You don't have an easy time of it with Jessica and the rest. Why do you stay?"

Her insides were going tight, and she hung onto the small bag desperately. "My son, because of my son."

"Something always holds us, if we allow it. There are better places to live, to raise a child. I'm part of Temple County, and I *have* to stay."

"We all have a choice," Sandy murmured, "of sorts, anyway. There's the house, Mr. Lassiter. You don't have to take me all the way in."

"Sure I will, Mrs. Coffield." The white gravel drive crunched beneath his wheels, and huge live oaks dappled shade across the moving truck. Earl stopped before the columned porch, before wisteria vines losing their leaves. The house needed a coat of paint, he saw. "Mrs. Coffield, Sandra—I only once actually saw your boy, but I know he isn't happy. If you—"

"Thank you," she said quickly, and left the pickup. "I'm back now, and I can—well, thanks again."

Earl drove off slowly, and when he looked into the rearview mirror, saw her standing slumped and forlorn on the shaded porch, seeming smaller. Avery Coffield's mistress, Elliot Coffield's wife; he hadn't pictured her like that. She should be younger, brassy, and sure of what she had to offer, the commodity she was trading. Sandra Coffield was none of that; she was a little girl lost behind a grown-up façade, and she was badly frightened. The Coffields would tear bloody strips out of her. The image of Sandra clinging, Earl whipped the truck back onto the road and headed for the mill.

"Ain't goin' near that mill," Sheriff Kobburn said. "Alvah ain't likely to be there nohow. All them Hobbs slippin' around with guns—uh-uh. Nobody wants Al-vah Lassiter bad enough to commit suicide."

"How the hell are you keepin' this quiet?" Scarpo said.

Kobburn rubbed his belly and sipped at iced bour-bon. "Couldn't shut down the killin's of Ben and his wench; that nigger doctor filed a report with the state *po*lice. But them Lovelaces now—one fell in the river and t'other run off the road; accidents. Got us a sure enough doctor comin' in today, white man from Mem-phis to put that nigger in his place."

"That Alvah," Scarpo said. "Didn't give a damn when it was him and them others, but he took off with my hot truck, wasted my driver and a load of alky. Now he sold a load belonged to me, and he's runnin' independent. That mother gets burned, guy that does it collects a bonus."

"Liable not to be that easy," Kobburn said. "We got federal men in town; strangers all over the god-damn place, and some big nigger hisself come from the Coast to stir up more trouble. I come by today to tell you we better watch it for a spell, maybe shut down the runs."

"You don't *tell* me nothin'," Scarpo said. "*Marone!* To think I coulda been in New Orleans all this time. Yeah, okay; I'll hold back the alky until it settles down."

"If it settles. Niggers fixin' to march down the street, and the shit'll hit the fan then for sure. About that bonus now—how much you figure?"

Scarpo looked at him. "Five big ones, if I get my truck back."

Kobburn grunted. "That might bring Lovelaces out in the open."

*   *   *

He came out of the woods moving quietly on foot, low to the ground and flitting from tree to bush until he was at the back door. Then Alvah went in with a rush, carbine across his chest, to stand in the Africa Baptist church and check every deserted pew. Padding down the aisle, he opened the door into the tacked-on rectory.

Two strange blacks snapped heads around at him. Alvah said, "Cool it; I'm lookin' for Lou Miller."

One of them said, "With a gun, man?"

Alvah lowered the carbine. "People after my ass, but it's got nothin' to do with Lou. I figured he'd be here."

"Figured wrong," the other said. "What you want with him?"

Alvah sensed the hostility, the watchfulness. "My business and his, brother."

"Brother, shit," one said. "*Mother*, more like it."

"Look," Alvah said, "Lou and me, we were asshole buddies in Korea. I want to see him and he wants to see me. I'll stay put until one of you gets a message to him that Alvah Lassiter's here. And don't come on strong with me, man."

"Lissen him, talkin' black. Don't go with that 'fay hide."

Shifting the carbine, Alvah said, "Lou used to pick his friends better. Jump salty with me, motherfucker, and I'll burn some spade ass, you dig? Now one of you bad mouths get your hat and tell Lou."

Eyes malevolent, one man got up carefully from a chair and Alvah made him room to pass. The other just looked as Alvah picked a chair and sat with the carbine across his knees. A long time ago, he had learned how to wait.

* * *

Every restless movement of Jessica's body showed impatience. She walked back and forth, crossing the small mill office several times, noting with some satisfaction that the typist was a nigra. Funny to see one, though; she'd just never thought there might be black typists.

Two white men came down the hall, talking animatedly to a tall woman, and Jessica tensed as she recognized Barbara Dexter. She turned to look out the window, but the woman had seen her anyhow.

Behind her, Barbara said, "If you're waiting for Earl, he drove to town."

"I'm certainly not waitin' on *you*," Jessica said.

"Might as well come into my office. Miss Gattling, it's time for your coffee break, isn't it?"

Imagine, Jessica thought, calling a nigra *Miss*, and one of those sharecropper Gattling nigras, at that.

"Yes'm," the typist said, and left the room.

"We're changing the offices around," Barbara said. "In time they'll look decent."

"I'm sure I don't care," Jessica said. "If Earl's not comin' back soon—"

"I run interference for Earl, handle many of his minor problems. Perhaps you'd care to tell me your business."

"It's personal," Jessica said. "Just go right on handlin' your minor problems, and I'll tell Earl when I see him."

She was halfway across the room when Barbara's voice stabbed at her: "Tell me, Jess—have you ever been truly satisfied by a man?"

"Goddamn you," Jessica spat, "don't *dare* call me Jess!" Then she turned and fled, heels beating a furious drumroll against the floor.

*   *   *

Calvin Davison wished he hadn't seen the look that jumped into Betty Jean's face when this Louis X walked through the back door of the clinic.

As if she has looked upon the visage of God, he thought, but Louis X wasn't even a disciple, unless it was of the devil. He was bizarre, demanding attention by his paramilitary dress, the flamboyantly bushed hairdo and golden earring. But Davison had to admit the man was more than simply flash; a spark burned in him, one that could reach out and ignite loyalty—or fanaticism—in others.

"Organize," Louis X was saying to a select few in the clinic. "Organize, plan, and attack. These 'fays don't listen to soft talk; they don't hear logic; they don't even hear the cryin' of little children. They're not *gonna* hear, until somebody kicks 'em in the ass and yells—hey, honkie! I'm *here*, baby, and I ain't goin' away just because you want me to, and I ain't stayin' in my place—the place you picked for me— because my place is right up there with *you*, baby; because I'm just as much a *man* as you are, and maybe a damned sight more!"

"Tell it, brother," a young man said.

Louis X spread his hands, strong and capable. He stood tall behind the table, a figure of power and hope. "Yeah, I'm tellin' it. And I say we got the start of an organization here, one we have to pull together in a hurry, account of the registration's comin' up. We have the strength, the numbers—man, we got 'em outnumbered two to one, and we about to show Mr. Charley that strength. No more kissin' ass; no more yassuh; no more doin' dirty nigger work for nigger pay!"

"Yeah!" someone shouted, and an older man chanted, "Amen!"

A rabble-rouser, Davison thought, who could pull

an audience with him, but to where? Yet so much of what Louis X said made sense, and maybe he was right about confrontations; nothing else had worked so far.

"When we vote," Louis X went on, "and we *will* vote, brothers—then Mr. Charley got to listen, got to shape up, or get himself blown away by the ballot box. Now, ain't nobody sayin' it's easy; ain't nobody sayin' blood won't get spilled, but they about to learn that nobody can tell black blood from white blood, when it's runnin' in the street."

Beside Davison, Dan Mason whispered, "Lord, lord."

Louis X pointed a finger like a gun barrel, sweeping his listeners with it. "The clock's run out for whitey, but he don't know it until we show him. We got to show him we have balls, that if he means to put down the brothers, *he's* goin' to get put down with us. Judge Lynch been hangin' over our shoulder all our lives, so dyin' ain't nothin' new to us; let's see how whitey likes it!"

"Yeah," they chanted, "yeah, yeah!" and Davison could feel a sweaty, violent excitement building.

Dan Mason stood up, square and blocky, a steadying figure the older ones looked to. He said, "I mean to register, but I don't want to stand against none of my white friends."

"You got no white friends, brother," Louis X said. "See where they stand when you try to get your vote."

Davison said, "All this talk of blood and dying; the goal is registration, not war."

"The war starts when we try to register," Betty Jean put in, "and it won't be us starts it."

"But we can finish it," Louis X said. "This time, we don't run like puppy dogs; this time we don't kiss they asses and beg 'em please don't whup us no more, massah. Now, I have cadre men who'll move into the field and recruit, who'll make sure every black in this county marches on that courthouse. Abdullah will take the northern sector, Gemal the south half; I'll be at the head of the town column—"

"And when the state police are drawn up?" Davison asked. "The guard, deputies from other counties?"

Louis X held up a black fist, threw it skyward. "They fire on us, put dogs on us, we *burn* this fuckin' town, burn it down on whitey's head!"

The shock of it quieted the crowd in the clinic, and Louis X kept his fist raised. "First, they get a sample we mean business. No black goes to work a week before registration, *nobody*—that means no house niggers, no field hands, nobody. Anybody cops out on that order, my boys discipline 'em."

Dan Mason said, "I work the Lassiter mill, and Earl Lassiter never done harm to no black here."

Louis X put burning eyes on him. "Never rubbed a pickaninny's head, never called you boy, never raped a black woman, never paid you less than a 'fay doin' the same job?"

Stubbornly, Dan said, "His daddy was a good man, and the youngun is, too. Payin' more'n any boss in the county, and the *same*, brother—the same for black and white."

Softening his voice, Louis X said, "To make this strike work, it's got to be all-inclusive. It has to show 'em how much they need us, depend on our sweat. You understand that, man?"

"I understand you come in here and talk about burnin' down this town, where you don't live. When you gone, we still be here, scratchin' around in the ashes for somethin' to eat."

"What's your name, man—Uncle Tom Somebody?"

"My name's Dan Mason, and I ain't ashamed to say it. Dan *Mason*, not X, Y, or Z, and comes to the marchin', I be there, but I be at my job, too. And the first nigger strikes a match to my house goin' to wish he didn't."

As they stared at him, Dan clumped out of the room and slammed the door. Davison said, "That man has a lot of respect around here."

"Not respect," Betty Jean said, "just patronizing from whitey because he's a good nigger. But he's still a *nigger*."

Louis X put his hands behind his back. "Been plannin' to call on the mill man, anyhow. Seems he could get hurt worse than the other 'fays; got a bigger payroll. Could be he'd see the light and shut down on his own, or talk some sense to the other whiteys."

Abdullah slid into the clinic and went up to his chief. Men began to shift restlessly, to whisper among themselves, and Davison thought a fuse had already been lighted, despite Mason's resistance and Reverend Brown's weak disapproval, despite his own mumblings.

Louis X lifted a hand for silence, and it came immediately. He said, "Lassiter man runs the mill? Well, I'm goin' off to meet his brother now. And by the way, seems like they's a fat sheriff tryin' to hide under a tree out there, so you can go either by the front door and tell him good evenin' to his face, or sneak out the back."

They all went out the front. Davison thought Betty Jean was going with them, but she stayed behind. Davison might have been wrong about Louis X signaling her with a jerk of his head.

**If you smoke
and are interested in tar...
you may find the
information on the back
of this page very worthwhile.**

A comparison of 58 popular cigarette brands with Golden Lights.

FILTER BRANDS (KING SIZE)

REGULAR	MG. TAR	MG. NIC.	MENTHOL	MG. TAR	MG. NIC.
Golden Lights			Golden Lights		
Regular	8	0.7°	Menthol	8	0.7°
Parliament	9	0.6	Kool Super Lights	9	0.8
Real	9	0.7	Salem Lights	10	0.8
Camel Lights	9	0.8	Multifilter Menthol	11	0.7
Vantage	11	0.8	Vantage Menthol	11	0.8
Viceroy Extra Milds	11	0.8	Doral Menthol	12	0.8
Marlboro Lights	12	0.8	Marlboro Menthol	14	0.8
Doral	12	0.9	Alpine	14	0.8
Multifilter	13	0.8	Kool Milds	14	0.9
Winston Lights	13	0.9	Belair	15	0.9
Raleigh Lights	13	0.9	Salem	16	1.1
Raleigh	16	1.0	Kool	17	1.4
Viceroy	16	1.1			
Marlboro	17	1.0			
L&M	17	1.0			
Lark	17	1.1			
Tareyton	17	1.2			
Pall Mall	17	1.2			
Camel	19	1.3			
Winston	20	1.3			

°FTC Method

FILTER BRANDS (100's)

100's REGULAR	MG. TAR	MG. NIC.	100's MENTHOL	MG. TAR	MG. NIC.
Golden Lights 100's	10	0.9°	Golden Lights		
Merit 100's	11	0.7	100's Menthol	10	0.9°
Benson & Hedges			Merit 100's Menthol	11	0.7
100's Lights	11	0.8°	Benson & Hedges		
Parliament 100's	12	0.8	100's Lights		
Marlboro Lights			Menthol	11	0.8°
100's	12	0.8°	Virginia Slims		
Winston Lights 100's	13	1.0	100's Menthol	16	0.9
Virginia Slims 100's	16	0.9	Eve 100's Menthol	16	1.0
Eve 100's	16	1.0	Silva Thins Menthol	16	1.1
Silva Thins	16	1.2	Belair 100's	16	1.1
Tareyton 100's	16	1.2	Pall Mall		
L&M 100's	17	1.1	100's Menthol	16	1.2
Benson & Hedges			Benson & Hedges		
100's	17	1.1	100's Menthol	17	1.0
Raleigh 100's	17	1.2	L&M 100's Menthol	18	1.1
Marlboro 100's	18	1.1	Kool 100's	18	1.3
Viceroy 100's	18	1.2	Salem 100's	19	1.3
Pall Mall 100's	19	1.4	Winston 100's		
Winston 100's	19	1.3	Menthol	19	1.3

°FTC Method

Kings only 8 mg. tar

100's only 10 mg. tar

They're as low as you can go and still get good taste.

Source of all 'tar' and nicotine disclosures in this ad is either FTC Report May 1978 or FTC Method.
Of All Brands Sold: Lowest tar: 0.5 mg. 'tar,' 0.05 mg. nicotine av. per cigarette, FTC Report May 1978.
Golden Lights: 100's Regular and Menthol —10 mg. 'tar,' 0.9 mg. nicotine;
Kings Regular and Menthol —8 mg. 'tar,' 0.7 mg. nicotine av. per cigarette by FTC Method.

© Lorillard, U.S.A.,1978

CHAPTER 34

"Hell, no," Kobburn said. "You ain't about to work outa my office and get in my way ever time I turn around. Find your own goddamn place." Suits and ties, he thought; what kind of lawmen did they think they were? City folks; he'd like to see them out sloshing around the river or busting through briar patches.

"Sheriff," the agent said, "we're accustomed to working with local enforcement agencies, but if you don't intend to cooperate—"

Kobburn leaned back in the chair and threw boots up on his scarred desk. "I don't know doodly squat about this here civil rights stuff, and it ain't my job. You work your side of the road and I'll handle mine."

The other man said, "Have you made any progress on the murders?"

"Old man Lassiter and his wench? If'n I have, it's my business."

"Not if it's concerning civil rights," the first agent put in.

Jesus, Kobburn thought; look at them, all duded up like they was about to play-act on TV. "This here's my county," he said, "and I do things my way. You go bustin' around in them woods and the *best* thing'll happen is you get snakebit or squall for help from a bed of quicksand. Folks out yonder don't cotton to

strangers nosin' around their property, and if somebody don't draw on you, they sure as hell ain't studyin' on answerin' questions."

"We're not interested in their stills," the agent said.
"That's no concern of the bureau."

Grunting, Kobburn said, "One guvment man same
as t'other. Do better was you to haul off that biggity
nigger afore he starts somethin' he can't finish. How
come you ain't on *his* back, him threatenin' to burn
down the whole town, incitin' to riot and such like?
If'n I can find that bastard, I'll stick him so far back
in jail they'll have to pipe daylight to him."

The older agent said, "That would be a mistake,
Sheriff. Louis X is a leader, a symbol, and nothing
would suit him better than to become a martyr. Your
town probably will burn, if he's arrested."

"He won't live to see it," Kobburn said, and wished
he hadn't. These FBI men came in here toting law
books and connections running clear back to Washington, and lord knows what they could get at him for.
Hastily, he said, "What I mean is, folks won't take
kindly to burnin', and when these peckerwoods get
riled up, you and me ain't enough to stop 'em; there
ain't state guard or state *po*lice enough to stop 'em."

"If everything is worked out properly, thought out
logically, it won't come to violence," the agent said. "A
peaceful demonstration, the exercise of civil rights. No
provocation on anyone's part, a quick sealing off of
trouble spots if they flare up—"

"Jesus," Kobburn said, "you talk like we got a army
here. Lemme tell you somethin'—the *army*'s out yonder, and when them niggers come marchin' down the
street hollerin' burn Temple city, that's when the war
starts. I ain't about to get caught in the middle."

"We thought as much," the agent said calmly.

"Go on," Kobburn said, "see if'n your law books fit to be tombstones."

The agents went to the door; the older one looked back. "We'll be around, Sheriff."

"Yeah," Kobburn said, and wondered how much they knew about Beevo's.

"There's always Beevo's," Jessica Coffield said. "I reckon your talents would be appreciated there."

Sandy kept her hands together. "This is my home, my son's home and heritage; it's where we intend to stay."

Jessica flung herself to the bar and tinkled ice into a glass, splashed bourbon over it, made a production of enjoying the drink. "You're only here on sufferance, only because Elliot allows you to stay. I thought we were done with you when he shipped you off to that crazy house. It's just a pure shame they didn't keep you locked up." Cutting a look at the other woman, Jessica said, "If you're all cured, have a drink. Folks that aren't crazy can take just one drink without hurtin' anything."

"No thanks," Sandy said. "I'll go up now and see my son."

"Might be there, might not. Seems Thomas Elliot takes to nigras more, and it's true that Auntie Kate's a better mama."

"Will Elliot be home soon?" Sandy asked. "They told me at the hospital they'd called him."

"Well now, the senator's kind of busy, runnin' hard just to keep even, I'd say. But he drops in, time to time. Oh; when you get drunk and go insane again, try to be quiet; Lila took to her bed, feelin' poorly."

Sandy got up and climbed the stairs, feeling weakness in her knees, blowing the tantalizing odor of bourbon from her nostrils. She opened the master-suite door and saw Jessica's things inside, the scarlet sheets. Down the hall to Thomas Elliot's room then, to sit trembling upon his narrow bed and wonder why he didn't have many toys. There was so much to learn about her son. She hoped he would give her the chance.

"Never thought we'd have another chance," Alvah said, slapping Lou Miller on the back. "Goddamn, when them gooks were poppin' away at us and I was leakin' all over you, I figured that was all she wrote, man. But here we are, just like the old days, you hard-ass fuckin' spade. Drink it dry and fuck 'em all, huh? Don't even save six for pallbearers."

"Or two for road guards," Louis X said. "Fuck 'em *all*, man; *semper fi*."

Alvah waved a Mason jar of bootleg. "Ain't this the place? Reminds me of that time we raised hell in that gook whorehouse; course, these gals talk English and they got indoor plumbing. Man, have they got indoor plumbing."

Louis X said, "Heard you been *gunji* with the locals."

"Ol' gung-ho Lassiter, that's me." Alvah drank from the jar and passed it. "Just caught up on some cats that burned my old man, and ain't done with it yet. Goddamn civilians tryin' to slip up on an old grunt like me; never happen, Marine. Where the hell those gals get to?"

"They be back," Louis X said and took a drink. "You gettin' along okay on that leg?"

Rapping it with his knuckles, Alvah said, "Do a thirty-mile hike on it; walk clear to Luke the Gook's

Castle. Hey—you remember how we cut up that chink patrol?"

"Never forget it, man."

"To the fuckin' Gyrenes," Alvah said, and spilled clear liquor down his chin. "Wish to hell I coulda stayed with you, buddy. Stateside is a drag, nothin' to keep a man goin', nothin' happening."

"I got out," Louis X said. "The fuckin' war was lastin' forever, so I got out."

Alvah blinked. "I wouldn't mind. Beats hell outa civilian life—if you can call it livin'."

Thoughtfully, Louis X said, "I got shook when you lost your leg. There wasn't nobody I was close to, you dig. And man, they kept feedin' more and more blacks in, using them up, burnin' them up, right outa boot camp, man."

"Hey, I don't remember that many blacks."

"Percentagewise, more than whites, a lot more. Then I got back to Japan on R & R, and saw all those fatcats coolin' it, bunch of office pinkies and desk riders livin' it up, while so many brothers were dyin' back in Frozen Chosen. I said screw it and got out; let them mothers fight their own wars."

Alvah frowned and took a drink, stretched out his bad leg. They were in a Clark County cathouse stuck off in the woods like all good cathouses ought to be, with hot black whores and pretty good whiskey. It was a time to remember, to say how goddamn good it had all been, because there'd never been a guy like ol' Lou Miller, never a pair of asshole buddies like Lou and Alvah.

"Got out in Dago," Louis X was saying, "and soon's I took off my blues, what do you think? I was just another nigger, man; step back in the line, *boy*—you want to go to college, *boy?*—better take this janitor job; you don't have the qualifications for college. Shit; what they were tellin' me was go back to hustlin', never mind I fought their goddamn war; never mind they jived dark skin into wastin' dark skin—you just another nigger now, and it's too bad you didn't get wasted, too."

"Wait a minute," Alvah said. "I never thought nothin' like that, and as for them fuckin' gooks—man, you saw what they did to our people."

"I got to wondering," Louis X said, "what I'da done to some strange cat, was he in my backyard. I mean, it's their country, man. Ol' Syngman Rhee, he any better than the guy up north? Their turf, baby, and we had no business on it."

Alvah looked at the whiskey jar, back up at Lou Miller. Ol' Lou with a funny hair style and a gold earring, not dressed in utilitites or greens or blues, but all in black. Funny how much it looked like some kind of uniform. He said, "Williams, and that crazy kid Johnson, and all the others—Lieutenant Grey; you tryin' to tell me they died for nothin'?"

"We win anything over there?" Louis X asked. "Anybody give you the time of day when you come back? Now they startin' the same bullshit somewhere else."

"We're *Marines,* man," Alvah said. "Marines don't have politics."

"Used to be Marines. You ain't and I ain't, and a damned good thing, else they'd have us in Nam, burnin' Oriental brothers."

Alvah stared at him, whiskey bitter in his mouth. "No goddamn gook was ever my brother, but you come close to it, closer than my own blood kin."

Louis X touched his shoulder. "I know, baby, but you one in a million, one in a hundred million." He leaned closer. "Tell me, Alvah, your real brother, the one runs that big mill—would he be sittin' here jiving with a nigger and screwin' the same whores? Before you answer that, man, here's somethin' else for you—how come you had to take me to a black whorehouse? Why can't we both fuck white women?"

Alvah swallowed whiskey he didn't want because there was no answer, and he didn't want to think about all the other things Lou Miller said. His leg ached some and the women came giggling back; he smelled acrid sweat nothing like the exciting scent of Korean girls. What the hell made a man wear a ring in his ear? Damn; nothing seemed to be coming out right.

"Thought I'd come right out with it, Mr. Earl," Dan Mason said. "We back to where we was; just me and a couple more—and them Hobbs. But they more at home totin' rifles around than in the mill."

Earl nodded. "And it's not pickets this time."

"It's that Louis X and his folks. For certain there's bound to be trouble now."

"Thank you for coming in," Earl said. "Do what you can; concentrate on getting out one order at a time."

When Dan was gone, Earl walked into Barbara Dexter's cubicle. "May I borrow your crystal ball?"

"I've heard," she said. "More labor problems."

"A black messiah. Why would he want people not working?"

Barbara tapped a pencil upon the desk. "Demonstration of power, or perhaps something else."

"Such as?" She always looked crisp, he thought, always sleek and efficient. Had he made an irrevocable blunder, classifying Barbara as only another bed-and-bored company whore? She wasn't playing around with anyone on the staff.

There were folders open on her desk, and she pointed to one of them. "Louis W. Miller, Los Angeles, *aka* Louis X. Record of juvenile arrests before service in the Marine Corps, Korea; record of arrests since, but the pattern has changed. Misdemeanors, petty felonies before, political after return to civilian life. But all isn't kosher soul food; Louis may be all his people hope, but he's also a hustler. Companies have been invited to donate to his cause, in return for fire protection and/or labor insurance."

Earl said, "My, the things you can learn in sociology. You'd know if Greater Atlantic has ever been so invited, of course."

"Not yet. I'm not saying this civil rights leader has a numbered account in Switzerland; he might be using the funds solely for his movement. His political activity costs."

Fine-looking woman, he thought; she'd be beautiful if she wasn't so defensive, so determined not to be seen as a woman, but a better man than anyone on the staff. Sandra Coffield could use some of that *chutzpah*: he felt sorry for her, having to face Lila, Elliot, and even Jessica's fury.

He said, "Anything to do with politics is costly, it seems. What will company policy be, when this messiah puts the bite on GAC?"

Barbara closed the folder. "I'd say a donation would be made, within reason."

"Balanced against losses and written off as operating costs. Pay the two dollars."

"Something like that. I imagine you'll be hearing from Louis X soon."

"Or his heir," Earl said, and turned to leave.

"You will be sensible, Earl? There's nothing to be gained by stubborn resistance."

"Stubborn," he said, "me?"

Barbara said then, "Oh; Miss Coffield stopped by, but she couldn't wait."

"I'll call her; thanks. Have one of the drivers pick up my stuff from the motel, please. I'm moving into my father's house."

After he was gone, Barbara opened her lower desk drawer and removed another folder. She opened and looked at it awhile, before making a notation there. She returned the folder and touched short, manicured fingernails to the telephone, and closed her eyes, breathing deeply.

Elliot steadied himself. "I'm simply trying to make you see my position, Jessica. It won't be easy, but I can make out all right if I can just find a little capital, to show the party I'm still very much in the picture."

"You shouldn't have tried to shake down Earl," Jessica said. "He can release the information he has and finish you for all time in this state."

Elliot nodded. "But he *hasn't,* don't you see? He's only a small cog in Greater Atlantic Corporation, and he's been told not to go any farther. That means GAC is convinced it's to their benefit to keep me in politics."

"Then see them for the money," Jessica said. "Don't whine to me about mortgaging the land. Whining doesn't become you, dear; I like you better as your normal, bastardly self."

"I'll send Sandy away," he said, "and the boy, too."

"She's cheaper stayin' here," Jessica said, "and next time she gets drunk, you can put her in the state crazy house; no more fancy sanitariums."

He ran a hand through his hair. "Where's Mama?"

"In bed wtih ladylike vapors, since she saw us fightin'. She won't do you any good; all she has left is costume jewelry."

"You bitch," he said, "you vicious, heartless bitch. Why are you doing this to me, *why*?"

"You know," Jessica said, "you damned well know."

"Elliot," Sandy said from the archway, and they turned to stare at her.

"I meant to come see you in a while," Elliot said, "but this is so important—"

Pale without makeup, hair combed loosely, Sandy Coffield walked into the living room. "Thomas Elliot barely knows me, but he was glad to have someone to talk to. He's such a lonely little boy."

"Do tell," Jessica said. "I'm goin' to mix a drink. Anybody else want one?"

Elliot said, "Sandy, this is vital to my career, to Thomas Elliot's future. I've been trying to make Jessica see—"

"How much you need money," Sandy said. "I have money, Elliot. Your father put it into my account when he asked me to come up here and marry his son. Avery—Avery didn't want me to ever have to beg for anything. Will fifty thousand dollars help you?"

"My God," Elliot breathed. "Fifty thousand—"

Jessica rattled glasses in the library. "You—my daddy gave *you* all that money? Paid you to be his whore. Paid you so much, when all this time I could have used it for The Shadows? Goddamn you, I'll—"

Elliot laughed. "Don't whine, darling. You're better as your usual bitchy self. Sandy, Sandy, I can't tell you how much this—"

Carefully, she said, "You'll have it transferred to you only when you sign over all interest in The Shadows to your son and make me Thomas Elliot's executor."

"We don't have to go through all that rigmarole, Sandy. The boy already has a good share, and when I—"

"It's the only way I'll give you the money, Elliot."

Jessica smashed something in the library, and when she stormed into the living room, her face was ugly. "Don't do it, Elliot. She wants it all for herself and Daddy's bastard."

His smile was thin. "You left me no choice, dear— you and your lover thought you had me between a rock and a hard place. Of course I agree, Sandy. We'll go to Will Jellico in the morning and have the papers drawn up. I'll be lieutenant governor yet."

Still holding herself tightly, Sandy said, "You ought to look in on your mother now. I think she's dead."

CHAPTER 35

It was a good time to be in the woods. The air was cool off the river, and sweetgum leaves were turning. This was when hound dogs would be straining, eager to run, and the belling of their voices would soon be heard in crisp and starry nights.

This was when they'd taken up their guns and followed Pa, he and Alvah learning on every outing, and if they didn't tree a coon or shake a fat possum from a persimmon tree, that was all right, too. It was just being there together, walking free and easy like you could go on forever, and smelling woodsmoke, boiling coffee over an open fire while they waited old Gip's bugling when he struck a fresh trail.

It was bringing fat rabbits back for Ellen to dress out, still-hunting gray squirrels, collecting muscadines and chinquapins against the winter, storing hickory nuts and drying fox grapes that tasted like raisins later on. And still some catfishing to be done, wood to be split and stacked. But the best time of the year, because the hard work was behind and there'd be sitting around the fireplace while Pa spun a yarn or two.

Earl hunkered down on a bank above the river and watched a softshell turtle stick its pointed nose above water. There'd been times he'd lain right here with the .22, and Alvah, because he was bigger and a better swimmer, splashing in to scoop up a headshot turtle before he sank. If you hit them anyplace else, they went straight down like big rocks and you'd never find them in dark water.

A good feeling, having enough smoked and salted meat put by for winter; hams hung in the smokehouse, hogshead cheese in crocks and plenty of white lard; cornmeal ground and onions strung, sorghum in gallon jugs; honey, if you'd found a bee tree. A good feeling.

It only changed after you took to noticing the other younguns didn't have holes in their shoes, nor patched elbows. It got worse when the sap rose in you but the best girls lived in fancy houses with nigger servants and only went out with guys who had cars. That was a different hunger, one that fatback and crowder peas couldn't feed, something that kept gnawing at you year after year.

Sure, it was a prideful thing to walk your own land, to know nobody could make you bend your neck to him, long as that was so. And a man wasn't properly buried, unless laid to rest in his own soil. But there was worn-out land with shacks on it, and rich bottom land with big white houses on it, and you couldn't fault a man for needing to better himself.

No need to take hold of more than you could carry, though; no sense to spread out so big you couldn't keep track. Enough was enough; if you made a million dollars, who said it had to be turned into ten more? You didn't shoot more meat than you needed, didn't plant more than you could harvest, and two cars didn't drive any better than one. Nobody needed a swimming pool, long as the river was here.

Getting up, Earl brushed his hands. A month ago, before first frost, he'd have picked up seed ticks and

redbugs; now they were dying off or hibernating for
coming winter. Too bad other irritants, other blood-
suckers, couldn't be put off until next spring. He
looked upriver where the dam bulked, and knew that
Hobbs cousins were somewhere near. Hell of a thing,
when you had to guard your back as well as watch
ahead, but with feelings running high in the county,
there was no telling what some peckerwood might try.

Walking down toward the swinging bridge, Earl
found himself wishing the old house could somehow
have been saved. He'd have felt more comfortable
there, but the woodyard covered the site now. Was he
consorting with ghosts, living in his father's house,
dreaming of those simpler, better times? Certainly he
was living with a kind of guilt, for three years in Boston didn't change all the programing of youth, of generations, of the land.

Blood answered blood, and even if it didn't make a
lot of sense, some things were the way they were. Alvah reacted without thinking, and the Hobbs came
without considering where their guns might lead them.
And when Earl had been manhandled by Scarpo's
hoods, Pa had never said a word, just showed up
where he ought to be.

But Alvah was going to get himself killed, and even
if that was what Alvah wanted without knowing it,
what kind of burden would his death lay upon Earl?
The final Lassiter, heir to those old tombstones and
sunken graves in the pasture, Pa and Grandpa and
Colonel Lassiter and all their get buried yonder, looking to Earl Lassiter for justice.

Crossing the hanging bridge, he went up to the
house and let himself in. The rifles waited over the
mantelpiece, and there was Pa's can of Prince Albert.
Earl took down the can and papers to roll a cigarette;

he was never very good at it since he and Alvah smoked cornsilk; the cigarette was lumpy. The blue-smoke smell of it made it seem as if Pa was still in the house, and Earl found himself listening for Ellen in the kitchen. Little Marcie had always been so quiet you never knew she was around.

He'd have to get a cook, if any black would come work for him; maybe one of Dan Mason's kin. Now there was somebody doing what was right to him, knowing damned well what it might cost. Dan was not only in danger from the peckerwoods, but from his own people, the young ones all jacked up by this imported leader come to lead them to equality, forty acres, and a mule. Or into a holocaust.

The hounds were gone, but Earl sensed someone coming. He started for his rifle but dropped his hand. No woods runner would walk right up to the house that way. If somebody was laying for him, the man would put a scope on him from three hundred yards or so, as they'd done to Pa and Ellen. As Alvah had lined up on two Lovelaces?

"Earl—you there?"

He opened the door to Jessica, looking trim and pert in tailored workclothes. Kissing him on the cheek, she laughed her way inside. "My! If it hadn't been for Dan, I don't think I could've gotten by your guards. It's kind of like you're in a state of siege."

"I am."

"Oh pish! You men are always makin' everything worse than it seems."

"Sorry to hear about your mama."

Jessica coasted to the table and put a package upon it. "Yes, poor Mama. She just never got over Daddy bringin' that woman into The Shadows, and then the child, and then—just when we thought we got rid of her forever, yonder she comes back from the crazy house, bold as you please. I swear, there's just no understandin' some people. When Mama saw Sandy again, she just took to her bed and gave up.''

"I meant to come to the funeral," Earl said.

"No," Jessica said. "It was quick and real private, just like poor Mama wanted. She's better off without all that disgrace. But I needed cheerin' up, so I brought over some sour mash, and if you have water and ice—"

The country could change and a race war loom, but Jessica was always herself. She looked very good in a summer tan just fading, that mass of hair bound back by a ribbon, the delicacy of her features improved by maturity, her body ripened and straining against tight jeans, mounding a simple shirt. Earl turned on a light and brought glasses, ice cubes.

"How'd you know I was here, Jessica?"

"Well, you weren't at the mill or the motel, so I—oh, Earl; must a girl give away all her secrets? With you, I guess that's so; I could never hold back anything from you."

He let her pour whiskey, then said, "You're holding back our boy."

Jessica frowned. "Are you so sure it's the right time, with all this trouble? And keepin' him in the same house with that drunken woman, and Elliot—after what you did to him—"

"Elliot did it to himself. He should have known I wouldn't be pushed. He tried to blackmail me, Jessica. I fought back."

"And I don't blame you one bit," she said quickly, "but it did put *me* in a terrible bind. Elliot almost mortgaged most of The Shadows, and the lord knows I'm havin' a hard enough time keepin' it solvent. But then, Elliot was always so lucky, and I'm not. He's still able to run for office."

Sipping whiskey, Earl said, "He found the money."

Jessica tossed off her drink and poured another. "Got it from that hussy. My daddy paid her to marry Elliot, just so he could have his whore under our roof, paid her fifty thousand dollars he took from what was rightfully ours."

"And she gave it to Elliot?"

Jessica slid down in the old hide-bottom chair and stretched her legs. "Traded it to him for his interest in The Shadows; said it was to protect her brat's future, but a woman like that—anyhow, that leaves me barely hangin' on. And I won't give her the satisfaction, won't let a—a nobody take over my house; I just *won't!* She doesn't belong there, Earl. You and I do."

"I used to dream of that," he admitted, "as a fairy-tale; the castle, the beautiful princess, but I never had a white horse, only Pa's old pickup."

She came to him, fitted her slim body between his knees. "Earl, Earl, I should have waited. I didn't love Adam Benning, but I had to marry him, to save The Shadows. You understand that; you love the land as much as I do. But when you came back, I filed for divorce. It won't take all that long, darling. And we're here right now, together now."

Not his Pa's bed, where Ellen had loved. Marcie's bedroom, then, simple in white, and Jessica writhed to him in that special, fiery way that bubbled his blood and dried his throat. Electric beneath his hands, the body perfect, singing with delights; the smell of her, the wildsweet flavor of her. Clenching, thrusting, trapping and devouring him, Jessica was all gauzy dreams of all summer nights.

"You're the best," she whispered against his throat.

"Am I good, too? Tell me, honey—am I the best fuck in the world?"

Earl wished she wouldn't say things like that. It was out of character for a princess. Cam, Stacey—all the girls up north, the procession of them that had warmed his bed, the hissed or moaned words were for them, as were all the practiced erotic tricks. It should be different with Jessica, and yet whatever she did thrilled him. The touch of her bare flesh was enchantment, the golden fall of her hair across his belly was a silken marvel.

"You're the best, Jessica," he said.

And later, when she brought him a drink and sat erect with her breasts tip-tilted and coral-ended, she said, "I reckon I know how some whores feel, askin' for money, and I hate it."

"For the boy?"

"For The Shadows. I don't need it right now, but before spring plantin'; two more irrigation pumps, a new tractor, and I hoped to get one of those mechanical cotton pickers; maybe a down payment on that until the crop's in. The gin needs repair, too, and I feel just terrible, Earl, and the only way I can say right out how bad off The Shadows is, I keep tellin' myself it's for both of us."

Earl said, "You never bring the boy into it, and you've never even told me his name."

"Thomas Elliot—Coffield. I mean, I wasn't married and didn't want to bring your name into it, even if they kept askin' who the daddy was. So I just took it all on myself. It was better for both of us, you only startin' out with that big company and all. You can change his name later, if you want."

Earl found his cigarettes and lighted one. It didn't smell like Prince Albert. "If they can't keep the mill closed down, you needn't worry about The Shadows, even if the people in Boston don't support me."

"Why shouldn't they, darlin'?"

"Greater Atlantic is a giant corporation, Jessica. It can write off investments like this one and never blink; it will, if the board thinks it's nonproductive. And people are scrubbed with even less thought."

Jessica's shoulders drooped just a bit. "But I thought, I mean, you're doin' so well—"

"Sand down a pine knot and polish off the rough, and it may look like an exotic wood, but it's still a hard knot. Nobody's about to close down Lassiter mill, Jessica; not blacks or rednecks, and it may come as somewhat of a surprise to the company, but that includes Greater Atlantic."

She turned to him, nestling the cones of her breasts to his chest. "I just knew I could depend on you, Earl." She was touching the tip of her tongue to his ear when they heard the echoing slap-slap of rifle shots.

Duane Hobbs' shot caught one of them running, turned the man end over end. Through the scope, he watched the blamed fool climb up and wobble on off, dragging one leg. Another one squalled like a shoat stuck in the fence, so Duane figured one of the boys hadn't centered him. Folks that come up on the dam carrying dynamite, and slap out in the open thataway, you had to let the idiots off light; no more sense than God give a cross-eyed possum.

"Pa!" one of the boys hollered. "Hey, Pa! Got me one of 'em hemmed up, and he's araisin' his hands. What'll I do with him?"

Duane Hobbs lowered his rifle and cleared his throat. "Bust his arm, I expect." He watched a skinny

man make a run for it. Fella could run passable well,
too; rabbited out maybe twenty yards before the bullet
snatched him around. Must be Lucius behind that rifle, Duane thought; the boy always did hold a mite to
the left. Damned near took out the fella's shoulder.

"All you idjuts!" Duane bellowed. "Ain't none of you
hurt bad, so I reckon you better light a shuck afore
that dynamite goes off. You got maybe two shakes of a
cow's tail."

Whole lot of scrabbling in the brush agoing on
then; bushes snapping every whichaway and them
fools hollering out, "Don't shoot, don't shoot." Duane
Hobbs cupped his hand to his mouth: "You, Matthew—and you, Mark! Light it off!"

Redyellow, the blast roared off through the trees,
too far from the dam to do more than tremble it some,
throwing dirt high and whipping pine tops, sending a
ripple out across deep water behind the dam.

"Hell, Pa," Lucius said when the noise stopped, "we
coulda centered 'em every one, 'stead of just skinnin'
'em up."

"If'n them was Lovelaces and Blakes," Duane
Hobbs said from behind his log, "been a heap of work
buryin' the fellas, since the buzzards won't have 'em.
And Earl asked no killin' less'n we purely had to."

Mark and Matthew came out of a patch of huckle-
berry bushes beyond the dam; one of them hunkered
down near the water. "Looks like somebody run the
wrong way. He's floatin' out yonder."

Duane Hobbs came down the bank, scanning the
woods across the way, just in case. Cocking his head,
he could hear falling down and whining and such, a
good piece off. "Dead man don't float when he's
fresh," he said. "Lucius, ease on out and tow him
in."

Lucius might be only a fair hand with a long gun, but he was slick as a conger eel in the water, and had always been right good at unsnarling set hooks and trout lines. Duane Hobbs watched the boy haul the body to the bank, then scrub at his hands and scrunch up his face.

"Been here a spell," Duane Hobbs said then, "and it's a woman. Shame the mud turtles got at her, but I reckon some'll know her by her clothes and that there color hair."

Matthew said, "Could be the dynamite lifted her off'n the mud."

"Could be," Duane Hobbs agreed, and whirled on his heel, rifle coming up in a smooth, flowing motion. But it was only Earl Lassiter busting down the path with a carbine in one hand and a woman by the other. "Didn't drop her," he said when they panted up. "Creased some fellas totin' dynamite, then set it off ourselfs, and here she come, floatin' up."

The gal made getting-sick noises, and Earl's face went kind of white, too. Duane Hobbs looked polite off into the woods until they took themselves in hand more. Then he asked, "Ain't kin, is she?"

"No," Earl said, "but I'd know that red hair anywhere. It's Jolene Kobburn."

CHAPTER 36

Davison said, "The autopsy showed she died of an overdose, Sheriff. I'm sorry."

Kobburn was uncomfortable in the clinic. He said, "Overdose of what?"

"Heroin," Davison said. "From the signs, she'd been on it a long time. Ahh, Sheriff—when will you claim the body?"

"Ain't pickin' it up."

Davison frowned. "But she's your daughter, man."

"Don't have no daughter. She died for me the day she took to whorin', just like her ma; just like her goddamned ma."

"But—don't you care how she's buried?"

"County'll take care of it. Plant her in the nigger graveyard for all I care."

Putting his hands into the pockets of his white smock, Davison said, "You're a strange man, Sheriff."

Face red and belly trembling, Kobburn set his jaw. "None of your nevermind what I do, how I act, you hear? Strange man, you say? I'm still a man, a *white* man, and fancy as you talk, you still ain't nothin' but a nigger. If that white doctor'd been in town, you'd never get to touch a hair on a white woman's head— live or dead."

Shouldering past Davison, the sheriff kicked open

the door. Betty Jean said from the hall, "That son of a bitch. And you keep talkin' about moderation."

He sat down heavily and reached for the phone, dialed it. "Mr. Lassiter, please; Dr. Davison calling."

"Why call him? Bury that poor damned junkie in the *nigger* graveyard."

Davison said, "Yes, that's right. The sheriff refused to claim her body, and I have to turn over the autopsy report to one of the FBI men."

Betty Jean said, "So they can hang it on Louis X, or some other black. Everybody knows we're all junkies and whores and pimps."

"That's good of you, Mr. Lassiter. Yes; I'll make the arrangements. Thank you."

"Mister, *mister*," she burlesqued. "Thank you, mister, suh. The poor bitch probably tricked Lassiter so many times he feels a little guilty."

Davison said, "He calls me doctor; I call him mister. Would any of your johns feel guilty enough to pay for burying you?"

"Okay; I deserved that. I just get so damned sick of turds like Kobburn, but that doesn't make Earl Lassiter a brother." Alvah is his brother, Betty Jean thought; Alvah with the stumped leg and stumped soul. He hadn't been a john, even though she used him. In the beginning there was a certain sharing, but Alvah was white and a crazy—drive too fast, love too hard, always needing more than there was.

It was far more than it had been, Ira Lowenstein thought, remembering that scruffy one-time sawmill. He'd seen pictures and drawings in the home office, but here was the reality of a big plant, of production that could be. Ira drove the rented Ford to the gate, where a slouch-hatted man sauntered from nowhere, rifle across one arm.

So it had come this far. Ira said, "I'm with Greater Atlantic and a friend of Mr. Lassiter. Do I need a pass or something?"

Pale blue eyes looked him over, a gaunt, sun-browned face nodded. "You 'pear harmless. Go on in; Earl's down to the woodyard. Keep in mind this is the onliest way out."

Damn, Ira thought; that one was straight out of the Hatfields and McCoys, and serious as all hell; the warning had been plain. Ira had known the feel of labor troubles before, but nothing like this. He saw a single stack trailing smoke, the others shut down; not enough production to pay the bills.

Driving to the edge of the yard, he left the car, out of place in his business suit and snapbrim hat. A few blacks moved about the piles of pulpwood, about an equal number of whites, and Ira blinked when he recognized the faces—Abbot and O'Keefe, Giorgio, the others—staff management personnel sweating and grunting as common laborers.

"Earl! Good to see you."

"Ira." Earl's handshake was warm and lingering. "It's been a while. Guess I should have expected you."

"May we go to your office?"

Earl laughed. "Good old Ira, always on a tight time schedule. Sure, come on up. How's Brenda?"

Fine, Ira said, and Boston was okay, no heavy snow yet. And at the small, cluttered office, Ira said hello to Barbara Dexter in passing. One terrific *shiksa*, he thought, and wondered how Earl was making out with all that woman. Following that train of thought, he naturally remembered the beautiful little piece who'd teased him, Jessica Something.

Earl drew coffee from a big electric pot, passed Ira a paper cup. "So you're a troubleshooter now."

"Sort of. They're worried, Earl. First your run-in with that state senator—"

"It paid; he's off our backs."

"Then this labor problem and no production. Racial, isn't it?"

"Boston knows that," Earl said. "But possibly they don't know more is coming."

Ira took off his hat, unbuttoned his coat. "Why this mill, why Lassiter? That's what they're asking."

"Ask why the blacks picked this particular time to demand their rights. We're caught up in history, Ira."

Blowing on his coffee, Ira said, "You mentioned something else coming."

"Another squeeze, another try at blackmail. I expect the black leader to demand money, in return for allowing the workers to return. And when—if—they do, that will inflame the white faction more."

Ira nodded. "I've read Louis X's file, and that's one reason I'm here. The company sees more than loss of labor through this man; it sees probable destruction. The man's dangerous, and it would be foolish not to acknowledge it."

Earl walked to the window and looked toward the gate. "So Boston means to pay blackmail."

"It's thought of as insurance. Earl, I'll tell you they were considering a shutdown until all this is over, but it's not the immediate investment they're concerned about. Temple County's a bridgehead, albeit an expensive one. Tupelo, Natchez, north Louisiana—all considered sites for growth."

Earl watched a long white car pull up at the gate, saw two of the Hobbs converge upon it. He said, "Each mill paying protection; word gets out."

Sighing, Ira said, "That's worrying ahead of time."

"How about paying off the whites, if *they* promise not to burn us out? Does that come out of the contingency fund also?"

"Nobody mentioned that possibility."

"Someone should have. They're as much trouble here. Last week, they tried to blow the dam."

Ira sat straighter. "We didn't get that report."

"Neither did the local law or the FBI. Questions were asked, but nobody answered, no more than any doctor reported treating the resultant gunshot wounds. Damnit, Ira—Boston is a long way from Temple County, and not only in air miles." Earl continued looking out the window, and wasn't surprised when his phone rang.

"Yes, Uncle Duane?"

"Three bushy-headed niggers down here to see you. Made 'em lay down rifles. Want me to run 'em down the road?"

"Send them up, please."

Duane Hobbs cleared his throat. "One of 'em's a bluegum nigger acts like his ass can spit bullets; mighty tempted to see can he do it."

"I need to talk to him now," Earl said. "If he comes back again, you're welcome to him."

Ira said, "Louis X?"

"And cohorts, disarmed. Come for their pound of flesh."

"Try to hold it to fourteen ounces," Ira suggested.

Jessica Coffield smiled. "I'm only suggestin' we get along better, seein' as how we're condemned to live together."

Sandy said, "I don't think we can."

Rattling ice in her tall, frosty glass, Jessica took a

long sip. "Ummm, that's good. All right, pure business then, and I know what a good business woman you are, gettin' all that money out of my daddy."

"I tried to give it back, but Avery refused. He said it would come in handy someday, and it did. I have no more money, Jessica, so what do you want from me?"

Drinking again, Jessica said, "Common sense. Through you, Thomas Elliot stands to inherit most of The Shadows, the way my daddy rigged it up, and because you bought off my brother. But Elliot's spendin' that money fast as he knows how, and if I don't get next spring's crop in, if everything keeps on fallin' apart around here, there won't be much for your youngun to inherit. Taxes are comin' due and what nigras are willin' to work, why they want more than they're worth. You'll have to sell off a piece of land here, and another there, and pretty soon the house, too."

Sandy rubbed her forehead and looked away from the drink Jessica continued to rattle. "I—I didn't realize things were that bad, and I'm not sure I believe you."

Jessica looked away, too, so she could smooth her face. "You and Elliot don't know, or care, a damned thing about runnin' a plantation. I'm tellin' you the truth; if I don't find some operatin' money, The Shadows will be nibbled away."

Hand trembling just a bit, Sandy lighted a cigarette. "But how can I help?"

At the bar, Jessica slowly refilled her glass from the shaker. "I can't for the life of me figure why, but you're about the only person Daddy ever trusted, and that might be because he was sick and old. But I have to trust you now—a little bit. If you ever think on breakin' that trust, I'll remind you that you can't be with Thomas Elliot every minute of every day, or take him with you when you go to those drunk meetings."

Sandy clenched the chair arms. "Are you threatening my—"

"Lots of accidents happen on the place," Jessica said, "especially to a youngun who runs around the woods half the day—snakebite, quicksand, fallin' out of a tree, drownin' in the river—most anything. And the next time you get drunk, why it'd be days before you even knew."

"I'm not going to get drunk," Sandy said. "I'm not."

Jessica's smile was sweet. "Keep tellin' yourself that. And keep what I'm about to tell you a secret. I have a boy just a little younger than yours, but I can't show him to the man thinks he's his daddy, and this man is my only chance for money to run the plantation. Now, he's never seen Thomas Elliot, so I can pass him off as my own, as *our* own."

Staring, Sandy murmured, "You—you want my son to—"

"To save his inheritance, that's all. You think Avery Coffield meant for his son—and my half brother—to grow up as nothin' but white trash? It's not like this little deception will hurt anybody. Earl will stop feelin' guilty, and even if it has to go on for a spell, Thomas Elliot will make out better with a daddy."

Sandy put a lighter to another cigarette. "I—this is a terrible thing to do; Thomas Elliot might become attached to—and the man—and what happens when the truth comes out? No; there must be some other way. I c-can't do it."

Jessica shoved the shaker across the bar, moved it closer to Sandy. "Think about it, dear. That's all I ask—just think it over."

* * *

Every time Alvah thought about it, he got pissed again. Not only had those wop bastards refused to buy his load, but they'd tried to hijack it. If he hadn't slapped one alongside the head with a wrench and knocked him into the other one, they might have put a bullet into him. As it was, he stomped them both pretty good, and had a pair of .45s in the glove box.

But where the hell could he unload the alky? Wops had the Gulf Coast tied up, and he might have to go clear to Nashville with it. That son of a bitch Scarpo, that pus-gutted Kobburn were in on this, trying to run him out of the county, and the nigger trouble just added to the pressure. So many feds around, and the state cops jumpy; niggers caused that.

Goddamn; Lou Miller was a good ol' boy, a Marine good as the best of them, maybe having to be, because he was a spade. But this Louis X—he was pretty close to being a nigger. Betty Jean, too, leaving him to shack up with one of her own kind. But she didn't geld him when she cut out; he'd screwed plenty of black wenches since.

Can't you make it with a white woman? she'd asked. Sure he could; look at Jolene; he'd banged Jolene good. Poor, dumb, dead Jolene. He'd only laid her because she was Kobburn's daughter.

Tooling the loaded truck around a curve, Alvah looked into the sunset. Nashville hell; it was too damned far. Maybe Scarpo's connections didn't reach far as Jackson. He'd dump the stuff there, even if he had to peddle it cheap to some ginmill. Alvah reached under the seat and held the Mason jar between his thighs to unscrew the top. He drank and drank again, half wishing a patrol car would try picking him up, wishing a lot of vague things he couldn't set straight in

his mind. Why the hell did ol' Lou Miller wear a ring
in his ear? Might as well be a bone in his nose.

Okay; Lou was part right about getting treated
second-class, but he could have stayed in the Corps; he
hadn't lost a leg. And L.A. or San Diego was a whole
lot different than Temple County; Lou ought to see
that. All that crap about not going to a white whorehouse; hadn't they shared the same gook women, took
turns with black ones in Clark County? White whores
weren't as good as gooks or niggers, and Lou ought to
know that, too. Alvah did. Besides, what white whore
in Mississippi would bed down with a black? She'd be
out of business so goddamn quick, and with her ass
busted, to boot.

What's all this jive about you ambushing 'fays, Lou
had asked. Run out of one war, go find another, Alvah said, and Lou said, Yeah, I can dig that, man.
Only mine's got a cause. Alvah came back with: Mine
is just be-cause, and they laughed, but somehow the
laughter wasn't the same as it had been in the rice
paddies.

He took another drink of bustskull whiskey and
turned off the main highway, heading for Jackson,
heading north.

"Northern liberal," Louis X said, standing arms-
crossed and with his lieutenants flanking him a pace
to the rear. "*Mistuh* Lowenstein, come down from
Greater Atlantic with orders."

Ira said, "You seem familiar with our operation."

"Tactics, baby," Louis X said, ignoring Earl Lassiter. "Know the enemy and hit him where he hurts."

"We're not your enemy," Ira said.

"Shit; all you mothers are."

Earl said suddenly, "Talk to me. I make the decisions here."

"Now, Earl—" Ira said.

Louis X kept looking at Ira. "What's the lid, baby? What you *think* is your best offer?"

"No more than fifty thousand," Ira answered, "and that's for a guarantee of noninterference for a period of—"

"Go down for double, whitey," Louis X said. "Cost you that much to stay closed awhile."

Earl said, "Not a goddamned dime. Now haul your ass out of here."

Now Louis turned glittering eyes on him. "You know what you sayin'—boy? Better listen to your boss, or won't nobody work this fuckin' mill, if you got one to work."

Opening a desk drawer, Earl said, "I don't have a boss. I own fifty-one percent of this layout, and if anything happens to Lassiter mill, *you* won't be around to see it."

Louis X dropped his arms; behind him, the others shifted. Ira said, "For God's sake, Earl—"

"Know your enemy," Earl said, hand in the desk drawer. "Hell, you don't know the first damned thing about me or my people. I'm not standing against black rights, but against *you*. You arrogant bastard, it's up to me if you leave here alive. Know your enemy, shit. You're so goddamned dumb you walk right into a nest of riflemen who can blow that ring through your ear at three hundred yards, and be damned glad of the chance."

Louis X shuddered and leaned toward the desk. Earl said, "I'm a lot closer than three hundred yards."

Lips working, fists clenched, Louis X forced himself back. "Gonna pay, you mother—pay for—had our guns, we'd—"

With his left hand, Earl picked up the phone and thumbed a button. Never taking his eyes from the taut trio, he said, "Uncle Duane, seems like a big white car ran into that water oak out front and got smashed pretty bad; rifles inside got all boogered up, too. I'll report the accident when I get around to it."

Putting down the phone, Earl said, "Have a nice hike to town. Don't come back."

Spittle flecked the corners of Louis X's mouth when he whirled and stamped down the hall. One of his lieutenants looked back at Earl and spat.

Ira Lowenstein said, "You—my God, Earl, why did you antagonize them like—"

"You heard him. We're the enemy, so it's just tactics, *baby*. You just don't kiss your enemy's ass, even if he's whipped you bad, and that hustling son of a bitch hasn't whipped me. He never will."

Wiping his face, Ira said, "I think you would have shot them all. That's no way to do business."

"Right now, it's the only way."

"Earl, Earl; think what you're doing. This mill, only a beginning; you could manage the others, a network of mills, rise so far in the corporation—and you do this, react like this. I've never seen you this way, never expected—"

"They didn't expect it, either," Earl said. "Louis X has learned the psychology of applied violence, and depends upon logical men turning away from it. He could be so paranoid he has to try and save face by attempting violence, but I think he's still a hustler at heart, and will look for an easier way."

"And if you're wrong?"

"Then I fight."

"On two fronts," Ira said, getting up and going to the water cooler. "The blacks *and* the whites."

"If I have to; for what's mine, for what *I* believe in. The Israelis know that; they learned from the ghosts of Auschwitz."

Ira drank water and shook his head. "I'm no Israeli, but an American businessman, and everything I've learned tells me this is a bad location, that we should take our losses and move. I think the company will agree. It won't be easy for you to finance this operation alone, *if* you manage to stay in business. And to think, I was the one who advised you to take stock options. Now I'm thinking about bankruptcy. Just yours, Earl."

Earl pointed at the window. "Out there is Lassiter land, and the mill is just sitting on it. We've been invaded before, but we're still here, and the land is still here. Do you understand, Ira?"

"No," Ira said.

CHAPTER 37

Shaking Ira Lowenstein's hand, Elliot steered him through the bustling campaign office and into a private cubicle where they could talk. He'd never known a Jew up close, but Elliot realized what this one represented, and was wary.

"What can I do for you, Mr. Lowenstein?"

"Go home," Ira said. "Work from Temple County." He sat down and opened a briefcase.

"But my campaign, my schedule—"

"Greater Atlantic will blanket the state effectively, Mr. Coffield. Radio and TV spots, press releases, billboards—our PR crew will film your speeches before you leave."

"Now just hold your horses, buddy. I ain't even wrote out all I mean to say, and—"

Ira cocked his head. "That's pretty good, exactly the image. PR stayed right with it. You'll find few departures from your usual points—more for the poor folks, soak the rich, keep the schools lily white, states' rights, all that crap."

Elliot sat on the corner of his desk. "Then why is Greater Atlantic interested?"

"Because we can break you. The Lassiter files, remember? The company feels you can be of considerable help."

"I have damned little choice," Elliot said. "But what can I do in Temple County right now?"

"Meet secretly with certain blacks; make them understand what you say is because you need the white vote, that what you do after you're in office will prove you a progressive leader blacks can depend upon."

Elliot whistled softly. "That's a tall order, but I see what you mean. If the nigras get the vote—"

"When they do," Ira corrected. "It's inevitable."

"They won't be able to break in at the state level," Elliot went on, "not right away. But the black vote can be important in the future, even vital."

"Yes," Ira said, "and blacks in your home county will remember what you did for them." He stood up. "Shall we meet with the PR people?"

Rumpling his hair, loosening his tie, and dropping into character, Elliot said, "My daddy didn't raise no damned fools. Lead the way, good buddy."

There was no other way, Sandy thought, not if she meant to stay sober. If only she hadn't given all the money to Elliot—but that was past, and something she couldn't change. She could wish for the chance to take Thomas Elliot out of danger, but they had nowhere to run. Climbing into the truck, she started it and eased away from the house, although Jessica was supposed to be out in the fields. Part of AA's serenity prayer went . . . *and courage to change the things I can;* that was important to her sobriety, and God only knew how much guts this took.

She was trembling as she drove down the gravel road toward Lassiter mill, and bit her lip when she saw the tangled wreckage of a Continental near the gate. Scrutiny by two silent, hardfaced men didn't help her nerves, and when Sandy passed through to climb the stairs to the offices, her knees were weak. She didn't need a drink; nobody *needed* a drink.

"I'm Barbara Dexter," the cool, poised woman said. "Mr. Lassiter's assistant. May I help?"

Once, Sandy thought, she had looked something like this woman. Oh, never so sure and strong, but taking more care of herself, choosing the right clothes. Was it so long ago? "I—it's something very personal. I have to see Mr. Lassiter."

"If you'd care to wait in my office," Barbara said. "He shouldn't be long. He drove in to see the county commissioners."

"You're commissioners second, businessmen first," Earl said. "It'll pay you to listen."

Sam Harvey peered down at his gavel. "Ain't no cause for us to hear anything you got to say, boy."

Will Jellico said, "None a'tall, long as your murderin' brother's runnin' loose."

"Send your sheriff after him," Earl said. "Or the state police, if you can prove Alvah killed anybody."

"Everybody knows he done it," Martin Nelson said.

Earl slapped the council table, and they all jumped. He said, "Alvah goes his way; I go mine. And my way is this—if some peckerwood so much as *tries* to burn me out, something else will go up in smoke—a bank, maybe; a general store, a fancy plantation house."

"Hold on there," Sam Harvey said. "You're threatenin' lives and property. You can't hold us responsible for every little—"

"Hell I can't," Earl said. "Whoever doesn't work for you, owes you in some way. So you let them know to stay off my land and away from my people. You're all good, churchgoing Christians, so you know what an eye for an eye means, and bigod, I'll collect with interest."

Burr Watson worried at his chin. "Earl boy, the niggers is the ones you got to watch."

"Wasn't blacks tried to blow my dam. You all see to the whites and I'll see the blacks get the same message."

"Yeah," Will Jellico muttered, "you close enough to 'em. But we been given to understand your big corporation ain't. Seems you're on your own, like."

"If any of you had a lick of sense, you'd understand this concerns everybody, only you're too mule-headed. But nobody's flat out stupid, so you'll take to heart what I said."

Sam Harvey watched Earl slam the door and said, "Don't know about the rest of you, but I can't keep a guard on everything I got, not clear around the clock."

"Like father, like son," Will Jellico said. "One down, two to go."

Burr Watson tangled and untangled his fingers. "He's got all them Hobbs out yonder; poison mean as cottonmouths."

"I reckon," Martin Nelson said, "we'd do well to look out for ourselves, at least until things get more settled."

"Amen to that," Burr Watson said. "Anybody got a bottle?"

A bottle of nail polish, bottle of perfume; Sandy rummaged around them in her purse to find cigarettes. In the hospital, nobody could have perfume; it had alcohol in it and somebody would drink it. She was so shaky, and couldn't find matches. Another hospital no-no; you always had to ask the nurse for a light. Why did she keep thinking of the hospital?

"Light?" Barbara Dexter asked.

"Thank you." Gratefully, Sandy drew smoke. "Have you known Mr. Lassiter long, worked for him quite a while?" How would Earl Lassiter react, and why should he believe a stranger? She wasn't even sure he was the man; Jessica had slipped only that once, and there could be other Earls nearby. But with money?

"Not long," Barbara said. "Are you an old friend?"

"N-no; I met him once, but this really is important. I'm Sandy Coffield."

Something to Jessica, Barbara thought, but hardly the same breed. This one showed a flaw, but not the same kind. She was a pretty woman, just missing loveliness, but exuding a soft sensuality that was very attractive. She'd be compelling, if her nerves weren't raw, the long, neatly molded body drawn so achingly taut.

No, she was nothing like bitchy, arrogant Jess, whose time was approaching. When the circumstances were just right—Barbara's lips curved in anticipation, and she covered the smile by asking Sandy if she'd like coffee. The woman accepted eagerly.

The stairwell door slammed, and Earl pounded up, his face dark. He banged his office door, too. Barbara said, "He's not in a great mood. Hang on and I'll try to smooth the way."

Sandy almost shook coffee over the paper cup when she sat and began telling him. His face seemed impassive, with only a momentary narrowing of the eyes as she somehow blundered through the reason she was here.

"I d-didn't think I could do it," Sandy said then. "And it's not really to protect you, Mr. Lassiter, even if I'm right. I have a selfish reason."

Not really a big man, but tall and lean-waisted, he

continued to stare at her. "You expect something from me, then. How much?"

When she flinched, coffee dregs did spill out over her hand and onto her skirt. "Damn!" Sandy said. It was too much for her sandpapered nerves. "You think I—I want *money*? Damn you, what I'm doing will probably cost my son his inheritance. But it's something I *have* to do, so I can be honest with myself. If I don't—if I—I—all right; *all right*. It won't make sense to you, but I'm an al-alcoholic, and trying like hell to stay sober, and if I screw up my life any more than it is, I'll be drunk in the gutter again. So I'm gambling with Thomas Elliot's future, and maybe even his l-life, because Jessica has already threatened him, and she'll do it, too, if I can't stop her. And—and—" Sandy tried for a steadying breath, tried to keep her eyes from overflowing. "And if you don't believe that, if you think I'm just some kind of cheap hustler, I—oh damn!" She fumbled for a tissue and dabbed at her eyes.

He moved around the desk, leaned close above her, one hand ever so lightly upon her shoulder. "Hey, hey now."

"D-didn't mean to—to cry."

"It's all right; good to let it out sometime." His hand was warm and gentle, but strong, and somehow she drew some of its strength through her cheek, touching it against softly haired knuckles.

Sandy sat up, knowing her lipstick was smeared, her eyes red and puffy. It felt good to cry a little, but if she didn't cut it off, she might never stop. Don't feel sorry for yourself, AA said, but don't be too critical, either; nobody promised you a rose garden; the world doesn't owe you a damned thing.

The world owed Thomas Elliot, though—a shot at life, anyhow. His mother owed him far more, and where did her responsibility to her son end, and responsibility to her sober self begin?

"Better?" Earl asked, and when she said yes, he went behind his desk again. She missed his nearness; he seemed someone she could lean on. *Just for a while, Sandy; you won't be shaky forever. But why should he be your crutch? You've just hit him with dirty dishrag news, and the guy has problems of his own.*

He brought her fresh coffee, lighted her cigarette, then sat back and said, "Jessica; did she actually give birth?"

"She said so, but that she couldn't show him—she said him—to you."

"Did she mention where—he is?"

Sandy shook her head and that made her nose feel more runny. "No. I'm sorry I even thought about doing what she asked, but I—if a piano wire was stretched this tight, it would snap. I'm scared, and trying to hold myself together, but I don't know how I can do that and take care of Thomas Elliot."

She was surprised when he brought out a can and papers, rolled a cigarette. Its smoke was like fragrant pipe tobacco. "My pa used to say getting your tail in a crack separated men from boys, or women from girls. You didn't take the easy way out. I know you're Elliot's wife, and you don't have to tell me if he's your boy's daddy."

Lifting her chin, Sandy looked him in the eye. "He's a Coffield, but not Elliot's."

"So; old Avery. A hard man to like, but you had to respect him, in a way."

"I did," Sandy said, "and I loved him."

"Must have," Earl said. The anger he'd shown slamming up the stairs was gone, and Sandy thought she could read hurt in his eyes. "Is The Shadows really so bad off?"

Sandy rubbed tissue at her nose. "I don't know; Jessica says it is. She seems to have gotten thinner, worked harder since Lila—since her mother died."

Thoughtfully, Earl said, "Jessica and Lila and Elliot—all of them knowing and blaming you. You caught hell, Sandra."

"It was no reason for me to turn into a drunk. There's never a reason for that, only excuses."

"And you'll go back to The Shadows, after telling me what Jessica meant to do?"

"Thomas Elliot is there. It hasn't been much of a home, but it's all he knows."

Earl snuffed out his handrolled cigarette. "There's a house across the river, my pa's house where I've been staying. Right now, it's better for me to stay nights at the mill."

"I don't know if I could—"

He said, "I've known Jessica Coffield all my life, or thought I did. I guess she'd do anything in the world to hang on to The Shadows; she's just like Avery in that. Okay, you loved him and he must have loved you, but that doesn't change Avery Coffield from what he was to everybody else—a tough, mean, bullheaded bastard. And he left behind a carbon copy in Jessica."

Sandy saw the raw anger come back, his fists clenching, a muscle twitching in Earl's jaw. "Goddamn her; all she ever had to do was be honest with me. I wonder who the youngun's daddy is. Could be anybody, I reckon—one of those athletic bums she was always showin' off. Any woods runner around here, and he'd been braggin' about layin' her; if his daddy had money, she would have made him marry her. Why

couldn't she show the youngun to me? Why the hell
did she try to palm off your kid?"

He wheeled away from the desk and went to the
window, hammering a fist into an open palm. Sandy
watched the hunching of his shoulders, the long effort
he made to bring himself under control. When he
again faced her, Earl Lassiter didn't slip back into
Temple County dialect, and there was an iciness about
him.

"He might be mine, and crippled or born blind.
She'd think I might not accept him, because Jessica
Coffield wouldn't. I don't know where he is, what he
is, but I'll find out. In the meantime, Sandra, I think
you and your boy will be much safer in my house. I'll
send a car and driver back with you, to get whatever
you need, and Thomas Elliot."

Twisting the empty paper cup into shreds, Sandy
said, "You may be right; I guess you are. But I can't
face Jessica alone—not yet. Maybe when I'm stronger,
have a better hold on myself—"

"I don't have much of a grip, either. If I see Jessica,
I might break her back." He looked out into the hallway. "But I have a specialist in human relations here.
You don't have to tell her anything; I'll give Miss Dexter instructions, and I think she can run good interference for you. In fact, I'm certain she can."

Sandy slumped in the chair. It was a relief to have
somebody else make a decision, to carry some of the
weight. Coming this far, she had used herself up.

Purring along in the big car, Sandy almost changed
her mind, but Earl Lassiter was right and reality had
to be faced, no matter how ugly. Auntie Kate would
join them later; she was attached to Thomas Elliot.
Sandy would have to ask Earl, and find a way to pay
the woman; one step at a time, she reminded herself.

Beside her on the back seat, Barbara Dexter looked just the way Sandy wished she could: strong and hard and very certain of herself. There even seemed to be something eager about her, and never a flicker of resentment at being ordered to do what must be a distasteful task, at being forced into the maelstrom of other people's emotions.

Up front, without turning his head, the driver said, "That big white house?"

Barbara Dexter answered. "That's it," and looked at Sandy. "Don't worry, dear. Take as much time as you need. Nothing will happen to you."

When the car stopped before the front door, Barbara got out first and walked up the steps before Sandy, who had gone numb. She didn't ring the bell, but turned the brass knob and swung back the carved door. Sandy followed her inside, into the shadowed depths of the house she'd come to fear, hoping with every step that Jessica wasn't in, that she was still working the fields.

But when she started up the stairs, Sandy heard the kitchen door and called out, "Thomas Elliot?"

Striding into the living room, Jessica stopped and slapped a riding crop against her boot. She didn't look up at Sandy, but across at Barbara. "What the hell are *you* doin' here?"

Slowly, Barbara Dexter smiled.

CHAPTER 38

Hefting the padlock in one hand, Scarpo glanced at it, at the door, and threw the lock away. The trucks were loaded with what he could salvage; goddamn hillbillies could have the rest and welcome.

Fats was in the car, Vinnie leaning on the door as the trucks were waved off. At the trailers, black and white whores huddled whispering, and a chill wind rose off the creek to chase oak leaves across the parking area.

"It'll blow over," Vinnie said. "We'll be back."

"You, maybe," Scarpo grunted. "I don't want nothin' to do with these crazies. They got no head for business. *Marone*, and they call us *paisans* emotional."

Vinnie looked up where the hill was peeling off its covering. "He's still out there somewhere, and he gets away with the truck, the alky."

"You wanna go after him," Scarpo said, "go. You got my blessin'. Here they got different rules and it's their turf. That Alvah's crazy, somebody'll burn him tomorrow, next week, sometime. In the city, what do they know? The guy hustled us and got burned. It turns out even."

"Kobburn," Vinnie said, holding open the back door of the car, "you think he'll move in?"

"A *stupido*; he might try. With all the feds, them TV guys and reporters, state cops, all that—he might try because he's dumb. When they squeeze him, he tries for a deal, but what can he prove? *Basta*; let's go home. I ain't never gonna eat another piece of cornbread."

"Cornpone and grits," the man from the attorney general's office said. "I don't worry about any real violence, but about getting poisoned."

The FBI man pushed back his plate and reached for a toothpick. "You haven't been here long. I've served a hundred years. They don't talk; they look through us—they don't want us here, so we're not."

"A sullen bunch, but I notice the streets are almost deserted. A show of force and they disappear—except for business-as-usual merchants."

The FBI man chewed his toothpick, glanced morosely into his coffee mug. "The last twenty years of this hundred, I've felt it building like too much steam in a rusty old pipe. If it blows, there goes most of our force, because that's all we have, mister—just a show."

"But surely, all the state police—"

"They're *Mississippians*. They look through you, too. When they start shooting, all those guns will be pointed only one way."

"You mean at blacks."

"I mean," the FBI man said, "I hope to hell this Lassiter can do some good, *any* good, that he can convince the militants to back off. Somehow, he seems to have cooled down the county commissioners and that's something. You know how difficult it is to tail a man when he knows every face in town? If it wasn't for some cooperative, mercenary locals—and I'm not all that sure about *them*—we couldn't keep tabs on anybody. Lassiter hasn't tried to duck, though. He's over at the clinic now. I hope they let him talk."

They were talking up a storm when he came in, but when they saw Earl, the crashing sea of frustration went suddenly quiet, turning into a puddle of black faces much more dangerous because they were silent. Earl walked to the front of the room and stood facing them.

"Hey, preacher—Dr. Davison—Mac Hutto—DeKay. I don't know all of you, but I guess most of you know who I am."

Betty Jean said, "Yeah, we know you, big man—*white* man."

"Hush, girl," Reverend Brown said. "We havin' a private meetin', young Mr. Lassiter, and—"

Betty Jean said, "Yessuh, Uncle Tom," and some young ones in the crowd laughed.

"Won't keep you long, preacher." Earl had never felt such concentrated hate, but he had to try and reach them. He said directly to the light-colored girl, "I want your registration to succeed. I may not like what happens after, but I understand it's something that must be."

Her rich lips curled. "Lawsy, lawsy, you all. What you call a turned-around Oreo goin' to claim he's black inside?"

Earl went on, "Coming at us head-on isn't the way. Folks are waiting for that, hoping for it. When the killing starts, it won't stop right away, but your civil rights movement may be stalled for a long, long time. When it does succeed, as eventually it must, most of you won't be here to see it."

"Shit," Betty Jean said, and Davison caught her

wrist. "Don't talk for me, girl. This man is making sense."

"I laid it out for Sam Harvey and the rest," Earl said. "They're after my hide as much as yours, and they've been told if I get burned out, if any of my mill people are hurt, I burn back, hurt back. I have to tell you the same thing."

A strange black leaped to his feet. "You threatenin' us, whitey? You come in here bad-mouthin' like you salty enough to do that?"

"Believe it," Earl said, locking eyes with the girl. "But fire and blood isn't the solution for either of us. The boycott is."

Davison's eyes went wide; Reverend Brown blinked and rubbed his head. Dan Mason said, "You mean don't buy *nothin'* from 'em?"

"Not a piece of bread, not a single egg. Buy out of the county, out of state."

"How we do that?" Reverend Brown asked. "So many poor folks, and they ain't been workin' much lately, and strangers ain't about to give no credit."

Earl said, "I'm hurting, too, but for two or three months, I can gamble on the boycott. Lassiter mill trucks will bring in staples, and Dan Mason will see to distribution and billing, at cost."

Betty Jean said, "What do you get out of this, man—all your sins washed away?"

"I don't owe anybody, or any race, a damned thing, especially guilt. I want my mill running at capacity, which will make me money, and supply steady, decent paying jobs for you. With a war going on, I can't do that."

"Sure," Betty Jean said, "make money from black sweat."

Dan Mason stood up. "Gal, if you got any brains,

they ain't showin' through your mouth. Mr. Earl growed up with a black mama and sister; his daddy and that black woman got killed because Ben Lassiter wouldn't stand for nobody botherin' a little black gal wasn't even his. As for sweat—if'n you ain't learned everybody in this world got to sweat, you don't know nothin'."

Betty Jean yelled at Dan Mason, and the young blacks supported her; Davison and the older ones didn't. They snarled at each other, while Reverend Brown tried unsuccessfully to make peace. Forgotten for the moment, Earl moved for the door. He'd had his say, and the rest was up to them. But where were Louis X and his muscle men?

In the outer office, Davison caught up with him. "It's a good idea, and thanks."

"Time is so damned important," Earl said. "Only a few weeks to make them feel the boycott before registration. I hope it's enough." He held out his hand and Davison took it.

Alvah took to the woods after the truck was hidden on a weed-choked logging road. Crouching beneath a sycamore tree, he listened to a rocking spiritual from the Africa Baptist church. It looked okay, but he waited awhile longer before limping through a grove of loblolly saplings that shielded his passage.

He was feeling pretty good, after unloading alky in Jackson, and lining up more from a black bootlegger who told him Scarpo had split. The guy also passed word Louis X wanted to see him at the old Wilson house near the church. That felt pretty good, too; maybe ol' Lou and he could bring it back, the close, hurry-up living when nobody knew if they'd see tomorrow. Everything was sweeter then, the candles brighter; whiskey was stronger and women screwed better. You loved your buddies because next time you went up against the gooks they fought with you and for you. When somebody didn't come back, you drank *soju* for him, had a piece of ass for him, and said he was a good fucking Marine.

Alvah straightened and peered at the sagging house across a dirt road. Must be Wednesday, he thought; prayer-meeting night, hand clapping and stomping in the church. Maybe he might have been a Christian, if he could have gone to black churches when he was a youngun. They had a lot more fun. He went quickly across the road and into shadows. Standing very still, he saw a deeper shadow against the porch and eased the .45 from his belt, eared it off half-cock.

"You Alvah?" the shadow whispered, and he said yeah.

"He expecting you."

"So he puts out guards?"

"Easy, man. It ain't for you, so go ahead on."

Inside, door shut behind him, Alvah hid the automatic and grinned across the room. There was ol' Lou naked as a jaybird, with two fine, bare-assed black wenches scuffling around the room and wiggling to radio music. Lou waved at him. "Party time, you redneck."

"Better believe it, you spade." It was going to be great, like Korea because guys with guns were looking for them both and this could be their last drunk.

And before long they were gook-squatting on the floor, passing the bottle and tapping a joint of grass, while the women looked at them like they were crazy. They talked of guys dead for a long time, bringing back their faces, remembering names, and Lou wasn't saying it was a white man's war.

"These chicks ain't trained like the gooks," Louis X said. "Got to teach 'em to *anticipate*, baby. Like when we had three of them fuzzy little cunts goin' at the same time. Remember?"

"Hell," Alvah said with a handful of round, dark breast, "who could forget that night?"

"Gonna set it up again," Louis X said. "She be here any minute, and we'll have us a night. See you still carryin' iron."

"Just this ol' .45 I took off a fella tried to hijack my load of alky, man."

Louis X jerked his head and the women drifted to the kitchen. He said, "That Mafia cat long gone, and somebody got to take over the business. Be pretty rich, all the black bootleggers feedin' you stuff."

"It'd be fine," Alvah said, his head buzzing a little.

"They do what I say, man. All you got to do for me is talk to your brother."

Alvah passed a hand across his eyes. "Earl? What the hell has he got to do with anything?"

Louis X poured it on him: not Earl's company, but belonging to a bunch of fatcats up north, guys who wouldn't miss a hundred big ones no more than pocket change; how come this Earl was acting up, not a good guy like Alvah. So much to do, baby, and a favor for a favor. The brothers were going to march, and it was just good sense for the mill to be protected when the shit hit the fan. Did Alvah dig it?

"I don't get along with Earl," Alvah said. "Not since we were kids."

"He still your *brother*, man. It's like you savin' his life; some people want his ass pretty bad. Have a drink, redneck. *Semper fi.*"

"Up your gung ho," Alvah responded and spilled raw whiskey over his chin. In the kitchen, two women giggled and Alvah remembered they hadn't been screwed yet. Lou Miller kept talking about the mill and Earl and how he was having a hard time keeping the brothers off, about the coming demonstration bound to turn into a revolution.

Looking over at his piled clothes, Alvah felt some of the glow fading. Blaring music began to hurt his head. They never had music in Korea, and their weapons were always within reach. When wind rattled the rice-paper doors, heated floors were warm and golden-skinned little gooks even warmer.

She came in through the kitchen, golden-skinned and shiny, darker women at each side. She stopped and Louis X came up to lock on to her waist.

Betty Jean said, "You didn't tell me it was him."

"Don't have to tell you nothin', baby, except it's for the cause. My buddy there got the hots for you, and I can dig that. You always fucked like a mink."

"The cause," Betty Jean said. "Louis—please—"

He swung her around. "Look here, redneck—you want this sweet ass first?"

Betty Jean trembled back from them. "No," she whispered. "Louis, I've done everything for you, for what it all means. But please, *please*—respect me just a little bit."

"Shit," Louis X said.

Alvah crawled to his clothes and put a hand into them, kind of scrunching everything to his chest. His back to them, he said, "Guess I better split."

"After I brought this chick just for you? We ain't talked about the mill, gettin' it to pay off."

Slipping on his pants, Alvah said, "And if Earl don't pay off, you want to know how to get inside, maybe have me help."

"Somethin' like that, man. I mean, a little fire,

blowin' a boiler—just to show that fatcat company we mean it. Then they come through."

Alvah had his boot on when he turned; the other stayed laced to the prosthetic unless he took off the whole damned thing. Funny; Lou never joked about it. A few years ago, he could have made the stump more bearable, like when they joked about the lice and stink and guys getting killed. Now Lou didn't kid around.

He said, "I wish you hadn't ask me, Lou."

Louis X shoved Betty Jean aside. "How come? How come I can't ask you for nothin'? You 'fay son of a bitch, you *owe* me. You owe me your whitey life, man."

Putting his shoulder against the wall, Alvah watched the door open, saw another black cat step in, the outside guard. There ought to be another out back, if Lou hadn't forgotten his tactics. The other guy said, "Trouble?"

"Come all the way in," Alvah said, "and put your hands on top your head. *Move!*"

"Do it, Abdullah," Louis X said.

Alvah showed the .45 when he draped shirt and jacket over one shoulder. He said, "I'm sorry, Betty Jean—for you and him and me. Lou, don't make me no sorrier. Please, goddamnit."

"I don't even know you," Louis X said. "You just another whitey, and I don't know no whiteys."

Backing out the door, Alvah closed it and angled off the porch quick as he could hobble, right on across the road and toward the church. Halfway there, he saw lights bobbing down the road, and hit the brush. Crashing through it, he went too far and missed the old logging road in the dark. Panting, he stopped to orient himself and put on his shirt, zip the jacket, changing hands with the pistol.

He limped back and to the right, finding the gnarled oak and the opening past it. When he reached the truck, he leaned his forehead against its cool door. He said to the night, to the sickness in him, "I never asked you to tote me off that ridge, Lou. I never asked you to fight your white man's war or sell out anybody. I never asked you for anything you didn't want to give."

Turning, he roared it out of his blackness into the blackness that meant more than night: "Goddamn you, Lou!"

And like an echo magnified many times over, like the closeup muzzle blast of a cannon, the giant sound smashed over him. For a shattering second, the sky blazed orange, and a hot wind lashed tree limbs around Alvah.

The church. The Africa Baptist church.

They were screaming. A crooked finger of fire poked up into the night. Alvah pushed away from the truck and started for the burning church. Then he stopped. Somebody had dynamited the prayer meeting, and his was the only white face around. They screamed and Alvah crammed the heels of his hands against his ears, staring at the rising fire.

CHAPTER 39

At the top of the stairs, Thomas Elloit said, "Mama?" and quickly, Sandy went to the boy, whispering, sweeping him along the hall with her.

Below, Jessica lifted the riding crop and rushed at Barbara Dexter. Calmly, Barbara blocked the swing with a lifted forearm, clamped steely fingers into Jessica's elbow, and flung the smaller woman to the floor.

Glaring hate, face contorted, Jessica spat, "I'll see you in hell for this!" She coiled her feet beneath her.

"Don't be more of a fool," Barbara said. "I'll just have to break your arm."

"You—you—" Jessica choked on her own anger. Rubbing her arm, she sat on cypress planking that needed polish, hair tumbled about her shoulders. "You can't take Sandy and the boy out of here. I'll call the law."

"Too late, dear," Barbara said. "Earl knows your scheme to defraud him. Try to lose graciously."

"She told him," Jessica hissed. "That drunken bitch told him. Why would he believe *her*?"

Leaning back against a carved table, Barbara crossed long legs and said, "Probably because he took his first real look at you. I did that the first time we met."

"*You!* Who the hell cares about you? You're jealous

of me; you're after him yourself, his money, the mill—"

"I don't want Earl Lassiter," Barbara said, "and never did."

Jessica twisted the riding crop in both hands, looking small and hurt and defenseless. "You must want somethin'. Look, in a way, you're close to him, but Earl will always come to me when I crook my little finger. Maybe we can work together, both get what we need."

Sandy came down the stairs carrying a suitcase, holding her son's hand. "I'm ready, Barbara."

"Go on," Jessica said, "get out of here, you bitch, and never come back. Don't ever set foot on The Shadows again."

Face tight and pale, Sandy led the boy for the door and hesitated there.

Barbara said, "Ramirez will drive you back. Tell Earl. I'm staying awhile, to discuss a few things with this woman."

"Are you sure? I mean—" Sandy wouldn't look at Jessica.

"It's all right."

"Mama," Thomas Elliot said, "where we goin'?"

"Away," Sandy said, "but you'll come back."

"Try it!" Jessica shouted. "Goddamn you, just try it!"

The door closed and Barbara Dexter said, "We're alone now, Jess, all by ourselves in this big house."

Jessica stared. "Don't call me Jess. Just you wait until I set the sheriff on you. I'm a *Coffield*."

"You're a sneaky little slut." In a deft motion, Barbara took off her blouse and swivel-hipped from her skirt.

"What—what are you doin'?" Jessica's eyes were

wide. "Takin' off your clothes like that, what are you—"

Unhooking her bra and tossing it aside, Barbara thumbed into panties and stepped out of them, sleek legs flashing. Erect, her hips thrown forward, she cupped her breasts, rolled erect nipples between long fingers. "You keep saying who you are, Jess. I'm about to introduce you to *what* you are. Get out of those clothes."

Jessica scuttled back on her knees, riding crop lifted, her other hand outthrust with fingers clawed. "You— you're crazy—flat out of your mind! Stay away from me, hear?"

"Scream," Barbara said. "Why don't you scream?" She took a long, gliding step and Jessica slashed at her legs. Barbara walked into the blow, took it across one full, strong thigh, and darted a hand to catch Jessica's flowing hair.

She jerked the girl forward into her lifted knee. Jessica tried to scream then, but the pain to her breasts caught in her throat and she could only whimper. Barbara's fingers ripped open her shirt, tore at her belt. Blindly, Jessica struck out, hit something, and tried to crawl away.

The kick flashed agony up her back and into her head. Rolling into a ball, she tried weakly to keep Barbara from yanking off her boots. Her jeans—oh lord!—her jeans were being ripped down, her legs flung around every whichaway. Sobbing, she crawfished onto her back and kicked wildly, but nothing seemed to hurt the woman; nothing stopped her.

Redwhite fireworks exploded behind Jessica's eyes and she tasted blood in her mouth. Rolling her head from side to side, she did her best to dodge the grinning, sweaty face. Her hair was pulled so hard she thought it was coming out by the roots, and then—and then—teeth locked into her lower lip . . . hands were everywhere, probing without gentleness . . . weight upon her, smothering her. She moaned into a panting mouth as tears ran down her cheeks.

And then, suddenly, overwhelmingly, it was happening. Fierce, wilder than ever before, tumbling her helplessly over and over in madwet foaming, it was happening and she couldn't struggle against it, didn't want to fight it, really never had. But she was afraid, and cried out.

"What you cryin' for?" Louis X asked. "Those brothers and sisters whitey blew up?"

Betty Jean wiped her eyes. "For them, for me; I guess for you."

They were in the rectory of the remaining black church, and he had his back to her, peering through the window. He said, "Whitey screwed up good when he hit the church. National Guard trucks be comin' down the street before long, and feds all over the place. Network TV crews here, hopin' to get more shots. They will, too."

"Louis," she said, "don't you *care*? God, there are dead and crippled people, and all you can see is more of the same."

He spun around. "Back on the Coast, you were more ready than anybody to talk big. It's past shuckin' and jivin' now, and we *use* what happened, baby. We use the hell out of it."

"Like you tried to use me with Alvah, use him to sell out his brother; anything or anybody to get your way."

"Goddamn right. Woman, you got any idea what it takes to keep the movement rollin'? I got to buy, grease politicians, get guns, ads, pay transportation, put on a show of feedin' ghetto kids—and it all costs *money*. Lots of money, more than two-bit contributions from brothers can cover. Lawyers, writs, fines—every damned day more money goes out than comes in. But every day is one step closer, and you fuckin' right—I use Alvah, you, anybody else to take another step. This shitty redneck town's just a start; then the county, the state—until brothers are marchin' on Washington and tellin' the man he can't wipe ass with us no more. Then they'll listen, because we *make* 'em listen."

Betty Jean hunched on a straight chair, dress ripped and stained with ashes, her face streaked. "Alvah didn't listen."

"Alvah, Alvah! You screw that cat too long? I'm talkin' about the whole black race, and you signifyin' over one flipped-out 'fay. He mighta been the one blew up the church, you ever think of that? He was right there and I don't put nothin' past that dude. Best time of his life was Korea."

"He was your friend."

"Nobody my friend like that. What the hell that company money mean to him? Means another day, another step for *us*, but he don't see that. Comes down to it, he Mr. Charley, too."

Betty Jean put away her crumpled hankie. "Everybody is with us or against us, then?"

"Now you groovin', baby. So get yourself back to the clinic and help Davison and them other Uncle Toms to see it. The doc, now—he won't need but a push, after workin' with all the hurt brothers."

"Then—please wait, Louis. If you blow up something of theirs, it'll just make the problem worse."

"Got to get worse before it get better," Louis X said. "Woman, don't be tellin' me what to do."

Sheriff Kobburn didn't know what the hell to do. Every time he turned around, seemed like he was falling over a government man or some goddamn fella with a camera. And them state troopers, stomping around like they owned the whole county.

His deputies were either acting like movie stars or talking too damned much, and every white man in town was deviling him like all this mess was his fault. Hell, they wouldn't even let him close to what was left of the nigger church, and wasn't much he could do, if they did; or would. Kobburn figured whoever chunked that dynamite was after that uppity nigger called himself Louis X, and it was a pure-D shame they missed him.

Get rid of that bastard and a few more, and things would simmer down in a hurry. The niggers wouldn't be talking about a demonstration then; they'd be worrying about saving their own black asses.

And how come Sam Harvey and the rest got on *him* account of no niggers buying in town? They think he could jerk every one of them upside down and shake out his pockets? Jesus, Kobburn thought, here he'd been looking to turning in his badge in a couple of years, soon as he had enough money salted away in the bank in Meridian. But that dago had to run off to New Orleans just when it was all going good.

Maybe if he gave Alvah to the government men, they'd look the other way when Beevo's opened up again. Somebody had slipped a note under the office door saying Alvah Lassiter'd been around the nigger church when it blew up. Be a feather in his own cap, though, was he to haul in that crazy son of a bitch by himself. Boxing Alvah up was something else, but there was always the fella and his bloodhounds over to Pachuta.

Chewing on a cigar, Kobburn put through a call to Pachuta, then hollered for Luther Travers to get his dead ass out and bring in some Lovelaces.

"What for?" Luther wanted to know.

"Goin' to need a bunch of deputies," the sheriff said. "You know anybody better to put on Alvah Lassiter's track?"

"Be damned, Sheriff," Luther said. "If you ain't slick. Alvah's about the onliest white man hereabouts that folks won't make a hooraw when he gets locked up for bombin' the church. Less'n it's his nigger-lovin' brother."

Kobburn nodded and chewed his cigar. "That 'un ain't stomped my toes yet. If'n he does, he's liable to find out they's more'n one way to skin a Lassiter."

Lassiter mill lay below him, the log road grown over with briars, winding out of the river hills and un-used since Pa's time. Alvah could think back and see Pa gee-hawing two big mules, snaking pine logs down to the flat where they could make crossties out of them with a broadax. Earl was too little to do more than get underfoot, but Pa let him hang around any-way. It took a heap of work for one crosstie, and when a load of them was hauled to the railyard, the L & N agent didn't give much.

Backing off the skyline, Alvah eased back to the truck and took a big drink from the fruit jar. Least-ways, he had a full load of alky it would take a man all his life to drink. It helped some, because he kept hearing those folks hollering in that burning church. It was like that time in Korea, when Joe Chink was holed up out of the cold in some mud shacks, and Navy Corsairs came down to lay napalm on them. They hollered and hollered, and Alvah had propped the BAR on a frozen rock and pumped a full clip into the fire, because it was a hell of a way for anybody to die, even a bunch of goddamn chinks.

What the hell you do that for, ol' Lou Miller wanted to know; you out of range anyhow.

Alvah shook his head and took another drink. Lou Miller was back in Frozen Chosen; he must be. Lou wouldn't have tried to hustle his buddy, or claim Alvah owed him.

"I don't owe you *shit*," Alvah said. "Been better off if you'd left me on that damned hill alongside my leg." Maybe he'd have lived to burn a lot of gooks and get medals like Pa, even a statue in the town square, like Colonel Lassiter.

Lou Miller had been a Marine, a foxhole buddy, somebody you could trust, a man who trusted you. That son of a bitch in the old house was a fake; that bushy-headed bastard with a ring in his ear was somebody else, because nobody could change that much. And why did he bring in Betty Jean, when Alvah had been just about set to lay the black wenches? No need for that; no cause to make a man feel bad. The old Lou Miller would have known that.

Wind shook the trees, wind with the smell of rain in it, and Alvah shivered. He took a drink, and another one, and figured he'd have to find some place to stay between alky runs. He didn't even know if he was going to make any more runs. He didn't know much of anything.

"Anything I can do, name it," Elliot said to Ira Lowenstein, "but I can't pull the Guard in here. I'm running in opposition, remember? The governor is the only one who can call them out, and I don't think he'll do it unless whites request help. If only a handful of blacks get killed, he wouldn't care; there's not enough black votes to bother him."

Ira said, "You spoke to black leaders?"

"Except for that Louis X; he's hiding out, but still in control, from what I could find out. He has tremendous appeal to the young."

"Then they'll march, anyway?"

Elliot doodled on a notepad. "A good part of them might not have, but the church bombing pulled the factions together. It was a mistake."

"It was murder," Ira said, "vicious, blind, and stupid. My God; I feel as if I'm trapped in a jungle."

"In a way," Elliot said, "in a way. It's easier to get in than out. You know, my campaign seems to be going well; the polls have me way up there."

Ira stared at him. "You know," he said. "I don't give a damn."

Elliot smiled. "But Greater Atlantic does, and that's what counts, isn't it? What the company thinks."

The company was going along with him, but temporarily, Earl knew. He also realized that even if he pulled this off, the board would already have him marked down as emotionally immature, a high-risk manager, and one who had shown a tendency to rebel against policy. Earl Lassiter, mechanical engineering wonder boy, had gone as far as he could in GAC.

He touched the phone, still warm from his hand, and pictured department head Victor Quinn talking. No, simply laying down the law; there had been no real conversation. Quinn was disappointed; Earl was being groomed for bigger things. And there would be no financial backing coming, Earl understood that? Otherwise, company resources were still at his disposal until further notice.

Yes, Earl understood; he also knew they would wait only until his position was so shaky they could move in, declare bankruptcy, and take over his stock. The whole state could explode into a bloody inferno and, a thousand miles away, simply be transposed into profit and loss columns, all so sterile and logical. And so far from reality.

Where was Barbara Dexter? He wanted her to contact the same agencies that had uncovered Elliot Coffield's secret love life. Even with the scarce data he had, operatives should be able to run down the whereabouts of Jessica's child. He knew the approximate date of her confinement, and he'd bet she hadn't gone out of state.

Earl pushed the phone button that connected him with the house. The car had brought Sandra and her child back hours ago, with word that Barbara would be along later. How much later, damnit?

"Sandra, this is Earl. Everything all right, finding your way around? That's good. Anything you need, any sign of trouble, call me here. I'm having a bed set up in the office. Did Miss Dexter give you any hint of when she'd return?"

He listened to the soft, husky voice tell him of a flareup at the Coffield house: Barbara had taken it in stride. Sandra sounded a little more at ease, less frightened, but she didn't know about Barbara. She did ask him to come by for supper.

"Good idea," Earl said. "See you later."

Ham sizzling in the castiron skillet, biscuits browning, fragrance of strong black coffee: Ellen's dark hands deft and sure, Pa sitting back with his paper and night coming down easy, greeted by katydids and lightning bugs. Marcie playing quietly in the kitchen, and a feeling of warmth, a closeness that had a slient gap to it, because of Alvah. All of that gone now, even the house. The new house held strangers, and Earl wouldn't walk from it to wrestle with wornout truck motors and a make-do post peeler. That Earl, young and full of dreams, was gone, too.

CHAPTER 40

Betty Jean eased one bent knee over his body, needing his nearness and warmth but trying not to wake him. Cal Davison worked harder than any man she knew, long, tiring hours at the clinic where he treated blacks and whites alike. Only whites too poor to travel to Meridian and see a real doctor showed up, or those who needed help quickly, but he cared for them as calmly and efficiently as if he didn't know.

Already carrying so much that it was stooping his shoulders and peeling weight from him, he borrowed heavily from sleep to remain a vital part of the movement. Frosty moonlight touched his face, softening worry lines, making him younger. Betty Jean wondered how his wife could have left this man, how she could have taken the son that meant so much to him.

Davison didn't talk about it much, but she saw the special tenderness he had with sick children, the unashamed tears when he was patching up young victims of the bombing. And Betty Jean knew he sent money to Chicago every month, though no letter ever came from there, even though the checks kept coming back.

So different from Louis X, and now she couldn't say who was right. She'd believed in Louis so long, and completely, but that faith was shaken when he brought her to Alvah as a bribe, as quick bait for a much larger bribe. Maybe the money *was* desperately needed, but she remembered the bovine docility of the other black women, whores for Alvah's use. Wasn't that what they were all trying to get away from, the prostitution of body and dignity?

But nobody could passively accept the horror of the bombed church, and Louis preached fighting back, shaking his fist and asking how long they could put up with lynchings. How many more little kids had to die before blacks started showing they had some guts?

How do you know who to fight, Davison asked, and Louis roared back: all of them! Burn their churches, their houses, everything!

Betty Jean put her cheek against Davison's chest, riding with the easy rise and fall of his breathing. That night a lot of people had been asleep like this, knowing nothing until the blast brought them up. Maybe only one bitter, twisted man had lighted that fuse. Alvah; could it have been Alvah Lassiter, striking back insanely at Louis? She remembered his face, the look on it when Louis was arguing with him. He had been ready to kill somebody, and the sheriff was after him.

"No," she murmured, and Davison put an arm around her. "What, honey?"

"Nothin'; I didn't mean to wake you up."

Davison sighed. "Sleep's been pretty spotty, anyhow. What time is it? No, don't tell me."

"Can I get you anything?"

His hand stroked her back, moving slowly up and down. "It's all right here, but I've been neglecting you."

"You give so much of yourself away, Cal. I just wish I could bring it all back for you."

Pulling her closer, Davison said against her throat, "You do, Betty Jean, you have."

Lifting over him, spreading herself for him, she gave him all that she was, but even as they moved together, even as the little glad cry burst from his throat, Betty Jean knew there was one great void in Cal Davison she could never fill. She could not give him back his son.

Her son made it right, Sandy Coffield thought. He was straight and sturdy, with a stubborn set to his jaw that reminded her so much of Avery. She watched him legging it across the yard, learning more of him each day, feeling Thomas Elliot's reluctance to trust her and accepting that. The group speaker at the hospital said it took us a long time to screw ourselves up so bad, so don't expect everything to smooth out just because we got sober. And don't go around acting like you've done something wonderful by staying away from the bottle; hell—you're just living now like you should have been all along. Don't expect applause.

Another night was behind her, and it had been a nice one. She had almost forgotten how to cook, but it all came back, and if the biscuits were burned a little, Earl seemed to enjoy them anyhow. Thomas Elliot was stiff, being around a stranger, but Earl hadn't pushed it, and when he talked to the boy, it was as one man to another. Elliot Coffield had never done that; he barely said hello or goodbye in passing.

After her boy was asleep, she sat awhile by the fireplace with Earl, drinking coffee and grateful he didn't ask questions, content to listen to his nostalgic ramblings about the farm and his father. Watching firelight play upon his face, she saw him as older than his years, perhaps wise, certainly solid, immovable, his roots buried deep in this back-country soil. Sandy was sorry when he left to cross the footbridge in the dark, and waited to see him again.

"I reckoned I better talk to you, Earl," Duane Hobbs said around a chew of tobacco in his cheek. "Them trucks bringin' in supplies; hear tell they're for niggers."

"That's right, Uncle Duane. They're not buying from the stores in town. Family heads will draw food here, from Dan Mason. He'll keep track. But if that makes it hard for you to watch who comes in and out—"

Shifting his tobacco, Duane Hobbs said, "That don't bother us none. Trouble gets in, it ain't fixin' to get out. Thing is—how come you doin' this?"

Earl took a deep breath. "So the blacks can register to vote, without a lot of killing on both sides."

"That's straight answer enough, I 'spect. Ain't what I thought to hear, though. You figured this all the way, backwards and forwards?"

"I have, Uncle Duane."

"Well now. Reckon you got the right to your way of doin'. Me and the boys talked it around some, and I 'spect we'll be agoin' on home. Lackin' Matthew and Mark; they'll stay, if'n you'll have 'em."

"Be proud to have them, Uncle." Earl hesitated, then said, "Smithson will have your checks ready, but I know that's not pay enough. If I get through all this—well, I'm beholden."

Duane Hobbs started for the door, then turned and leaned against it. "Your ma always had a mind of her own, and them boys—Matthew and Mark, they can be muley as the next, looks like."

"I'll watch out for them best I can. Uncle—the boys and me; we might be a sign pointing the way."

"Nigger votin' is Temple County worry," Duane Hobbs said.

"Might be Clark County next."

Duane Hobbs pushed himself away from the door, rifle over his arm, shapeless hat hiding his eyes. "Face that when it comes. Take care of yourself, hear?"

"You, too, Uncle." Earl knew he would probably never see Duane Hobbs again. If he visited them in Clark County, the family would be polite but not anxious to claim him as kin. But two had stayed behind, and that was a brightness, whether they remained out of clan loyalty or because they believed as he did.

The phone rang three times before he picked it up. He'd have to remind the staff to use the phone no more than necessary; the switchboard operator in Temple would certainly be listening in. In fact, all Temple County lines might be tapped; the FBI was good at that.

"Earl," she said, "I should have called last evening. I'm perfectly all right, and if you don't actually need me today—"

"Barbara." There was a throaty lilt in her voice he'd never heard. "No, I don't need you. But where are you? The car came back without you and I wondered—oh; there *is* something. The agency you used for—our friend upstate. I can't tell you why, on the phone."

"I understand," she said. "There's a folder in my files, under R—for research. I think Mr. Blanski can handle this for you, since he's not too busy with sales."

"Yes, all right. Barbara, where are you?"

"Visiting," she said, "at The Shadows," and chuckled as she hung up, leaving Earl blinking at the phone.

* * *

Putting down the phone, Barbara Dexter said, "Come here, darling."

Jessica said, "I—I don't want to. I mean, there's so much to be done in the fields, and—"

"Don't," Barbara said evenly, "*ever* tell me what you want or don't want. I know exactly what you need, Jess. Bring me that riding crop."

Mouth working, Jessica whispered, "P-please," but she picked up the little whip and trembled it to the woman.

"On your knees," Barbara commanded. "There; that's better. Oh yes, much better. You're such a lovely little slut, Jess, so very beautiful. But you and I know how ugly you are inside, don't we? *Don't we?*"

"Yes," Jessica whispered.

"All my life," Barbara crooned, "I've been waiting for you. I was sure that night when I had to shake you. I was certain after that, and it was so difficult for me to wait. It wasn't as hard for you, because you didn't know. But now you do."

Still holding out the crop, Jessica tried to keep her body from quivering. "I n-never did anything like that before. I never even thought of it. Why—why don't you go on back to the mill and let me alone? You've got Sandy and the brat, and I promise—"

She shrank back when Barbara took the whip. Barbara said, "Sit up straight, bitch. Look at my body and tell me I'm beautiful, too."

Jessica swallowed and threaded her fingers together upon naked thighs. "Yes, of course; you—you're beautiful."

Barbara flicked the riding crop against a breast and Jessica stifled a scream. Barbara said, "Put more feeling into it, Jess. Say—it—again—and—again." She punctuated each word with a little sharp blow, not hard enough to bring blood.

Screaming, Jessica rolled from her knees and leaped up to run. The scream was choked off by a strong arm around her neck, and she felt the pressure of that gleaming nude body against her own, the hard nipples boring into her shoulders, knew the hot, spicy breath in her ear. Jessica folded at the knees, and Barbara had her by the hair.

"A little mistake, darling," Barbara said, standing above her. "But you'll learn. Indeed, you're just beginning to learn that you have no choice."

"You have a choice," Earl said to his assembled staff. "I realize you're all under contract, but there are circumstances the company will recognize when you get back to Boston. So, those of you who don't care to stay won't carry an onus."

They shifted in their chairs, looked at each other and away, glanced at Earl and away. Earl said, "It's dangerous here, and will probably get worse. I've lost most of my guards, and that leaves the mill open to attack. In fact, you're taking a chance driving back and forth from the motel. The company doesn't pay for that."

Dark and squatty, one of the drivers leaned forward. "I ain't exactly management, Mr. Lassiter, but I'm here. So I'll say I drove a jeep in Korea, for a crazy recon outfit. I'm getting paid a hell of a lot better here. Ramirez stays, and if you got a spare weapon, I don't mind walking the fence."

The other driver held up his cap and shook it. "Yeah."

Smithson stood up. "I been here since the mill went

up, when your daddy was in charge. I liked ol' Ben Lassiter and mean to stand by his son."

Earl said, "You have a family somebody can get to."

"Wife and two younguns," Smithson agreed. "Squirrel-huntin' time comes, they bring in more than me. They'll make do."

"Thank you," Earl said, and thank you again as the chorus grew. If anyone wanted to fly back north, nobody admitted it. He shook everyone's hand and said he'd work out some kind of guard shift, that he thought it better if they moved into the plant for now. He felt warm all over when they cleared the office.

Ira Lowenstein said, "Company men or Lassiter men, what's the difference? Me, I just ride herd on our captive statesman."

Sitting at his desk Earl said, "Elliot Coffield? I wondered at the big splash he's making. His file; you're using it against him."

"With him," Ira corrected. "He understands the situation."

"You can't trust him."

"What's to trust? He works for the company now, and when he doesn't, he's unemployed."

"Troops," Earl said. "Can Elliot get troops in here before the lid blows off? The state police will hang back, or break a lot of black heads, and the people here know it. But they might hesitate to go against the Guard."

Ira shook his head. "Only the governor can order an alert, and that fine gentleman is liable to show up here with a club in each hand—a memorable picture for his white constituents."

"And a sure ticket back into the state house, or Congress."

"Bite your tongue," Ira said. "Earl, it's a fine thing

you're doing, giving away food so the blacks can keep their boycott going. Not intelligent, but fine."

"I'm not giving it away," Earl said. "They're signing for it, and they'll pay it back. It might take a while, but I'll bet every man will settle his bill, if only a dollar or so at a time."

"You're that sure? If this was done in Boston—"

"Ira, there's a difference. How many times have you been into a black ghetto up there? How many blacks do you know personally? I'm not following the old paternalistic line when I say there's a different situation here. I *know* blacks; some were my friends, some weren't. I grew up with a black woman I respected as I would my own mother, and with a girl I loved as a sister. All right, so that's not usual in Temple County. But what I'm trying to point out is that while we may not socialize with blacks, we respect individuals among them, and are respected in return, if we deserve it. We despise them as a race, because that dogma has been imprinted into our very genes, programed more solidly into us than any computer tape. Some of us are questioning that data, maybe only a few, but we *are* taking a look. Up north, you tend to glorify the black as a race, but you have damned little to do with them as individuals, as *men*."

Ira stood up with his briefcase. "Me, he's lecturing on prejudice," he said half to himself, "and maybe I should listen. You're right, Earl. I only hope you're lucky, too. I'm not moving into the mill, because I'm respectable—or acceptable—as a campaign worker."

"Just as well," Earl said. "I didn't want an extra guest for dinner tonight."

CHAPTER 41

"He come through yonder," the dog man said, "just like you figured, Sheriff. But then he got in a pickup, just about here. See them deep tracks? Must of been totin' a load, to cut that deep."

Kobburn hitched up his gunbelt. "Keep them dogs on the trail and see where he come out."

"If'n he hit a county road somewheres, won't be easy to trail him no further."

Behind Kobburn, an FBI man said, "The suspect entered Highway 54 about two miles from here. And we've already taken impressions of the tire tracks."

"That so?" Kobburn grunted. "Well, Joe Dixon, I reckon you can range them hounds up and down the highway, for a spell."

One of the Lovelaces, Jerry or Frank—Kobburn couldn't tell them apart so good, they all looked pretty much alike—rubbed a shirtsleeve over his new badge and said, "Most likely, he's hid out a far piece from here. Can't keep that four-wheel Ford hid, tho'; squats down lower'n any other."

"Damn, Lovelace," Kobburn said, "don't you think I know that?" He put his back to the FBI man and pretended to consult a notebook. "Got some other clues to check out."

"We'd appreciate running that note through the lab," the FBI man said.

"Can't," Kobburn said. "Throwed it in the stove. Just said Alvah Lassiter was at the church that night. What the hell can fancy lab doodads tell you about that? And who told you I got such a note, anyways?"

The government man didn't answer, and Kobburn swore to himself he was just about to kick some asses; Luther Travers and C.J. Franklin better learn to shut their mouths, did they want to hang on to their badges. "Get to gettin', you all," he said aloud, and lumbered back to his patrol car.

He had more than Alvah on his mind. Sam Harvey and the rest had dogged him into setting up kind of a roadblock on the Quitman highway to keep watch for Lassiter mill trucks. Stop them, they said, then find some excuse to haul in the drivers—resisting arrest or something; search the trucks for contraband, dynamite and the like. Just be sure that nigger food gets ruined in the process.

Thing was, after that first run north, Lassiter trucks hadn't been on the road anymore; not that highway, anyhow. Martin Nelson and Burr Watson was some upset, Kobburn thought, as he bypassed town and headed out the creek road. They was getting hurt worst, being storekeepers. Funny; you wouldn't figure niggers to spend money enough to count.

Pulling up behind the place, he waited until Billy Dee Blake limped out the back. Bill Dee acted like a mule with a sandburr under his tail, since somebody'd put one through his leg at the dam. "Hey, Billy Dee."

"Hey, Sheriff. Got most of the gals back, but it ain't easy gettin' whiskey. Them 'leggers all runnin' scared account of so many govmint men."

"We'll find it," Kobburn said. "Have them whores clean up the place and pretty soon we be open for business. Might keep a lookout for Alvah Lassiter; be plumb out'n his head to come back here, but you never can tell."

Billy Dee worried a plug of tobacco and spat. "Got me a twelve-gauge pump leanin' ahint the door wishes *any* goddamn Lassiter shows his face."

"Take care of that leg." Kobburn took the cigar stub from his mouth and gazed at the chewed end. "Be back afore long to test out a couple our whores; man can't go too long 'thout some nigger nooky."

He drove slowly back to town, feeling pretty good, considering. Nobody'd seen that bushy-headed nigger in a week, and could be he got the message when the church blew up. Wasn't nobody else causing trouble couldn't be handled, and once the Lassiters was out of it for good, the niggers would go back to work and stay in their place. He looked over the clinic when he drove by, and grinned because that uppity nigger doctor kept going about his business like Floyd Kobburn hadn't put the meat good to his high yeller wife. Davison had him another ass-shaking wench now, warming her up for a real screwing. Some day soon, Kobburn thought; some day real soon.

"Didn't expect it so soon," Earl said, "and I'm glad you drove here instead of using the phone."

"We don't have it all," Donner said. He was a worried little man in a rumpled suit, tie off center, heavy glasses. He didn't look like a detective. "But enough to track down the kid. She used her own name at the hospital and on his birth certificate."

Earl said, "What's his name?"

"Thomas Elliot Coffield, and when we get a line

into the bank, next time somebody comes by to pick up a check—"

"Are you certain of that name?"

Donner looked pained. "Got the photostat right here. On a hunch, we checked out safety deposit boxes, and what do you know, she used *your* name for one. Take a court order to get in, though."

"Thomas Elliot Coffield," Earl repeated. "I suggest you go through every birth record in the state about that time, and look for another boy by the same name." Sandra wouldn't lie to him, he thought; she had no reason. Was the boy hers, or Jessica's? Had she lied?

"Whatever you say; take a couple more days."

Earl rose and shook hands. "Thank you, Mr. Donner. I'd like all reports delivered in person, when you're finished."

He looked down from the window and watched the investigator get into a nondescript car. The mill yard was much busier than it had been for weeks, banged-up trucks coming in steadily with their loads of pulpwood, practically all driven by blacks. Nobody pushing them, Dan Mason had said; they doing it on their own, account of they don't want no charity. You notice every truck got somebody riding shotgun; they know what they doing.

When he buzzed Barbara, she came quickly, looking good, a glow about her Earl couldn't define. He said, "We're getting new workers. Are any white?"

"A few; they're mostly named Smithson. Related to our personnel manager, I think."

Drawing coffee for them both, he gave her a cup and sat on the edge of his desk. "As a precaution, everybody is staying here at the mill—except you."

She lifted her chin. "Are you telling me I must?"

"Of course not."

She continued to look directly at him. "I'm a guest at The Shadows. I like it there."

"With Jessica? I don't understand how you two can get along."

"Jess has to be—understood, that's all."

Earl sipped coffee. "Jessica tried to blackmail me; maybe she succeeded a long time ago, or maybe she'll try again. What hurts me hurts Lassiter mill, and indirectly, the company. So if you're too close to pry into what she's doing, Smithson will make out your severance check."

There was a moment of silence, so he could hear the whisper of nylon as Barbara crossed her legs.

He said, "A boy I was supposed to have fathered, not the one Jessica meant to show me; not Sandra Cofield's child, although that's possible. I have to know if there are two boys, know which woman is lying."

Her coffee untouched, Barbara stood up. "All right. I'll find out."

"If you can."

Her smile was more a grimace, cold and a little forced. "You've made it my job, and I'm good at what I do." Barbara Dexter walked out the door.

The doors of the Templar Club swung busily, the clink of glasses steady but subdued in the rattle of talk. Will Jellico went at his julep glass as if he meant to chew it, but Sam Harvey stared moodily into his own drink.

"You fellas ain't bad off," Burr Watson said, "but me and Martin are losin' our shirts. I mean, business off sixty percent since they stopped buyin'—*sixty* percent."

"Just about right," Sam Harvey said. "They outnumber us more'n two to one. You think I ain't got trouble of my own? Them damned government men; they put the state examiner up to auditin' my books."

Will Jellico rattled ice in his glass. "I don't get paid for all the writs and injunctions I get out, all the time I spend in law books, and runnin' up to the capitol. And with Beevo's shut down—but I ain't hollerin' quit, bigod. I been thinkin'—been a spell since the Klan rode."

Sam Harvey jerked. "Them FBI men—"

"Peaceful demonstration," Will Jellico said, "and the Klan ain't against the law no more'n a nigger march."

Martin Nelson said, "Store don't bother me much as my land. Can't find nary a nigger to work Moss Bend. They keep this up 'til spring, and I won't have no seed in the ground."

"I just don't know," Burr Watson said. "*I'm* the one has to sit up in the courthouse with government men lookin' over my shoulders and niggers comin' at me deep as the Tchufuncta in high water. I'm in enough of a fix already."

"That Lassiter bastard," Will Jellico said. "Earl, I mean. Th' other one did us a favor being at the church. Earl Lassiter wasn't feedin' the niggers, they'd come to heel right quick. Got to cut off them trucks."

"Tryin'," Sam Harvey said. "Time Kobburn sets a roadblock here, trucks come a new way, or don't come a'tall. Reckon them pulp cutters runnin' in staples, too?"

"Wouldn't put it by 'em," Martin Nelson said. "Can't get used to seein' our own niggers ridin' with guns acrost their laps. Expect it from them outside bushy-headed niggers, but not our own. Ain't seen that bunch in a spell; reckon they at the bottom of the river?"

"Uh-uh," Sam Harvey said. "We'da heard. Somebody might tell Kobburn and his deputies to stay out in the woods followin' Alvah, long about tomorrow night."

Will Jellico snickered. "Bigod, it's about time."

It was time for supper, but Earl hesitated. He'd gotten used to going across the river to eat, to talking easy with Sandra and the boy. Thomas Elliot had already found the best fishing hole, and was hinting about a .22 to go rabbit hunting. A boy needed somebody to show him things like that.

Sandra had changed the house some, so it looked brighter, felt warmer when he came in. He thought of her, of how the shine in her eyes would dull if he asked her. But Jesus, she'd married Elliot Coffield and bedded old Avery Coffield and lived with Jessica.

Crossing the mill yard, he looked to the gates and up on the hill. The Boston bunch never figured on anything like this when they left the city, walking guard and the like. He hoped nobody shot himself in the foot. After registration, he might pull in most of them, because already the mill was picking up, and when the dust had settled, it should boom. Earl crossed the bridge and walked slowly through the pines, even slower across new ground his pa had broken. Near the house he smelled woodsmoke and frying fish, that channel cat Thomas Elliot was so proud of hooking.

She was glad to see him and good to see with a strand of bronze hair loose against her cheek, a sparkle to her not many women had.

He didn't ask her then, not with the boy retelling

how he dragged the cat to land, not with firelight caressing her throat and getting caught in Sandra's hair. Earl ate and said how much better it tasted when a man brought in the meat himself; he drank chicory coffee and thought of what she'd told him about herself: the husband killed in Korea, some of her life before that captain. She didn't speak of Avery now, because she knew Earl didn't like him. He wanted to know more about her, so damned much more that had nothing to do with alcohol or other men.

When Thomas Elliot was off to bed with a "we'll see about the .22 rifle," Sandra brought out some brandy Pa had been partial to, and poured some in his coffee. Feet propped, Earl rolled a Prince Albert and started to ask her. He didn't; he just looked at her and said something else.

"It doesn't bother you, to have me drinking?"

"Not now. At first I thought I was being deprived of something, but now I realize I have a choice. I can drink, and go back to what I was, or I can stay away from it and—see what happens, *know* when it happens."

He should be comfortable, Earl thought, full as a tick, watching a fire, tasting brandy and good blue smoke. He shifted in the chair and lowered his feet, put aside the coffee.

"All your problems are still out there," he said. "Jessica and The Shadows, possibly nothing for your son. What do you think will happen, Sandra?"

"Something wonderful," she murmured. "I live each day as it comes and don't worry about the next one."

"And if this wonderful thing doesn't come along?"

She smiled and brushed back her hair. "I've learned to wait."

The gesture did it, the round smoothness of her upper arm reflecting the fire all pink and warm; the lifting of a full breast against her simple dress, Sandra's mouth damp and shiny. She sat on the rag rug, legs tucked beneath her. Earl came out of the chair and to her, dropping to one knee to take her in his arms. For a throbbing moment, he simply held her and stared closeup into clear, soft eyes that didn't mirror surprise. Gently then, Earl kissed her.

She tasted of uncertain youth, and forgotten dreams, her mouth flavored with honey, her tongue a shyly exploring flame. There was hunger in the body that fitted to his own, a pulsing richness, and Earl hadn't known there was such need in him until he went blind with its urgency.

Moving inches back from him, Sandra held her hands upon his shoulders; melonslice tremble of a mouth; great, wide eyes. With a moan, she lifted his hands to her breasts and pressed hard upon them. "Please," she gasped, "oh my God, please," and he didn't know why she was begging.

There was no awkwardness about them as they moved from their clothing, only quickness, and his face was buried in the golden globes of her breasts, his hand cupping the hotwet fleece. Sandra was silken, she was soft. She caressed him, clamped him tightly in her hand as if she was afraid he might leave her. Fine, long racehorse legs; mobile hips; a belly scented with the essence of woman; moving ticktock, circling, lifting to guide him into her—desperate beauty and a fierce tenderness.

Devouring him, she absorbed him, only to give him birth again and again. So fluid and seeking, such a magnificent fitting, precisioned in velvets and a precious, binding oil.

He was larger than himself, bigger than dreams, a

focused and greedy strength reaching into the coiling attack of her, probing for the searing core of her, and Sandra took him gladly, gladly. The eruption shuddered him, flung him with her along a whitesparking lava flow that rushed dizzily down a steep mountainside. Cooling crimson, cooling flower pink, it left them misted in peace.

Earl heard faraway drumming, and her heart answered. He could not move, would not let her go. A century later, she moved, or was it the mountain they had climbed? Cupping her, kissing her, he listened to Sandra say please again, softly as the echo of an echo—please, please.

Lifting his head, he stared down into her face. "What, Sandra? What, darling?"

"Please love me. Even if it's only for a little while, please—oh, really love me. Only for tonight; only for now."

"I will," he said. "I do."

"Earl," she said, "Earl," and her love-making was not to him, not for him, but what she wanted, needed to do.

She wasn't Jessica Coffield, or Cam or Stacey or anybody else. She was Sandra, and there had never been another. They lay soft in each other's arms while firelight applauded and jealous wind rattled the windows. A nightbird cried.

A muffled thunderclap shook the house, shook them apart, and upon its passing, a siren howled warning.

"The mill," Earl said. "It's the mill!"

CHAPTER 42

Up on the hill, Alvah rolled out of his blankets at the explosion, snatching for a steel helmet that wasn't there, fumbling for his M-1. Incoming artillery, that scream you knew so well and never got used to. Where the hell was his rifle, and the rest of the fire team?

"Lou," he whispered into the dark, "hey—Lou!"

But nobody answered and Alvah realized he was alone on the ridge without knowing how he got there, his mouth all fuzzy and his head banging from too much *soju*. Goddamn gooks must top their rice whiskey with diesel oil.

He took a drink anyhow and found a .45 in his blankets. That made him feel better, and he squinted off into the valley where a village was burning. Bastards were using white phosphorous again. The shriek of artillery turned into some kind of siren that made his head hurt worse and more *soju* tasted like the bottom of a rice paddy, but it cleared his eyes.

It was cold up here, and Alvah shook with it, pulled a blanket around his shoulders. That wasn't a village, but the mill, and the whole thing wasn't afire, only one building. The siren shut off and he was glad. Christ; he could have sworn he was in Korea and chinks were hitting the position. Not Korea, he repeated to himself, not Korea but Temple County, because the images kept overlapping, and when he knew for sure, he was disappointed.

Down there, guys were running around and a truck pumped water. Alvah could hear faint yelling from where Pa's house used to be and put down the whiskey to rummage in his jacket for a smoke. Now why in hell had he pulled the blanket over his head to light it, and why cup the spark in his palm every time he took a draw?

So brother Earl's mill was on fire. The thing had first blown up when a boiler let go, or something. Yeah; something. Little brother had his educated ass in a sling now. Somebody just showed him he couldn't go against the grain of the whole county like Pa did.

Alvah took a drink. Like Pa, and it was shitty for a combat man good as Ben Lassiter to get wasted from ambush by some sneaking civilian. Goddamn gooks shed their uniforms and mixed in with refugees, and somewhere back there, out came a grenade.

Shivering, Alvah covered the cigarette and pulled at it. It took him a while to get it straight in his mind again, because the guy was coming up the hill like he didn't give a damn, busting through brush and stumbling around. Damned wonder he wasn't waving a flashlight; stupid civilian, or just acting like one.

Waiting until the guy was almost on him, Alvah rose out of the ground and chopped him with the .45. He kind of squeaked and fell over. Alvah checked him out for grenades and didn't find any. Squatting over the guy, he looked down the hill, but didn't see anyone else against the light below, didn't hear another infiltrator. That didn't mean they weren't there. Christ; he could use some help. It didn't do for a man to be out on his own like this, cut off from his platoon, from his friends.

Taking another drink, Alvah shook his head to clear it. That was the mill burning, nothing else, and he *was* alone. The guy groaned and Alvah stuck the muzzle of the .45 into his ear. "Don't make no mistakes."

"Uhhh," the guy groaned. "Oh man—my head—*wh-what?*"

"You didn't fire the whole mill," Alvah said. "Looks like they gettin' it under control."

"You—busted my head, man. Uhhh. I—I—"

"Scatter your fuckin' head all over this hill," Alvah said, "you don't keep still and tell me somethin'."

"Hey—*don't*—"

Twisting the gun muzzle, Alvah said, "Tell me."

"Didn't—didn't nobody get killed. Oh Jesus, they didn't say nobody be up here at night."

"You ain't talkin' fast enough," Alvah said.

Rapidly, the man said, "He say come in with the workers, do like they do, slip off and hide 'til night and light the dynamite. Oh man, mister—you ain't goin' to pull the trigger?"

"Fuzzy-headed son of a bitch with a ring in his ear," Alvah said, "calls hisself X. That him?"

"Yessir, yessir. Oh sweet Jesus—"

"How come you didn't set it off in the main shops?"

"He—he said just teach 'em a lesson, that's all."

Alvah sat back and struck a kitchen match, holding light over the black's bloodied face. He said, "Now I know you, boy. I know your face so goddamn good I'll never forget it. Next time I see you, I put a bullet between your eyes. Hear me?"

"Y-yeah, yessir."

"Light a shuck," Alvah said. "See how far you can run, case I change my mind."

Hesitantly, the man wobbled to his feet and backed

up the hill. Holding both hands to his head, he whimpered and turned to run, hunched against the slap of a heavy bullet that didn't come. Alvah listened to brush snapping until the sounds faded. He had a drink and ducked under the blanket to light another cigarette. Staring down the hill, he watched the flames.

Flames reached out at Earl but he fought them back with the hose, and beside him, Dan Mason worked an extinguisher. Other men flung shovelfuls of dirt, and the water truck circled between the shops and the main buildings, throwing a steady stream.

"Ain't that bad," Dan Mason grunted. "Just the post peelers, but good thing we was stayin' here."

Playing the hose over sizzling embers, Earl said, "How'd it start?"

Dan wiped his face and dropped the empty extinguisher, picked up a shovel. "Had to be a purpose; nothin' yonder to blow up 'til it got to some gas."

"Wind's helping," Earl said, "unless it changes."

He saw Ramirez wheeling the pumper truck to run it to the river for another load, saw Butler riding with him, smoke-blackened. They'd gotten on it quick, administrative people rushing down with extinguishers, grabbing shovels from the storeroom. Over there, Matthew Hobbs had found another hose and stood guard over the main shops, lips peeled back in the heat.

Someone was on this side of him, bending, scooping, throwing dirt. Firelight played in loosened bronze hair as she worked. He said, "Sandra—here, take this. I'll use the shovel."

She was sweaty and gasping, and a spark had burned a hole in her robe. Barefoot in the mud, hair all tangled and chewing her lower lip as she aimed the hose, Sandra had never looked more beautiful.

Earl needed the labor, needed to slam the shovel point into the ground and strain to hurl dirt into the dying fire. Fiercely, he worked, sweat pouring down his cheeks and smarting his eyes, worked until his arms ached and his naked chest heaved desperately for air. Bastards, bastards, *bastards*.

"We 'bout whupped it, Mr. Earl."

Panting, he leaned on the shovel and stared at blackened, hissing ruins. The old mill, where he'd put together the first peeler out of junk parts and wished for no more than some good steel; over there, the room where he'd slept, so as not to bother Ellen and Pa.

Ellen and Pa gone, the old house razed, now the peeler mill. Alvah gone God knew where, little Marcie shipped off from home; everything known wiped out to make way for the new that might not last. Was it worth it? Was anything worth it?

Sandra was at his shoulder, touching him with gentle fingers. "You'd better get something on; you'll catch cold."

Beyond her, bright-eyed and face smeared, Thomas Elliot stood with a bucket in his hands.

Sandra said, "I couldn't stop him, and he stayed out of the way."

Earl nodded. "Thank you, boy."

"A boy," Jessica said, "a boy, damnit, and I never even laid eyes on him."

Barbara Dexter lounged on the sofa, toying with her drink. "Why not?"

Jessica put the library bar between them. "Do I have to tell you *everything*?"

"Whatever I ask, dear. Are you turning rebellious?"

"N-no." Jessica poured a sidecar from the silver

shaker. "How did this happen to me, and right here in my own house. I never—I can't—"

"Why didn't you see your child?"

Gulping at her glass, Jessica said, "Because I didn't want to, that's why. I knew what it was, so did the doctor, the nurse. The way they looked at me—"

Lithely, Barbara uncoiled her legs and walked to the bar. "Did you hide him because there's something wrong with him?"

Jessica took another swallow and said defiantly, "He was just right; just *right* for what I wanted. And Earl would pay for his keep, support him until I needed the little bastard someday. I knew I'd need him, because Elliot—that goddamned Elliot was runnin' everything and lordin' it over me—" She reached for the shaker.

Barbara tapped pointed nails on the bartop. "You actually planned an illegitimate child to use against your brother? But how would that affect him?"

"Playin' at politics is just about Elliot's life—that and his boyfriends. Oh, I got him good when he was about to sell off The Shadows, got him real good. I thought he was about to kill me."

"You digress," Barbara said. "Come to the point."

"Had him right by the balls," Jessica said. "If he's got any. Birth certificate in my own name and put away safe, the youngun put away, too." She drank greedily and her mouth was wet when she showed teeth at Barbara. "Affect Elliot, *affect* my selfish, bitchy brother? It would knock him right out of politics for good."

"Jessica," Barbara said, "you're trying my patience."

"All right, *all right*! Maybe you'll let me alone if I tell you, and go back where you came from. I hope so, oh—I hope so. You want to know about Thomas Elliot Coffield? Yes, that's what I named him, the same as my daddy's whore named *her* bastard, what do you think of that? And every time I think about it, I laugh so hard—but Elliot didn't laugh, and I'll bet my daddy isn't laughin' there in his front seat in hell, either."

Wild-eyed, Jessica hammered on the bar with both small fists. "Because *my* Thomas Elliot Coffield is a nigger! Nigger, *nigger!*" She laced fingers over her mouth, but couldn't stop laughing.

"Nobody's laughing," the FBI man said.

"But it's so ridiculous," the man from the Attorney General's office said. "A caravan of adolescents in bedsheets driving so solemnly through town. Do they actually think they can frighten anyone in that Halloween getup?"

"Look along the street. How many black faces do you see?"

"The *Klan*, for godsakes; I thought it had gone the way of the Bund."

"Law enforcement went that way," the FBI man said. "Look again; no police in sight, no state troopers. Some of them might be under those sheets."

"Boogey men trying to bluff people out of exercising their constitutional rights."

The FBI man said, "When I was little, I saw a burning cross. I should have run home, but the other boys wanted to sneak up closer. A man had been lynched and the cross wasn't the only thing burning. Ever since, I wish to hell I'd run home."

The lawyer looked down the street. "The procession seems about over."

"Not until they burn that cross. Then it may be just

beginning." He watched the last car drive to the corner, past the Templar Club, and wondered at the glow in the sky some distance away.

Sheriff Kobburn threw away his cigar butt. "What you reckon's on fire yonder?"

Deputy Travers squinted into the night. "Klan burnin' out some niggers?"

"Uh-uh, too far out along—hey now! Lassiter mill, I bet a pretty." Kobburn laughed. "Workin' out just right."

Luther Travers laughed, too. "Slicker'n owlshit, Sheriff. Onliest thing bothers me is Alvah. Bootlegger thinks he seen him t'other day, but not for certain sure. Raggedy-ass, scraggly beard; 'legger said he looked wilder'n a pissant."

"Always was," Kobburn said. "Son of a bitch had a lick of sense, he'd be clean out'n the country. Wonder if Earl's hidin' him out. But Earl Lassiter's gettin' his comeuppance now; white man backin' niggers to vote. Comes of ol' Ben keepin' a wench right there in the house, I reckon."

"Talkin' about wenches," the deputy said. "That nigger doctor draws some good 'uns. First that hot lil' ol' wife, now another high yellow looks like she'd flat eat a man up."

Kobburn nodded and looked through the patrol car windshield. "Been eyin' that some. Come out of Beevo's whorehouse, but hell; that don't make no nevermind. They take to whorin' natural. Onliest ten-yearold wench still got her cherry is 'cause she can outrun her brother."

Luther Travers chuckled. "Nine-year-old, more like it."

"Hold on," Kobburn said. "Somebody's comin' up

the road. Hit him with the spot, Luther. Don't want nobody slippin' up on us."

The beam pinned a wobbling black who threw up his arms, and Travers said, "Just a drunk nigger."

"Out tonight, with the Klan ridin'?" Kobburn heaved himself from the car, pistol in hand. "You, boy! Walk over here real slow."

Travers said, "Got his head skinned. What you been up to, boy?"

"Just—just hoorawin', sir. Fell out a truck and they run off and left me."

Kobburn grunted. "Mean to tell you ain't heard the Klan's out?"

"Ku Kluxers?" the black said. "Oh lordy, nossir, nossir, I sho' didn't. Hadn't been for them fools drinkin' and tusselin' with me—mister sheriff sir, can I please ride a piece with you? Just one of Mr. Nelson's niggers, sir; don't mean nobody no harm. Oh lordy, the Kluxers is out."

"Made it this far," Kobburn said, "go ahead on. Ain't havin' no nigger bleed all over my back seat."

"Yessir, thank you, sir. I be on my way quick, sir."

"Oh shit," Kobburn said and put up his pistol.

The man walked down the road quickly as he could, pressing a kerchief to his split head. When he rounded a curve, he cut off into the woods and sat down. It was easy to shuck rednecks like the sheriff; just do Stepin Fetchit for them and they bought it every time.

But that crazy mother back up on the hill was something else. Jesus; he could still feel the chill of the gun muzzle in his ear, still see those bloodshot, sunken eyes in the flare of the match. That son of a bitch was clear off his track, mumbling about chow trucks and Joe Chink and things that didn't make a bit of sense.

He pushed the kerchief harder against his scalp and

knew he had never been closer to death, that Louis X couldn't spook him now.

Whispering it to the night, he said, "Screw Louis X. I ain't goin' to tell him. Won't be here to tell him."

CHAPTER 43

A black called Johnson hadn't reported for work today. Earl looked at Dan Mason's handwritten list and thought the bomber might have been Johnson—if that was his name—or anyone else. He could have the workers counted in and out, their lunch boxes searched, increase night security inside the plant, and still he was vulnerable.

For all his big talk in town about eye for eye, he could hardly say eenie-meenie and choose a black home to burn. The saboteur could be white, or maybe Louis X was collecting for a wrecked Continental. But the militant hadn't blown up the Africa Baptist church, unless he was more cruel and Machiavellian than any man had a right to be.

The county commissioners, feuding Lovelaces, and redneck purity were set against a black firebrand, ordinary folks wanting what was long overdue them; both were lined up against Lassiter mill. The county was a tricky chessboard where black and white pieces made moves without rules. Would it be any better when all chessmen were integrated brown, or would there be elitist shades of the same color?

Earl rolled a cigarette and looked into the hallway. Barbara Dexter hadn't come in yet. He struck a match to the Prince Albert and watched the smoke dissipate;

the vote would be like smoke, promising equality that
was a long way off, but a beginning. Intermarriage
and "mongrelization," the white man's greatest fear,
were farther still. Perhaps another two hundred years
would bring acceptance, one of the other, but Earl
doubted it. Tribal pressures were too strong, as the
clannish ethnic neighborhoods in Boston proved,
where Irish blocked out Italians, and Polish snubbed
Puerto Ricans, and most excluded blacks and Jews.

Here in the South, where handed-down history was
more meaningful than a modern news event, men
spoke bitterly of the Reconstruction period as if they
personnally remembered when illiterate blacks were
thrust into positions of power by carpetbaggers. It
would happen again, they said, niggers stomping on
whites and grabbing all they could carry, no white
woman safe on the streets, rape and pillage.

Perhaps it would happen; power corrupted without
prejudice and on a less obvious plane, the same things
were going on already, black woman raped, black man
exploited. A backlash was long overdue.

"Oh hell," Earl said, "this is Barbara's field, not
mine. Social scientists know all the answers."

"Pardon?" she said from the hall, and he motioned
her into the office.

"I saw the fire last night," she said, "but nobody
came to help; no sirens, no police."

"No Barbara Dexter," he said.

"What could I have done?"

"Something, nothing; I don't know. Did you get anywhere with Jessica?" Her name had an aftertaste in
Earl's mouth.

Barbara went to the coffeepot. "She has a child, but
it's not yours."

He waited while she drew coffee and brought it to the desk. "Just that?" he said.

"I think it's all you have to know."

Standing up, Earl carefully lifted the paper cup from her manicured hand. Then he hurled it across the room to splatter against the wall. "Don't screw with me," he said. "My mill has been blasted, my brother is being hunted like an animal, this whole goddamn county is about to explode. Don't *screw* with me, Barbara."

She flinched from the tight anger in his face. "I-I'm not responsible for any of that. You asked me to do something personal for you, to find out—"

"No; I *told* you to do it."

Barbara said, "Jessica Coffield isn't for you, for any man. All her life, she's used men to her own ends, made fools of you all. Worse, she's made a lie of herself."

"What the hell does that mean? You still haven't answered me. The boy—what's wrong with him, whose is it?"

She stared into his eyes. "Why do you want to know, so you can cuddle jealousy and hate to yourself, rationalize why the childhood dream princess never really cared for you?"

She was diamond-hard, he thought, and as brilliant, and knew how to use her sharp edges to cut. Earl said, "If I need analysis, I'll hire a graduate shrink. Now, one more time—*the boy*."

Barbara crossed arms over her beasts. "Jess told me in confidence, and I think—"

Earl cut her off. "*I* think the detective agency will bring me a report very soon. I don't know how you and Jessica are mixed up, why you're living there, and

I no longer give a damn. You're fired. Get the hell out of here."

Her face went pale. "Earl—the company expects me to stay through this crisis, and if I'm shipped home—"

Putting his back to her, he went to the window and looked down at a cleanup crew working over the ruins of his peeler section. He hadn't expected all his regular hands to show up today, much less new workers, but there they were, clearing rubble while experienced mill hands were at their usual jobs. Surprisingly, there was a knot of whites working off to itself, and Earl recognized pieces of it: the Wilson brothers, Jody Thompson; hardscrabble farmers who sometimes cut a little wood, or when times were hard, ran off a little whiskey. Were they here to help a Lassiter or to put a nigger lover in his place?

Barbara said, "Goddamn, you're tough. All right. Jess wanted Sandy's boy to fool you; you were asking too many questions and she couldn't use her own child. That one is also named Thomas Elliot Coffield, but he's a mulatto." She waited, and when Earl didn't turn to face her, went on, "She swears she only laid one black—Dr. Davison."

To the window, Earl said, "They'll kill him, even after all these years—shoot him, drag him behind a truck, and string up his body to set it afire. All Jessica has to do is claim he raped her and she was too shamed to admit it. Oh, they'll be righteous in their wrath, fierce protectors of southern womanhood—but after the blood dries and the stink of burned meat is gone, no man will say howdy to Jessica Coffield, and decent women will cross the streets to keep from meetin' her, and they better not even lay eyes on her nigger youngun. Jesus! What was she *thinkin'*, what went on inside her head?"

"She thought to protect The Shadows from Elliot's ambitions," Barbara answered slowly. "It was more a way of revenge on her father. Jess hated him for bringing another woman into the house. She could compete with a bloodless mother, but not with Sandy."

Earl went back to his desk, opened a drawer, and took out a bottle. "Paper cups," he said, and when Barbara brought them, poured whiskey.

"I can use it," Barbara said.

He drank the shot of bourbon in one gulp, and rolled a cigarette, spilling tobacco. "Avery Coffield never did a goddamned thing he didn't think clear through to the end. It was just his bad luck that a set of balls got hung on the wrong one of his kids. Jessica is her daddy all over again, and you can bet she saw Davison as more than a lay, more than a picked stud to the catch colt she planned to drop on Elliot someday. The doctor figured in it, too."

Barbara frowned. "I don't think she'd plan so far in advance."

"You mean that's something you didn't pry out of her. But why Davison and not some hardup young field hand whose brains were all in his pecker? The field hand could never pose a threat to The Shadows, to the goddamned Coffields; as a black leader someday, Davison could."

Earl drank again, crushed out his cigarette, and eyed Barbara. She poured her own drink. "Earl, aren't you striking back at her for—for rejecting you? Is it possible her thinking could be so devious, so farsighted? With Jess, it's more an instinct, a reaction to what she might see as—"

His laugh was short and grating. "Jessica has all the instincts of a cottonmouth and twice the poison. You know how us ol' country boys react to cottonmouths?

When we're young and immortal, we pin 'em down
with a stick and grab 'em by the tail; then we swing
'em around and around, and pop their heads right off.
When we get older, we come down on 'em and break
their backs; *then* we beat their heads flat."

Barbara shuddered. "I don't see the—"

"Then *look*. You developed a sudden interest in Jessica Coffield and that's your business. I stayed in Boston quite a while, around different folks, so I'm not
shocked—Christ, after everything Jessica's done, how
can I be? But don't let *your* emotions cloud logic; I've
been stupid enough for both us."

"Earl," she said, fingernails digging into her thighs,
"I'm only—damnit, I'm human, too."

"So is Dr. Davison; so is that black Thomas Elliot,
hidden away and ignored all his life; so are the problems in Temple County—*human* problems, not neat
little cause and effect in some textbook." He leaned
forward, hands knotted atop the desk. "I want that
boy brought here and kept out of Jessica's reach; I
want an affidavit stating that Jessica has no idea who
the father is. And I want all that in a hurry."

He paused and Barbara Dexter reached for her cup
of whiskey, hand shaking just a bit. "She—she isn't
completely under control, and if she's been lying to me
about using Davison—"

Earl said, "If you can't carry out the assignment,
keep right on going, all the way to Boston. Leave Jessica Coffield to me. I'll just have to break her back
and beat her goddamned head flat."

Drink forgotten, Barbara Dexter stared at him and
realized he meant that literally. She had a sudden,
vivid image of Jess writhing helpless on the floor, then
going still, all that lovely hair blotted with scarlet.

Eyes closed, Barbara swayed for a moment, then stood up. There was so little time.

"Time they see what they up against," Louis X said. "Handful of blacks don't mean nothin'; a hundred don't. But thousands, now—that shakes whitey to see so many brothers marchin' at once, see all that *power* out there."

"But the police'll come down," Reverend Brown said.

"Good for TV, better for us. A few busted heads are nothin' alongside what they did to your church, preacher. You forgettin'?"

"No," Reverend Brown said. "Never forget that. All right, I march with you."

Louis X touched the ring in his ear. "Now you're black, brother. I got all my people ready; you get yours."

Reverend Brown rubbed a wrinkled hand over his balding head. "I wish there was some other way."

A long way ahead of the others and off on his own in the deep woods, Virgil Lovelace grinned when he found the tire track. Ol' Alvah couldn't cover his trail complete, just like he kept telling that bunch heading off on the wrong scent; a loaded-down pickup just natural had to leave sign somewhere. Here it was, not swept out by pine limb. Ol' Alvah was getting a mite careless or pretty tired.

Looking up at the hill, Virgil figured that to be about right, too. Fox might run a far piece, but when the hounds got close, he holed up. Good place for ol' Alvah was near to the mill, near to home where he could holler for help. Sheriff Kobburn said stay clear of that mill, account of them sharpshooting Hobbs, said government men would search it legal since Alvah was a bombing suspect. Virgil Lovelace grinned some more and bit off a plug of Brown Mule tobacco. Government men, city folks, couldn't root out Alvah Lassiter in a month of Sundays and Christmas throwed in to boot. Beside, ol' Alvah wasn't owed to nobody but a Lovelace. Rifle easy in his hand, deputy badge hidden under his jacket, Virgil moved carefully along the abandoned logging road.

Being out on the stump was much harder than staying put and letting Greater Atlantic run his campaign via television, Elliot Coffield admitted. The only problem here was keeping his alliance with certain blacks a secret. If that ever got out, he was through as a statesman, regardless of how much money poured into his election fund. The machine would immediately drop him from the ticket, anyhow. Right now, they were ecstatic over the unexpected richness of the campaign.

Elliot rocked back in his office chair and smiled. The governor-elect wouldn't be so happy, a few years from now, when Elliot booted him out of the mansion. Maybe, Elliot thought, he could bypass the capitol and go directly for Congress with Greater Atlantic backing. Why not?

There was a little, buzzing fly in the political ointment, though—Sandy. Just today, Sam Harvey had asked him what Elliot's wife and son were doing out there at the Lassiter place, how come they moved out of The Shadows. Elliot said something quick about Jessica and Sandy not getting along, then got humble about his wife's drinking problem.

She get drunk enough to leave you and take up with

Earl Lassiter? Sam wanted to know, not satisfied. It had been a nice piece of acting, Elliot thought, taking Sam Harvey aside and being so ashamed, so worried, and asking man's advice from a wise old friend. What could he do about it, without upsetting the campaign and giving a nigger-loving Republican a chance to take over the state? It might not be all it seemed, either; his sister told him Sandy was staying there in the house, all right, but a Yankee psychologist was there most of the time with her. Sam had seen that long-legged Yankee woman? Sure, that was the one, her with the big tits. Anyhow, she was trotting back and forth between Sandy and Jessica, trying to iron out things. Earl Lassiter just let Sandy move in to annoy Elliot and start gossip; everybody knew he was sleeping at the mill.

Elliot sat up, straightened his coat, and brushed a hand over his hair. The talk would spread, of course, unless he got Sandy and the boy out of there. But Earl and Greater Atlantic—still, there should be a way, some compromise. He touched a buzzer and Mark Manley hurried in; dear Mark, so faithful over the years; fading a bit now and a little shopworn but completely loyal.

While the door was open, Elliot said, "Hey, ol' buddy," and when it closed, "My dear, tell me—just what *is* going on between my sister and that woman from the mill? You're out at The Shadows more often than I, and I'm sure *nothing* escapes you."

Escape, Jessica thought; get the hell away before this mixed-up thing got worse. Clear out until planting time, and by then the stinking pulp mill ought to be out of business and the niggers whipped down; Barbara Dexter would be gone back north where she be-

longed and things would be the way they used to be,
how they were meant to be. Jessica Coffield was her
own boss, always had been from the time she could
talk. She wasn't one of those—those—

Hurling clothes into a suitcase, Jessica hauled it
downstairs and into the living room. The nerve of that
bitch, questioning her, threatening her. Not that the
information mattered, because when Sandy and her
brat took off, all chance of convincing Earl went with
them.

There was still Elliot, damn him. He was spending
plenty of money running for office, more than Sandy
gave him. It was coming from somewhere, and as long
as a certain little nigger bastard was where she could
bring him out into the light, Jessica meant to get hold
of money. If not right now, then after Elliot got
elected.

In the meantime, there was Dr. Davison. Lord
knows how much he was making off his clinic, but she
was sure it was enough to keep her—and pay for his
youngun's upkeep—until Temple County was back to
normal. He'd be damned glad to pay for his hide, or
get himself hung to a tall pine. She picked up the
phone. Patting a booted foot, she waited till Davison
came on the line. "This is Jessica Coffield at The
Shadows. I think you ought to come runnin', Doctor.
It's about—your son."

When she put down the phone and turned, she saw
Barbara Dexter standing just inside the front door.
Jessica fled into the library and jerked her daddy's
shotgun from a rack. She just had time to break it, see
that both barrels were loaded, and snap it shut again
before Barbara was striding purposefully toward her.

Jessica brought up the gun. "You—you better not!

You better stop right there. I—you won't lay a hand on me again, not ever again."

Barbara kept coming.

Earing back both hammers, Jessica said, "Don't! I'll shoot—I swear *I'll kill you!*"

CHAPTER 44

Just a hair too late to do anything about it, Virgil Lovelace got a twitchy feeling between his shoulders. That's when the voice said softly, "Howdy, gook."

Virgil didn't move a muscle, but the time stretched out and he said, "I ain't no gook." Oh lord; ol' Alvah Lassiter was ahint him and not giving him a chance in the world to turn around.

"Can't understand a word I say," Alvah whispered. "You a dumb one. Tolled you in by leavin' that track, didn't I?"

Hands tight on his rifle, Virgil said desperately, "Alvah—Alvah! Look now—I didn't have nothin' to do with killin' your pa."

"White man couldn't learn to talk gook in a hundred years," Alvah said, "outside a few whore-house words." He coughed. "You sneakin' bastard—go on, run for it. *Ka-rah!*"

Wasn't no use, Virgil knew and rolled his body as he dived for the ground. It was like a mule kicking him low in the back, but he got his gun around and triggered off a shot. Pain wrapped around his backbone and jerked his head back and he fought to breathe. Dirt got in his eyes and he tried to wipe it out.

The man squatting over him didn't hardly look like ol' Alvah; hairy like a possum, sick-eyed as a wormy hound. Blood alongside his head, though. Virgil pawed at his eyes and grunted to breathe. "Got—got me a piece of you, anyways."

Alvah mumbled, blinked his eyes. "What the hell you doin' over here? Thought all you bastards hid out when the war started."

"Son of a bitch," Virgil said. "Never dropped your pa, but—but hit your nigger mammy clean. Ahh; oh sweet Jesus—"

Alvah wiped at his head, looked at blood on his hand.

Twisting on the ground, Virgil hissed, "Busted the wench center—then—your pa come crawlin'. Son of a— *ahh*—got the nigger church—*ahh*—too. You know that—that bushy-headed nigger put the blame on you? Oh lord, lord—"

Swaying upright, Alvah stared down at the man, faintly interested in the way Virgil's feet were gouging ruts in pine straw.

"Finish me off, Alvah," Virgil gasped. "Can't—can't stand it no more. F-finish me off, you son of a bitch."

"You already dead," Alvah said, and dragged him off the trail, rolled him down into a gulley. He was wiping out marks when he got dizzy and had to sit down. Every time he coughed, his head hurt, but no more than his stump. If it hadn't twisted on him, the gook wouldn't have gotten off a shot.

It wasn't any good out by yourself, and Lou Miller never showed up—that bushy-headed one—put the blame on you—church going up and so much screaming. Never could stand screaming.

Ellen, Ellen—goddamnit, I'm sorry; didn't mean to, but the sap was rising strong in me and listening to you and pa in the bed at night—I'm sorry, Ellen.

He had to get off the ridge. He was hit in the leg

and head-shot and this was a different kind of fucking war anyhow, with no glory to it.

I'm sorry, Pa.

Painfully, he limped up the hill. He didn't need Lou Miller's help, because he could find the squad, and there was a drink in the truck.

"Squattin' ahint a truck," Jody Thompson said after he flung the man into Earl's office. He held up a bundle. "Had this on him. Dynamite."

The Wilson brothers filled the doorway behind Jody, and behind them, the Hobbs boys. The man on the floor got up to one knee, eyes darting for a way out.

"Who is he?" Earl asked.

"One of them Johnsons from over to State Line; shirttail kin to Lovelaces. Bastard meant to blow us all up."

"No such a thing," Johnson said quickly. "Just shut down this nigger lover's mill, get back at him for his brother killin' folks."

Earl said, "Who gave you dynamite? Who sent you?"

The man's unshaven jaws worked; his eyes flicked here, there, hunting for a hole. "Go to hell. The rest of you folks—you're white men; how come you workin' for *him*?"

Jody Thompson said, "Mainly account of your kin. Hangin' badges on polecats don't sweeten 'em up none."

One of the Wilsons said, "Stoppin' *our* trucks, pickin' into our plunder, biggity as all getout. Wasn't takin' sides 'til then. 'Sides, winter's comin' on and cash money's scarce."

Johnson bobbed his head, Adam's apple jerking. He

pointed a grimy finger at Earl. "But this 'un wants niggers to vote!"

The other Wilson shrugged thick, meaty shoulders. "Makes me no nevermind. Never voted in my life 'cause it don't make a speck of difference who gets in; rich gets richer and poor man gets cornholed just the same."

"Boys," Earl said, "I'd appreciate it if you'd haul this dynamiter over yonder to one of the grinders and ask him again who put him up to this. Reckon it wouldn't hurt the pulp much, if you had to grind up his legs in it."

Jody Thompson grinned. "Reckon not."

Johnson's darting eyes went still. "They'll kill me, do I tell."

"Make a whole corpse thataway," Jody Thompson said.

"Give me a runnin' start?"

Earl nodded, and Johnson said, "Law put me up to it. Sheriff figured you'd blame niggers and go at 'em."

"Kobburn," Earl said. "You all heard it."

"Turn him loose," Matthew Hobbs said from the hall, "and nobody'll ever hear it again."

"Don't mean to take it to court," Earl said. "Haul him out and put him on the road, but see he don't head for town."

Jessica Coffield kept pointing the shotgun, even after Barbara stopped. Her hands were shaking, but she kept her feet planted firmly.

"This won't help," Barbara said. "You'll only need me more than ever, but I'll be gone."

"No, damnit, *I'll* be gone, somewhere you can't ever do that to me again."

"I do nothing you don't want, nothing you don't crave."

Jessica backed up a step and eased down the shotgun hammers. "You crave it, you mean. You're cruel and vicious and—and—"

"Perhaps I am. That's why we fit so well, Jess. I need to punish and you need to be punished."

Jessica's elbows touched the bar. "No, *no*. Just go on and get out of my house."

"So you can bargain with the black doctor, get money for his life? Oh, that will make you more guilty than ever, Jess. You'll run and try to find a man to make you feel good again, but it won't work. You need me." Barbara smoothed the dress over her hips, her eyes fixed upon the other woman. "When you were small and did something to make your father whip you, wasn't it good? Didn't it thrill you, didn't you keep doing things to make him angry? So good; always so good."

Jessica shook her head, the shotgun muzzle pointing floorward now. "He—he wouldn't, after a while. He made me grow up and then he wouldn't."

"But I will, darling, and you can do it with me because it's all right."

Bringing up the gun again, Jessica said, "Get out of here, damn you!"

"All right," Barbara said, turning slowly and moving from the door. "Goodbye, Jess."

"Don't call me Jess!" Jessica shouted.

"Goodbye," Barbara said.

Jessica put the gun atop the bar and dug her fingers into her belly, twisted them there. "Barbara—come back! C-come back—*please*. Don't leave me."

* * *

"Leave here and you're liable to wind up dead," Betty Jean said as Davison reached for his jacket. "Can't trust them and you know it, especially their women. Why'd she call *you*, anyhow?"

Davison said, "It's about my son. I have to go."

"How does *she* know—Cal, I'll go with you. It could be somethin' else, a set up, a trap." Betty Jean put a hand on his arm. "You—this white woman—"

"A long time ago. Just once, and she—it sounds crazy, but she forced me into it. She couldn't have, if I didn't want to, I guess." He was looking at the wall. "My wife was still here, but so damned afraid of everything, and I—I—black and white, black on white, *in* white. Oh hell."

Her eyes were deep and moist. "You still want her?"

Davison turned then. "No; you made me forget. But she sounded threatening, and my son—"

"Come on," Betty Jean said. "I'll stay in the car and if you—*no*; damned if I will; I mean to be right there with you. Some things with a woman, another woman can handle better, even when they're different colors."

It was going along just great, Kobburn thought as he cruised slowly out toward the creek road. The government men were running around like chickens with their necks twisted, so damn sure Alvah Lassiter blew up the church, and that kept their long noses out of his business. Pretty soon Earl would come squalling in about somebody dynamiting his place, and the FBI would be busier than ever. Funny Earl hadn't made a report on the fire at the mill, but you couldn't never tell about them Lassiters; in fact, he was kind of counting on Earl being as muley as old Ben. When he pitched into the niggers for blowing up his place, it would get him the same thing it got his pa. And the goddamn commissioners would get off a good sheriff's back; might be, everybody'd get lucky and Earl would down that bushy-headed nigger first.

Kobburn chewed his cigar as he turned the patrol car onto gravel. Niggers was keeping their heads down anyhow, nothing stirring for all their big talk, but it might be better could he get his hands on Louis X and make another example. Hell, they'd been so quiet the state troopers pulled out and gave Kobburn back his county. If them black bastards dared march on the courthouse, they'd wish to hell they never heard of no registration.

Yonder was Beevo's, and Kobburn puffed his belly in pride. Cost him a pretty to restock it, what with all the bootleggers shutting down and most the whores scared shitless, but money would roll in afore long, and this time, nearly all of it was his. Kobburn stopped the car and changed the cigar from one corner of his mouth to the other. When Earl Lassiter give up on feeding niggers and they started buying at stores again, Kobburn just might have him a talk with Sam Harvey and the others. Look here, he'd say, I saved your asses, so I reckon Beevo's is rightly mine, without no payoffs to nobody else, and if you don't like that, you can just—

There it went! Mighty solid blast, too; more than a man'd figure on just two sticks, but ol' Rusty Johnson must of laid them up next to a boiler. Shook the ground pretty good.

Joe Blake stuck his head out the back door. "What'n hell was that, Sheriff?"

"Mill, I 'spect," Kobburn said. Then his mouth fell open and the cigar dropped out. It was the wrong way for Lassiter mill; that blast had come from town.

* * *

Town, Sandy realized, a second after she dropped the dish; *town,* thank God, and not the mill. There was no danger to Earl. Knees trembling, she bent to pick up broken chinaware. What if something happened to him—would she shatter like this, go all to pieces? And what might happen to Thomas Elliot? He was just opening up, unconsciously imitating Earl in little mannerisms, identifying with the first man who'd paid attention to him.

It's not Thomas Elliot you have to worry about, Sandy told herself as she dropped shards into the trash can; it's *you.* If you don't stay sober, there's no way you can be there when your son needs you. And Earl never promised you tomorrow; you only asked him to love you for a little while, for right now.

Up and down Main Street, they came running to the fire truck, but after the first look, blacks faded away. Sam Harvey stared through the bank window and thought, good lord, suppose we were all over there having a drink. His teeth clamped together so hard that cords stood out in his neck. Bigod, they went too far this time. Floyd Kobburn better pull in all his deputies and quit chasing shadows in the woods; he sure as billy hell better protect this town; he bigod *better,* or see that badge on somebody else.

Will Jellico ran into the bank, shoving through women bunched up at the window. "Told you, goddamnit! I *told* you, Sam—but you kept sayin' take it easy, take it easy. Now look what they went and done, the black bastards. Blowed up the *Templar Club,* goddamn their black hides to hell!"

Sam Harvey grabbed a skinny arm and jerked Will Jellico to the back office. "Shut up, hush up! Don't everybody have to know our business; don't know

who's gettin' paid these days. Where in hell's the sheriff?"

"Settin' on his fat ass somewheres. Sam—Billy Dee
Blake was stockin' the bar."

"Sam Harvey kicked the door shut. "He ain't comin'
outa that mess. Lord, you suppose they figured *us* to
be in there?"

"Another half hour, we woulda been, and they
knowed it. Tit for tat; us for them niggers in the
church. Son of a bitch! One white man, even sorry as
Billy Dee Blake, is worth more'n a dozen black bastards. Where's them Lovelaces, all them special deputies we been payin' for?"

"Chasin' their tails in the woods, but they goin' to
be right here, every damned one of 'em. Oh damn;
that club's stood a hundred years, onliest place a man
could be with his own kind—well, they tore their asses
this time, split 'em right down the middle. I don't give
a damn every government man in Washington comes
slippin' around Temple County, them murderin' niggers don't march on our courthouse!"

"Better they bombed the courthouse," the FBI man
said. "Better they bombed nothing at all, but they
might as well have blown up the Confederate statue in
the square. It has the same symbolical meaning as the
Templar Club."

"They're only striking back," the man from the Attorney General's Office said, "and now surely the governor will have to mobilize the Guard."

The FBI man said, "Up there in Jackson, there's a
Templar Club, too. It isn't called that, but that's
about the only difference. The governor's a life member, and so is the head of the state police."

"I'm calling Washington."

"If you get through, everybody here will know your conversation word for word. Better let us patch you through by radio, but if you're thinking of federal troops—it'll take more than this."

The lawyer said, "How much more?"

"That's what's bothering me," the FBI man said, "and how much time before we get an answer. Nobody wants to hear."

CHAPTER 45

When nobody answered Davison's knock, Betty Jean pushed open the front door, despite his hesitation. She moved in front of him, such a natural protective gesture she didn't even think about it. The house was something out of antebellum movies to her, with the superior stateliness of Tara and all it implied: hoopskirts and house niggers, field hands and pickaninnies.

Davison was nervous. "Maybe she's out back."

"And maybe there's an ambush." Betty Jean caught a noise, a soft sound. She dropped her voice. "Over there, but Cal—we ought to get out of here."

"If someone's hurt—"

She caught up a fireplace poker and got in front of him again. The other room was filled with shadow, but she saw them on the floor, coiled and squirming together like white snakes. Betty Jean's mouth twisted, and at her shoulder, Davison sucked in a sharp breath. With a vast and cynical relief, she said, "Go back in the other room. This is somethin' I know about."

Lifting her voice, she called, "All right, girls—break it up! Fun's fun, but nobody's makin' any money and the johns are waitin'."

They came apart hissing in outrage, in shock. Betty Jean smiled coldly at them while they pawed for clothing, their faces turned away. She picked a big leather chair and sat in it, the poker across her knees, feeling much, much better; feeling in control.

"Never was my bag, girls," she said conversationally, "but I don't put it down if you dig it. Of course, folks around here don't see it that way. Let's talk about that phone call, and Dr. Davison's son."

The sons of bitches were sitting up and taking notice now, Louis X thought; maybe they were thinking about a black church and black people dying and seeing how it damned well could happen to *them*.

From the Holiness Baptist window, he could see the lone camera crew running around, buttonholing whites for interviews. The rest of them would hustle back quick, more newsmen in town than pigs, and that was exactly what they needed, nationwide coverage to reach clear to Washington. And tomorrow, when the pigs and 'fays beat on the brothers to break up the march, when dogs and cattle prods were used, the whole country would see it, hear it, *feel* it.

"You can't mean to go ahead," Reverend Brown said. "Not now."

"Best time, old man. Mr. Charlie is shook up good. He sees the brothers ain't just takin' it from him no more, but fightin' back. He goin' to be scared and pissed, and try to bust up TV cameras, but he can't get 'em all, photogs and radio and newsmen."

The preacher said, "But folks goin' to get hurt, maybe killed."

"Two hundred years," Louis X said, "we been gettin' killed for nothin', old man. This time, it's for *somethin'* and the brothers know it. They all ready for me to lead 'em. Every house close to town all filled up with brothers and tomorrow we march on the courthouse. You can hide out, if you want."

Reverend Brown rubbed his head. "I be there, too. If the Savior got nailed to the cross for me, reckon I can—"

Louis X snorted. "White man's savior, not yours. He'da been black with some guts, they never take him and he wind up drivin' nails hisself."

"You ain't Him," Reverend Brown said, "but maybe you meet Him afore long; maybe we all do."

Reaching down to pull back a canvas tarp, Louis X lifted a sawed-off shotgun and stroked it. "That happens," he said, "I bring plenty of company, and I come smokin'."

Smoke down in the valley where artillery landed, Alvah saw. He sat in the truck and chewed the last of his rations and drank some more whiskey. Pouring some on a kerchief, he patted his head and winced. Hell, that wasn't artillery on a village; something went off in town. He just got mixed up sometimes, like he kept confusing Lou Miller with the spade called himself Louis X.

And the squad truck—no, his alky-running pickup—ought to be moved out; it had been here too long, and some chink patrol might stumble over it any time. He coughed hard, a spasm racking his guts, and hung on to the wheel until it passed. No sense dragging Earl into things, if Kobburn and the Lovelaces ran up on him close to the mill. The youngun was doing all right, coming up in the world; pretty good for a hard-dirt farmer never had two nickels to rub together. Pa would be proud.

Pa knew how it was to lay it on the line, to get up and walk into the guns when every nerve in your body screamed stay down, stay down. But his war was different; all goddamn wars were different, and since they

fucked up Korea so bad, and there was no place in
Nam for a crippled Gyrene—

He got out and pulled camouflage off the truck,
climbed back, and kicked over the engine. If they were
still out yonder, he'd run roadblocks before, and figured on pulling in next to the village where the squad
would be goofing off. The corpsman could take a look
at his head.

"Sheriff," Sam Harvey said, "you meet them niggers
head-on and turn 'em back. You got enough deputies,
and if you ain't, there's enough folks madder'n hornets
be happy to pitch in."

Kobburn hitched up his belt. "Not with them
govmint men here. Best us legal-appointed lawmen
handle it—me and C.J. and Luther and them Lovelaces; plenty enough to head off a bunch of coons.
Hell, cut down on them burrheads up front, and afore
they quit kickin', the rest'll be runnin' for the woods
lickety-split."

Will Jellico said, "Be carryin' *my* pistol, and so'll
everybody else. You certain sure they mean to march
anyhow, after what they done to the club?"

"They marchin'," Kobburn said. "I got ways of
knowin'. Now, if some of the boys was to bust them
TV cameras and stomp on every other picture taker
they find, we be better off. Be a good thing folks get
to fightin' among themselfs, and sort of run over them
govmint men accidental, so they don't see too much."

"We can arrange that," Sam Harvey said. "Boys,
pretty soon everything's goin' to be right back to normal."

"Normally," Davison said, "it would be better for
me not to come here, much less bring along Betty

Jean. But Mr. Lassiter, your assistant told us you're involved in finding a—looking for this boy—oh hell; my son."

"You don't *know* that," Betty Jean said quickly.

"Sorry," Davison said. "I guess I do. Does that bother you, Mr. Lassiter?"

Earl said, "Nothing bothers me about Jessica Coffield; not anymore. Did Miss Dexter tell you what we know?"

"And all Jessica knows," Betty Jean said. "That woman is the damnedest—"

Davison cut in: "Betty Jean got all the information, and there'll be no trouble about the releases you sent Miss Dexter for."

"*Miss* Dexter," Betty Jean said. "*Miss* Jessica; couple of closet lezes ballin' it up."

"Betty Jean—"

"Never mind," Earl said. "I suspected as much. Doctor, I wanted to see the child didn't suffer more than he has already, and I thought of protecting you."

Betty Jean said softly, "I believe you mean that."

Earl looked at her. "An agent should be here tomorrow, but I probably won't need his information now. You know where the boy is, where Jessica has her evidence? Good; when Miss Dexter brings back the forms, we can start things moving. Do you want the boy, Doctor?"

Davison said, "He's mine. He sure as hell isn't hers, but he's my blood. Nobody has to know anything else. If Betty Jean can accept him—"

She took his hand. "Like you said, he's yours, Cal."

"After the dust settles, then," Earl said. "Or, if you're not going to march—"

Face twisting, Davison said, "I have to; damnit, I

have to. Not only to try and hold down the militants, but I belong in the ranks. Can you see that?"

"Yes," Earl said. "You can do nothing else. Neither can I, Doctor. I'll be there, too."

"Standin' where?" Betty Jean asked.

"Not standing," Earl said, "walking with you."

Betty Jean couldn't say anything.

For a while, Sandy didn't say a word. Then she put a hand on his shoulder. "If that's how you see it, Earl."

"If a white outsider did it, they'd get him first. Since they know me, I'm hoping they'll hesitate and take time to listen, maybe even to think. And Davison promised to try and keep Louis X and his ilk in the background. Davison has treated a lot of whites and they respect him; they know the preacher, too. With the doctor and the reverend up front, and nobody threatening—I don't know, Sandra. It's just an off chance."

Driving herself from him so she would not cling, Sandy looked out and saw Thomas Elliot come out of the pines. He was growing straight and tall, with a good set to his shoulders; he carried his new .22 rifle proudly and carefully. Don't treat this like a toy, Earl told him, and don't practice on living things; anything you shoot, you'll eat; understand that, boy? And gravely, Thomas Elliot had listened.

"If anything happens," Earl said, "I'm setting up a—"

"I don't want to hear it!" Sandy snapped. "I don't care about anything. I'm a nurse; I can go back to work and take care of my child. We don't need anything from—from—" Her composure broke and tears came.

Holding her in his arms, he said, "There may not be

anything left, anyway. What there is, you're welcome
to. And don't say no, Sandra. All of us need." Earl
held the length of her trembling body against his own,
stroking her hair. Outside, he saw Thomas Elliot coming to the house, a small, lonely figure against the setting sun.

The sun rose hesitantly on one of those sharp, piney, and ghost-frosted mornings when everything living seemed reluctant to stir from warmth. Then a
mocking bird shook itself into drowsy flight and was
cursed by an irascible gray squirrel. In the town, curling woodsmoke gave lie to sleep, and as the sun lifted
higher, there were sounds: a subdued cough, metal on
metal, the slam of a door, a slow building of individual noises that blended into a taut humming. Temple County had never really been asleep, and now it
was dropping the pretense.

Sheriff Kobburn waddled down the courthouse steps
and looked over the sawhorse barricade. Opening a
plaid jacket, he exposed his gunbelt and the pistol
butt; across one beefy arm lay a twelve-gauge pump.
He grinned left and right at Deputies C.J. Franklin
and Luther Travers, and they hiked the muzzles of
their own riot guns in salute. Six Lovelaces and three
Blakes spread out along the barrier, their badges reflecting sunlight when they turned.

Woulda been seven Lovelaces, Kobburn thought,
but seemed like Virgil lost his nerve in the woods and
cut for home, but a dozen white men were plenty. He
turned and looked up at the courthouse windows
where the commissioners were hiding, and made a big
show out of lighting his cigar.

Behind the Holiness Baptist Church, Louis X hid
the sawed-off beneath his loose coat and watched Ab-

dullah and Gemal do the same. "Davison and the preacher, they figured to start early so we wouldn't be up front," he said. "When the march comes down Main Street, we cut over and take the lead."

At the far end of Main, where houses weren't painted and leaned against each other, blacks moved slowly, men in scrubbed-thin overalls, women wrapped against the chill with legs defiantly bare. Some were little more than children.

"Just walk easy," Davison said. "Stay orderly and pay no attention to what they yell at us. Don't yell back, don't throw things, don't give them an excuse."

"Where Louis X?" somebody asked. "Where the leader?"

Betty Jean called back, "Here are your real leaders! Listen to 'em."

The crowd rippled, surged in upon itself. "Who he? What the hell *he* doin'—"

Earl Lassiter came through them, dressed in fresh khakis, his head bare. "Doctor, Reverend, Betty Jean. Looks like a nice day for a walk."

Then he saw her, wedged between two tall blacks who paid her no attention. She was slight and stood very straight in starched gingham, matching ribbons holding her pigtails—*Marcie!*

Somebody muttered when he flung the men aside, but Earl didn't give a damn about anything else, only this frail and so vulnerable girl where she wasn't supposed to be.

"How'd you get here, Marcie? Why did you come? Damnit, I *told* you—"

Defiantly she faced him. "Saved my lunch money and rode the bus. Up in Jackson they was talkin' about the march so much that ol' Greyhound just about full of colored folks."

"Not you," he said. "You're a kid, you have no business—"

"I got the right," Marcie said. "It was my mama and Ben—uh—my mama and Pa got killed. I got the *right*, Earl Lassiter."

Davison's hand was on his shoulder. "We're going to move in a minute. Good lord! What's that child doing here?"

Earl stared at her, the stubborn set of her chin, the small hands fisted at her hips, eyes that were so much older than her years. In Ellen's quiet fashion, she had also been immovable. Earl said, "This is Marcie Nash, and she has as much right to be here as anyone else, more right, maybe."

"Nash," Davison said. "Oh."

Earl said, "Do this for me, Marcie. Stay back in the crowd some. That way, if anything happens to me, you can come on up and take my place. Is that okay?"

"Okay," she said, and for a second, her resolve wavered. "Earl—"

He bent to her and kissed her cheek. "Don't get hurt when they start chunking rocks."

"You neither," she said.

Reverend Brown climbed onto a box. "Childrun, we about to need all the help we can get. Let us pray."

"Bullshit!" a young voice yelled.

"Let us pray," Reverend Brown repeated, bowing the many heads of the crowd.

At the courthouse, Sheriff Kobburn said, "They bunchin' up, boys; won't be long."

Deputy Travers squinted down the street. "White man with 'em."

"Hell," a Lovelace said. "That ain't no white man; it's Earl Lassiter."

The truck was tucked in with a pile of stripped

wrecks behind Bubba's gas station, only another chunk
of dusty, dented metal. Alvah creaked awake in the
front seat and rubbed his leg. It took two drinks before he could work a slit in his swollen right eye, and
when he put a handful of whiskey on that side of his
head, it didn't do much good.

Rummaging in the ashtray, he found a butt and got
it going. When he got out to piss, the bum leg wobbled and he almost fell. Where the hell was everybody?
He was goddamned tired being alone.

Alvah got hurting into the truck and finished off
the canteen of *soju*—no, it was a Mason jar of stumpjuice, and broke when he dropped it outside. Stupidly,
he stared at shattered glass, then looked up the street,
slowly getting his good eye into focus.

Up in the courthouse, Sam Harvey said, "They
comin', a whole passel of 'em."

Burr Watson said, "I didn't know there'd be so
many. You said I didn't have to open the registration,
Sam; you promised."

"Shut up, you little bastard," Will Jellico said.

And Martin Nelson said, "I'd be proud to have the
state police back."

Davison walked slowly, his head up. Betty Jean was
beside him, and Reverend Brown holding his Bible.
Davison thought of the son he had never seen, and of
the other one lost to him. He saw the sawhorse barriers
and the line of waiting men, the wink of sunlight on
gun barrels. And he saw Louis X and his men break
suddenly from a side street to take over the march.

"No!" Davison yelled. "No, don't start it—"

Sheriff Kobburn was caught strutting in front of the
barricade. He flung away his cigar. "Yonder they
come, them bushy-heads! They totin' guns, sure as
hell!"

Long strides eating up the distance between them, Louis X shouted, "Hey, pig, pig! Come on, brothers— off the fuckin' pig!"

Upstairs, Sam Harvey said, "Where'd that truck come from? It'd take a lunatic to come rollin' up the street this mornin'. Damn! Ain't that—"

His good foot jammed to the floor, Alvah threw the truck at them. There was old pus-gut Kobburn and some Lovelaces and they'd killed his pa. There was a bunch of gooks and a fire team in trouble.

"Lou!" Alvah yelled. "Hey, Lou—you goddamn spade—" But it wasn't Lou after all. It was some bastard with a ring in his ear.

They cut down on the truck with shotguns and handguns and a couple of rifles; they blew out the windshield and shattered the hood, the cab. But it plowed through men and the barricade and halfway up the courthouse steps before it slewed over and rolled back. That's when the load of raw alcohol touched off. The gas tank followed. It didn't exactly explode; there was a big *whoof*! of bluewhite flame that swallowed everybody close to it.

Sheriff Kobburn screamed when the fire got him and tried to run. So did Louis X, but they were already blind and ran into each other. Holding on as if they could hold to life, they fell together and kept burning.

Others died there, the black shotgunners, Deputy C.J. Franklin and Deputy Luther Travers. But folks remembered Louis X and the sheriff best.

CHAPTER 46

Thomas Elliot Coffield squatted on his heels and dropped a little rock into the water. "Ain't goin' to be ready for Mama's party."

"I just as soon jump in the river, anyhow," Thomas Elliot Davison said.

"That ain't the idea, T.E. The idea is, you and me get to use it before all the rest."

"Before biggety ol' U.S. *Senator* Coffield, T.E?"

Coffield laughed. "Oh, he ain't so much. We let him come around 'cause he used to be married to my mama."

Davison said, "Ain't he your daddy?"

"By name, T.E. You know damn well who my daddy really is."

"Know *mine*," Davison said. "Doctor's better'n a senator, any ol' time. Good as a mill owner, too."

Coffield dropped another rock. "You can't come in the front door for the party, but you'n me'll have our own in the kitchen. First, we got to do somethin' about this here swimmin' pool. Say—you know where that irrigation line cuts across the field? I bet we could tie in a pump down yonder and fill up this pool in a hurry."

T.E. Davison frowned. "I don't know. Been mighty dry, and that land behind the mill needs its water."

"Hell," T.E. Coffield said, "that belongs to Auntie

Marcie, but she's been off to college ever since Daddy give it to her. She's got some white croppers on it, and they don't 'mount to much."

"Still'n all," the black boy said.

"You *scared*, T.E.?"

"Me? Dare you, and anybody take a dare, steal a hog and eat the hair."

They ran across the lawn and past where the old Indian spring used to be before it dried up, and out into the cotton field.

Earl Lassiter caught a flicker in the corner of his eye and paused to watch them go. He smiled and shook his head; always together, those two. Picking up the silver shaker, he rattled its icy mixture and said, "Mrs. Lassiter, care for some lemonade before I pour whiskey in it?"

"Can't take the time," Sandy said. "It looks like the flowers are wilting, and the gumbo doesn't taste just right, and the kids—"

"Thomas Elliot will be back," he said.

"The others," she said. "I swear, I don't know what gets into them when I have a party planned. Lorena's so much bigger than little Ben, but she's always whining how he hits her, and—"

"Probably does," Earl said.

"They'll tear down the house one of these days."

"No," Earl said. "The Shadows outlasted a lot of folks; I guess it can get by a few more younguns." He rattled the shaker when Sandy bustled off, and found himself counting—four, five—he broke off the count. No traditional sidecars, no Jessica, no Greater Atlantic Corporation. He was exactly where he wanted to be, in the white house, and Jessica had taken the money and was where she wanted to be—wherever that was.

"Here's to," Earl said, and poured himself a drink.

* * *

"Drink, Sheriff? Beevo said, showing most of his gold teeth. "Got some prime stuff here, and more prime black stuff in the back rooms."

"Uh-uh, Beevo," Dan Mason said. "I don't take a favor, I don't owe none. You keep it quiet, don't bring in no white gals, I look the other way. Get too big for your britches, I come down on you."

"Damn," Beevo said, "you'd come down on a brother?"

"You ain't my brother," Dan Mason said. "My mama died birthin' me."

"You knows what I mean."

The sheriff pushed back his big straw hat. "Knows folks got killed so's a man like me can wear this badge. Took killin' off troublemakers on both sides to make folks see the middle way. And look here, Beevo—ain't you or no other nigger about to lead me by the nose; no white man, neither. You got that plain, Beevo?"

"I got it," Beevo said. "Won't get no trouble here, Sheriff."

Dan Mason sighed. "That's good, 'cause right now I got to go talk to them white croppers on lil' Marcie's place. They hollerin' somebody upriver takin' water out'n the irrigation ditch."

Out on the creek road, dust swirled fine and thick behind the patrol car, then settled heavily upon the roadside where native tough and wiry Johnson grass outlasted the drought, as always.